"WOULD YOU ALLOW
ME TO KISS YOU?"

Her cheeks turned a vivid red. "Just to see what it is like and so that I'm not such a ninny if a man does try to kiss me. I know it's a lot to ask, but I don't want to make a fool of myself when the time comes. Is it *very* revolting?"

Dear God, why are you doing this to me? Is this a test? Because I fear I'm going to fail it. Sorry.

"Kissing is not revolting. Not with someone you're attracted to, at least."

"Oh. Then it shouldn't be too revolting with you. I do like you."

John swallowed and gave her a strained smile. "No, it shouldn't be too revolting, but I don't think . . . that is to say . . ." She kept looking at him with wide eyes, her mouth slightly open, her lips full and delicious and—*oh, Lord*, he thought, *I am doomed.*

Other Books by Jane Goodger

Marry Christmas

A Christmas Scandal

A Christmas Waltz

When a Duke Says I Do

Published by Kensington Publishing Corporation

The Mad Lord's Daughter

JANE GOODGER

ZEBRA BOOKS
KENSINGTON PUBLISHING CORP.
http://www.kensingtonbooks.com

ZEBRA BOOKS are published by

Kensington Publishing Corp.
119 West 40th Street
New York, NY 10018

All Kensington titles, imprints and distributed lines are available at special quantity discounts for bulk purchases for sales
promotion, premiums, fund-raising, educational or institu-
tional use.

Special book excerpts or customized printings can also be
created to fit specific needs. For details, write or phone the
office of the Kensington Special Sales Manager: Kensington
Publishing Corp., 119 West 40th Street, New York, NY 10018.
Attn. Special Sales Department. Phone: 1-800-221-2647.

Zebra and the Z logo Reg. U.S. Pat. & TM Off.

ISBN-13: 978-1-4201-1152-1
ISBN-10: 1-4201-1152-3

First Printing: August 2012

10 9 8 7 6 5 4 3 2 1

Printed in the United States of America

Prologue

The man stood, his black cape whipping around him in the cold, blustering wind, and stared at the grave of the only woman he had ever loved. The monument held a winged angel looking down solemnly at him, as if feeling the very pain that squeezed his heart. He stared at the words BELOVED WIFE and his stomach clenched; bile threatened to flood his throat. Behind him sat a stone manor house, empty and as cold as the North Sea that stretched endlessly before him.

He bent, and with a long elegant finger, traced her name, the carved granite icy to the touch. It had been years since her death, years of suffering her loss, of wondering why she'd left him when he'd loved her so. He would never forget the terror, the madness of searching for her, running from room to room in his massive manor house, only to finally realize she was gone.

God, how he had loved her. And yet . . . she'd left him alone, without a word, without a single sign she had loved him in return. He'd told her more than once it didn't matter that he had a wife and children; it mattered only that they loved one another. But she left in the middle of the night as if the hounds of hell were chasing her, left him to suffer silently, as his heart hardened. Christina. Beautiful, lovely Christina, who had told him she'd hated him. But he knew better.

It took him years to find her, and when he did, it was only to discover she'd married another. Spread her legs, allowed another to touch her, to plant a seed inside her. The thought that she'd pushed out another man's child nearly drove him past the edge of sanity. He pictured that madman, rutting between her legs, grunting like the pig he was.

Years and years ago she'd died, been buried in this cold ground, but he'd been unable to come until now. Beside her tomb was a freshly dug grave with a simple marker where her husband had been laid not five months ago. The usurper was dead, and now the house and the land where his love was buried could be his.

Even if he could only have her cold bones, the home she'd lived in, the walls she'd touched, the floors she'd tread upon, it would be enough. It was all he had, after all.

Behind him, the agent cleared his throat.

"Are you ready, Your Grace? I do believe you'll be pleased with the home. It's quite authentic, you know, though it will require some improvement, I daresay. The views of Bamburgh Castle are quite stunning. Yes, indeed."

He raised his eyes from the gravestone and stared blindly ahead, feeling a rage grow, which he quickly tempered to mere irritation. He loathed dealing with lower beings. It made his skin crawl. He was willing to deal with this man only because the agent was the only way to obtain what he so desired.

"Of course, we cannot see the east wing today because of the daughter," the agent continued. "She is quite terrifyingly fierce about her privacy. I've never actually seen her myself, but . . ."

The man jerked his head and stared at the agent, who stopped abruptly, his mouth open, frozen mid-syllable. "She had a child with him? Their daughter is still here?" he asked.

"Yes, sir. Her relatives have been contacted, but they've yet to arrive to remove her. Apparently, she's refused to leave."

A slow smile spread across the man's face, and the agent gave him an uncertain smile in return. A daughter. A living, breathing piece of Christina just a few dozen yards from where he stood. He looked toward the manor as if he might see her, peeking through the curtains, a shy little girl just like her mother. Sweet. *Innocent.* Did she have Christina's wispy blond hair? Her blue eyes? Or did she have the drab, dull brown of her father?

Did she smile like Christina? Did she have the same intoxicating scent? Would she sigh when kissed or struggle? . . .

He realized with sudden and joyful insight that he did not only want the house and the land.

He wanted the daughter.

Chapter 1

Bamburgh, England, 1862

Melissa looked out her first-story window and glared as a coach pulled up bearing the man who would take her from the only home she'd ever known. Her breath fogged the glass, and she wiped it away impatiently. She wished at that moment she had special powers and could make the coach burst into flames, forcing the man to run from her home in terror, never to return.

"I hate him," she said, trying to shut out the efficient bustling of her maid behind her.

"Yes, miss."

"Go and tell that man that I'll not be coming down."

"Yes, miss." But the maid kept packing, ignoring her mistress even as she agreed with her.

"Mary, really."

Mary, who was nothing like what a young girl should have as a personal maid—she was quite old and not at all attractive—paused just long enough to give Melissa a chastising look, before placing another stack of books into an oversized chest. Mary had been with Melissa as long as she could remember and was far more friend than maid, which probably explained why the woman continued to ignore her orders.

"I'm not leaving. Chain me to the wall if you must," Melissa said dramatically, picturing herself as a secular Joan of Arc.

Mary raised one eyebrow, then slammed another stack down into the chest.

"Really, Mary, you can't care for me at all if you'll allow *that man* to take me away. Papa never would have allowed it. He wanted me protected. He wanted . . ." She paused, because the thought of her father was simply too painful. He'd been dead just six months now, leaving her bereft and completely alone, but for Mary. She wondered if there was another soul in England who was as alone as she. She had no mother, no father, no siblings, and now, no home. She swallowed down the lump that instantly formed in her throat.

"Your father wanted you to be a normal young lady. He just didn't have the courage to let you go," Mary said, her tone holding the barest hint of disapproval. Whether it was disapproval of her father or of her childish behavior, Melissa didn't know.

"He was protecting me," she said for the hundredth time. She'd said those same words so many times since her father's death, they'd lost their meaning and even she had come to doubt them.

In all the time she'd been kept safe, she'd never once thought of herself as a prisoner. She'd been completely content to live her life, knowing she was protected and loved, and knowing her safety made her father happy. No, the doubts about her life had set in after her father's death when she'd overheard some well-loved servants characterize her as "the poor little lass, kept prisoner all these years." And then another servant had mysteriously added, "It's those eyes." Actually, the comment had been whispered, as if the maid had been afraid she might be overheard.

Melissa's first reaction to those overheard words had been rage. How dare they criticize her father for keeping her safe, for allowing her to live without threat of death or danger?

But the words she'd overheard wouldn't let go of her. Did the servants truly pity her? Did they think her secure existence more of a sentence? Had her father stolen from her, stolen her childhood, her freedom, her very life? She'd asked Mary, and the older woman had shaken her head in disgust. "Just silly words that you should pay no mind, miss," she'd said.

But as the weeks passed, and Melissa began to learn just how desperate her situation was, she couldn't help wondering if her father had not done all he could to protect her. She didn't like the idea that her father had feared for her, or had been afraid of something himself. As soon as those thoughts entered her mind, she pushed them away. Her father had loved her, wanted only the best for her. Surely he'd known better than the servants who worked for him.

Melissa paced in front of the window, stopping every so often to check whether anyone was departing from the coach. Ah, there he was, jamming his ugly hat upon his head. The devil himself who thought he could rip her from her home, bring her to God knew where, make her enter society with all its dangers.

Marry her off.

Oh, God.

She still had the letter from the fiend, his evil words cloaked in a veneer of concern. Bah! The only thing that man was concerned about was getting rid of her. How artfully he'd written it. The letter had fairly dripped with sympathy and understanding, while hidden in those kind words was her sentence. She would leave her refuge. She would marry. She would never see her beloved home again. Not that she could actually ever remember seeing it from the outside.

That thought made her frown. She hated thinking ill of her father. Yet those words: *Poor little lass, kept prisoner all these years.* Over and over she could hear them, hear the real sympathy in that voice, picture another maid sadly shaking her head.

Poor little lass and her mad father.

She watched as the man held his hand out and helped a woman step down, as footmen stood guard beside the coach in their drab, dark green uniforms. Hmmm. She hadn't known there'd be a woman. The way he was treating her, the way she was dressed, it was evident she was not a servant. When he looked up, she instinctively backed away a pace and gasped.

Mary was beside her, and not being nearly so cautious as she, pressed her forehead against the cool windowpane. "Oh, I see," she said, looking at her charge warily.

"I hate him," Melissa said, but with far less venom than before. The man looked strikingly like her father, and so it was nearly impossible to truly hate him, after all. Mary went to pat her shoulder, but withdrew before making contact. Her weary brown eyes looked as if she might dissolve into a fit of tears.

"I don't want to go," Melissa said, her own voice

tight from unshed tears as she stared blindly out the window.

"I know, miss, I know." Mary stood beside her, wringing her hands together as she often did when upset about something. She'd made that same gesture the morning she'd come to tell Melissa that her father had passed away overnight.

"I'm frightened." Melissa finally whispered what she'd felt in her heart for so long. Stark fear.

"It'll be all right. You'll see."

"But what if I die? What if my father was right?"

Mary let out a soft chuckle and peered at Melissa's stricken countenance. "We all must die sometime. But I'm fairly certain that day isn't going to come for you for quite some time. Your uncle will protect you now, and then your husband. Really and truly, miss, you don't need protecting at all."

"Then why . . ." She'd never questioned her father out loud. Never. Her life had been her life. She'd never thought it strange, never realized there was anything different. Until now.

"Because he loved you so," Mary said, instantly understanding her confusion. "He'd lost everything and would have done anything to protect you. I don't think he ever considered what would happen to you when he died, how unprepared you would be."

It had been eighteen years since she'd walked through the threshold of her suite of rooms. Her father had made certain her life was filled with books, learning, and entertainment—all provided by himself and the rare tutor he'd allowed in. She knew how to comport herself in a drawing room, even though she'd never been in one. She could waltz and do the polka and perform intricate country dances, even though she'd never been in a ballroom. She could play the pianoforte, though she'd never heard a master play. She was perhaps one of the best-educated young women in England, but had no one with whom to share her vast knowledge.

She'd never questioned why she needed to learn all these things, knowing only that she was pleasing her father.

The first person she'd seen in years, other than the servants and her father, had been a solicitor, informing her that the estate was being sold to settle her father's debts, that there would be nothing left for her but a small inheritance. Enough, the lawyer had told her, for a dowry and to fund a single season in London, during which she could find a husband. After that, she would be at the mercy of relatives she'd never seen.

The second person she'd seen, though only from a distance, had been the man who would buy her home. He had explored the property at his leisure, while Melissa had paced in front of the window like some angry specter. She had raged at him through a closed door and had banged on it furiously when the Realtor had returned to inform her that she needed to remove herself from the house in one month.

"The house is sold, miss," Mary had told her. "You've no choice now."

"It can't be sold. It's mine."

"No, miss. Not anymore."

Now the time had come to leave, and Melissa was truly terrified. There were so many things to fear she couldn't name the one that left her most paralyzed.

Her breath became short gasps, and Mary clapped her hands in front of Melissa's face, recognizing the coming panic.

"You'll be fine, miss. Fine."

If only Mary were coming with her, but she was going to Nottingham, so far away, and she knew Mary couldn't leave her family behind, not even for her. Mary's daughter was about to have a baby, her first, and Melissa couldn't ask her companion to leave.

Melissa nodded, more to please the older woman than to acknowledge her words.

"So. When they come, you'll go?"

At that moment, a knock sounded on the door. Melissa took a deep breath and pulled out a handkerchief to dab at her tears. "I'm ready," she said with a jerky nod. It was, perhaps, the biggest lie she'd ever told.

Diane Stanhope stepped down from the coach and breathed in the sharp, fresh air, relieved beyond measure to no longer be confined in the coach with George Atwell, Earl of Braddock.

The man made her exceedingly uncomfortable. Saying he was not a conversationalist would have been a vast understatement. He'd offered but four sentences to her since they'd departed from Nottingham just days earlier. They were: The train is departing. I'll go arrange your room. We'll stop here to change horses. We've arrived.

Everything else, those one-word answers and grunts, had been responses to her inquiries. He'd stared out the window at the landscape passing by, dragging his gray eyes away from the view reluctantly when she'd ask him a question. This was her penance for being an old maid of independent means. She was deemed an appropriate companion for those young girls who needed a chaperone and were unfortunate enough to have no living female relatives who could perform the duty.

Lord Braddock had approached her at a ball, and she'd been foolish enough to believe he'd been only asking her to dance. What he'd actually wanted was to see if she was available to chaperone his niece, the daughter of a reclusive brother who'd recently died. She should have known better, but for that one moment she'd actually thought this man whom she'd been watching for ten years had finally noticed her.

How humiliating.

But also, educating. She was thirty-two years old, had never had an offer of marriage, had never actually been officially courted. She'd spent the last few years watching over her own niece and doing a very bad job of it, if one were to be completely honest. Elizabeth had managed to fall in love with—and lose her innocence to—an artist's assistant. It was only luck that the man had turned out to be eminently marriageable. Indeed, Diane had been so blinded by her own jealousy of her niece's good fortune, she hadn't seen the signs that Elizabeth was in the throes of a love affair until it was far too late.

Now, Diane was to guide another girl toward marriage. How on earth should she be expected to do so when she'd failed so dismally? The truth stared back at her every time she looked in the mirror. Even her great fortune had been unable to overcome her plain looks.

And yet . . . when Braddock had asked her to dance, she'd felt pretty, she'd felt flattered, she'd felt that cruel stirring of hope she'd thought was long dead. Lord Braddock was such a handsome man, not to mention fabulously wealthy. She'd thought his quiet nature held a thoughtful soul. But she was beginning to think that he was quiet because there was nothing going on inside. How could a man stare silently out a window for two days? Had his now-dead wife left him from sheer boredom?

Or was it that he resented her company? She knew that feeling: to be stuck in a corner of a room listening to the prattle of some old woman who felt the need to relate every event of her life no matter how tedious. Was that how he felt about her? Was he thinking: Good God, how long is this trip going to take?

Was she that objectionable?

At least for the journey home she could get to know her new charge. Braddock knew nothing of his niece but that she had led an even more reclusive life than that of her father. In fact, Lord Braddock believed that the girl hadn't actually left her home in years. It was incomprehensible. Was there something wrong with the girl? Was she damaged in some way? She knew of a few aristocratic families who kept their ill-formed children hidden from view for years. No doubt there were children born who were never acknowledged, never seen in public. Perhaps this girl was one. She certainly wouldn't know, as Lord Braddock had said nothing of his niece, and it was possible even he did not know the poor girl's circumstances.

"Miss Stanhope," Lord Braddock said, startling her with his deep voice. They stood in the shadow of a once-graceful manor, the wind from the sea cold and damp.

"Yes?"

"I wonder if I could ask you for full discretion."

Ah. So the girl was damaged in some way. "Of course," she said.

"Melissa is not my brother's daughter. Her actual father's identity is unknown. Perhaps I should have said something to you before, but I feared if you knew the circumstances of her birth you would decline."

Diane lifted her chin. "Lord Braddock, I have never been a proponent of the Bastardy Clause," she said. It was rather brave of her to admit such a thing, given that the clause had overwhelming support and was stalwartly defended by most of society. Most, that is, but for those poor souls who became impregnated and were then tossed out to fend for themselves and their babes, shunned by even their families.

"I have had little stomach for it myself, but I fear Parliament has no interest in any sweeping changes. You are a rare woman, indeed," he said, his gray eyes warming a degree. "You understand it is paramount that no one know of her illegitimacy. To society she will be my niece, my brother's daughter, now orphaned."

"You have no idea who the father is?"

"It would make no difference in the eyes of society, but, no, I do not," Lord Braddock said, and she was amazed at the venom in his voice. She knew little of Braddock's political leanings, but she had not thought him an advocate of the poor or of women.

"Very good, my lord."

"When my brother met Christina, she already had the babe, and she was in a desperate situation. It is remarkable she did not turn to a baby farmer, given the state of destitution she was in. My brother wrote me—he was quite eloquent—and it was then I began to question the worth of the Bastardy Clause. Rupert loved the child as if she were his own, but she, in fact, has no legal right to any properties, not even the small inheritance my brother left to her. It is imperative that no one know this fact."

Something in Diane's heart tugged. How many men would have taken a bastard into their homes simply because she was loved by their brother? This fierce protectiveness was something unexpected. "You know nothing of your niece?"

"Only that my brother would have done anything to protect her. My brother was a good man, though I did not always agree with his method of protecting Melissa." He looked up to a window, and Diane followed his gaze, only to see an older woman looking down upon them curiously. "She's been a virtual prisoner in her rooms for eighteen years."

"A prisoner?"

"She has not left her rooms for eighteen years. Indeed, no one has seen her as far as I know, but for servants and my brother. He went a bit mad when his wife died, forbidding me or anyone else to come to his estate. Christina died of some fever that nearly decimated the village, and he couldn't accept the idea of his daughter's dying as well. He thought to protect her, to save her. And to keep her hidden."

God only knew what such isolation had done to the child, Diane thought. "Why did you not tell me before now?" she asked, her eyes sweeping over the house.

"I feared you would not help me. I have no idea what we shall encounter. She could be mad, herself. Unkempt. Wild. Untrained. I don't know, and I didn't think I could face such a thing without a woman such as you."

"A woman such as me?"

His cheeks turned ruddy once again. "Someone stern and serious. Someone un-frivolous, solid."

"Ah." Yes, she was certainly all those things. "Shall we proceed, then?"

He nodded, and indicated that she should precede him up the three steps leading to the front door, which was adorned with a large, black wreath. "When we introduce the girl to society, there is a small chance the circumstances of her birth will be discovered, or at the very least questioned. I wanted you to be prepared."

"We shall simply tell them the truth," she said. "That her father recently died, and that her mother died when she was a small girl. It is all anyone needs to know."

Diane looked up at him and tried to stop her heart from stirring, an effort that failed dismally when he gave her a small smile and said, "Thank you." He might have said something romantic for the way her heart stirred.

"It is nothing," she said, and gave the bell a hard, determined turn.

A butler opened the door almost immediately and bowed. "Lord Braddock, we've been expecting you," he said, stepping back and opening the door widely. "Miss Atwell is in her rooms. If you'll follow me."

The butler, who was surprisingly young to hold such a lofty position, led them briskly down a series of hallways and waited patiently for the pair of them to catch up as he stood outside a set of doors. The hall was stacked with several chests, indicating an efficient staff—or one in a hurry to get rid of the house's last resident.

Diane followed behind the butler, her stomach a jumble of nerves. What would they find behind that door? Would her new charge be disheveled? Would she speak? Would she scream and scratch and claw at them?

The butler knocked politely, and Diane, with Braddock standing slightly behind her, waited. The door opened, revealing a plump, older woman, whose eyes were filled with compassion, and Diane's heart picked up a sickening beat. Was she looking at them with compassion because of what they were about to face?

"Miss Atwell?" the woman asked, turning back to the room.

Behind the maid stood perhaps the loveliest girl Diane had ever seen. Her eyes were large, an unusual and almost unnatural violet, and were uptilted exotically. She was frighteningly beautiful, and a deep dread filled Diane. She was to protect *this creature* from the randy young men in London? She was to ease this girl into society? It would be impossible. She would create a stir simply walking into a room.

Melissa stood in the center of the room, holding a small pelisse, wearing a bonnet that was stylish and current, even though it was of unrelieved black. She wore black from her head to her toes, and Diane couldn't help wishing the girl could at least be in half mourning, but it had only been six months since her father's death.

"I am ready," she said, nodding to Diane and her uncle, her voice low and husky. She walked toward them sedately, making Diane feel foolish for her avid imagination. Diane gave Lord Braddock an assessing look and saw the same look of stunned relief that no doubt showed upon her own countenance.

"I am Miss Diane Stanhope," she told the girl when it appeared Braddock was going to remain silent. "I'm to be your chaperone. And this is your uncle, Lord Braddock."

"So pleased to make your acquaintance," she said, her diction perfect, her manner cool. "My coat, Mary?" she said, nodding to her maid, who gave the young woman a smile that could only denote fierce pride.

How difficult must this moment be for the girl, Diane thought. If Braddock was correct, she had not crossed the threshold of her door in eighteen years. She must be nearly frightened to death, and yet she appeared calm and collected.

Their small party backed into the hallway, and Melissa followed, the only sign of her distress coming when she approached the doorway. She hesitated, just for a moment, and pushed through the entrance like someone walking beneath a dripping eave after a rainstorm. The only other sign that the girl was finding this at all difficult was the sudden paleness in her face. She walked with fluid grace until reaching the door, which stood open to the cold, late winter day. Milky sunshine eased through the low clouds, casting the sea beyond with a pearlescent glow that softened the appearance of the cold, harsh waters of the North Sea. Melissa stopped dead, almost causing Lord Braddock to run into her.

Melissa stared out the door, her unusual eyes wide and filled with a fear that Diane was only just beginning to recognize. The poor, poor dear. She held out her hand to the young woman, who simply turned her stricken eyes to Diane's hand, staring at it as if she'd never before seen such an appendage.

"Take my hand," Diane said softly. But the girl simply clenched her own hands more tightly together against her stomach and marched forward like a convicted felon walking toward a dangling noose. When she reached the shallow steps, she proceeded down them, one at a time, planting both feet on each step, as a small child might do.

Diane shot a look to Braddock, whose eyes were filled with a striking combination of compassion and anger. When he realized Diane was looking at him, he pressed his lips together and shook his head almost imperceptibly. Yes, he was angry at his brother. But all his compassion was for Melissa—that much was clear.

Diane moved closer to Braddock so she could speak without Melissa's hearing her. "We must be patient," Diane said. When he looked down at her, his gaze softened, and he gave her the smallest smile and nodded.

When the footman offered Melissa his hand to help her to step up into the awaiting carriage, Melissa instead pulled herself awkwardly up into the vehicle.

Diane followed gracefully, sitting next to the girl, and Braddock pulled himself up and sat across from them.

Melissa stared straight ahead, her body so rigid, Diane thought that if she gave the girl a little push, Melissa might totter over like a statue. She laid her gloved hand on the girl's arm, and Melissa instantly stiffened. Diane immediately withdrew her hand and glanced at Braddock, who looked a bit helpless at the moment.

"Are you ready to travel, Miss Atwell?"

Melissa nodded, a jerking movement that clearly told Diane just how terrified the girl was.

"This is your first time in a coach, is it not?" Braddock asked with false joviality.

This time, Melissa's lips curved up into the smallest of smiles. "If I have, I cannot recall it. I've never even seen a horse so close up. Not that I can remember. They're terribly large, aren't they?"

"I daresay they are," Braddock said. "But these are gentle and good horses, and we'll make certain the driver takes things slowly until you're accustomed to the movement." Then he opened the door and gave instructions to the footman. He knocked on the roof with his walking stick, and the carriage jolted forward slowly.

"Oh," Melissa said, her hands clutching the seat on either side of her. She sat stiffly, head directly forward, but her eyes darted to the window, where a slice of landscape was visible through the velvet curtain.

Gradually, she began to relax, and by the time the coach had reached the main road, Melissa was able to lift one hand and pull back the curtain. Slowly, a smile spread upon her face, and she leaned forward to get a better look.

"Why, this is marvelous," she said, her eyes still on the passing landscape. "Oh, look, Bamburgh Castle. It's enormous," she breathed. She looked back at her traveling companions. "Did you know that Grace Darling saved thirteen souls from the S.S. *Forfarshire* when she was only just my age?" she asked, mentioning a local legend.

"It is one of my favorite stories," Diane said with enthusiasm. Indeed, it was the story of Grace and her bravery that had helped Diane cope with some of her lesser problems in her youth.

"Your father knew her, I believe," Braddock said.

"Oh, I know. He told me all sorts of stories about her and her father and their life in the lighthouse," Melissa said, her eyes shining happily. And then, as if she was just remembering that her father was no longer with her, she grew quiet and subdued, and she dropped her eyes to her hands, folded in her lap.

"This all must seem very strange to you," Diane said.

"I'm certain this is only the beginning," Melissa said, forcing her mouth into the briefest of smiles. "I must say I'm a bit concerned about entering society and . . . all that entails."

"My dear, we have months and months before we shall introduce you," Diane said, resisting the urge to hold her hand. She had the distinct feeling the girl did not like to be touched.

"And if I don't wish to be introduced?" she asked, her question directed to her uncle.

"You will," he said, his abrupt words tempered only slightly by a forced smile.

Diane gave him a slight look of exasperation, for he'd come across as cold and demanding. Which was precisely how Diane had perceived the man. However, her instincts now told her he felt far more than he allowed others to see. Or perhaps this was just the wishful thinking of an old maid who found herself fascinated by a man she'd never thought to be near for longer than the space of a single dance.

Chapter 2

Melissa sat at the breakfast table, jerking slightly whenever someone entered the sun-filled room unexpectedly. She'd been in her uncle's home now for two days and still could not stop herself from starting each time someone entered a room unannounced.

Diane told her she would get better, to give herself time. The problem was, Melissa wanted nothing more than to return home, go back to her rooms, and never come out again. No. That wasn't quite the truth. What she wanted, more than anything, was to be able to run free, to lift her face to the rain, to ride a horse thundering across a field, to stand at the edge of a cliff and stare out to the sea. However, she was an intelligent girl, and she knew that it would be beyond difficult for her to achieve any one of these things when she couldn't even act naturally when a servant entered the room.

She was about to take a bite of a dried-out bit of sausage (her cook had done a much finer job with breakfast, she thought), when she was startled nearly out of her seat by the entrance of a young man. He strode into the breakfast room, hair tousled, cheeks ruddy, and threw himself into her uncle's open arms. The two men embraced with laughter and back-slaps, both grinning like boys who'd been separated for weeks.

"Welcome home, Father," the young man bel-lowed, then grabbed a piece of ham off his father's plate and popped it into his mouth. This must be, she realized, her cousin, John Atwell, Viscount of Willington. Diane had told her yesterday to expect him. So here he was. She stared at him, as she did all new people, Diane had pointed out, taking in his strange appearance, his hair, the way his beard grew in, his loosely tied cravat. She'd never been in the same room with a man so young, and she found she couldn't help but stare, in spite of Miss Stanhope's admonishment that she stop the disturbing habit. But how could she control her curiosity? He was com-pletely unlike anyone she'd ever seen in her life, with unlined skin, sharp features that age hadn't yet soft-ened, and a vibrancy that made her uncomfortable.

Her father had never appeared before her other than impeccably dressed. He'd been a stickler for such things, apparently. This young man came bustling in as if blown by a gale, full of smiles and a vitality that made Melissa smile. This was what she wanted to be like. Fearless. Carefree.

Lord Braddock regained his composure and took his seat. "This unruly young man is my son and your cousin, John," he said. "John, Melissa Atwell." He looked to Diane. "And you, of course, know Miss Stanhope."

"Of course, a pleasure, Miss Stanhope," he said, bowing over her hand.

Then John turned his attention to her, and she

could feel her cheeks heat beneath his inspection. She found she didn't like meeting new people, because they had a tendency to stare at her as if she had two heads.

"Charmed," he said, tearing his eyes away and coming over to where she sat. He held out one hand, and Melissa simply stared at it, her cheeks growing even redder.

"A pleasure, Mr. Atwell," she said, moving her hands to her lap. His eyes grew slightly colder as he withdrew his own hand and gave her a slight bow.

"Actually, it's Lord Willington." His demeanor was definitely cooler now, and Melissa felt foolish beyond measure, but she hadn't a notion of what she should do or say. Behind him, her uncle made a small noise. "Of course, I insist you call me John. We are, after all, first cousins."

Melissa forced herself to look up at him and smile, but that only made him narrow his eyes slightly. They were cold and gray like his father's, holding none of the humor they had just moments before.

"You wrote to me once," she said, her smile wavering slightly. "It was on the occasion of my eighth birthday. I still have the letter." It was, in fact, the only letter she'd ever received from anyone, and she'd cherished it for years—and still did, if she were completely honest.

Her cousin shook his head. "I don't remember sending it, but I'm certain I must have."

"You told me about fishing at your lake in the country and how pretty the perch were. And then," she said, laughing a bit, "you told me how wonderful they tasted when your cook fried them up. I was horrified, really."

John laughed, all coldness gone now, and he gave her the strangest look, one she couldn't begin to interpret. Then again, many people gave her strange looks that she couldn't interpret. She'd noticed it on their way from Bamburgh, how people stared at her, and she'd begun to worry there was something odd about her appearance.

"After breakfast, I need to speak with you, John," her uncle said.

John turned away and gave his father a cheeky grin. "I promise whatever you've heard, it isn't true."

Her uncle, whom she'd thought of as stern and overly serious, burst into laughter. "What is it, then, that you've done but are prepared to claim no knowledge of?"

John shrugged, and Melissa found herself fascinated by the exchange between the two men. How differently they acted toward one another than either did with others.

"A young man was apparently seen attempting to climb the Duke of York's column," John said with forced seriousness. "I swear, it wasn't me."

"This time."

"I was present, but just as I was about to join this anonymous man . . ."

"Norris, no doubt," her uncle interrupted, and John grinned again.

". . . just as I was about to show this man how it was done, I heard your voice in my head warning me about my frivolous activities."

His father grunted, but looked amused. "That's the voice you should always listen to."

"Of course, Father," John said, moving to the sideboard and piling his plate with an impossible amount of food.

Melissa looked down at her own plate, at the now-cold sausage and dry toast, and pushed it slightly away. Miss Stanhope saw the movement and stood.

"Miss Atwell, if you will follow me," she said.

Melissa sighed. Miss Stanhope took her job much too seriously. Each day after breakfast, she reviewed her education to be certain she'd be ready to enter society. Melissa completely dreaded the thought of entering society. The thought of walking into a roomful of strangers was enough to make her break out into a very unladylike sweat.

What Melissa wanted to do was simply explore the garden and perhaps go for a walk in Hyde Park. She wanted to feel the sun on her face, the breeze in her hair. She wanted to see children romping near the lake there; she wanted to feel the grass beneath her hands. People did such things every day and didn't die of some disease. As long as she didn't touch anyone, as long as no one touched her, she would be safe.

John, feeling full and contented, rapped sharply on his father's study door and entered without waiting for an answer. His father smiled up at him and shoved away whatever document had been occupying him. It had always been like that. No matter when he had interrupted his father as a boy, his father would almost always put aside what he was doing and give John his complete attention.

"You wanted to see me?" he asked, curious. His father rarely asked to see him in a formal way as he had that morning. They usually caught up between mouthfuls, talking about the latest political news—or which horse was expected to win at Ascot that year. Or whether he'd won at cards the night before, or if another one of his friends had succumbed to Cupid's bow. More than one conversation of late had been about just that subject, and John was more than grateful his father had never once hinted it was time for him to choose a wife. Thank God for Norris, he'd thought more than once. The second son of the Viscount Hartley, Charles Norris was his closest friend and one of the few friends he had who had the same dispassionate view of marriage as he.

"I'd like your impressions of Melissa," his father said bluntly.

John threw himself into a chair and hooked a knee over one of its arms, ignoring the slight look of disapproval his father gave him. "She's going to give poor Miss Stanhope fits, that's for certain. I predict a proposal within a month of her debut, even wearing those clothes."

"Yes. She is lovely," Lord Braddock said, but there was clearly something bothering his father. "I would trust you with my life, John, so I am about to tell you something that must never leave this room. Do you understand?"

John had rarely seen his father so serious. "I understand. This is something about Melissa?"

"She is not my brother's daughter," he said gravely. "My brother knew who the father was but refused to tell me. But from all indications, it was a peer. His wife, Christina, was near death when my brother found her, and Melissa wasn't much better off. He made me promise to protect her, never to let anyone hurt her, and to keep the secret of her birth safe. I promised without hesitation given my stance on the matter."

"Of course," John said. He was well aware of his father's work with Dr. John Brendon Curgenven. The doctor had just begun an investigation into baby farms, often operated by greedy women who purchased the babies from desperate mothers only to let the infants starve to death. Poor women, with nowhere else to turn, would give their babies to these monsters, fully believing their children would be put up for adoption. In too many cases, the children were allowed to die. It was a barbaric practice that many in Parliament were aware of but chose to ignore. Getting anyone to care about the fate of these poor children was more than difficult given the social and political climate.

His father was a founding member of the Association for the Preservation of Infant Life, a group that had urged the elimination of baby farming. He met regularly with Dr. John Curgenven, an outspoken opponent of the current laws. He himself had sat in on several meetings and was appalled at the reports of infanticide being carried out each day in London. Now John understood his father's commitment had much to do with his love for his brother.

"So," John said, drawing out the word. "She is not truly my first cousin."

"Don't even think about it. She is your cousin to everyone you meet, and you know damn well that she's off-limits, no matter her parentage."

John let out a laugh. "She *is* rather delectable, Father. You must agree." It was a vast understatement.

When he'd first laid eyes on her, he had found her ethereally beautiful—and it was more than just her eyes. It was her creamy complexion, her curling black hair, which framed her face so charmingly, the way she studied him—even the way she blushed when he'd offered her his hand. His reaction had been immediate and physical, one he had doused as soon as he learned who she was.

"Delectable," his father muttered. "And I must agree with nothing. However, you must agree not to look at her with anything other than brotherly disinterest."

John didn't know why he would argue, except to drive his father to distraction. He certainly had no interest in the girl, no matter that she was perhaps the most beautiful creature he'd ever seen. Virgins wanted marriage, and God knew he wasn't ready for that particular adventure. "Must I agree, Father? What if I fall madly in love with her?"

Now, it was his father's turn to laugh, because they both knew just how absurd that suggestion was. For one, John would never be allowed to marry a first cousin, even if such marriages were generally accepted by the upper echelons of society. His father was a long-standing member of the Royal Commission currently debating the issue, and an outspoken opponent of first-cousin marriages. He was a personal friend of Charles Darwin, a naturalist with rather radical ideas about natural order. His father believed such unions weakened the line and made it more likely that unwanted traits would be passed on. John's father's views were well known among the ton, which at times made for social difficulties.

But none of that held as much weight as the absurd

notion that John would fall in love. Fortunately, the two men agreed on the utter ridiculousness of love between a man and a woman. There could be lust, yes. Men lusted after women, perhaps grew fond of them, but in both their experiences the emotion most people thought was love was nothing more than an illusion. The two men believed in science, not fiction. And this thing all the poets expounded upon was pure drivel. If there was an exception, they had yet to see it. The only pure love was that of a parent for a child and a child for a parent. Everything else was nonsense.

"All right, then, John. But I cannot express to you how important this girl is to me. My brother loved her and protected her for eighteen years from the prying eyes of outsiders. He kept that poor girl imprisoned in a suite of rooms all that time," his father said heavily.

"My God." No wonder the girl seemed a bit socially awkward and almost otherworldly. "She actually seems amazingly normal, then, considering."

"Yes, but I don't think we've yet discovered all the effects of this confinement. You have noticed she doesn't like to be touched."

John remembered her odd reaction to his hand. "Yes, I have."

"That's because my brother was convinced she would die of disease if she was touched by anyone. And I think he was equally convinced her real father would somehow do her harm. My brother went a bit mad, I think, when his wife died."

"Do you really think the true father would have taken steps to have an illegitimate daughter returned to him?"

"I don't know, but Rupert was convinced he might. But if we all protect her, perhaps we can have her safely married off before there is any possibility of discovery."

John drew his leg around, giving his father all his attention. "I cannot imagine anyone wanting to hurt Melissa."

His father shook his head slightly. "I don't know, and I don't want to find out. I only know that my brother asked me to protect Melissa, and I swore to him I would. I want you to be Melissa's guardian angel until we get her safely married. Protect her from gossip, introduce her to good, gentle men who will care for her. Keep her away from anyone who offers up speculation about her birth. Help her to adjust to the real world. Can you do that for me?"

John smiled at his father. "You can count on me, Father."

Chapter 3

Diane perused the *Times*, searching for an event at which they could ease Miss Atwell into society. She wasn't so foolish as to think the girl was ready for a dinner or a ball—or any event in which she would have to interact a great deal with people she did not know. Melissa might appear to have all the polish of a debutante, but her lack of experience with social interaction would make even the most insignificant appearance rife with potential difficulties for her.

Diane tapped one finger against her mouth, scanning the *Times* for an appropriate venue, and wondering if there was a single place where Lord Braddock could take the girl without creating unwarranted interest. It was certainly a dilemma—this need to launch her and the equal need to do so with caution. She even considered bringing Melissa to Nottinghamshire, where she would have far more sedate entertainments than in London.

Melissa would cause a stir no matter where they brought her, Diane realized with a sigh. She was just that beautiful. And the fact that she'd never before been seen in society would cause even greater interest. How on earth could they explain why she had not been seen? Of course, Diane knew the best explanation was none at all. To react to such questions with surprise and confusion. *Why has she not been introduced? My goodness, what a forward question.* Diane smiled to herself, for she had used such tactics more than once in her life.

She was about to put the paper away when she noticed an advertisement for a new Julius Benedict opera debuting at the Covent Garden Theatre. She slowly smiled. The opera would be perfect, as they were unlikely to encounter anyone who would demand an introduction. She didn't know whether Lord Braddock had a box at the opera house and was about to go find him when he walked by the small sitting room.

"Lord Braddock, a word if you please."

As always, when Lord Braddock walked toward her—or even looked at her, for that matter—her heart sped up a notch. She couldn't stop it any more than she could stop his look of complete boredom. That thought nearly made her smile, but she stopped herself just in time, because each time she smiled, Braddock gave her the oddest look.

He was a formidable-looking man with broad shoulders and a physique that had yet to show his age. She'd wondered more than once through the years how a man who had to be in his fifth decade could appear so well formed when so many men had gone to fat or were forced to wear girdles to keep their burgeoning stomachs in place. She'd admired him from afar for more years than she'd like to admit and had danced with him only that one time when he'd inquired about her chaperoning Melissa. Still, her heart sped up. Still, she felt like a nervous young girl whenever he walked into a room.

"I'm sorry to interrupt you, my lord, but I believe I've come up with a good venue to introduce your niece. The Covent Garden Opera House. I was hoping you had a box there?"

Braddock frowned. "Is this something I would have to attend, then?" he asked.

"It would be best," she said. "I take it you don't like the opera."

"It's the people who attend such events I don't care for," he said dryly, then frowned even more heavily when Diane laughed outright.

She quickly sobered. "I do believe it would be beneficial to her to make her entrance into society at such an event. Little would be asked of her but to stand beside you and look charming."

His brows drew together, and Diane couldn't help thinking that the man would look far more attractive if he actually smiled once in a great while. "Are you worried about her entrance?"

"Yes, I am," Diane said, trying to keep the exasperation out of her voice. "The poor child has been hidden away for nearly two decades with nary a soul to talk to but her father and servants. While she's been taught how to act and what to say, she has never had the opportunity to put such lessons into practice. I fear if we introduce her into a situation where more interaction is needed, she will find it overwhelming."

"Has she said as much?"

Diane shook her head. "She has no idea whether she should be nervous or not. She has no experience with society. She may do splendidly, but it would be best to have you there by her side should things go awry."

He tapped a fist lightly against his chin in thought. "John can go, too," he said finally. "That would at least make it more palatable for me and perhaps more entertaining for Melissa."

Diane stared at him, wondering if he knew he'd just insulted her. "I'm sure that would be best," she said. "And you do have a box?"

"I do, not that I can recall ever sitting in it beyond the grand reopening of the place. *Santanella*, I believe it was. I fell asleep."

Again, Diane laughed and suffered that *look* from Braddock. Really, it was too much. Was she to go around frowning her entire life because some unfortunate feature on her face made him nearly wince in pain each time she smiled?

"Lord Braddock," she said in her coolest voice. "Is there something about me that offends you?"

The look on his face was so astounded, Diane nearly smiled again. "Offends, Miss Stanhope?"

She could feel her nostrils flare and knew from looking in the mirror that such an expression definitely was not attractive. "Every time I smile, you look as if you've swallowed something unpleasant. It is quite disconcerting, and it's gotten to the point that I take great pains not to smile in front of you. I wish you would either tell me what so offends you or try to ignore whatever it is you find so distasteful." Despite her resolve to appear stern, Diane was slightly mortified to realize that her throat was beginning to close up, and that if Lord Braddock said a single unkind thing she would likely be unable to utter a sound.

"You think . . ." It was Braddock's turn to smile, leaving Diane completely confused. It was not at all amusing. Not in the least.

"Miss Stanhope, please let me put your mind at ease. You are not a beautiful woman," he said. "In fact, most men would probably describe you as rather plain."

She stood there, his words hitting her like soft blows to the heart. She'd seen it more than once, men who thought that women past a certain age were impervious to hurt. But it wasn't true; her battered heart was proof enough of that. She schooled her features to show not a single emotion, as he blithely talked about her complete unattractiveness.

As if suddenly realizing what he was saying, the great lummox, he abruptly stopped talking. "I see I am not saying this correctly," he muttered, then took a deep breath. "When you smile, Miss Stanhope, you become another woman altogether. You must know this is true. It transforms you. When you smile, you become rather"—he stopped, his cheeks going ruddy—"stunning."

"Oh," she said, through a throat suddenly gone tight for another reason altogether. "Well. Thank you." She smiled, then immediately covered her mouth, horribly self-conscious. "Now, I'm afraid, I'll *never* be able to smile in front of you." She'd gone quite red in the face, her eyes twinkling above her hand. Braddock grinned back, as if enjoying her discomfort.

"You mean to say you thought I was offended each time you smiled?"

Diane nodded, feeling foolish. "You did make the oddest expression," she said, laughing. "The first time I thought I must have something rather horrid stuck between my teeth."

"The Browning ball," he said, and Diane couldn't stop the foolish rush of happiness that he had remembered. "I do apologize if I made you feel self-conscious."

Diane smiled again, this time not hiding her face. "Apology accepted, sir. Now, about the opera. It is Monday. Are you available?"

"Yes," Braddock said, clearly wishing he were not.

"Thank you, my lord. I'll go tell Melissa. No doubt her first outing will be nerve-wracking."

Melissa sat on a small settee in the well-equipped library, looking up at Miss Stanhope, who was lecturing about the proper behavior of a young lady attending the opera. Looking up, but not listening. All her life she'd listened to people lecturing about how to act but had never gotten the chance to put such lectures into action. She *knew* how to act, what to say, how far to curtsy, how not to fidget.

"Miss Atwell."

Her head snapped up. "Yes, Miss Stanhope?"

"I have the distinct feeling you were not listening to me."

And then, feeling a slight edge of irritation, she repeated precisely what her chaperone had been saying. "One mustn't clap until the conductor drops his baton. To do so is the most obvious sign of ignorance."

The older woman's cheeks grew a bit pink, and Melissa felt immediate remorse. "I am simply trying to help," Miss Stanhope said.

Melissa held back a sigh. "I do know that. It is only

that I've heard such lectures my entire life. I want to start doing things, not just talking about them."

"Of course you do, dear," Miss Stanhope said kindly. "But I wonder if you would bear with me for perhaps a few more minutes. I've asked your cousin to come in this morning. Ah, here he is now."

Yes, Melissa thought, here he was. This burst of energy and fresh air, this young, vigorous man, this stranger whose eyes could be cold or warm, but were always slightly disconcerting.

"How may I be of help?" he asked, striding forward and giving the women a small bow, a rakish grin on his face.

"You may escort your cousin to the door and return," Miss Stanhope said.

Melissa stiffened and immediately fought the panic building in her. She hated the thought of touching someone, even with her protective gloves on. "Of . . . Of course," she said, and began to stand until she noticed Miss Stanhope's staying hand.

"Please let Lord Willington assist you," she said gently.

It was a simple thing, really. She need only place her gloved hand into his. He waited patiently, hand extended, that intense look on his face once more. Melissa stared at his hand as if it were a coiled snake ready to strike.

"Miss Atwell," her cousin said. "Will you please join me for a trip to the door."

Feeling foolish, Melissa forced herself to place her hand in his and stood. His hand was large and strong and solid, and he held hers as if this wasn't a momentous event, as if this was something one did every day. And, of course, for most people that would be true.

For Melissa, who couldn't remember the last time she'd voluntarily touched another person, it was disconcerting indeed. He then placed her hand in the crook of his arm rather forcibly, and began walking, practically dragging her along, his arm holding her hand like a vise while she tried to tug it free.

"Can we please try that again," Miss Stanhope said. "And this time, please do try not to look at your cousin's hand as if it is holding something offensive."

Melissa pressed her lips together and sat.

"Miss Atwell," her cousin said, holding out his hand. This time, there was only the slightest hesitation before she placed her hand in his. She was lifting herself when Miss Stanhope said, "Again please."

Something passed through Lord Willington's expression, something that looked too much like the pity she'd seen in the Bamburgh servants' eyes far too many times. Lifting her chin, she slapped her hand into his extended one, rose, then grabbed his arm almost defiantly. She could feel his muscle flex beneath her glove, could feel his heat, and she fought the impulse to pull away again.

"Again. And this time without the violence," Miss Stanhope said, her voice tinged with humor.

Melissa turned toward her chaperone in a quick, angry movement. "Really, Miss Stanhope, I do understand why you are insisting on this exercise, but I can assure you that I will be fine tonight when Lord Willington escorts me to my seat. I feel rather ridiculous," she said, but she sat anyway, her posture rigid with anger.

"Miss Atwell, may I escort you to the door." He stood before her, one eyebrow raised in challenge, and held his hand out to her.

She gave him the full effect of her smile and rather enjoyed the stunned look on his face when she did so. "It would be my pleasure," she said in her calmest tone. She took his hand and rose gracefully, then allowed him to place her hand in the crook of his arm.

"Much better," Miss Stanhope declared, as if Melissa had done something truly remarkable. "You mustn't hesitate, else gentlemen will either think you unpardonably rude or themselves offensive in some way."

"And we wouldn't want that," John quipped with a grin.

"No, we wouldn't," the older woman agreed. "Now." She took a bracing breath. "Would you please stand next to me, my lord, and face your cousin." He did so, giving Melissa a wink. She couldn't help but smile again.

"Miss Atwell, I would like to present you with Lord Willington. Lord Willington, Miss Atwell, Lord Braddock's niece, who is here for her first season."

Again, John held out his hand, and Melissa, without even a smidgeon of hesitation, placed her hand into his, wincing only when it appeared he was about to kiss her. Instead, he simply bowed over her hand, released it, and stepped back.

"You flinched," he said, and Melissa pursed her lips.

"I thought you were about to . . ."

"I was. Until you flinched."

"I did not flinch. And a gentleman should not kiss a young woman's hand during an initial introduction. Isn't that right, Miss Stanhope?"

"That is true," her chaperone agreed, "but there are some cheeky young men who do not follow such rules, and you must be prepared. As long as you are wearing your gloves, you may allow it, but you are perfectly in your rights to glare at any young man who is so forward." To show her the look, Miss Stanhope glared at John.

John stepped back in mock fear. "If you could master such a look, dear cousin, no man would ever attempt such a kiss again."

To Melissa's surprise, Miss Stanhope laughed.

"Miss Stanhope?" A young footman stood at the entrance. "Lord Braddock would like to see you in his study."

"If you will excuse me," she said. She looked from one to the other as if uncertain whether to leave. "You may continue practicing," she said, following in the servant's wake.

"I'm not a child," Melissa grumbled, knowing she sounded very much like a child.

"So. It's true," John said when Miss Stanhope was gone.

"What is true?"

"My father told me you'd stayed in a suite of rooms for years, that you've never been in the world. I find that completely fascinating."

Melissa stared at him. He appeared sincere, but she could not be certain. Small nuances in conversation that seemed so easy for other people to identify were quite difficult for her.

"There you go, staring. You're going to have to find a way to stop doing that," John said.

"Was I staring?" Melissa said, mortified. "I thought I was just looking."

He was instantly remorseful. "No, no. You weren't staring. Well, perhaps a bit. You do have this rather intense way of looking at a chap. I suppose it is because of your lack of experience dealing with different people. Truly, you are remarkable."

"Oh." She immediately dropped her gaze and looked down, only to have John laugh aloud. "I do wish you would stop doing that."

"What?" he asked, all innocence.

"Laughing at me. Even when you're not laughing at me, you're laughing at me. Like now," she said accusingly, pointing a finger at him. "Your eyes. You are laughing at me, aren't you?"

"Yes," he admitted easily. "I am. You must understand that I've never met anyone quite like you. As a man of science, I find your circumstances quite interesting."

She suddenly felt rather crestfallen. She'd never thought of herself as different or strange. It had never occurred to her that when she finally did go into society, it would be difficult. After all, her father had hired the best governesses and tutors to make certain she would know what to do. "Am I so very unusual?"

"Of course. But in a very nice way. You see, women are a deceptive bunch, never saying what they mean, always hiding what they're feeling. You, on the other hand, are delightfully easy to read." He peered at her face. "Right now, for instance, you are feeling quite self-conscious and embarrassed that *I'm* staring at *you*."

"I fear I shall be an utter failure and embarrass Miss Stanhope, as well as my uncle."

John shrugged, as if such an occurrence wasn't in the least consequential. "What is the worst that could happen? You refuse to give your hand to some oily gentleman who is only interested in your dowry? I hardly think that would be a tragedy."

"But what if I refuse to give my hand to a man who would otherwise have fallen madly in love with me?"

Honestly, Melissa had never considered such a thought. She'd never considered leaving Bamburgh, never mind falling in love and marrying. Such things always seemed to be reserved for characters in the books she'd read, not for her.

John threw back his head and laughed, and Melissa wasn't certain whether she should be insulted or laugh with him. Was it so ridiculous that someone would fall in love with her? It suddenly seemed as if it were something she very much would like. She didn't want to be left alone to molder away into her old age. Did she?

"Love," he said, still sputtering. "Men don't fall in love, my dear. They only want two things. And money is one of them."

"And the other?"

"Good God, you cannot be that . . ." He stared at her again, and Melissa thought she saw another bit of pity. "Then again you probably are," he muttered.

"I am what?"

"Innocent. A man wants women, especially beautiful ones like you. He'll want to . . . do things."

Melissa felt her cheeks turn pink. "I may be innocent, but I'm not stupid. You are talking about fornication, are you not?" She felt ridiculously proud that she did know what he was referring to—which probably was even more a mark of just how naïve she was.

He let out a choking sound. "Yes. I was."

"Men want only money and to fornicate?"

It was his turn to blush, something that Melissa found extremely satisfying. "I suppose that is putting matters a bit simplistically, but yes, that's about right."

"So I cannot expect a man to fall in love with me?"

"Love between a man and a woman does not exist," he said.

"That's not true. My father loved my mother very much. He spoke of her all the time, spoke of how he loved her. And I loved my father. I am a woman, and he is a man."

"Paternal love is a different thing entirely. We are conditioned to love our children. I am speaking of romantic love. I don't mean to be cruel or indelicate, but it is far easier to love a ghost than a real woman. Love, or what we think of as love, does not last longer than the day your heir is born. And then you find what real love is."

Melissa smiled and shook her head. "Do you truly believe that? That all these people who pair up are doomed to be unhappy and live a life without love?"

"Yes. And that such a life is not the tragedy romantics like you make it out to be. The real tragedy is the poor souls who believe in love wholeheartedly, only to be bitterly disappointed time after time."

Melissa tilted her head. "An interesting theory, but I think it's complete hogwash. I think you believe this only because you have not fallen in love yourself."

"Not theory. Fact. It's been proven again and again. And I refuse to fall in love, for I recognize that state of mind for what it is, a transient emotion fueled by lust."

"So all the poets, even Shakespeare himself, were wrong. Everyone who believes he or she loves someone is delusional. Is that what you are saying?"

He shook his head, his gray eyes sparking with passion for his subject. "Not at all. People do *believe* they are in love. What they don't recognize is that real love, such as the love of a mother for her child, lasts.

But the love between a man and a woman is a fantasy, and one we cling to rather pathetically while our souls slowly wither and die from our disappointed expectations."

It was Melissa's turn to laugh. "You cannot be serious. You are jesting with me."

"Not at all," he said with complete earnestness. "I am a man of science. I observe behaviors, of animals, of humans. And my conclusion, and that of my father as well, is that the idea of romantic love is false. It simply does not exist."

For some reason, Melissa felt unaccountably sad. Not because he had convinced her—he had not—but because he seemed to believe this nonsense so wholeheartedly. He was dooming himself forever to be unloved.

"I think you are wrong. I think you cannot escape love. Even you. I do hope I'm around to watch it happen. I shall delight in it."

"You will have a long wait, I fear. In the meantime, I shall help you find your own path to disillusionment and heartbreak if you wish. I know quite a few eligible bachelors who are certain to fall at your feet and beg for your hand in marriage."

Melissa smiled. "Will I have to actually give them my hand?"

"I'm afraid, dear cousin, you will have to give them more than that. But for now, let's work on your not flinching when a man escorts you about a room."

She wrinkled her nose at him, but couldn't help smiling. She only hoped that all young men were as entertaining as her cousin.

* * *

Lord Braddock found the recent turn of events extremely unsettling. For years, it had just been himself and John, and he was happy for it. His wife, God rest her soul, had died more than twenty years ago, and he'd had no desire to go out and find another. Henrietta had been a mistake and it was more than that she had not enjoyed the marriage bed. The thought of begging another wife to lie with him was quite more than he could bear. It was humiliating, unmanning, and frustrating beyond tolerance. He'd never forced her, but rutting above a woman lying unmoving beneath you wasn't particularly enjoyable, despite the sexual release it afforded him.

No, he was quite happy with his mistress. She was not demanding, but was very willing when he was in London, which was most of the time these days, thanks to his duties in the House of Lords. No, Martha was the perfect woman. She never demanded anything but pleasure. She was never jealous, never spoke of love or missing him or any other such nonsense.

Frankly, he would be quite content to enter his old age living in his town house or manor in Cambridge and never returning to his country estate. John thrived there, but Lord Braddock felt as if he were suffocating.

"You needed to see me, my lord?" Miss Stanhope said, striding into the room without even a knock. This was precisely the type of woman he liked to avoid, the very type that fancied themselves in love with him, who would beg for love, then lie like a corpse in the marriage bed. He suppressed a shudder at the thought.

It wasn't as if Miss Stanhope wasn't desirable; she was. But she wasn't the type of woman one tupped and then said good-bye to. If he ever got her into his bed—which he had absolutely no intention of doing—he'd be forced to marry her. No doubt she'd want children, despite her age, and expect affection and attention. He was done with all that, thank God.

"Yes, I wanted to speak to you about whom you plan to introduce Melissa to once the season does start. My son has come up with a rather lengthy list of prospects. I'm familiar with many of the families, if not the young men themselves, and wonder if you could offer any insight of your own."

She pinched her nose unattractively, no doubt uncomfortable since their confrontation about her smile and trying desperately not to make any expression remotely similar to a smile. She wore a stiff, unrelentingly gray gown that covered her from her toes to her chin, with almost no adornment but for a small ruby pin by her throat. He wondered idly who had given it to her, for it was not an inexpensive piece.

"If you have the list, I will look at it later," she said, thrusting a hand out, much like a schoolmistress would to take an assignment.

"I would like your immediate opinion, if you don't mind."

This seemed to fluster her for some reason, and her cheeks, which were a tad too sharp in her otherwise pretty face, turned pink. "I've left your son with Miss Atwell alone in the library."

"And?"

"And it is certainly not proper for them to be alone together."

Lord Braddock narrowed his eyes. He knew precisely what she was implying, and he didn't care for it. "Why ever not? They are cousins."

She let out a small huff of air through her nose,

like a miffed little dragon. "They are not cousins, and your son is aware they are not. It is not at all proper for an unrelated, unmarried man and woman to be alone together for an extended amount of time."

Lord Braddock folded his hands in front of him on his desk, and something about his demeanor must have disturbed Miss Stanhope, for she stiffened ever so slightly. He supposed, he thought placidly, that she detected his anger.

"My son, Miss Stanhope, is perhaps the most honorable and trustworthy man I know—including myself. He is fully aware of Melissa's situation and would die before compromising her or disobeying me. I would trust him with my life."

Miss Stanhope looked both chagrined and startled by his ferocity. "I certainly did not mean to suggest . . ." She stopped, because that was precisely what she had done—suggested that his son would dishonor him. "I believe you are being imprudent," she said, lifting her chin. "To trust them is one thing; to thrust them together in this way is foolhardy. You must know that it only takes the hint of impropriety for tongues to wag and for reputations to be ruined."

What a brave little dragon she was, Lord Braddock thought, and wondered if that was why she was still unmarried. Had someone spread idle gossip about her? If someone had, he hadn't heard of it, not that he ever paid much attention to such stuff. But when he'd been making inquiries about who might make his niece an excellent chaperone, Miss Stanhope's name had come up more than once.

"In my house," he said succinctly, "there are no wagging tongues, Miss Stanhope. My son has earned my trust; I do not give it freely. And do not think I am blind to Melissa's feminine attributes. It is for precisely this reason that my son is so important to her finding a proper match. He is her guardian, and as I have appointed him as such, I will not allow you or anyone else to spread false rumors about him or besmirch his character."

Ah, that bothered her, for her nostrils flared and her eyes flashed with an anger that was quite striking. "I do hope you are not suggesting that I would be the bearer of such gossip."

He smiled, though he knew it was not a very pleasant smile. "I would never suggest such a thing," he said, and calmly handed her the list.

Diane took the list, resisting the urge to throw the paper back into his hard, mocking face. He was just as cold and heartless and unforgiving as she'd always thought him to be, she decided, turning away and walking to the window where the light was better— and where she was away from him. No, that wasn't true. She'd actually allowed herself to think, in her weakest moments, that Lord Braddock was a kind, understanding man whom she could admire. Inexplicably, her eyes burned as if she were on the verge of tears, which was ridiculous. Simply because she'd been set down by an arrogant, stiff, uncompromising, and foolish man? He'd made her feel silly for suggesting there was even a hint of impropriety in allowing his son to be alone with his niece.

She stared blindly at the absurd list, at names she'd seen for years, of men who'd looked past her as if she were nothing more than a potted plant. Oh, how she loathed that men and women believed unmarried women of a certain age had cast off all their dreams of marriage and children. As if she was a dried-up old woman.

Here she stood, in the presence of a man she'd admired for years, made to feel foolish simply for pointing out a real danger. Any tender thoughts she'd ever had of him—and they were very few indeed—seemed completely preposterous at the moment. Affronted, was he? Angry? Well, she was angry, too, for having her real and legitimate concerns dismissed out of hand. As if Lord Willington was such a paragon. Even priests were tempted by beautiful women. She was about to point out that fact, but when she looked up he was staring at her thoughtfully.

"I should not have belittled your very real concerns," he said slowly. "It's a flaw of mine, you see, to know with absolute certainty that I am right. I *am* right in this case, but I do believe I could have been a bit more politic during our conversation."

Drat. Just when she was getting up a good temper, he had to apologize. At least it sounded very much like an apology. She nodded, not knowing what she could say that wouldn't get him angry all over again. Instead, she walked to his desk and laid the list on the smooth, polished wood.

"Any of these would do," she said, then walked from the room.

Chapter 4

The Covent Garden Theatre was one of the newest and largest theatres in London, having been rebuilt in 1858 after a devastating fire. The result was a magnificent structure in a classic style that resembled more a grand government building than a theatre. Staring at it, Melissa had a nearly overwhelming feeling of being in a dream—and it wasn't a good dream.

Everywhere she looked, there were people, horses, carriages, vendors, buildings, noise, dogs—and smells. She felt as if she were being crushed by it all and had to fight the urge to squeeze her eyes closed and hold her hands over her ears like a child.

At first, the carriage ride had been fascinating, but it was all too short. She had little knowledge of London, but her first thought, when they'd arrived at Covent Garden from her uncle's house on Piccadilly, was that they could have walked to the theatre. But now that they had stopped in a long queue of carriages, it was all too much. The theatre was so large; it loomed over them as if it might crash down upon their tiny carriage. And the noise, it was unbearable. She clutched the seat with her gloved hands and stared blindly at her uncle, who sat across from her, completely at ease. *Don't scream. Don't scream.*

Melissa was so tense, her entire body started to ache. This was not what she had expected when Miss Stanhope had told her about a night at the opera. Miss Stanhope had explained that it would be a night of little social interaction, a way to slowly introduce her to the society she would someday be a part of. She described a calm, sedate setting in which nothing would be expected of Melissa except to nod at those who were introduced to her. She would look beautiful, she would be admired, and the night would be a rousing success. They had taken special care choosing her gown, selecting a deep blue velvet with cream lace and pale blue underskirt. A rope of pearls was woven through her dark hair, creating a lovely effect—at least that's what Miss Stanhope had told her.

It would be a wonderful night, one requiring little of her but to look calm. This was what Miss Stanhope had told her, and this was what she'd believed. She could stand and nod at people. She could carry on a conversation. Of course she could.

But now, she realized with something close to panic, she could not. She was terrified at the thought of being amongst so many people, of their looking at her, touching her, bumping into her. Outside was a seething mass of people, of all shapes and sizes. It was too, too much to contemplate.

"Melissa."

She blinked and turned toward her cousin, who was staring at her intently, his gray eyes visible in the gloom of the carriage. "Are you well?"

That single question, the concern in his voice, calmed

her almost instantly. "Quite well," she said, and almost sounded as if she meant it. It was the proper response to such a question, was it not? Certainly she could not tell these people she was about to run screaming from the carriage toward Bamburgh.

She felt Miss Stanhope's sharp gaze on her, and she schooled her features. She would not humiliate herself or her uncle. It was such a simple thing they asked. She glanced out at the people, walking about as if being there were a normal, everyday occurrence, when it was truly a terrifying leap of faith. All those people. Surely one or two of them was ill. What if one of them touched her? What if some disease was, at this very moment, crawling upon one of their arms, ready to jump off and onto her as she brushed by? She hadn't even stepped from the carriage and Melissa wanted to go home.

"Have you heard anything about this opera?" she asked as if the quality of the opera was of utmost importance to her.

"Today is the debut," Miss Stanhope said. "But the company is wonderful. I've never yet been disappointed by a performance."

The carriage jerked to a halt, and soon the sound of the steps being lowered could be heard, just seconds before the door was efficiently opened by a liveried footman. Miss Stanhope departed first, giving Melissa a pointed look, a silent reminder to allow the footman to assist her down. Melissa felt foolish and awkward, as if every little act of hers was going to be carefully reviewed by her chaperone and uncle. Taking a bracing breath, Melissa stood and calmly gave the footman her hand, trying with all her might not to cringe at the warm strength of a strange man's hand holding hers.

Every day women were touched, and they did not die. Every day, they breathed in the air that others breathed, they jostled and bumped, embraced. And they did not die.

She felt the gravel beneath her feet and dropped the servant's hand, feeling unaccountably relieved and proud of herself. No one would ever know what it had taken to act so completely nonchalant when stepping from that carriage. No one would ever know the panic she had to fight, the fear.

Turning, she watched her uncle and cousin step from the carriage with graceful, masculine ease, looking about the crowd for acquaintances.

"Melissa, if you'll allow me to escort you," John said, holding out his arm much as he had in the study. As always, he gazed down at her, his eyes crinkling as if he knew what she was going through and he was giving her courage.

She gave him a big smile, as if he'd offered her his kingdom instead of an escort, and he grinned back.

"I thought you were going to lose your accounts in the carriage," he whispered in her ear.

"I haven't the slightest notion of what you mean," she said, but she smiled up at him to let him know she did.

"They won't bite, you know. At least not all of them. And I'll let you know which ones do."

Melissa squeezed his arm until he yelped, then looked up at him innocently. With John, she could be calm and almost confident. Clutching his arm, she felt as if there were a protective barrier between her and the rest of the people milling about. As they made their way into the opera house, her uncle was stopped several times and was forced to make introductions. Just as Miss Stanhope had told her, she simply nodded and murmured a few polite words and they went on their way.

"Not so difficult, you see?" John asked, looking down at her with a small bit of concern.

"I was being foolish in the carriage. I know that."

"Not foolish," he said. "Just a bit overwhelmed. Am I right?"

Melissa nodded, thankful that he understood, at least a little, how she was feeling. She didn't know why or how he understood, but was glad he did. On his arm, the fear that paralyzed her all but dissipated, and she idly wondered if she would one day be able to fight the panic on her own. Or would she need to drag him about for the rest of her life the way she used to drag about her little blanket when she was a child?

Melissa had never been in a building so large. As they walked beneath the entry, she expected to walk into a grand hall, but instead found herself being led into a crowded lobby. The air was filled with cigar smoke that clung to the ceiling in a fine haze, and so many bodies in one room made the space rather stifling. She seemed to be the only one who noticed this, however, so she kept silent as they made their way slowly up a set of stairs and along a long, curving hallway.

"Our box is number seventeen, and if you don't loosen your hold on my arm, I fear it will drop off from lack of blood. There you go. The odd numbers are on the left, the even on the right, should you get lost. Here we are," John said, stepping through a narrow door and into the box, where eight velvet-covered chairs sat.

"Oh," Melissa breathed. It was magnificent. A huge gas-lit chandelier hung high above the theatre, casting the entire cavernous room in a soft, golden light. The oval-shaped room rose three tiers above where she stood, and below was the main auditorium facing a large stage, now hidden by a thick, red velvet curtain. The ceiling was dominated by a golden starburst from which the chandelier hung. A small thrill went through her. This was what she'd dreamed about when she was in her room and had read about the operas that others attended. She didn't remember longing to go, but she'd always wondered what the grand London theatres actually looked like. And here she was, standing in perhaps the grandest theatre in the world, gazing up at the brightly lit ceiling.

John watched her, fascinated. She went from nearly terrified to excited and amazed in the space of a few minutes. She was gazing at the ceiling, and he glanced up to see what was so completely appealing that she didn't seem to be able to tear her eyes away from it. Yes, it was rather pretty, but his eyes moved down to watch her. She was beautiful tonight, with her chin up-tilted, her eyes sparkling with excitement. In the box next to them, he could see young Lord Waddington craning his neck to get a better look at her. Waddington was a fool and likely already half besotted with Melissa. From the look on his silly face, John had no doubt of that fact. He stepped between the awkward young man and Melissa and frowned his disapproval. The young man had the good grace to blush and move hastily back, and John sighed. This business of introducing Melissa to society was going to be rife with danger. She had the kind of face and form that would attract all sorts of men—from the perfectly respectable, to the perfect fools, like Waddington there. He wished his father would simply arrange something for the girl and be done with it. The only problem he could think of was he couldn't think of a single person who would suit. He'd made a list earlier, when he'd first met the girl, and had come up with all sorts of prospects. But now, as he considered the vast majority of the men he'd thought appropriate, he rejected them out of hand.

He had to get to know her better, he realized. She wasn't the shy, introverted girl he'd first thought her, a biddable female who was naïve as well as innocent. No, she was braver than half the men he knew. He watched her now, her lively eyes taking in a world she couldn't have even imagined a few weeks ago. Everything was glorious and new to her, he realized. She'd never been to a ball. She'd never danced with a man other than her own father.

She'd never been kissed.

John tore his eyes away from her delicious little mouth, not liking where his thoughts had veered off to of their own volition. He shouldn't be thinking about anything except finding a suitable husband for her. He certainly shouldn't be thinking about her mouth or any other parts. On that thought, his eyes drifted slightly downward, and his mouth went slightly dry as his gaze rested on her rounded breasts, straining against her gown as she leaned forward to watch others arriving in their boxes.

"Don't fall," he said, sounding irritable. She simply smiled at him.

"You don't need to hover over me, you know. I'm

perfectly fine," she said, but moved back a bit to mollify him. He grumbled beneath his breath and sat down just as Lord Braddock and Miss Stanhope stepped into the box.

"Oh, look, my brother is here with my niece," Miss Stanhope said, her face lighting up. She was one of those women who looked rather plain until she smiled. Her smile really did create a remarkable transformation, and John followed her gaze to a booth that was nearly across from them.

"Your niece is the new Duchess of Kingston?" he asked, his interest piqued. He knew none of the details, but there had been a bit of a scandal involving the duchess and her husband. Something about the new duke's being the rightful heir after years of being abandoned by the old duke.

"Your niece married a duke?" Melissa said, her voice giving away her awe that she was sitting next to someone who was related to such an important member of the ton.

"Yes, indeed," Miss Stanhope said. "A true love match."

Melissa immediately glanced at John with a knowing look.

"And how long have they been married, Miss Stanhope?" John inquired politely.

"Oh, they are very much newlyweds. It's only been weeks."

John allowed a smug smile to cross his features before turning his attention to his father. "Melissa wants a love match, Father. Do you have any possibilities? I was thinking of Lord Waddington. He's in the box next to us and already looks quite smitten."

"Lord Waddington?" Melissa asked with sudden, and exaggerated interest. "Someone has fallen in love with me already?"

His father gave John a hard look before leaning toward his niece and talking in quieter tones. "John doesn't believe in love. He is having fun with you."

"Yes, Uncle, I'm aware of his views. And I was led to believe that you shared them."

"I'm afraid that is true. While I don't want to squash your girlish dreams, I cannot say I've ever witnessed true love, whatever that is."

John noticed Miss Stanhope stiffen slightly.

"If people could eliminate all notions of love, the world would be a much calmer—and dare I say happier—place," she said. "I firmly believe marriages should be handled with diplomacy and tact, rather than allowed to descend into romantic balderdash."

Melissa moved her eyes from one person to the next. "Am I the only one, then, who believes in love? Is this a commonly held belief?"

Miss Stanhope's rigid stance softened. "No, it is not. And as in anything, there are exceptions to the rule. I do hope that my niece has found everlasting love, for example. Indeed, I'm not certain I've ever witnessed a love such as theirs in my entire life. So, I suppose it can happen. I simply don't believe in overlooking perfectly good prospects because of a lack of love. Many men would make very fine husbands if not for all the silly twits who overlook them in a misconceived search for love. And I am not saying you are a silly twit."

Melissa laughed. "I quite agree with you. But I

also believe that one can fall in love even in an arranged marriage."

"I am quite gratified to hear you say so," Miss Stanhope said.

"You have never been in love, then?"

"Of course not," she said as if the idea was perfectly absurd. John's father, who had been ignoring the conversation, turned his head slightly.

"But you are so lovely," Melissa said, and Miss Stanhope's cheeks turned a bright pink.

"Thank you, my dear," Miss Stanhope said stiffly. "Unfortunately, the men who were looking for wives during my seasons did not quite agree with you."

"I'm beginning to suspect that men are less intelligent than women," Melissa said in a stage whisper that clearly John and his father were meant to hear. He laughed at her audacity. No, Melissa was not a shy girl. She would do very well when she got over her fear of people.

Just then the lights flickered, and those not already seated hastily made their way to their seats. The four of them sat side by side, with John to Melissa's right, Miss Stanhope seated next to her, and her uncle on the far left. The lights had been dimmed only a moment when the orchestra began playing. And from then on, the girl was in rapture, her eyes never straying from the stage, from the actors and singers. At one point, John thought he detected a tear coursing down her face, something rather confusing as the opera wasn't at all tragic—at least not yet. By the intermission, John was about to fall asleep, and so was surprised when Melissa turned, bubbling over with enthusiasm for the opera.

"Oh, it was lovely, wasn't it? Are all operas so wonderful? I could hear every note, every word, as if they were sitting right in front of me. And the costumes! How do they move about so freely wearing such ornate clothing?"

John laughed, her joy infectious. "Such enthusiasm for mediocrity is really not the thing," he drawled, but he couldn't continue his farce and so ended up laughing again when he saw the look of horror on her face. It was obvious to him she was to become an opera lover. God help the poor man who married her. He suppressed a shudder at the thought of attending more than one opera a year.

"Lord Willington, would you be so kind as to get your cousin a refreshment. I would very much like to say hello to my niece. I haven't seen her in weeks, you see."

"Of course," John said, standing and giving Miss Stanhope a bow. "Would you like some punch, perhaps, Melissa? I think it will be a bit of a crush out there, and it might be best for you to stay put."

His father stood and stretched a bit. "I'll be two boxes down talking to Quimby. He's being stubborn about Rolt's Act, trying to water it down too much, and I want to get him to see sense while he's away from his cronies. I'll keep an eye on Melissa while you're getting refreshments."

"I'll be perfectly fine here reliving the first act," Melissa said, looking over her program for *The Lily of Killarney*. She'd never thought an opera could be so very exciting, and she couldn't wait to find out if young Creggan was actually going to murder his secret wife, Eily, so he could marry the wealthy Ann and save his lands.

Now that she knew the characters, she wanted to put their names with the names of the performers, and she looked over the program with interest. It was all so exciting and she wondered what the cast was doing at this very moment. How brave to walk out on a stage and sing your heart out to a large crowd of people. It must be so thrilling to hear such applause, to be part of something so absolutely astounding.

Down below, the seats were nearly empty, and several members of the orchestra were either relaxing or tuning their instruments. Outside, she could hear the rustling of dresses and quiet murmurs of people passing by. She looked toward the box where Miss Stanhope had gone to visit her niece, the duchess, but it appeared to be empty. Was she the only person still seated? Where had they all gone?

That was when she comprehended where at least some of them had gone, and realized she needed to find a water closet or be exceedingly uncomfortable for the remainder of the opera.

Feeling slightly rebellious, Melissa stood and moved toward the exit, peeking out at those who walked by. Everyone seemed so calm, so sure that he or she belonged, so completely unaware of his or her surroundings. Melissa reminded herself that this was practically an everyday occurrence for most of the ton. If they had to go use the necessary, they did so. Right now, Melissa truly wished she had told Miss Stanhope of her needs.

Two elderly women were passing by, chatting rather loudly to one another, when Melissa stepped out of the box. "Excuse me, ladies," Melissa said with an air of apology. "This is my first time at the opera house. I wonder if you could be so kind as to direct me to the necessary."

"Oh, I daresay you won't have time for that," one lady said. "It's all the way on the evens, you see."

Melissa looked doubtfully down the hall where the even-numbered boxes were, hoping to see Miss Stanhope or John walking her way. "Thank you."

Melissa stood uncertainly in the hallway just outside the box, nodding absently to the increasing number of passersby. Oh, why hadn't she thought about going minutes ago?

Just as she made up her mind to start walking toward the evens, the lights flickered, indicating the second act would be beginning shortly. Suddenly, Melissa found herself in a sea of people, all hurrying to get to their seats before the act began—and she was heading against the flow, jostling and bumping into people. She kept her arms against herself, her fists held tightly against her chest, as if she were fending off an enemy. Panic flooded her, and she found it difficult to breathe, to move. She pressed herself against a wall as people moved around her, some staring at her strangely. She squeezed her eyes shut and tried with all her being to hold in the scream she so wanted to let out. They were breathing on her, touching her, rubbing their clothes against hers. Calm, calm, calm, she said to herself over and over. But no matter how much she pleaded with herself to open her eyes and make her way to her uncle's private box, she was paralyzed.

From what seemed like miles away, above the roaring in her ears, she thought she heard her name.

"Melissa, good God, what happened? Melissa!"

She opened her eyes, and there stood John, staring at her with concern and fear. Without thinking, she flung herself into his arms and allowed him to half drag her into their box, which had been but a few steps away. She was shaking uncontrollably, pressing her forehead against his chest, clutching his lapels as though if she let go, she'd plummet down to the gallery below.

"It's all right," he murmured. "You're safe now. Safe. It's all right." He continued to calm her, his voice low and steady, as slowly she began to relax against him.

"What has happened?" Her uncle. She clung even more fiercely as she felt John shrug.

"I found her just outside, terrified of something. I don't know what."

"N-nothing," she managed, lifting her face up to look at him. "It was nothing. I . . ."

"I don't think she was ready for such a crowd. Is that it, then?"

She nodded, then pressed her forehead against him, and he tightened his hold on her. "I'm s-so sorry."

"I don't want you to worry about a thing, not a thing," her uncle blustered. Then, "Where the devil is Miss Stanhope? She's supposed to be with her charge, not gallivanting all about the opera house socializing."

"I was eight boxes away, conversing with my niece and my brother," came a terse reply. "You, if I do recall, said you would keep an eye on her."

"Well, you should have stayed here."

Melissa straightened up, shaking her head. "Please,

Uncle, it's not Miss Stanhope's fault. It is mine and mine alone. I had no idea I would react in such a way. I have no experience at this, you see. I should have stayed in the box as you directed me, but I needed to . . ." She flushed pink. Even she knew one did not mention aloud going to the necessary in front of members of the opposite sex.

"No need to worry," Miss Stanhope said in her no-nonsense tone. "The crowds have dispersed. I can direct you. And perhaps we should call it an evening, my lords?"

"Of course," Lord Braddock said rather quickly.

"I thought it was a great bore, too," John said, then gave Melissa a wink.

"We'll meet the two of you in the lobby," Lord Braddock said. "And, please, Melissa, don't worry about a thing. We'll muddle through this just fine."

By the time the carriage pulled up in front of her uncle's Piccadilly town house, everyone had agreed London was a bit overwhelming for a girl who had been as isolated as Melissa had. The plan was for Miss Stanhope, Melissa, and John to head to their country estate in Flintwood, with Lord Braddock to follow in a few weeks' time when his business in Parliament was concluded. Melissa did not object, for she truly thought their plan was best. It would allow her to get used to being out and about at small, inconsequential amusements where she would not be faced with such large crowds of people. By May or June, she would be ready for the season—and finding a husband.

During her long lessons on etiquette and deportment, Melissa had never questioned the necessity of such knowledge. She simply went along with the lessons because her father asked it of her. But now she realized everything she'd learned was in preparation for a day she hadn't thought would ever come.

The thought of having a husband, of being out in the world by herself, was more than daunting. It was terrifying.

Chapter 5

Melissa sat up in bed and hugged her knees, watching in pure delight as snow fell outside her window, big wet globs that would surely turn to rain if the day warmed. But for now, it was a lovely sight, especially knowing this would be the first time in memory that she would be allowed to go out into it.

Snow in Bamburgh was a rarity, but on the few occasions it had snowed, her father had forbade her to touch it for fear she'd catch a cold. But over the years she had snuck to a window and touched the impossibly soft and frozen fluff that clung to her sill. She'd even felt the snow kiss her cheeks once before Mary pulled her back in horror.

"It was lovely," she'd said, closer to tears than she would ever admit. She'd looked outside and seen one of the stable boys pick up a bit of it and fling it against the stable wall.

"You'll catch your death and then what will you do?"

Melissa had shrugged. "Die I s'pose."

Her father had overheard the entire exchange and stormed into her room, his face a mask of fury. It was one of the few times in her life she'd ever seen her father angry; never had that anger been directed at herself. He'd grabbed her shoulders and given her a hard shake, then dropped his hands immediately. "Don't you ever say such a thing again. Ever, do you hear me, Melissa Ann? Do you?"

Tears had coursed down her cheeks then, tears of anger and fear and terrible guilt that she had made her beloved father angry with her. But over the years she'd watched countless times when people trudged through the snow, as horses plodded through it, great clumps lifting into the air. She'd even watched her own father walk from the house to the stables, and he'd never fallen ill. It made no sense to a little girl, and even less sense to her when she was grown. By then, she accepted her life without resentment or anger.

But now, Bamburgh was behind her, along with her father's incessant fears, and she could do as she wished. If she wanted to touch the snow, she would. If she wanted to don a pair of boots and take a walk in it, she could. She pushed down a sharp stab of anger at all her father had taken from her. She would not be angry with him. He'd loved her. He'd only been trying to protect her.

But it had only been snow, a small rebellious voice said.

She rushed to the window and looked out to see John below talking to one of the servants who had a shovel in his hand. Without thinking, she threw open the sash and called down. "Is it lovely?"

"It's bloody cold, that's what it is," he called back, smiling.

"May I come down?"

"Of course," he said, looking slightly taken aback that she'd asked.

Melissa quickly closed the window and turned to find her maid, Clara, behind her tidying up the bed. While she missed her old maid, Mary, Melissa liked having someone who was not only efficient but who treated her like a normal young lady. Mary had always taken great care not to touch her and had always worn pristine gloves when she was attending her. Even when dressing her hair, Mary had donned a clean pair of gloves. It was something Melissa hadn't thought about until moving to her uncle's. She realized, with a bit of self-disgust, she hadn't thought of a great many things while living her cloistered, quiet life in Bamburgh.

"Clara. Could you please help me into my warmest clothes? I'm going out into the snow."

"Oh, miss, it's terrible cold out there," she said, shuddering, and Melissa had an awful sinking feeling that she would be denied. "I have some nice woolen mittens you can borrow. And your boots. Be sure to dress warm."

Melissa grinned, feeling a sharp sense of freedom. No one would stop her. "I will. I've never been in the snow, you see."

"Never?" Clara asked, amazed. "I met a girl from Italy once who had never seen snow."

"Oh, I've *seen* it. I've just never been *in* it."

"Let's bundle you up, then."

In a matter of minutes, Melissa was warm and cozy in a woolen dress, boots, muffler, and thick woolen mittens that Clara had fetched from her own supply. "Gloves won't do in this cold. It's getting colder by the minute out there. Me mum makes the nicest mittens, doesn't she? I've got more than I could ever use. It doesn't matter that I've only got the two hands, she's forever knitting more."

"Be sure to tell your mother thank you for me. These are wonderful," Melissa said, waggling her fingers inside the mittens. Outside, the temperature had dropped, and the snowflakes that had been thick and wet now fell and danced in the wind before settling onto the ground. She flung herself out the front door, not caring that she looked like a hoyden, not caring that she was supposed to be a twenty-three-year-old young lady who should be acting far more sedately. She'd been sedate for so many years, and now she wanted to experience life.

It was snowing and it was . . . oh, goodness, it was hitting her face, cold little bites on her cheeks and eyelids and neck. She pulled her muffler about her a bit tighter. It was cold, she thought, then laughed out loud.

"You are always laughing at something, aren't you? What is it now?" John asked, his dark hair frosted white with the snow.

"I've never been in the snow," she said, then turned her face up to it again.

"Look," he said, scooping up a bit of snow into his gloved hand and patting it until it formed a sphere. Then he tossed it at her, hitting her with a muffled thud on her shoulder and leaving behind a round snow print. Melissa opened her mouth in delighted shock, glancing from the snow on her shoulder back to John's grinning face.

"Let me try," she said, grabbing up some snow. The grass was still peeking through the white stuff, but it was disappearing quickly from view. Melissa did a very poor job with her ball, but she threw it at him anyway. He ducked with a laugh. "No fair, you must stand there and take it like a man," she announced, then bent down and retrieved more snow. With a bit of a devilish look, she gathered up as much as she could before packing it down and throwing it, hitting him squarely in the face. He stood there like a statue, his face covered with the remnants of her snowball.

"Oh, I didn't mean to . . ." She started laughing. "Honestly, John, I was aiming for your shoulder. I never meant to hit you in the . . ." He calmly wiped the snow from his face, where it left behind cold rivulets of water. His face had gone quite red, and Melissa hoped it was from the cold snow and not from anger.

"I'm afraid that requires retaliation," he said calmly, then bent down again. Melissa didn't wait to find out what he was planning. She took off across the lawn, her feet slipping and sliding in the snow. Melissa, having spent much of her life indoors, was perhaps not the most agile runner, and she found very quickly that running in the snow added a degree of peril. Hearing footsteps behind her and gaining quickly, she tried to make a quick turn but instead found herself flailing about right before she tumbled, face-first, onto the frozen ground.

"Melissa!" John cried, coming up next to her. She couldn't answer. Could. Not. She was laughing too hard. Oh, had she ever in her life laughed like this? Laughed at her own silliness, at the pure joy of being completely absurd. He was kneeling next to her, his face still wet from her snowball, laughing with her. His eyelashes, thick and straight, were clumped charmingly together by the melted snow, his gray eyes dancing with humor. She suddenly felt strange, impossibly hot even though she was sitting on the snow-covered ground. It was as if everything in her body thickened: her blood, her breath. It was the strangest sensation she'd ever felt in her life, and she instinctively knew it was because of John.

"I thought you surely hurt yourself," he said, still laughing.

"Only my pride," she said, thankful that the strange feeling was abating. "And, oh, my dress." It was a snowy, wet, muddy mess. "It's filthy," she said, rather delighted with that as well. She wished she could roll around in mud and laugh and laugh all day. Except it was extremely cold sitting there on the ground. She began struggling to get up, but he offered her his hand. She grabbed it without hesitation, and he hoisted her up rather too fast, making her crash against him and threatening to toss them both back onto the snowy earth. Her face was just inches from his. She could see a bead of water on his cold-flushed cheek, see the dark shadow of his beard, even though it appeared he'd already shaved that day, see that his gray eyes were rimmed with the darkest blue. And that feeling was back full force, a feeling that made her wonder what it would be like to press her lips against his. Not one month ago, such a thought would have made her wrinkle her nose in distaste. Put her mouth against a man's? Never. But for some reason, the need to press against John, to kiss him, was nearly overwhelming.

John pushed her gently away, his smile appearing rather strained. His laughing eyes were shuttered, his jaw tight. Melissa felt unaccountably foolish. She was not good at hiding her feelings, as she'd never had to practice such subtle deceit before. It was possible John was quite aware of what she'd been thinking— and he very clearly didn't like it.

"Did I hurt you with the snowball? Is that why you are angry?" she asked, praying he would allow her to pretend ignorance.

His cautious look was immediately replaced by one of his smiles. "Yes, as a matter of fact, you did. Wounded me terribly. But I suppose falling headlong into the snow and ruining your dress is enough recompense."

A whinny from the stables drew Melissa's attention. "Could you show me the horses?"

"I suppose you cannot ride?"

"I did have a hobby horse when I was a girl and rode her like blazes. I was a princess saving an errant knight."

That made him laugh, and Melissa relaxed slightly. "I do believe it's the other way 'round, my dear."

"Not in my world. However, the thought of riding a real horse rather terrifies me, if I must be perfectly honest."

"You must."

She shot him a withering look. "They are so monstrously big."

They stepped into the gloom of the stables, and Melissa breathed in air laden with hay, wood, leather, and horse manure. It should have been an unfortunate combination, but Melissa found the aroma not at all offensive. It was markedly warmer in the stable, and the snow on her coat immediately began melting.

"My goodness, how many horses do you have?" she asked, wandering down the middle of the stone floor, far from the reach of any horse that might want to attack.

"We've twelve here, including the carriage horses, and a few others at my father's estate near Cambridge. You shouldn't be afraid of horses, you know. They're rather like big dogs."

"I'm afraid of dogs, too," she said, backing away from one stall where a black horse with a white mark on its forehead leaned out.

John immediately went over to the beast, murmuring softly, then rubbed its head. The horse seemed to like the attention, and Melissa stepped a bit closer. "Sir Jake is like a kitten," he said, taking something out of his pocket and feeding it to the animal.

"I thought you said horses were like big dogs," Melissa said, keeping her eye on the horse in case it decided to burst through its stall.

"All right then, in an effort not to confuse you, I'll say Sir Jake is like a puppy. All love and gentleness. Come here, I'll show you."

Melissa stood, eyes wide, staring at the horse, which seemed completely uninterested in her presence.

"I would never let you approach a horse I didn't think was completely trustworthy. There are some who are a bit more ill-mannered that I would not allow you to pet, but . . . ."

"Pet? You want me to *touch* it?"

To her horror, John gave the horse a hug. "You've wounded his heart irreparably," he said. "Good ol' Sir Jake is very sensitive. Now, come here. Don't be such a coward."

Melissa marched over to him, her arms crossed.

"Take off those silly mittens and hold out your

hand like this," he said, demonstrating by holding his
hand, palm up, completely flat. It was said as if this
were a simple request. Well, if he was not going to
take great issue with it, she wouldn't either. She took
one mitten off and held out her hand, frightened to
her very core. Her hand shook noticeably, and she
shot a look to John, who was staring at her with an
intensity that was exceedingly disturbing. Without a
word, he dropped a bit of carrot into her palm, then
grasped her sleeve at her wrist and gently guided her
hand toward the horse.

Melissa stifled a scream as the horse's great head
dipped toward her hand, but John held it fast. To her
wonder, the horse gently took the food from her
palm, hardly touching her with its impossibly soft
muzzle.

"Oh," she whispered, smiling as she watched the
horse crunching on the very same morsel that had
just been in her hand. It was miraculous.

"There's my gentle boy," John said, rubbing the
horse's head again.

"May I try again?" Melissa asked, still grinning and
feeling ridiculously proud.

John dug into his pocket and dropped another
carrot chunk into her hand. Melissa noted he took
care not to touch her, and for the first time in her life
she felt that loss. In her memory, she could not remember ever being touched by anyone, skin to skin.
Always they wore gloves, even her father.

But she had touched a horse—or rather a horse
had touched her. The thought should have been
terrifying, but it wasn't. Again, she held up the piece
of carrot, but this time of her own volition, and Sir
Jake took the offering happily. "It tickles," she said,

feeling foolishly happy. She'd thought she would find John smiling at her, but instead he was looking at her with such sadness, she felt her stomach drop in a sickening lurch.

"Do not do that," she said, backing from him and the horse.

John shook his head. "Do what?"

"Look at me with pity." Melissa could feel hot tears pressing against her eyes. "I'm not something to be pitied."

John looked instantly contrite. "I'm sorry, but it was wrong what was done to you, and I do pity you. You are a woman grown who has never played in the snow, never fed a horse a carrot, never . . ." He stopped, and she could see the muscles in his jaw clench. "There is a lifetime of experiences you have never had, and that *is* something to be pitied. If your father were alive, I would thrash him for what he's done to you."

The more he spoke, the tighter she gripped her arms about herself, as if she could somehow stop the words from entering her soul, from tearing the pure image she had of her father from her heart.

"My father loved me," she said quietly, and watched as John's ire deflated.

"Even if that's true, and I'm certain it was, it does not alter the fact that what he did to you was wrong. I understand his reasons. But it was still wrong. You cannot even touch me—or anyone, for that matter—without flinching. I fear for you, Melissa, I do. The ton will not be kind to you, and the men . . ." He stopped suddenly and looked away.

Her throat was so full, she could hardly speak, and

the tears in her eyes finally spilled over. She truly hadn't thought she was so different from other girls. She knew she'd have a lot to learn, but was she so very different that a man would not want her?

"Thank you for showing me the horses," she said quickly, forcing the words out from a throat that ached terribly. She hurried from the stable, conscious of her awkward gait as she tried to run. She heard him calling from behind, but she only went faster, slipping a bit, unused to the snow, unused to running, unused to everything that everyone else took for granted. Tears fell quicker now, and she prayed he wouldn't run after her.

Oh, God, to think she'd wanted to kiss him. And he likely knew it. It was beyond humiliating to think that he knew. He pitied her, and the fact that she'd wanted his kiss likely made him pity her even more. She was such a stupid, freakish girl. With a sob, she reached the front door, only to realize she couldn't let anyone see that she'd been crying, something that made her cry all the more. She stood there and tried to gather herself together, shivering from the cold.

John watched her go, angry with himself, and particularly with her father. Every time she discovered something new, each time something ordinary delighted her, it only fueled that anger. Even the way she ran from him, lifting her skirts too high, slipping and sliding and nearly falling into the snow again, made him angry. He let out a curse, and Sir Jake snorted back at him.

"I've made a muck of it, haven't I, old man?" he

asked the horse, who seemed to look at him accusingly. "I s'pose I should go apologize then, shall I?"

With a sigh, he pulled up his collar against the cold and trudged after her, taking long, loping steps and keeping his head down. It was even colder now than before they'd entered the stable. He turned the corner around the house and was surprised to see her, still standing at the entrance, seemingly staring at the door. Then he heard her sniff and realized she was still crying. Damn.

"I'm so sorry, Melissa," he said, and watched as she immediately stiffened. "I had no right to say anything about your father. Indeed, your unusual circumstances have made you unique. An original. If I'm charmed by you, I'm certain others will be, too. Look at poor Waddington the other night at the opera. Smitten, and he hadn't even seen your lovely smile yet."

She turned her head toward him just a bit, but it was enough for him to see that she was smiling. He took that as a good sign and walked up the shallow steps to stand by her.

"I am sorry, you know. It's only that I've been charged with keeping you safe and getting you ready for the season, and I take those responsibilities very seriously."

She dipped her head slightly, just enough so that her neck was exposed to the falling snow, and he watched as several landed and melted just below where her dark curls showed beneath her hat. He had the sudden image of himself kissing her there, where the melted snow was leaving tiny, cold droplets, and he squeezed his eyes shut to banish that completely inappropriate and delectable image.

His father had put her under his care, and he had promised to protect her and care for her. That charge did not include kissing her, as he wanted to do now. As he'd wanted to do when they were playing in the snow. He'd seen the way she'd looked at him, watched the awareness grow, the confusion in her violet eyes. Hell, he should be thinking of her as a sister, not as a desirable woman who would likely taste as sweet as she looked. . . . Damn, there were those errant thoughts again. Part of him wished his father had never told him the truth about Melissa's parentage and had allowed him to believe they were closely related. While he told himself she was off-limits, his body knew the truth—that she was a lovely, desirable woman who desired him. He suspected she was completely innocent. He certainly didn't want her discovering her desires with him. The sooner they got her ready for the season and married off, the better. In fact, perhaps they could have a small get-together at Flintwood House and invite the top candidates from his list, thereby avoiding her season altogether.

"Do you truly think it's possible that I could be ready for society in time for the London season?" she asked, her voice tinged with uncertainty.

"I do. And I will help. We will dance and play cards and take walks and do all the things you will be expected to do with the swains who will no doubt start arriving as soon as word is out about Lord Braddock's beautiful niece."

"That would be lovely," she said, turning to him and giving him another of her stunning smiles.

No, he thought, it would not be lovely. It would be rather torturous. But he would do it anyway, as he had promised his father he would. He had given his father his word, and nothing would stop him from fulfilling his duty—certainly not his ridiculous and sudden attraction to her. He would find her a suitable, gentle husband who would care for her all the days of her life.

And he would watch and be glad of it.

Chapter 6

"Part of your duties as the wife of a landowner is to make certain your husband's tenants are well cared for," John said, sitting beside her in his smart little surrey as they toured the Flintwood estate. "A good wife will know her husband's tenants, will be certain the sick are cared for and that they have enough food in their stomachs."

"And what does a good husband do?" she asked, trying to bait him.

"A good husband listens to his wife when she tells him what needs to be done," he said without hesitation. "Having a title is a great responsibility. A lord must maintain his estate, to make it profitable even in times of difficulty, to keep it in a condition worthy of his heirs."

Melissa looked at the lands surrounding Flintwood House, seeing things she hadn't noticed during the days since they'd arrived. The stone walls were in perfect repair, the livestock she'd seen looked fat and healthy, and all the cottages sturdy and well kept. She wondered what it would look like in summer, in full growing season. It must be lovely.

On their journey from Bamburgh they'd passed by other farms that had looked very poor indeed compared to those in Flintwood. They were passing one particularly large, charming cottage, its snow-covered yard dotted with hundreds of footprints, surrounding a large and jolly-looking snowman.

"Oh, look," Melissa said, pointing out the cocky-looking fellow wearing a battered bowler on his frozen head. "There must be children." Melissa dared not tell John that she'd never actually seen a child close up. He would only look at her with that odd combination of anger and pity that made her feel uncomfortably aware of how different she was from most young women of her class.

"Shall we stop in? This is the Picket house. Huge brood of children, which is why they have one of the largest houses. Oldest boy works in our stables when he's not helping his father. Good lad, he is."

"How many children?" Melissa asked, trying to keep her tone level, but failing miserably.

"Nine. And mostly boys. I think the last was a girl, born less than a year ago, if I recall."

"A baby?" she breathed, not able to keep her enthusiasm from her voice.

"That's right," John said, sounding excited rather than pitying. "You've no doubt never seen an infant, have you?"

She shook her head, slightly mortified.

"Well, you're about to see a baby and more." He pulled a bag from beneath the seat and held it up to her. "Peppermint sticks. They go mad for them," he said, flashing a grin and leaping down from the surrey and going 'round to help her down. In his enthusiasm, he grabbed her about the waist and pulled her down effortlessly. "Come, now. And do try not to stare. It might frighten the children."

Melissa wrinkled her nose at him. "You can be extremely disagreeable when you want to be," she said in mock anger, but laughed when he gave her a look of pure innocence.

Before he could bound to the door, it swung open, and it seemed as if twenty children piled out of the house at once, not just seven. It was obvious John made their house a regular stop, for they were climbing all over him trying to get at his bag of peppermint sticks, which he held aloft and out of their reach.

"Children, leave poor Lord Willington alone," a harried-looking woman said. She was dressed more fashionably than Melissa would have pictured for a farmer's wife; clearly they were one of the more well-to-do families. Only her hair, which burst willfully from her bun, seemed even the slightest bit unkempt. And while her tone was rather stern, Melissa could tell that she was nearly as charmed by her own children as John was. The children quickly settled down and looked up at John like seven little angels, patiently waiting for their candy.

John gave them one each, then gave three to Mrs. Picket—one for her and one for Mr. Picket and one for their son who would be home later that day.

"Mrs. Picket, I'd like to introduce you to my cousin, Miss Melissa Atwell," John said. "Miss Atwell, Mrs. Picket. This is Toby, Thomas, Henry, Paul, Lizzie, Nathan, and . . ." He looked around, making a great show of searching for the little toddler who was hiding behind his legs, giggling madly. "Mrs. Picket, I do believe you are missing a child."

The other children laughed. "Jamie's in your stable," the little girl piped out.

"No, no. Isn't there another lad? A little one. I swear you had one called Philip. Mrs. Picket, is he lost?"

The little boy threw himself in front of John and yelled out, "Here I am." His face was already sticky from his candy.

Melissa stood back, overwhelmed at the sight of all these children. They were so . . . little. Little noses, little hands. Their skin smooth and creamy, their hair wispy and clean. Melissa heard the sound of a baby, and while they all herded into the large front room, Mrs. Picket disappeared, returning in moments holding a chubby little blond-haired baby.

"This is little Louisa," Mrs. Picket said, gazing down at her infant.

"How old is she?" Melissa asked, her eyes riveted on the child.

"Nearly eight months now and already trying to pull herself up to walk so she can keep up with her big brothers and sister," Mrs. Picket said.

"She's lovely," Melissa said. "Truly, all your children are." She wanted to touch the baby, to see if her skin could be as soft and velvety as it looked, but fear that she might hurt the little thing stopped her.

"They can be a handful, but we're truly blessed," Mrs. Picket said. "We were just finishing up our lessons, if you'd like to watch a while."

The children gave a collective groan, but without being told trudged into the next room, where two large tables were set up.

"We'll let you get to your work," John said, to the

sound of more disappointed groans. "I know the children won't be able to concentrate while we're here. It was good seeing you, Mrs. Picket. Tell Mr. Picket I'll be by Saturday next to talk about getting that new American horse plow."

"I'll let him know. It was a pleasure meeting you, Miss Atwell," Mrs. Picket said, leading them to the door.

After John helped Melissa into the surrey, he turned to her. "That might have been a bit overwhelming as an introduction to children. Have you survived?"

"It *was* a bit overwhelming. They all seem so . . . alive," she said, struggling to come up with the proper description for the Pickets' children. "And small. Like little people."

"Oh, they'll grow. Have you seen her oldest? Jamie is just fourteen, but he's nearly as tall as I am. A big, strapping boy."

Melissa looked at him with curiosity. "You truly like the children, don't you? It's not only duty for you, is it?"

He looked taken aback by her question. "Of course I like them. They're good children."

Melissa had never considered that she might have children someday. It was something so beyond her experience; she hadn't given it a thought. But after visiting the Picket household, she was better able to wonder at what it would be like to be a mother, to have children, to hold a little baby who depended upon you for everything. It gave her a small insight into what it must have been like for her mother.

Her mother had died so young, she only had the vaguest memories of her. Her father had been a calm, stern, and loving presence in her life, and for all his flaws, she'd never felt unloved. Now, as a woman on the cusp of having her own husband and children, Melissa wondered how it would be to lose a beloved spouse and be faced with raising a child alone.

One of her most vivid memories was of asking her mother whether she would be able to attend a ball like Cinderella. Her mother and father had been sitting by the fire—her father reading a book, her mother knitting. They'd looked at each other as if she'd asked whether she might travel alone to America, and then her mother's eyes had welled up with tears. It was fear Melissa had seen in their eyes, the kind of fear that had made Melissa feel horrid. She'd made her mother cry and her father look like he just might join her. Melissa had never again asked about balls or princes, and when her mother died, she had stopped believing in fairy-tale endings.

They rode in silence on the way back to Flintwood House, Melissa so lost in thought, she didn't even notice the sky had cleared, making for a brilliant sunset.

"Look," John said, lifting his chin to a sky gone a stunning peachy-yellow. Melissa gasped at the beauty of it, and when she turned, she found John looking at her with the oddest expression on his face.

"I'm inviting a couple of my friends here in two weeks," he said gruffly.

"That sounds like fun for you," Melissa said uncertainly.

"They're coming for you, to see if you'll suit." He jerked on the reins, and they jolted forward. "I think you'll be ready by then to meet them."

"Yes, I believe so," she murmured, though she wondered why he suddenly seemed angry with her. No doubt having his friends to the estate to meet her was a bit of a nuisance for a young man who likely wished he were in London.

He stopped the surrey outside the stables and greeted Jamie, who came out immediately to care for the horses. John lifted her down and looked pensively at the darkening sky, now a deep rose. "They're both good men. Either one would make a good husband for you."

She remained silent, staring at his profile. "Am I to be carted out like a horse for viewing?" she asked with a bit of a laugh. "It seems rather orchestrated to me. Then again, I really never gave marriage a thought."

"That's the most intelligent thing you've said yet."

She shook her head. "I shall prove you wrong by falling madly in love and staying that way until we die, lying side by side, holding hands."

He shoved his hands in his pockets. "Don't you even care who they are?"

Melissa shrugged. "No. Even if you told me their names, it would mean nothing to me."

"Their ranks, then?" He stared at her as if he was challenging her, but about what, she had no idea.

"You seem bent on telling me about them, so do."

"Charles Norris is the second son of Viscount Hartley. His brother is frail and has no heir, so there is a very real possibility Charles will gain the title. He's nearly thirty, a Cambridge man, very intelligent and serious."

"Does he notice beautiful sunsets?" she asked teasingly.

He gave her a sharp look, then continued. "Graham Spencer is a marquess. His seat is in Avonleigh. His father died two years ago, and he is quite respected and forging his path in the House of Lords. I hear he is already a force to be reckoned with. My father greatly admires him."

"He sounds perfect. If I marry him, I'll be Marchioness of Avonleigh. Oh, I like the sound of that," she said. "Avonleigh. It sounds like something out of a fairy tale, doesn't it?" She deepened her voice. "Now arriving, the Marquess and Marchioness of Avonleigh." Then she did a curtsy. "Yes, Your Highness, I am the Marchioness of Avonleigh. Delighted to meet you." Melissa giggled at her silliness and laughed even harder at John's look of male disgust.

"Avonleigh is in the wilderness of Northumberland and Charles's estate is just an hour's ride from Flintwood. He's mad about horses and hunting."

"Delightful."

John offered his arm, and Melissa sensed a bit of challenge in that gesture. So she took it unhesitatingly. "What if I don't like either one?"

"There are others on my list," he said shortly.

She gaped at him in amused disbelief. "You actually have a list of potential husbands? How many are on it?"

"Fourteen. But I've culled the herd a bit, now that I know you better."

"You have, have you? What if you culled the one man I was meant to be with?"

John let out an audible huff of air. "Really, does it matter who you're married to? You'll spit out the heir and the spare, grow bored, have discreet affairs, and carry on with your life. Honestly, Melissa, as long as the man doesn't beat you or gamble excessively, he'll do."

"Will he?" she said softly. "I daresay I shall be a bit more selective than that."

"Then you'll be wasting your time."

Melissa didn't know how to respond to John when he was being so cynical. How could a man who stopped to stare at a beautiful sunset, who remembered to bring children candy, be so opposed to the idea of true love? What had happened to him to make him so cynical? If he was telling her the truth, he'd never been in love, so it was not some great lost love that had blackened his heart forever. If no woman had broken his heart, then . . .

"Your mother."

He looked at her impatiently. "My mother what?"

"She's the one who broke your heart. And your father's apparently. That explains everything."

He let out a sharp laugh. "You are wrong. In order to have your heart broken, it must be thoroughly engaged."

She furrowed her brow at that. "You didn't love your mother?"

"She didn't love me," he said with cold certainty.

"But you told me that the only true love exists between parents and their children."

He nodded. "Yes, that is the usual case. Just look at Mrs. Picket and her brood."

"And what of Mr. Picket? Does he not love his wife?"

"Of course not," he said quickly, but something in his face changed, a flash of uncertainty or remembrance, that disappeared as quickly as it had come.

John pulled back a large swallow of brandy and stared at the fire in his room, feeling out of sorts. If he were in Town, he'd be out with his lads, going to a club, playing cards, letting off some steam. He was not a disagreeable person. In fact, most people thought John was rather too affable. He was not the sort of man who said the things he'd said to Melissa earlier that day—things he knew deep down he didn't believe.

Any man, as long as he didn't beat his wife, would be suitable for a woman such as Melissa? Was he *insane*? Right now, he couldn't think of a single man on his very long list who would suit her. She was far too unusual, too . . . something . . . to be with just any man. Avonleigh, indeed. He half wanted to write his friend and tell him to stay away. She'd not marry him if he had anything to do with it. He was too . . . Well, he liked politics far too much, and Melissa knew nothing of politics. And Avonleigh liked smaller women with more curves. Melissa had curves, it was true, but she was slim and rather too tall for Avonleigh's taste. Now that John thought more about it, they would never suit at all.

What Melissa truly needed was a man like Picket— but with a title. Despite what he'd told her that afternoon, he thought the Pickets might be that rare couple who did love one another. Perhaps he should adjust his beliefs to include only members of the ton. Yes, Mr. Picket adored his wife. He'd once ridden ten miles in a cold, driving rain to a hothouse in Sheffield to get her a single rose for their wedding anniversary. John knew because he'd met him on the way home. The farmer had been a bit ruddy-faced about the whole thing, but John would never forget what he'd told him that day: "Without her I'd be nothing more than me. An' how sad would that be?"

Nothing more than me.

John frowned fiercely, swirling the amber liquid in his snifter and breathing in the sharp fumes before taking another swallow. It would be good to get her off his hands. Perhaps when his father returned from London, John would take his leave. They wouldn't need him again until the season started in earnest. Who knew? Perhaps she'd find Charles Norris to her liking. Women were constantly flocking around him, and he'd been the target of more than one marriage-minded mama. He would do.

For some reason, John's stomach churned at the thought of them together. Charles was a sophisticated and experienced man who would no doubt have little patience for a girl so completely innocent. And Charles could be a bit of a snob, something that hadn't bothered John overmuch until now. Still, they might suit.

He drained the glass and let out a curse, wishing the task was done, that she was married and off his hands. Wishing the thought of her married didn't bother him so damn much.

Chapter 7

Miss Stanhope sat, her back straight, posture perfect, as she played the piano and watched John and Miss Atwell go through the intricate steps of the quadrille while obviously trying desperately not to laugh. Melissa, who had spent much of her life performing steps with "ghost" dancers, at first had calmly moved in time to the music in perfect form.

But poor John was having quite a difficult time of it, and instead of becoming frustrated, was having great fun talking to his imaginary partners. He entertained the two women so thoroughly, they could hardly get through the first figure without being completely overcome by laughter.

Diane stopped playing when it became quite clear that Miss Atwell knew the dance far better than the young lord did.

"I think we've covered the quadrille quite enough," she said, making a very poor attempt to be stern. "Perhaps we should focus on the polka or the reel."

"Or the waltz," Melissa said, still grinning. "I've

never before danced the waltz with a partner. My father never learnt it, you see."

John looked delighted. "Before we begin, however, I absolutely insist on a demonstration of how it is possible to dance the waltz without a partner."

Melissa lifted her chin with exaggerated dignity. "It's very simple, considering I don't have to worry about someone's blundering about and stepping upon my toes."

John gave her a little nod of his head, silently acknowledging her wit, then turned to Diane. "Could you play something by Strauss? I find Brahms depressing."

Melissa perked up, feeling ridiculously happy to be dancing with an actual partner. But she would be a good sport first and demonstrate how very easy it was to dance alone. John sat in a nearby chair, lazily draping himself over it, so that he rested his temple against one knuckle, seemingly bored with the entire exhibition.

Melissa assumed the position driven into her by her dance instructor, her back painfully straight, her chin held erect, her eyes forward, and embraced her imaginary partner as if it weren't the most ridiculous thing on earth to do. She thought she heard John make a noise that sounded suspiciously like he was trying to stifle a laugh. Ignoring him, and smiling like mad, she began dancing as soon as Diane started the piece, only to break into gales of laughter when she chanced a look at John, who had quite lost his battle to appear bored.

He stood. "That, my dear, is a tragedy of the first rate," he pronounced. He turned to Diane. "Please begin again, Miss Stanhope."

Melissa felt a familiar rush of trepidation when he walked toward her and extended his hand, but quashed it immediately. Grasping his left hand firmly, just to show she wasn't afraid, she was slightly more hesitant when she felt his other hand upon her back, warm and solid, just below her shoulder blade. She shook her head slightly, angry with herself, then placed her own left hand upon his shoulder.

"Courage," he whispered, bending down near her ear. He nodded to Diane, and then Melissa was swept into a waltz like none she had ever imagined. All those times, dancing by herself as the dance instructor called out corrections, could never have prepared her for what it felt like to dance with a man who knew how to waltz. It took only a few moments before she was allowing him to lead her around the room, sweeping past Diane, who looked on with approval as her fingers flew over the keys.

Melissa quickly responded to his slightest pressure, following his lead, feeling herself become part of the dance, part of her partner. It was glorious, to be held like that, to move around the floor in complete unison with another human being, to feel his breath upon her forehead, and then, when she lifted her face, upon her cheek. He smiled down at her.

"You are amazingly good for a girl who's never done this," he said. "Marvelous, really."

Melissa flushed, feeling happier than she had in memory. How wonderful it would be to be wearing her prettiest ball gown, to dance in a room full of people, all swirling about, laughing, talking. She would not grow fearful, not if John was with her, looking down at her and smiling the way he was now.

Diane stopped playing and was positively beaming

at her. "You, my dear, are certainly ready to dance at your first ball," she said. "Now we must get you used to crowds and social interactions, and our work will be done. But I'm afraid those lessons will have to wait 'til tomorrow, if you don't mind. My correspondences are much overdue, and I really must dedicate some time to that this afternoon. But tomorrow I suggest we meet again, my lord, so we can practice the various social interchanges that might occur."

"I see no reason I cannot handle that now," John said affably. "I have some estate business I must attend to tomorrow and will have little time to dedicate to Melissa. But I certainly don't want to keep you from your correspondence."

Diane seemed to pause, then nodded, and Melissa had the distinct feeling her chaperone felt uncomfortable allowing John to handle this aspect of her education. When Miss Stanhope was gone, he noted the chaperone's hesitancy.

"I believe Miss Stanhope is taking your education as a personal mission and would be very displeased with herself if something should go wrong."

"As happened at the opera?" Melissa said, suddenly feeling dejected.

"Precisely. But that won't happen again. I'll stay by your side until you feel comfortable, I promise. In the meantime, you can practice with my friends and me. They'll be here in two days, you know."

Melissa wrinkled her nose. "I shall feel like a horse being inspected."

"And so shall they, I've no doubt."

Melissa hadn't thought of it that way and suddenly felt better about the whole thing. "I suppose I hadn't thought that young men of the ton often feel the same pressure to marry as women. You don't think they'll find me too old, do you?"

"While you are rather long in the tooth, I do believe you do not yet qualify as a spinster."

Melissa knew he was jesting, but until recently hadn't fully understood that twenty-three was quite old to make one's debut. Most girls were married and had children by her age—or else were considered on the shelf, according to Miss Stanhope. She would know, Melissa reasoned, because her chaperone was definitely a spinster.

"All right, then. Prepare me for my first ball." Melissa was aware she sounded very much like a green recruit preparing for his first battle—a bit frightened but with a courage that was likely misplaced. She stood before him very much like a soldier before a commanding officer, back straight, arms to her side.

John rested his right elbow against his left arm, and tapped his index finger against his mouth as if deep in thought. "Ah, I know. We'll go through different scenarios and see how you respond. Let's see. A spotty-faced young man with an overgrown Adam's apple who smells strongly of sausage approaches you for the first waltz of the night. What do you do?"

Melissa nodded, as if this were the most important of questions. "While I do adore sausage, I look at my dance card, which is already nearly full, and tell him the first waltz is already taken by my cousin."

His eyes sparkled with good humor. "Very well. But what if it is not taken?"

"Then I graciously thank him and agree to the dance."

"Or?"

"Immediately seek you out to be certain we dance the first waltz together."

He clapped his hands together. "Brilliant."

Melissa curtsied very nicely and said, "Thank you, sir."

"My lord, to you, underling."

"My Lord Conceit, how very sorry I am if I have inadvertently discounted your rank."

John rubbed his hands together and paced back and forth a bit before stopping. "All right. Scenario two. A very handsome, very rich young man who dances like a master and to whom you are quite attracted in a very improper way . . ."

"You!" she said gleefully.

He gave her a dark look. "Not me. Now pay attention. This stunner has asked you to take a walk in the garden with him."

"Hmmm. How rich?"

John growled. "Be serious, miss."

Melissa let out a puff of air. "I immediately seek out Miss Stanhope and advise her of my plans."

"Precisely. Now, what if you cannot find Miss Stanhope?"

"I regretfully decline."

"Ah," he said, raising one finger. "This man, this Adonis, is very persuasive. And he convinces you that it is perfectly proper to go out to the terrace and look at the stars. You're within sight of an entire ballroom. What could possibly be wrong with that?"

Melissa narrowed her eyes. "This sounds like something you may have done."

John shrugged, but pressed her. "What do you do?"

"Honestly?"

"Honestly."

"I'd probably go."

John didn't look happy about her answer, but he didn't say she was completely wrong either. "Not the best choice, but I'll allow it this time. Now, what if he should try to kiss you?"

Melissa's face immediately heated. "I wouldn't allow that," she said, shocked.

John tilted his head. "Why ever not?"

Was he tricking her? Trying to have her believe such a kiss would be within the realm of proper behavior when it was not? Or was a simple kiss from a handsome man, given freely, acceptable?

"Do I want to kiss him?" she asked.

His eyes drifted to her mouth, then shot back to her eyes. "Yes," he said, sounding slightly annoyed.

"Well, he is handsome. And rich. I'm assuming he has a wonderful title. He wants to kiss me, and I desperately want to kiss him. . . ."

"I did not say desperately."

". . . and I *desperately* want to kiss him," she repeated, just to needle him. "So, yes, I do. I kiss him." She nodded as if certain she had the right answer.

"No. You do not kiss him," he said, sounding horrified. "You don't even know the man! If someone saw you, you'd be marching down the aisle with a complete stranger within a fortnight. Good God, Melissa."

Melissa pouted good-naturedly. "But he's so handsome," she said wistfully. "And you've told me it doesn't matter really whom I marry, as long as he is wealthy, doesn't beat me, and can give me children."

"I apologized for saying that."

Melissa lifted her eyebrows. "But if it's what you truly believe, I'm afraid I cannot accept that apology."

"You," he said, pointing an accusing finger at her, "are insufferable."

Melissa shrugged to tell him that his opinion of her didn't matter in the least. She was having far too much fun at the moment to get into an argument with John.

"I would never allow a man to kiss me for the simple reason that I would foul it all up, so you needn't worry."

This, apparently, got him curious. "Foul it up?"

"As you so succinctly pointed out not five minutes ago, I am rather long in the tooth. A man would certainly expect a woman of my advanced years to know how to do such a simple thing." To her horror, Melissa felt the sharp burn of tears in her eyes. Suddenly, the fun had gone out of the lesson. "I've never even touched another person. Not really. How am I expected to be a wife? To kiss someone? To allow someone to touch me? . . ."

She let out a short sob, then swallowed, and closed her eyes, mortified that she had blurted out her greatest fear. How could she allow a man to touch her anywhere he wished when she'd never even held a man's hand? She pressed her gloved hands against her cheeks, feeling the smooth silk against her flesh. In quick, angry movements, she tore the gloves from her hands and threw them to the floor.

John's heart nearly broke for her at that moment. He knew she didn't want his pity, but by God, how could he not give it, watching her fall apart in front of him.

"Sometimes I want to go home so badly I could

scream," she said fiercely, staring at the floor, her fists clenched against her stomach.

"Melissa, come sit by me," John said, walking over to the settee. She looked at him uncertainly, then joined him and sat, very much like a petulant child. John slowly took off his gloves and placed them between them on the settee. "Now, give me your hand."

She looked up at him, and he nearly got lost in those magnificent violet eyes of hers, still shining from her brief bout of crying. Instead of giving him her hand, she clenched her fingers tighter in her lap and gave her gloves, still lying on the floor, a look of longing. Taking a shuddering breath, she said, "My father thought that disease entered the body through the pores of one's hand," she said, gazing at her own small, pale hands. "I wasn't allowed to take my gloves off except to bathe and at night. And no one was ever allowed to touch me without wearing them. Not even my father. He . . ." She shook her head and fresh tears fell. "He didn't want me to die, you see."

Bloody hell. "I believe your father, while well meaning, was a bit misguided. It's far more likely that we get disease through tainted food or water than by simply touching someone, unless they've been mucking about a pigsty. While I'm no expert on disease, I can say logically that his theory is wrong, or else everyone you know would be dead by now. The servants, my father, Miss Stanhope, me. Gloves are worn so that clothing does not become soiled, or to keep one's hands warm. Now. Give me your hand, Melissa."

He laid his hand, palm up, in the space between them. She looked down at her hands for a long moment before finally, and with great hesitation, laying her palm on his. Her hand was small and cool, and he could feel slight tremors as he closed his fingers slowly 'round hers.

John watched her face, ready to withdraw if he saw any fear in her eyes. All he saw, though, was wonder, and something inside him gave a sharp, almost painful tug. She looked up at him, then back to where their hands were still clasped.

"It's so warm. And soft," she said. Then her brow furrowed, and she lifted his hand up as if inspecting it. With the index finger of her other hand, she trailed her fingertip across the callouses in his palm.

"From riding," he said gruffly, agonizingly aware that her touch was beginning to physically affect him in a way that was completely unexpected. How could her moving her finger across his palm be so incredibly erotic? He wanted to jerk his hand from her grasp, but he knew if he did, he would only frighten her more. So instead, he gritted his teeth together and prayed his body would stop betraying him. Unfortunately, the more he thought about how he didn't want his body to respond, the more it did. When she moved her thumb across his wrist, he became achingly aroused, and he let out a strained laugh and slowly withdrew his hand from her curious grasp. Imagine making love to such a woman, his tortured mind thought, if that innocent touch could cause him to grow painfully erect. It was monstrous that he should react to her so, that he would allow his mind to picture her in his bed, exploring his body the way she was exploring his hand.

Bloody, bloody hell.

"John?"

"Yes?" he choked out, moving slightly away from her.

"Would you allow me to kiss you? I . . ." Her cheeks turned a vivid red. "Just to see what it is like and so that I'm not such a ninny if a man does try to kiss me. I know it's a lot to ask, but I don't want to make a fool of myself when the time comes. Is it *very* revolting?"

Dear God, why are you doing this to me? Is this a test? Because I fear I'm going to fail it. Sorry.

"Kissing is not revolting. Not with someone you're attracted to, at least."

"Oh. Then it shouldn't be too revolting with you. I do like you."

John swallowed and gave her a strained smile. "No, it shouldn't be too revolting, but I don't think . . . that is to say . . ." She kept looking at him with wide eyes, her mouth slightly open, her lips full and delicious and—*oh, Lord,* he thought, *I am doomed.*

"Perhaps one kiss," he heard himself saying. Apparently his body liked that decision, for he leapt to life in an embarrassing way. Thank goodness, they were seated and his jacket hid the evidence of his torture. Melissa smiled, very much pleased, like a child getting a sweet after cajoling a parent.

"Who kisses whom? I think you should kiss me, because I expect you know what you're doing." She seemed utterly happy with how this afternoon was playing out, while he felt nothing but deep depression and torturous arousal.

"All right then, let's get this over with." She leaned forward, eyes wide open, her lips pursed tightly. Despite himself, John smiled. "No, silly goose, relax your mouth." John's throat went dry at the sight of her mouth, the perfect shape, the full lower lip that was made just for kissing. *But not by you*, said a voice in his head, a voice he ignored.

He leaned forward, staring into her eyes until they blurred before him, and pressed his mouth against hers. Oh, this was very, very bad. This was the worst possible thing he could have done, for she was unbelievably soft. He moved his mouth over her lower lip, just the slightest movement, and she gasped. John forced himself to pull away when all he truly wanted was to deepen the kiss and taste her. She'd only wanted the one kiss, after all, just to show her what it would feel like when she got her real first kiss. But she was looking at him with drowsy eyes, and her mouth was still soft and pouty and only inches away.

"Perhaps two," he said thickly, and moved toward her again.

She moved back. "No. I'm all set. Thank you."

John clenched his fists together to stop from dragging her into his arms as she leapt up, a big grin on her face.

"I don't know what all the fuss is about," she said cheerfully, slicing innocently into his ego.

"It was a rather brief kiss," he grumbled.

"Still, it allowed me to know what to expect."

"There is more," he said, and wondered if he'd lost his mind. He had no business kissing her in the first place, never mind begging for more.

"I'm certain there is," she said with a cheeky smile. "Thank you, my lord." She flounced from the room, leaving him aching and hard and rather flummoxed, if he were completely honest. That kiss, as innocent and brief as it had been, had aroused him far more than it should have. He wasn't a man who was affected by a woman unless he was lying naked in bed with her. To have such a strong physical reaction to so insignificant a kiss was astounding.

John stood, adjusting himself with a grimace, and walked to an outside door and directly into the cold morning air without a single thought to the freezing temperature.

Melissa skipped from the room as nonchalantly as she could, praying he would never know just how affected she'd been by her lips touching his. She left the room, calmly closing the door behind her, before pressing her back against the wall and putting a trembling hand to her lips. Surely her reaction could not be normal. People kissed every day—on cheeks, on the lips. She'd seen from her window maids and footmen sneaking kisses in the orchard. It was a curious thing and something she'd never imagined for herself. But now, oh now it was all she could do to remain in the hallway and not go running back into the library to beg for more. This could not be normal. It simply could not.

Perhaps she'd waited too long for her first kiss. Perhaps every bit of desire in her was frothing to the surface. Then, another horrible thought came to her: what if she reacted this way to every man? A good girl did not allow a man to take liberties. She'd learned this from one of her governesses—Paula, it was. Paula had seemed a bit worldly, full of bitter advice about life and what Melissa must be wary of. But she'd never told her anything about the rush of warmth that would flood her body, that strange sensation of wanting—something. No, Melissa knew what she wanted. She wanted John to kiss her again, the way those footmen would kiss the maids.

Melissa took a shaking breath and stepped from the wall. She'd never truly had anyone to talk to about such things. Paula had warned her not to allow "liberties," but Melissa hadn't known what that meant. She still wasn't entirely certain. She didn't know how to act with a man, what to allow, what to feel. Perhaps this desire was perfectly normal. Or perhaps she was a Wanton Woman. As Paula had warned her, Wanton Women were those who allowed men liberties. Was she one of those, then? She tried to think back on what Paula had told her, but could only remember feeling bored with the entire conversation. Paula enjoyed her lectures, and this had simply been one more droning lecture. How she wished she'd paid more attention, asked questions. She still remembered the horror of getting her menses. No one had warned her, so she'd thought she was dying. She'd kept the secret, not wanting to worry her father, for two days. Finally, a maid found a bloodied rag and explained briefly—and with pink cheeks—that the woman's "curse" would visit her monthly. It all had to do with Eve's tempting Adam with an apple, and none of it made much sense. That had been her only discussion about her changing woman's body.

Melissa walked to her room, battering herself with questions she had no answers to. As she walked by Miss Stanhope's room, she spied the older woman bent over her desk working on her correspondence, the scratch of her pen audible even from the hall. Looking at her, Melissa had a sharp stab of melancholy, for her chaperone seemed so very alone. How was it that someone as nice and pretty as Miss Stanhope hadn't married? Had she ever had a beau? Had she ever been kissed?

"Miss Stanhope?"

Her chaperone blew lightly on her paper and placed her pen in its holder before turning to her. "Yes?"

"Have you ever been kissed?" Melissa blurted out, then gave an inward wince.

Miss Stanhope's eyes widened, and her cheeks turned slightly ruddy. "Why do you ask?" She said the words calmly, but Melissa detected an underlying concern. She instinctively knew she should not tell Miss Stanhope about her very brief and very devastating kiss with John.

"John was quizzing me, you see. Making up scenarios about what I should or shouldn't do at a ball."

"Oh?"

"He pretended he was a gent asking for a walk in the garden, and I replied that I must first fetch you."

Miss Stanhope smiled, the movement softening her features, which moments before had looked rather taut. "That was precisely the right answer."

"And then I asked him what I should do if a man were to kiss me." She shrugged. "I don't know why I should allow such a thing, but is there a reason I shouldn't?"

"I expect it would depend upon how long you had known the young man. It's perfectly acceptable to allow your fiancé a kiss, for example, just as long as it doesn't go on too long. One kiss is allowed."

This troubled Melissa, for she didn't want to marry someone whose kiss she couldn't tolerate. "What if it's loathsome?"

"If you care for someone, it is never loathsome.

And I would suggest you not become engaged to someone you find loathsome."

Melissa wandered over to a shelf filled with porcelain flowers, tiny, delicate knickknacks that were intricately made. There must have been thirty of them, a hard little bouquet. "These are lovely," Melissa said, while her mind still mulled over what Miss Stanhope had told her. She held one finger up to touch a blossom.

"Those are quite delicate," Miss Stanhope said, rising as if Melissa were an errant child bent on destruction. Melissa withdrew her finger immediately.

"Wherever did you get them?"

Miss Stanhope marched to her side and moved one slightly, even though Melissa hadn't touched it. "I made them myself," she said as if embarrassed to admit such a thing. "I suppose I fancy myself an expert on English flora and fauna and wanted to capture each bloom in perpetual glory. Never changing. Always pretty. I take them with me wherever I go." Her tone became wistful, and again Melissa was struck by how lonely she seemed. Was it so awful to be a spinster, to be relegated to chaperoning younger, husband-hunting women?

"You never did answer my question," Melissa said softly.

Miss Stanhope sniffed. "Of course I've been kissed."

Melissa suppressed a smile and raised one eyebrow. "I hadn't known you were engaged," she said, knowing she had just caught Miss Stanhope in the rather awkward position of admitting she'd been kissed without the benefit of an engagement. The flush on the older woman's cheeks told her she was right, but she felt no triumph. "I'm sorry, that wasn't at all good of me."

To her surprise, Miss Stanhope laughed. "It's much

easier to spout rules than to follow them," she said. "I daresay I've become just what I'd hoped to avoid—a proper missish old maid." She let out a sigh. "Yes. I've been kissed. And rather well, to be honest."

"What happened?"

"He found someone else with a bigger dowry and a prettier face. I was not at all the thing during my seasons." She spoke the words with nonchalance, but Melissa could detect hidden pain.

"But you're so pretty."

Miss Stanhope searched her face for a lie and, apparently finding none, let out another sigh. "I was terribly thin. My pointed features were a bit harsh, I think. Needless to say, the years went by, and there were fewer and fewer kisses. And here I am." She let out a strained little laugh and walked to the window, which was letting in the milky light of an overcast day.

"I never thought of getting married," Melissa said, "but I suppose I shall. To be honest, it terrified me."

"And now?"

"I do believe I'm getting used to the idea. I think I would like children. They are adorable, are they not?"

Miss Stanhope stared out the window. "It is the most difficult thing," she said, so softly Melissa could hardly hear her. She looked up and gave Melissa a sad smile. "To realize you will never have a baby to hold." She turned her back to Melissa, and Melissa feared Miss Stanhope was hiding tears. But when she turned back, moments later, her eyes were dry.

"But I have freedom that other women do not. I have my own house, my own life. I can do as I wish," she said with a nod toward her collection of flowers.

"And you've been kissed," Melissa said.

"Yes. And more than once. But I daresay all kisses are not created equal."

Melissa sat in a wingback chair and pulled her feet up like a child. Miss Stanhope gave her a look, but said nothing as she sat, back straight and proper, at her writing desk.

"Which was your worst kiss? And your best?" Melissa asked, thankful she finally had someone to talk to about such things.

Miss Stanhope seemed to consider the question for a while, a secret smile playing about her lips. "Well, I have to say they were from the same man, a Lord Reginald Bissle. Very smart fellow. Always dressed to the nines. Almost a dandy, now that I recall. Which is probably why he wanted a bigger dowry."

"The kiss," Melissa urged, losing patience.

"Ah, that." Miss Stanhope pressed her lips together in thought. "Devastating," she breathed as if the kiss were anything but. "That's the word I would use." She ended the sentence with a sharp nod.

Melissa furrowed her brow, and she felt her own cheeks redden. That was precisely how she'd thought of John's kiss. "But how could that be bad?" she asked.

"Because he was the only man to make me feel as if I were . . ."—she stopped, and in her eyes Melissa saw a fleeting look of pain and regret—". . . the most beautiful girl at the ball."

"You probably were, but just didn't realize it," Melissa said fiercely, feeling protective of the young girl Miss Stanhope once had been.

"Perhaps I was that night. I thought I was madly in love, and the most handsome man had just kissed me." She let out a small laugh. "I was very young, you see. Younger than you by several years. I was never so foolish again as to give someone my heart knowing his was not engaged."

"But how could that have been a bad kiss?"

Miss Stanhope chuckled. "I never forgot it. Even when other men kissed me, I always compared their kisses to Lord Bissle's, and they always came up lacking." She shook her head at her own foolish thoughts. "Now, enough of this sordid talk, my girl, I have correspondence to finish."

Melissa leapt up from her chair and gave Miss Stanhope's smooth cheek a kiss, feeling inordinately happy and normal performing such a gesture. "Thank you, Miss Stanhope," she said.

The older woman flushed with pleasure.

Melissa beamed her a smile. "I'll see you at dinner then." Melissa left the room, her steps light, happy to know she wasn't the only girl in the world to be devastated by a single kiss.

Chapter 8

Charles Norris, second in line to a viscountcy, arrived riding upon what John said was an Arabian. It just looked like a horse to Melissa, but she could tell from his tone that this particular Arabian was something special. It was a whitish gray with darker legs, and Melissa secretly thought it rather a homely thing. The man upon the horse, however, was decidedly better-looking. His hair was burnished gold—too light to be considered red and too dark to be considered blond. He was still too far away to see his features distinctly, but from what she did see from a second-floor sitting room window, he seemed like a fine-looking man.

"I'll take him," Melissa said, teasing John, who had been in a foul mood all morning.

John shot her an annoyed look. "You haven't even met him."

"But he's rich and handsome," she pointed out with a grin. "Oh, do stop being so grumpy, John. Mr. Norris is the only young man I've ever met other than you, and I've been looking forward to it." Then she lowered her voice to a whisper. "Do you think he'll try to kiss me?"

"Not if he wants to live," John grumbled, and seemed even more annoyed when Melissa laughed.

"You're a far stricter chaperone than even Miss Stanhope. One look from you and all my suitors will go running away."

"Norris is not your suitor."

"He's not my suitor *yet*."

Despite his obvious attempt to remain ill-tempered, John let out a laugh. "I've no doubt that Norris will take one look at you and fall to his knees to propose marriage."

"I shall say yes if he does," she said, just to see how John would react.

"That would sit perfectly well with me."

Melissa ignored the dull ache his comment caused and forced a smile. Even though she knew he was teasing, she suspected it must be tedious to have to watch over her when he could be in London doing whatever it was young gentlemen did.

"May we practice the introduction? I'm terribly nervous." This was a lie; she wasn't even a speck nervous, though she knew she should be. She lowered her voice. "Mr. Norris," she said in her best imitation of John, "I'd like to present you to my cousin, Miss Melissa Atwell. You'll find her far more agreeable company than myself as I have a burr stuck on my . . ."

"Melissa," he said, a clear warning in his tone.

"So charmed to have this opportunity to make your acquaintance," she continued, still in a deep voice that was now meant to sound like Mr. Norris. Melissa curtsied to the imaginary Norris. "It is a pleasure to meet you, Mr. Norris. It shall be so nice to be

in the presence of a pleasant young man." Then she
clasped her hands to her heart. "Marry you? But, sir,
we've only just met."

"Please do marry her, she's quite annoying,"
Melissa said in her best John imitation.

"In that case, yes, I will marry you." Melissa began
laughing at her own antics. She had often carried on
conversations very much like that one with imaginary
brothers and sisters when she was young and so felt
quite adept at it. She looked up from her imaginary
fiancé to find John gazing at her with bemusement.

"There is no one like you in all of England, you
know," he said, shaking his head a bit. "You'll be married before the year is out." He held out his arm for
her to take. "Now, my lady, if you will allow me to
escort you to your future husband."

"Of course," she said, regally taking his arm. Then
she stopped and stepped in front of him. "Oh, dear,
what if the marquess also wants to marry me? Will
there be some sort of contest to determine the
winner? Oh, a joust would be marvelous."

"Your conceit astounds me," John said dryly.

She wrinkled her nose, and he tapped it with his
index finger. "Not every man is going to fall at your
feet or find your wit witty." He took up her arm again
and proceeded to walk toward the stairs, where they
were met by a harried-looking Miss Stanhope.

"One of the gentlemen has arrived," she said,
giving Melissa a quick look-over. Apparently satisfied,
she pulled Melissa away from John.

"It's Norris," John said.

"Yes, I know the family." Miss Stanhope seemed
well pleased, so apparently this Norris fellow was
a more than satisfactory contender for her hand.

Really, it all seemed so silly, Melissa thought. What were they to do, decide whether they suited in the space of a week and then marry? Was that what all women did? "We will greet both gentlemen in the main drawing room at precisely seven. Until that time, my lord, you may do what you wish with them."

John gave Miss Stanhope a small bow and winked at Melissa. "I thought we could start the parade now, but of course I bow to your expertise, Miss Stanhope," John said. "It wouldn't be right to give Norris an unfair advantage by letting him meet my lovely cousin ahead of time. They might be engaged before Avon-leigh even makes an appearance."

Poor Miss Stanhope was quite taken aback. "I daresay it won't happen as quickly as that."

"John has assured me I shall be fighting men off. Perhaps I should carry a stick."

Miss Stanhope looked from one to another and finally huffed out a sigh of exasperation. "Finding a suitable husband is no joke," she said sternly, and John and Melissa immediate schooled their features. "As lovely as you are, my dear, your dowry is quite small, which is something you should keep in mind. Conceit is not a virtue, you know."

"Not a moment ago I admonished her for much the same," John said with a wicked glint to his eyes. Melissa pressed her lips together but remained silent, hurt more than she would ever admit by Miss Stanhope's criticism. She did not believe for a moment that either man would be taken with her. What did she have to offer a sophisticated man of the ton? She knew no one, had no connections, had never run a household or been taught to. She was no more useful than a blank piece of paper without a pen. Melissa might not be an expert in marriage, but she did know that young peers tended to be attracted to women who brought more to the arrangement than a pretty face and a few pounds. In the space of a few seconds, her happiness and expectations were dashed as the reality of her situation set in. Miss Stanhope's subtle reminder that she was not nearly as desirable as she'd been pretending to be was an unwelcome truth. She was the daughter of a second son, a recluse who had never gone out in society, and an impoverished gentlewoman who had become a governess, one of the lowest members of society.

Her face flushed with suppressed hurt and anger, she said, "I have no illusions at all, so you need not fear. I am perfectly aware that I have very little to offer anyone and that my desirability is extremely limited." John and Miss Stanhope shared a look she could not interpret, but she supposed it was because she'd sounded rather piquant, even though she hadn't meant to appear so put out. Perhaps she was angrier than she realized.

"I didn't mean to offend," Miss Stanhope said, and darted another look to John.

Melissa smiled a bit shakily. "I know you did not. I am sorry. That didn't come out quite the way I intended. John and I were simply having a bit of fun. I do understand who and what I am and that I shall be lucky to find any husband at all."

"Norris and Avonleigh are good men," John said forcefully. "I trust them implicitly, and you are worthy of both of them. Do not ever forget that."

Melissa felt her throat burning and swallowed past the pain. "But I am no one."

"You are my first cousin," he said in a voice edged with steel. "That is all they need to know."

"What else would they want to know?" she asked with a little laugh. "I suppose I could show them my needlepoint. Or my collection of books on philosophy." Melissa had the distinct feeling that there was some underlying current, as if more were being hidden than said. Miss Stanhope and John kept exchanging looks, as if holding their breaths and waiting for something terrible to happen. "Is it because of my upbringing? Because I have not been in society?" she asked, completely confused.

John relaxed. "You may bring out your needlepoint only if you wish to impress a man's mama, and the books on philosophy only if you want to drive a particular suitor away. And as far as your unique childhood, I see that as no barrier to becoming wildly successful in your debut," he said.

"Certainly not," Miss Stanhope agreed. "Now, my dear, you should rest before meeting our guests. Shall we all meet in the drawing room at seven, then?"

Melissa was slightly disappointed to not meet their guests immediately, but she headed to her rooms, still unable to shake the feeling that more had gone unspoken than spoken.

John watched her go, once again resisting the urge to call her back. Why was getting a pretty girl married so darned complicated?

"I'm not certain we're being fair to her," John said softly.

"Of course we are," Miss Stanhope said sharply. "Life is filled with harsh realities, realities that so far she's been completely shielded from. I cannot think of a single reason she should know the facts of her birth."

"Still, I never realized how difficult it would be for me to lie to Melissa about who she is. It seems so dishonest to allow her to continue to believe she is my uncle's daughter, especially given the chance that someone will discover her low birth. It does trouble me, far more than I thought it would."

"I fear you would be very much more bothered if word got out that Melissa was illegitimate and not your uncle's daughter. She does not need that taint when she is looking for the best match possible. It's not as if she has a dowry to overcome such a thing. Indeed, even a large dowry cannot overcome all undesirable qualities."

John suspected Miss Stanhope was bitterly referring to herself. "I'm certain Melissa will find a good match. I personally will see to it. Good day, miss." He gave her a small bow and headed down the stairs to greet his old friend, only to find Norris with a young woman on his arm.

"Laura, a pleasure," John said with real delight. Norris had brought along his sister, a pretty girl with sparkling brown eyes and light brown hair.

"I was fiercely bored at home and begged Charles to let me come. I do hope you don't mind. He told me you likely didn't have the proper mix anyhow." She smiled up at him so charmingly, he couldn't even pretend to be put out.

"You are absolutely right," John said, dropping a kiss upon her cheek. The three of them had grown up on neighboring estates and were as close as family. Laura had always trailed after the boys, getting into all kinds of trouble as she tried to keep up with them. After their coats, hats, and gloves were taken, John led the pair to the drawing room where the three sat.

"Still climbing trees, are you, now that you're such a fine old lady?" John asked.

"As a matter of fact, just last week a kitten got stuck in a tree, and I helped it down."

"It was on the first branch," Charles put in, holding his hand up about shoulder high.

"Well, I would have climbed the tree if the little scamp had gone any higher. And I'm not so old. Only eighteen. Or soon to be. And I shall expect you to ask me to dance at every ball this season."

John gave her a look of horror. "Don't tell me you've gone and fallen in love with me again. So tiresome."

Laura made a face. "I was twelve and quite delusional. I actually thought you were a fine young gentleman. I'm sorry to disappoint you, but I'm already in love and half engaged."

John shot a query to Charles who was looking disgusted by the conversation.

"Brewster succumbed," Charles said as if the man had died.

Laura waggled her hand at her brother. "Not yet," she said, indicating her empty ring finger. "And I no doubt have your scowls and ill humor to blame for that. But I've every indication that my Thomas will propose to me any day now." She looked ridiculously happy at the prospect, and John mentally crossed Brewster off his list of contenders for Melissa's hand. In fact, Brewster had been one of his top choices for Melissa.

"Despite your delirium, I'm quite glad you've

come. You do know that my first cousin, Miss Atwell, is here preparing for her first season?"

Laura clapped her hands together. "Yes, Charles told me and I cannot tell you how happy I am. Someone younger and greener than I whom I can take under my wing. I shall feel very old indeed."

John cleared his throat. "Actually, Melissa is twenty-three. She's been living in Bamburgh these last years and has had no entry into society."

"Bamburgh. Goodness. That's the end of the world," Laura said, aghast.

"Yes. And so she doesn't know a soul in Town and is a bit shy. You can meet her tonight right before dinner."

"John's invited me here to get a gander at her before the season begins so I will have an advantage," Charles explained.

"You and Avonleigh," John put in.

"Avonleigh is coming? Good God, that only helps my case."

Laura swatted her brother's arm. "Lord Avonleigh is one of the most desired men of the ton. You're just jealous."

"If he's so wonderful, why didn't you set your cap for him instead of Brewster?" Charles asked.

"Because Thomas is perfect for me. Lord Avonleigh is far too stern for my taste. And too handsome. Imagine having women staring at your husband everywhere you go. No thank you."

"Yes, indeed. Brewster is a bit of a horseface, isn't he?"

Laura narrowed her eyes but did not take her brother's obvious bait. "My point is, big brother, if

Avonleigh is coming, you don't have a chance with the girl."

Charles laughed. "Avonleigh is nearly as opposed to marriage as our John here."

"Are you saying you are not?" Laura asked, clearly surprised.

Charles shrugged, and something about that shrug put John on alert. Could it be that Charles was actually contemplating marriage? Even though he'd invited his friend for the express purpose of meeting Melissa, he found this realization somewhat disturbing.

"Let's simply say that I'm not as opposed as I was a year ago. I'll be thirty next year. Practically middle-aged. Before you know it, I'll be too old to attract someone other than widows or spinsters."

"I daresay your money would attract just about anyone," John said dryly.

"Is that why you're opposed to marriage?" Laura asked.

"I'm not at all opposed to marriage. I'm simply waiting for a match that will be mutually beneficial."

"How romantic of you. You're not still harboring the belief that love doesn't exist? I thought that was simply juvenile angst."

A footman entered carrying a tray of tea and small pastries. He set it down quietly on a table, stopping conversation for the moment. John was relieved he wouldn't have to again lecture someone on the subject of love. He'd learned it was impossible to convince someone under the delusion of love that the emotion did not exist.

"Shall I pour?" Laura asked.

"I was planning to break out my brandy, but tea will do for now," John said, and watched with strange contentment as Laura went about the ritual of pouring and serving the tea.

The same footman appeared moments later. "Sir, Lord Avonleigh and Lady Spencer have arrived."

"I don't recall asking for sisters," John murmured good-naturedly.

John noted that Laura pressed her lips together in displeasure. The two women did not get on well, as Laura was a buoyant spirit who often ignored society's rules, and Lady Spencer was a bit of a stickler. While not entirely unpleasant, she was a girl who understood her place in society—and everyone else's, as well. The daughter and sister of a marquess, Lady Spencer had debuted two years ago and had rejected three suits, because she was holding out for something better than a mere mister or baron.

"No doubt Lady Spencer is well aware that you did not plan properly for this little party of yours. Three men and one single woman is simply not the thing, you know," Laura said with the slightest mockery. "Now we are even. Three men. Three women. And you do know that Lady Spencer is madly in love with you."

John gave her a withering look. "She may join the line of ladies in 'love' with me," he said dryly. Laura rolled her eyes and shook her head.

"She would be the perfect match for you, my lord. You are both wealthy. Both sticklers. Both boring beyond bearing."

John chuckled. "I take exception to that last. I am not boring."

Laura smiled and conceded that point. "No, sir, you are not boring. And I do not believe she would suit at all. She would suck the joy out of you, then stomp on it with those heels of hers."

"My, my. I didn't know your animosity went quite that deep."

Laura let out a sigh. "I'm being rather ill-tempered, and I apologize. I will try to be pleasant as long as possible."

"Thank you," John said with a bow, then stood as the pair entered the drawing room.

Lord Avonleigh and Lady Juliana Spencer were the epitome of English aristocracy. Avonleigh was a tall, imposing man, who appeared far older than his years. He'd inherited his title two years earlier at age twenty-five, and it seemed to everyone who knew him that holding the title had aged him. Avonleigh now stood at the fringes of the large group of young men who'd invaded London several years earlier, looking for entertainments that mostly included women, drink, and gambling. Most had since taken a more serious bent, but Avonleigh had embraced his title with a fierceness that was both unexpected and curious. He had been the prankster among them, but now took life entirely too seriously. John had hopes that something—or someone—would snap Avonleigh out of his tedious duty and perhaps bring a smile to the chap's face.

Lady Juliana Spencer, on the other hand, had never been anything but a proper lady. She wore her title like a mantle that protected her from underlings and anyone who was not a member of the ton. She was only nineteen but acted like a dowager. Unfortunately, she wielded power like a dowager as well, a position she seemed to savor quite a lot. John disliked her only because she frowned so heavily upon anyone who stepped even slightly out of the bounds of proper behavior. And John and his friends often did so. John couldn't help but wonder why Avonleigh would have dragged his sister to the country, but he found out nearly immediately.

"I do hope you do not mind my bringing along Juliana," Avonleigh said smoothly. "She didn't want me proposing to anyone she hadn't yet met."

Lady Spencer didn't even hint at a smile. "Since yours is a bachelor home," she said with a level look at John, "I suspected you would not have thought of having the proper numbers."

"That's why I'm here," Laura put in, cheerful as ever, although John thought he sensed a brittleness in her tone. Lady Spencer simply turned her head slowly to acknowledge Laura's input. "I didn't want the poor girl overwhelmed by all three gentlemen at once."

"Surely, the numbers are wrong now with Miss Norris and I both here. The girl's chaperone will most certainly be joining us, will she not?" She spoke as if she suspected there was no chaperone.

"Miss Stanhope will certainly not mind if the numbers are off," John said.

John thought he heard Laura let out a snort of suppressed laughter, and he made a special effort not to smile at Lady Spencer's ridiculous starchiness. *My God,* he thought, *she is worse than before.*

Lady Spencer was not an unattractive girl. Quite the opposite, in fact. But it was nearly impossible to warm up to a girl who rarely smiled, and when she did, only because she ought to. John often wondered what had made brother and sister so fiercely serious. At least Avonleigh had escaped for a while and had had a rousing good time before slipping back into his staid, serious life. He realized that Melissa would suffocate with such a man, and he mentally crossed Avonleigh off his list. Melissa could not marry a man who would not delight in her, who would chastise and correct her, and who was related to such a joyless woman as Juliana.

"When do we meet this long lost cousin of yours?" Avonleigh asked. "I have nuptials to plan, you know."

Laura laughed, but stifled herself quickly at the look Lady Spencer gave her. "My brother has no interest in marriage," Lady Juliana said, her voice sharp.

"Not so, little sister," Avonleigh said, and it was clear Lady Spencer did not care to be called "little sister," for her nostrils pinched. "I must do my duty and have an heir eventually."

John gave his old friend a curious look. "Are you serious?"

"Why else did you invite us here if not to present us as possible husbands?"

"If you marry, Avonleigh, I'm afraid my days as a bachelor will be numbered. Even my father will begin to take exception to my single state."

"I know," Laura said, fully animated again. "We can make a game of it. List all the single women of marriageable age, put their names on a wall, and the three of you can throw darts at them. You shall marry whomever the dart lands on."

Juliana gasped. "That is preposterous."

"And we can do the same for you, my lady. But with men, of course," Laura said, clearly enjoying herself. "It'll be grand fun."

John let out a laugh. "Stop teasing her, Laura. You know she has no sense of the absurd."

"Can we have more than one chance?" Charles asked. "I daresay I wouldn't want to marry just anyone."

"Oh, we'd be careful to include only those women you favor." Laura's eyes twinkled merrily, and John suspected she was delighting in antagonizing Juliana.

"Fair enough," Charles said good-naturedly. "Sounds as good a notion for wife-finding as anything else."

"We can draw for who goes first," John said, joining in the fun.

"I should go first since I'm the only one of us who is seriously contemplating marriage," Charles said. "We shall need a paper and pen. And scissors to cut out the squares. You do have darts, do you not?"

"Avonleigh, make them stop," Lady Spencer said, seeming to be truly upset.

"Do you truly believe even these fellows would allow such a thing?" he said, and gave his agitated sister a gentle smile that seemed at odds with his serious nature. "They are simply having fun with you, Juliana. That is all."

Her pale cheeks bloomed with two spots of color.

"I do not understand such jesting," Lady Spencer said, and lifted her chin.

"Which is why they so delighted in it," Avonleigh said, calmly, but he'd made his point with the others, who immediately ceased their teasing.

"We apologize, don't we?" John said, and the others nodded, though John suspected Laura was less than sincere. "Melissa will be down right before dinner. In the meantime, ladies, you may rest in your rooms or walk about the gardens. It is unusually warm today, and I do believe the sun shall make an appearance."

With that, the small group dispersed until that evening.

Lord Braddock felt strangely out of sorts. Perhaps it was because he was in London while John was home in Flintwood taking on duties that should fall on his shoulders. He trusted John and Miss Stanhope completely to get his niece prepared for the season, but he felt uneasy somehow. It was as if he'd missed some important fact, something critical that he'd forgotten to take care of.

Part of it, he knew, was due to Miss Stanhope and her prickly nature, which seemed so at odds with what he'd seen of her in the past. She'd seemed so serene, almost otherworldly in her calm, which was one of the reasons he'd selected her as Melissa's chaperone. He'd not expected her to fight him on any front, particularly not when it came to his niece. And his reaction to her smile was rather curious. George was not a man who put too much weight on what he deemed to be the natural physical reaction of a man to an attractive woman. But his physical reaction to Miss Stanhope was bordering on the bizarre. Perhaps it was just as well he was staying in London while she schooled Melissa in proper behavior.

Lord Braddock was far happier in the bustle of London at any rate. When he was rusticating at Flintwood House, he could never fully relax, for there were always so many more productive things he could be doing in Town. He'd just finished a meeting with his solicitor, ensuring that Melissa would be taken care of financially upon his death. His brother, God rest his soul, had left his daughter nearly nothing but

debt. That would not happen should Lord Braddock
suddenly die.

Braddock was on his way to his townhome not
three blocks away when he spied the Duke of Waltham
departing a bookstore and was sorely tempted to stop
and turn around. Braddock didn't care for the man,
mostly out of solidarity with his brother, who had
loathed him for reasons unknown. Braddock had
heard rumors of unsavory activities and mistreatment
of his female servants, particularly the young ones,
and the duke's rages were nearly legendary. The man
at times seemed unhinged. Braddock didn't know
what had happened between the duke and his
brother, but it had gone dangerously deep and had
nearly led to a physical altercation years and years ago.
His brother had always claimed Waltham wanted him
dead, but had refused to tell George why.

He had never been a man to put stake in rumors,
but Braddock knew there was something off about
the duke, something one could not easily pin down.
It was almost as if Waltham had a scent that one was
unaware of smelling until it made one nauseous.

"Braddock. Good day to you, sir," Waltham said,
sounding overly friendly considering George's brother
had counted him his greatest enemy. "I understand
condolences are in order."

Waltham gave Braddock an appropriately sorrow-
ful look and George got the distinct feeling the duke
was being disingenuous. "Thank you. I'm certain the
news of my brother's death saddened you greatly.
Good day, sir."

George was about to move on, glad the encounter
was over, when the door to the bookstore opened and
a young girl stepped out, smiling broadly at Waltham

and holding a book up in front of her. "Oh, Father, thank you. Missy will be ever so jealous when I show her I got the very first copy."

George was quite certain at that moment that every function in his body, his breath, his heart, his very brain, stopped functioning when he saw that girl. She was lovely, with curling dark hair, a creamy complexion, rosebud lips. And violet eyes. She was, quite shockingly, Melissa's twin.

George looked from father to daughter, his world slowly crumbling about him. It could not be. *Could not.* Melissa could not be the offspring of this scoundrel. But the facts were, at that moment, nearly undeniable. The duke had those same disturbingly beautiful eyes, the same dark, curling hair. The resemblance was unmistakable.

"Caroline, this is Lord Braddock. Braddock, my daughter."

George schooled his features and gave the young girl a small bow. "A pleasure, Lady Caroline," he said with utmost formality, which for some reason tickled the girl.

"Caroline has not yet made her debut," Waltham said, looking down at his daughter with slight distaste. "Her manners require some improvement. Go to the carriage, my dear." Just like that, the girl's smile was gone, as if Waltham had wiped it clean with that sneer. "Be thankful you had only a boy." He paused. "But I understand you have your niece now. Is she in Town with you? I should like to meet her. Our families have been at odds long enough."

George thought he might vomit. He silently cursed his brother for not letting him know this rather important detail of Melissa's birth. Did Waltham know?

Oh, God, did he know Melissa was his illegitimate daughter?

"She is not in Town," George said. "If you'll excuse me, I am late for an appointment. Good day."

George walked past Waltham, feeling his skin prickle as he drew near the man.

"By the way," the duke said silkily. "I've purchased your brother's home. Perhaps his daughter would like to see it sometime. Out of nostalgia. I'd be more than happy to let her."

George stopped dead. Then he turned slowly around, his eyes hard, his smile dangerous. "If you don't mind, Your Grace," he said with steely politeness, "I would like you and your family to stay away from my niece. My brother would have wanted it that way."

With that, he turned and continued down the street, but he swore he could feel those violet eyes on him as he walked away.

Diane looked at her reflection and let out a sigh, rather dreading this evening. Once again, she would be the fifth wheel, the unnecessary appendage. The old spinster who faded into the scenery, not even significant enough to pity. Tonight there would be three men, three women, and her. Tonight would be yet another night when she would be nothing more than an extra seat filled with a breathing body.

How she loathed such nights. She closed her eyes and turned away from the mirror, wondering fiercely how her life had come to this. The worst bit was that she still felt the same as when she'd made her debut, full of life and fun. And hope. She still felt that cruel hope that someone would fall in love with her, would fall to his knees and beg her to marry him. It was nonsense, of course. But as much as she protested the existence of love and the foolishness of young girls in the throes of their first passion, she still secretly believed it might happen to her. Diane left her room and checked in on Melissa, who was still having her hair done by her maid. She looked lovely in her dark lavender dress, and Diane was glad the girl was in half mourning now.

Diane walked into the drawing room with a smile pasted onto her face and allowed John to make introductions to Lord Avonleigh and Lady Spencer, whom she had never met. They were polite, but dismissive, as if she were a governess and not the wealthy daughter of an earl. Perhaps she was being overly sensitive this night, but she hadn't felt quite so bothered by her position in years.

John pulled her aside after introductions were made. "How is Melissa?"

"She's a bit nervous," Diane said. "I expect her down any minute, and then I'll let you young people have your fun."

John gave her a look of concern, which Diane waved away. "I'm perfectly content to eat in my rooms," she said.

"Perhaps I can write my father and have him return early."

Her heart gave an unexpected leap, which mortified her. This infatuation she had with Lord Braddock was beyond ridiculous. "My goodness, you don't have to bring him home on my account," she said, oddly moved that John would think to do so.

"The numbers are wrong," he whispered, glancing over at Lady Juliana. "I shall never be able to show my face in London again if I do not immediately remedy the situation. I'll write him tomorrow, shall I?"

Diane heard a small noise near the door and watched as Melissa entered, head held high, eyes sparkling and seeking out her cousin. While all eyes went to Melissa, Diane watched the reactions of the others in the room with amusement. Laura put a finger beneath her brother's chin to close his mouth, which had gaped open in utter and instant infatuation as soon as he laid eyes on Melissa. Avonleigh narrowed his eyes and became subtly more rigid. Lady Spencer lifted one eyebrow, sensing a challenge to her role as reigning beauty. And Laura smiled in welcome. Diane always had liked that girl.

John felt fierce pride when Melissa walked in, and noted with a bit of alarm the reactions of the other men in the room. Charles in particular looked as if he'd been hit by a runaway carriage. John strode to her side and took her arm, whispering in her ear, "Not even a flinch. Good girl."

She smiled up at him, but he could see by the fire in her eyes that his jibe had hit its mark, and she squeezed his arm almost painfully. "Could you please simply introduce me to my future husband?" she asked quietly, and his smile faltered as she let out a delighted laugh. How was it he was always forgetting what his role was?

He brought her to Charles first, rather disgusted by his friend's obvious admiration. "Charles, Laura, may I present my cousin, Miss Melissa Atwell. Melissa, my dear friends, the Honorable Mr. Charles Norris and his sister, Miss Laura Norris."

"I'm so pleased to meet you both," Melissa said, bravely holding out her hand for Charles to take.

Charles bent over her hand gallantly, and John could feel her holding her breath to see if he'd actually press his lips upon her gloved hand. He didn't, and she relaxed.

"Well done," he whispered by her ear, inadvertently breathing in her intoxicating scent. Lemons, he thought, and something spicy.

"Is it true you lived in Bamburgh?" Laura asked as if Melissa had lived in China her entire life.

"Yes. It's very isolated, but I'm so looking forward to the bustle of London."

"You must allow me to be your social director this season. I'm engaged, or nearly so, and I can help you find your way around the ton."

"Thank you, Miss Norris. I'm afraid I don't know a single soul in London. Or anywhere else."

Laura's eyes widened. "You mean to say you've never even been to London? Not even for a single season?"

Melissa laughed. "I've never even been to a ball."

"Oh, you poor dear," Laura said, sounding both horrified and delighted by such information. "I will take you under my wing and get you married in no time. And please call me Laura."

"Thank you, Laura. And congratulations on your engagement," Melissa said. "Of course you may call me Melissa."

"She's not engaged," Charles put in. "You really must stop telling people that you are. Poor Brewster will hear about his engagement before he gets to ask."

"Oh, very well," Laura said, pretending to pout.

"Just so you know, it's not the thing to announce one's engagement before it occurs," John said to Melissa as he winked at Laura.

"You're just jealous because no one will have either one of you," Laura said.

John pulled Melissa over to Avonleigh and Lady Spencer, who stood rather stoically near the more animated Norrises.

"Melissa, may I present Graham Spencer, Marquess of Avonleigh, and his sister, Lady Juliana Spencer."

Melissa dipped a little curtsy and gave Avonleigh her hand. He bowed over it, staring at Melissa in a way that made John want to step in front of her and protect her. "A pleasure to meet John's long lost cousin," he said, putting a subtle emphasis on the word "cousin." John instantly became alert.

"Thank you," Melissa said, sounding slightly uncertain. She turned to Lady Spencer expectantly, likely thinking she would be much like Laura. "It's so nice to meet you, my lady. Please do call me Melissa," she said.

"Indeed." The smile she gave Melissa was more than frosty, and John instantly stiffened. If Lady Spencer dared insult Melissa, he could not guarantee he would act like a gentleman.

Melissa darted an uncertain look at him, clearly sensing that this woman's welcome was less than friendly. Laura came to the rescue, stepping in with her cheeky grin. "Lady Spencer and I were discussing the season and thought it would be fun to come up with the names of eligible bachelors for you."

"We were doing no such thing," Lady Spencer said. "However, we could do so now." Some of her frostiness melted, and John felt slightly relieved. Perhaps he was simply imagining Avonleigh's strange reaction to Melissa.

The three young women sat together in one corner

of the room, no doubt debating the various men who would be candidates for Melissa's hand. "Thank God I never had a sister," John said to no one in particular.

"It's rather maddening to think of little Laura as a married woman. Every time I picture Brewster touching her, I want to slug him. But I s'pose I should just let her grow up," Charles said morosely. "Sometimes when she walks into a room, I wonder who that pretty girl is, and then I realize it's Laura."

"Brewster's a good man, at least you have that," John said. "Funny. I thought I knew all sorts of good men until I had to come up with a list of them for Melissa."

Both men laughed. "We're none of us good, that's the problem," Charles said.

John felt a rush of misgiving. Charles was right. Who did he know who could possibly make Melissa happy, who would treat her the way she ought to be treated? At that moment, he couldn't think of a single soul.

"It looks like you won't have to suffer through a season after all."

John stood at the railing of the terrace next to Avonleigh, watching as Melissa and Charles walked together toward the small lake. She stopped and laughed delightedly at Charles, who was looking down at his cousin as if everything that came forth from her lovely mouth was pure poetry. John had known Charles for more than twenty-five years, and he'd never seen him act this way with a female before. It was downright horrifying.

"He's behaving like an idiot," John grumbled.

"Most men do when they think they're in love," Avonleigh said dryly.

John glared at the couple, who continued their stroll to the lake. Though he could not hear their words, he could tell they were talking animatedly, for their conversation was punctuated by laughter with irritating regularity. Diane sat at the other end of the terrace, bundled up from head to toe as if it were the coldest of days and not an unusually warm spring afternoon, and appeared to watch the scene unfold with pure contentment.

"You seem rather protective of your cousin, given that you've just met her yourself," Avonleigh said.

Again, John thought he detected that emphasis on the word "cousin."

"It is my duty to protect her," he said. "My father wants her to be safe."

"From what, I wonder," Avonleigh asked.

"From society and its cruelty, I suppose. She's led an extremely sheltered life and could be easily hurt. I'm here to make certain that doesn't happen." John could feel Avonleigh studying him and knew his warning shot had been heard—and understood.

"Ah. I see the way it is. You fancy yourself her protector."

"Of course. I'm her cousin."

"And those duties include watching her every move." Those words hung between them like some sort of accusation. "She is lovely. Those unusual eyes, I think, will cause quite a stir. Quite unlike anything I've ever seen in your family."

John's gut twisted, for it became quite clear that Avonleigh was more than hinting about Melissa's birth. "Just say what you are thinking. I hate sub-terfuge, Avonleigh."

Avonleigh let out the sigh of a much beleaguered gentleman being forced to do something he does not want to do. "Does she know she is Waltham's daughter?"

Stunned, John turned his head sharply to Avon-leigh, who continued to look lazily at the strolling couple. "Why on earth would you make such a claim?"

Avonleigh gave him a look of utter confusion. "Are you saying you didn't know or at least suspect?"

"I don't care for this discussion," John said.

"And neither do I. But the girl is innocent, and no doubt you would hate to see her publicly humili-ated by the ton's vicious gossips. I tell you, people will know she is not your uncle's daughter, and I daresay proving it will be a rather simple matter if someone does offer for her."

John swallowed heavily. "I know only that she is not my uncle's daughter, something she does not know," John said quietly. "I tell you this because you are my friend. This information will go no further."

Avonleigh shook his head in disbelief. "As soon as she is presented, people will wonder at her birth. You cannot mean you did not know."

"I have no idea to what you are referring," he said, becoming frustrated with Avonleigh. "Surely there are other violet-eyed people in the kingdom. Her own mother could have had eyes that color. No one will question her birth simply because of her eye color."

Avonleigh gave him a grim smile. "It isn't only her eyes, which, by the way, are a Waltham family trait, as your father's friend Darwin can explain to you. When

I saw her walk into the room, I thought she was Waltham's daughter come to visit."

"Lady Anne? I see no real resemblance, to be honest." Lady Anne was a rather plump woman with dull blond hair and brown eyes. She was, in fact, the very image of her mother.

"No, the younger one. Caroline is her name. If you'd seen her, or if your father had seen her, you would never have attempted this. Melissa could be her twin. Same hair, same eyes. Miss Atwell is simply an older and more beautiful version of Lady Caroline. Anyone who has seen her will immediately note the similarities. Frankly, it's uncanny."

John looked at Avonleigh sharply. "I forgot there was another daughter. Has she come out?"

"No. I only happened to see her last fall at a house party in Sussex. While she is not well known in society because of her age, there are those who will immediately see the resemblance."

"I don't care that they do," John said. "They will never question my father publicly, even if they do so privately. Melissa is my cousin, my uncle's daughter."

"And what of Waltham? Do you not think he will say something?"

John pressed his lips together, his heart sinking. He'd heard there had been some animosity between his uncle and Waltham but had not known why. He wondered if somehow Melissa and her mother were the cause of the rift. Still, Avonleigh could be overstating things. "We rarely attend the same social events as the duke."

"Do you plan to tell her of her birth?"

"No. It is not my place to. My father wants her

protected. Our hope is that no one will realize she is not his niece. Or at least that no one will mention it."

Melissa laughed again, and both men lifted their eyes to her. God above, she was lovely. She held her hand on Norris's arm and looked up at him with a smile that no doubt was making Norris dizzy. John knew that smile, knew how it could affect a man. He should warn her not to smile so openly.

"Why don't you offer for her yourself and prevent the scandal? She is no relation, after all."

John's gut clenched, and an unexpected and unwanted longing pierced him. "The truth of it does not matter. What matters is that society know she is my cousin—and that is what they shall know."

Avonleigh gave him a curious look, then laughed. "Oh, that is rich," he said, hardly in control. "She is your *first* cousin, of course. And your father is a leading opponent of such marriages. That does put you in a difficult position."

"Hardly," John said.

"Oh? And the reason that you cannot keep your eyes from her is simply because of your role as her protector. My God, man, you flinch each time she smiles into Norris's face."

John turned fully to Avonleigh, his expression stony. "I don't care for what you are implying."

Avonleigh lifted his hands, proclaiming innocence. "I'm implying only that you are attracted to a female who is, except for her sad birth, completely available to you. Except she is not. Don't you see the irony in that?"

She laughed again, and John couldn't stop his eyes from flashing even though he knew Avonleigh studied him. He swore if she did so again he would run to the pair and yank her from Norris's arm.

"I'm sorry, John," Avonleigh said, suddenly serious. "I was teasing you only because I didn't know."

"Didn't know what?" John said between gritted teeth.

"I didn't know you truly love the girl. I am sorry."

John tore his eyes away from Melissa and Charles and stared at Avonleigh as if he'd lost his mind. "You are mistaken, my friend."

Avonleigh gave him a small bow that held only a hint of mockery. "Of course."

Chapter 9

Lord Braddock's unexpected arrival caused a major stir among those staying at Flintwood House, because the earl rarely did anything unexpected. A flurry of activity quickly calmed when the lord went directly to his study and summoned his son. John immediately sensed something was wrong. He spent a few minutes making certain his appearance was acceptable and racking his brains for anything he might have done that would have warranted such unusual behavior from his father. The last thing on earth John wanted to do was disappoint or fail the one person in the world who had always supported him wholeheartedly. For a moment, John felt like a ten-year-old boy who couldn't remember doing something naughty but was certain he must have.

"You wanted to see me, Father?" John said, eyeing his father cautiously.

"We have a problem," he said heavily, and the lump in John's gut grew. "My brother was not forthcoming with me, and now we are put in an untenable situation. He told me only that Melissa's father did not know of her existence, but he failed to tell me who the man was. It was a grave oversight. I don't know what he was thinking to keep such a secret from me."

"Waltham," John said.

His father's brows shot up in surprise. "However did you know?"

"Avonleigh said Melissa bears a striking resemblance to Lady Caroline, Waltham's younger daughter."

"It's rather uncanny," his father said with an air of defeat. "I saw the girl myself. I thought it was Melissa with Waltham, even though logically I knew it couldn't be." He shook his head as if still in disbelief. "We cannot hope to avoid gossip now. And it is paramount that Melissa be made aware of this. I've found it is always best to approach these sorts of matters directly rather than with denial."

"Surely you don't mean to tell people who her sire truly is," John said, his entire being rebelling against the idea. He'd never met Waltham, but his reputation as an unscrupulous and ruthless man was well known. John refused to think what such a man would do to find his daughter—a daughter kept from him by his greatest enemy.

"Not at all. But when people comment on their likeness—and they will—we shall agree. That is all. It certainly wouldn't make sense to deny their likeness. In this way we will deflect any gossip."

John frowned, not liking the idea that people would be talking about Melissa, perhaps even calling his father and him foolish for maintaining she was a true Atwell. "I don't want her hurt," John said.

"And if we take this tack, she won't be. At least not as much as she might have been if we hadn't discovered the resemblance before her debut. It's a wonder no one commented after we brought her to the opera."

"Maybe they did, but we did not hear of it."

Lord Braddock scrubbed his face, and John noticed for the first time that his father, usually impeccable, looked as if he'd just risen from bed after only a brief sleep. "I tell you I do not relish telling the girl that the man she's thought of as her father is no relation. The stigma of being a bastard might be overwhelming for her. Everything she has always believed is a lie. But we must tell her."

"Must we?" John could not bear the thought of Melissa being hurt, and the news that she was a bastard would certainly hurt her. There was nothing less forgiven by the ton than low birth.

"She's avoided the taint of being a bastard her entire life, so do not think I have come to this decision lightly. At least her mother was poor gentry and not a maid. Or worse. However, people talk, and there is a real danger there are some who remember her mother. She came from a good family that had fallen on hard times, and I know people will remember them—and her. There are also those who may recall that Christina worked as Waltham's children's governess."

John stared blindly at the floor, feeling restless and angry about the entire situation. He wished he could tell society to be damned, but he knew he could not. "I fear all this deception will come back to haunt us, Father. Lie after lie," he said, shaking his head. "But I think at least we cannot lie anymore to Melissa, no matter how it may hurt her. May I be with you when you tell her?"

"Of course. Do you know where she is at the moment?"

"No doubt with Miss Stanhope in her sitting room." He stood, but hesitated to leave. "She is unique, Father. Any man would count himself lucky to have her. She is not the shy little thing she was before we came here. She is . . ." *lovely beyond words.* He stopped, for his father was giving him the most quizzical look.

"She is . . ." he prompted.

"She is likely to get an offer before the season even begins."

His father looked happily stunned by the news. "From whom? Not Avonleigh."

"Norris. He's making an utter cake of himself whenever she's around. It's rather nauseating."

George laughed. "Thank goodness that hasn't happened to you, dear boy. I've seen better men than Norris fall victim to a woman. Is Melissa as enthralled?"

"She seems delighted by the attention and the novelty of having a man pursue her," John said. "But I don't believe her heart is engaged." Just the thought of Melissa's falling in love with Norris made him feel rather ill. Good God, if they married, she and John would be neighbors, and something about that seemed unthinkable. "I'll get her, and you can ask her yourself."

"It's important you not appear too eager to see Mr. Norris."

Melissa didn't want to disappoint Miss Stanhope, but she was hardly eager to see the man again. Perhaps it was because she'd had so little contact with men growing up, but she had scant interest in the man other than for practicing her social skills. "I'm afraid Mr. Norris does not know the importance of that particular rule," she said dryly.

"You don't care for him?" Miss Stanhope asked, her brows rising.

Melissa shrugged, which caused Miss Stanhope to frown. Shrugging was something a lady did not do. The list of things a lady did not do was growing daily. "I think he is a very nice man, but I do not think I should like to be with him for the rest of my life." It was his nose, she thought, considering the matter. His nose had the oddest little cleft in it, right at the tip. Melissa could not look at him without being aware of it. He was a nice man, very solicitous and flattering. Yes, it was flattering to have a man be so obviously interested in her. Enraptured might be a better word. And that made her suspicious. Why would a man like that be enraptured with her? From all accounts, Charles Norris was, if not a rake, then very knowledgeable about life and women. Or was he simply trying to be nice to her at the behest of John? That would have made more sense to her.

It seemed as if Mr. Norris was always hovering about her or staring at her. It made her feel exceedingly self-conscious. It really was too bad, because she liked his sister, Laura, very much, and it would have been nice to be part of their family.

He was handsome, with soulful brown eyes; his golden hair, streaked with both lighter blond and darker brown, was quite pretty. He had a nice jaw, strong and masculine, and while he wasn't as tall as John, he was tall enough so that she had to tilt her head slightly when speaking with him. And yet . . .

his arms were odd, too. And his hands. They seemed too . . . soft. Not feminine, but not manly. Then again, she'd only ever seen her father's hands and John's. Since they were all related, it made sense theirs would be the hands she liked. Strong, broad, and gentle without being soft.

She gave herself a mental shrug, knowing an outward one was unladylike, and pushed away the real reason she didn't find Charles Norris attractive, why the thought of kissing him was so unappealing. It had nothing to do with him and everything to do with John. How she wished she had never kissed him. It had been such a foolish thing to do, but then she hadn't known how it would affect her until it was too late. She allowed herself a small, silent sigh. Perhaps she would have to kiss Charles just to make certain. At that thought she wrinkled her nose, which caught the attention of Miss Stanhope.

"Is something wrong?"

"Oh," she said, gazing down at her needlework. "I put in the wrong stitch." It was, of course, a blatant lie, for if she had one skill in the world, it was needlework. Miss Stanhope narrowed her eyes but accepted her explanation wordlessly. Honestly, it was almost as if the woman could read minds. For a girl who had never much thought about men, all this thinking about them was giving her a bit of a headache.

It was at that moment that the man most in her thoughts stepped into the room following a soft knock.

"Good morning, ladies," John said.

They both dutifully responded in kind.

"Was that Lord Braddock I saw disembarking?" Miss Stanhope asked, keeping her eyes trained on her needlework.

"Indeed it was," John said with curious enthusiasm. "Now we are all even, Miss Stanhope. I do hope you no longer feel the need to deprive us of your company."

"He needn't have come home on my account," she said, her tone slightly sharp.

"Oh, no, indeed. He's come on another matter entirely," John assured her, but two spots stained Miss Stanhope's cheeks, and Melissa felt a tug of sympathy for her. How nice it would have been if Lord Braddock had returned just to make her stay more enjoyable. "He'd like to see you, Melissa, if Miss Stanhope can spare you."

"Of course," the older woman said.

Melissa leaped up and quickly put her needlework in her basket before practically running toward John, who gave her a bemused smile. "You are like a puppy," he said fondly.

"I'd much rather fancy myself a cat. From what I've read, dogs are entirely too drooly."

He chuckled and led her out the door.

"How is Uncle?" Melissa asked. "We were not expecting him, were we?"

"No."

Melissa, walking beside him, tilted her head. John seemed rather pensive, and she wondered for the first time if something had happened. Something horrible. Something involving Charles Norris's asking to court her, or worse, to marry her.

"Do you know what Uncle would like to see me about?" she asked.

"Yes."

Oh, he was so maddening. She would have questioned him more, but they were already at her uncle's study. Letting out a huff of impatience, she preceded her cousin into the room, smiling shyly at her uncle. Always when she saw him, she felt that same pang, for he looked so much like her father. Behind her, John closed the door softly, and Melissa became even more alarmed.

What was the protocol for rejecting a man's suit? Was she allowed to say no? Would her uncle let her reject a perfectly fine, perfectly acceptable man simply because she didn't care for his nose?

"Take a seat, my dear," her uncle said heavily, and Melissa's fear grew tenfold. She sat clutching her hands in front of her. She looked quickly over to John, who took a chair beside her, but he was gazing at his father—and looking quite miserable.

"I have something difficult to tell you," her uncle began.

Melissa furrowed her brows. Certainly, telling her a man wanted to marry her would not be difficult.

"The man you thought was your father, my brother, was not in fact your father."

Relief swept through her, and she let out a laugh. "Oh, yes, I know," she said, practically giddy that this meeting had nothing to do with Charles Norris.

Her uncle looked stunned. "You know?"

"Of course. Ever since I can remember, I've known. My parents made no secret of it. But my father has always been my father, so it made little difference to me."

"But surely you understand how society . . ."

"Father," John interrupted, and shook his head. He turned to her, and seemed to force a smile, which Melissa found rather confusing. What was all the fuss? "Would you mind waiting outside for a moment, Melissa? Just for a minute."

Without a word, Melissa stood and left the room, wondering what the two men could possibly have to discuss. Was it possible that they themselves had just learned the truth? She leaned against the paneled wall, hearing their muffled voices but not able to discern what was said. Their voices, low rumbles, made her smile. No doubt they'd thought she'd dissolve into tears upon hearing their news. Rupert Atwell was the only man she'd known as her father, though her mother had often talked about how lucky they both were to have found him. Their meeting had always seemed like a fairy tale to her. Her mother, alone and with a small baby girl, had stumbled along Bamburgh's coast, homeless and desperate, and had been discovered by her father.

"I fell in love with her—and you—that very day," her father had said.

Though quite young when her mother had died, she still remembered how her parents had loved each other. Vague images of cold, blustery days sitting before the fire while both parents read often comforted her after her mother died. She remembered the windows rattling, and her mother's worried look at the storm outside, and her father with those strong, reassuring hands, taking her mother's smaller, more delicate one, and comforting her.

The door opened, and John appeared again, with that same forced smile plastered on his face. "Please join us," he said, and she walked back into the study, slightly amused by their attempts to protect her.

After she'd been seated, her uncle, looking even more dour than before, asked her the one question she did not have the answer to. "Do you know who your true father is?"

Melissa felt herself bristling a bit. Her father was her true father. "No, nor do I care."

"I understand," her uncle said, giving John a helpless look.

"I take it you know his identity?" Melissa prompted, suddenly feeling nervous. She had never given her true father's identity more than a passing thought.

"By pure happenstance, yes."

"I don't want to know," Melissa said in a rush. She felt that knowing her father's identity would somehow change who she was, what she was.

"I'm afraid that's not possible," John said softly. "I'm afraid that everyone will know who your father is—or at least they will wonder."

"And we cannot have that," her uncle said, his tone brooking no argument.

"Father," John said in warning, before turning back to her. "Did you know your mother was a governess?"

Melissa creased her brow. "Yes," she said slowly. "I do believe they talked of it, or my father told me, years ago it was."

"And do you know where your mother worked? In what household?"

Melissa shook her head, gazing from one man to the other, completely confused by their demeanor. It was as if they were about to tell her that her father was Satan himself.

"Have you ever heard of the Duke of Waltham?"

"No," she said, stunned and relieved. Her father, a duke? It was a pleasant surprise. "My true father is a duke? Oh my, isn't that grand. Will I get to meet him, then?"

"No!" They spoke in unison, both looking exceedingly uncomfortable.

"Melissa, you do not understand the implications of this news," her uncle said. "It is not something to celebrate. Indeed, it is . . ."

"Father, let me," John interjected. "You see, Melissa, we discovered your likely parentage quite by accident. It appears you bear a rather striking resemblance to Waltham's younger daughter."

"My sister," she said, quite happy to learn she had a sibling.

John gave his father another of those helpless looks, and her uncle let out a small moan. "Yes, your sister," her uncle said. "But, unfortunately, you can never publicly claim her as such."

"Why ever not? And if I look so much like her, won't everyone know anyway?"

"That's just the thing, Melissa. We cannot claim we do not see the resemblance when it is so remarkable. However, we also cannot let anyone know Waltham is your father."

Melissa shook her head in confusion. "Why?"

Again the two men shared a helpless look. "Well, because . . ." her uncle started, his voice fading.

"Because of the duchess, you see," John said in a rush, sounding rather triumphant.

"The duchess?" her uncle asked.

"Yes, Father, the duchess would know her husband has been unfaithful, and it would surely humiliate her. Do you see now, Melissa? If we were to announce your sire, all world would know that the duke was unfaithful to his beloved wife. That single indiscretion twenty-four years ago could cause both such terrible heartbreak." Her uncle let out a strange sound, but John continued. "The right thing to do, therefore, is to agree with everyone who mentions this likeness but completely deny you are the duke's daughter."

"That might work," her uncle muttered, and John smiled genuinely for the first time that day.

"What if the duke sees me?"

"Doubtful. We have no plans to attend any event he'll be attending. Indeed, we shall avoid the family completely. And if the worst happens, only you and he will know the truth of the matter. No one else."

Melissa frowned, not wanting to lie.

"No one will ever ask you outright," John said. "No one would dare."

"Surely they will suspect," Melissa said, thinking of the poor duchess and her broken heart.

"Let them. Let our truth become the real truth," John said with force. "They might question us privately, but they will never do so publicly." But a look passed between John and his father, and Melissa knew he was not as confident as he sounded.

After Melissa had left, John remained in the room with his father.

"I should thrash my brother if he were alive," his father said darkly.

"And I should join you. However, we must play the hand we've been dealt. At least the news didn't destroy Melissa."

It was a stunning development to learn Melissa

knew she was a bastard and that she had absolutely no idea it was something most people would find devastating. John could not allow anyone to crush the girl. It would be so easy to do, to make her believe that she was somehow tainted. He would not have it, not even from the father he worshipped.

"As difficult as it is to believe, being a bastard is not a stigma to her, Father. Remember, she has been completely isolated from society. She has no idea that being a bastard is anything to be ashamed of, and I think it would have been a grave error to inform her now."

His father shook his head, a defeated gesture that tore at John. "I think we are both being naïve to think she will not get a very quick lesson in just how the ton treats bastard children."

John clenched his fists at the thought of someone hurting her. "But she is not a bastard. We will not acknowledge it, and so it will not be. Don't you see, Father, nothing has changed. She has no shame, nor should she. Only we have the power to make her feel less than she is. And right now, she is quite happy to learn she is a duke's daughter."

"Yes. She seemed rather pleased," his father said, shaking his head. "I fear this is going to turn on us. It is going to be a disaster."

John sighed heavily. "Likely so. But there is nothing we can do about it. We have no alternative. We cannot announce that we have Waltham's daughter living with us, a daughter we've been passing off as your brother's daughter. I cannot think of anything we can do to protect her completely. Perhaps a convent?"

He was joking, but his father actually appeared as if he were considering such a drastic plan. "Father, we are members of the Church of England. I hardly think a convent is feasible."

"Yes, but it certainly would solve everyone's problems."

"I would marry Melissa myself before I allowed it," John said, waiting in vain for the dread that always followed when he mentioned marriage. It strangely did not come.

His father let out a laugh. "I daresay it hasn't come to *that*. Everyone in the ton is aware of my stance on marriage between first cousins. They know I would never allow such a thing. I would be labeled a hypocrite, and all my hard work on behalf of the Commission and Mr. Darwin would be for naught. And if we admit that Melissa is not your cousin, we label her a bastard, and she would be ostracized and even your children would suffer."

"I wasn't serious, Father, so don't get yourself all riled up," John said, but something shifted in his mind. He felt a sharp stab of disappointment that was disturbing and unaccountable. What rubbish.

Still, a small voice, a voice that he'd been ignoring for weeks, whispered how unfair it was that someone he could finally imagine being with for the rest of his life should be forbidden to him for no other reason than propriety. Melissa was not his cousin, and he truly didn't give a fig about her birth. But he would not destroy his father's honor, his very standing in the House of Lords, with such a selfish act.

He could not deny he was attracted to Melissa, for he was. He wanted nothing more than to drag her into his arms, to feel her soft lips against his. That small kiss in the drawing room had been a tantalizing taste of what he really wanted. The thought of that kiss, the thought of what he'd wanted to do, had kept him up more than one night. He could not bring himself to imagine her married to another, touching another. But it did no good to pine for her, if that was what he was doing. Pining was too strong a word, he decided, pragmatic as always. If he had an attraction to Melissa, he would get over it. The best route to ending this ridiculous attraction was to get her married. No matter how his heart rejected such a solution, his mind knew it was the only one.

Chapter 10

Melissa, her cheeks flushed from being outdoors in a blustering March wind that carried with it the finest of mists, spied John sitting in his father's study brooding. That made her smile. A brooding lord. How cliché.

"You look like Mr. Rochester, sitting here all alone. Brooding," Melissa said, laughing.

"With a mad wife in the attic?"

"Have you read *Jane Eyre*? I thought only ladies did," she said, sitting down next to him on a settee and staring into a lively fire.

"You smell of the outdoors," he said.

"I know. Isn't it wonderful? I remember my father coming in after a cold, blustery day and smelling him. And now I can smell like that any time I want."

He gazed at her warmly, then turned abruptly away. "Where were you?"

"Oh, out walking. With Charles. I mean, Mr. Norris. He does love to walk. But I don't mind. I still need the exercise, and it was lovely outside. The finest mist was falling, tiny little beads that you could hardly feel, and yet my cloak was nearly soaked when we came in. Miss Stanhope was quite cross, I think, that we walked so far and she got so damp. But I think the next time it rains, I shall rush outdoors and swim in it."

He closed his eyes briefly, before turning to her again, his eyes going to her hair. One hand touched the very top of her head, an odd smile playing about his lips.

"Were you not wearing a hat?" he asked, gazing at his fingers, wet from her hair.

Melissa looked down, feeling guilty. "I was, yes. But it was so lovely to feel the mist on my face and my hat was quite blocking it, so I took it off. Miss Stanhope was very disappointed in me, but I just could not resist."

"And now your hair is wet. I suppose a little mist won't hurt you."

Melissa was glad he didn't chastise her or, worse, tell her she would certainly catch a cold because she'd committed the sin of getting damp.

"So. You were walking with Charles."

"Yes."

"Are you . . . Do you like him, then?"

John became very still, as if her answer was quite important. No doubt he wanted her settled quickly, but she didn't want to give him false hope. "He's very pleasant," she said. He was pleasant. And rather boring. And stared at her too much. And hovered. And smiled. It was all too much.

"I think he likes you very much. Could you see yourself," he swallowed, "marrying him? Could you see yourself in love with him?" He smiled, but it was a strange smile, oddly forced.

"I don't know," she said, honestly. "I . . ." Then, she

let out a sigh and said in a rush, "I wish I had never kissed you." She stared at her hands, twisting the still damp material of her skirt and leaving behind clusters of wrinkles.

"It was hardly a kiss. It was nothing," he said, forcefully.

"Oh, I know that." She bit her bottom lip, not noticing John's eyes drifting down to settle on her mouth. "It's just that I . . ."

"You what?" He sounded impatient, but when she searched his face, she saw nothing but mild interest.

Now she was completely mortified. "I should not have said anything. But, you see, it was likely because it was my very first kiss, and I've no doubt made it more important than it was. It was just for practice, I understand that, but I felt . . . It made me feel . . ." She closed her eyes briefly, then opened them to stare blindly at the fire. "I think there is something wrong with me," she whispered miserably.

"No."

She nodded. "There is. I don't think I'm normal."

"Tell me what you felt."

She looked up at him, her lips parted, her eyes beseeching him to understand. "I felt that I didn't want you to stop," she said in a rush. "I let Charles kiss me and . . . nothing. Like kissing the back of my own hand. Not repulsive, certainly, but not like . . ."

"I think you should stop talking now. I think you should go."

A hot rush of humiliation flooded her, and she stood abruptly. "It was only the briefest of kisses. Not even as long as our practice one. It didn't seem improper, and Miss Stanhope was just 'round the bend so nothing untoward could have happened." He sat, his expression stony as he stared into the fire. "I'm sorry," she murmured, but she had no idea what she was sorry about.

He looked up at her, and his expression softened. "No, I am sorry. You did nothing wrong, Melissa. Nothing. A small kiss from a gentleman is not such a terrible thing."

Then why did she feel terrible?

"I think I shall go and change out of these damp clothes," she said, lifting her limp skirt. She walked from the room, berating herself for being such an idiot. To admit her feelings to John, no doubt mortifying him, how could she have done such a thing? She never should have said a word.

That night there was dancing. The men pushed the furniture out of the way, and two footmen rolled up the huge carpet covering the parquet floor, giving them a miniature ballroom. Laura coaxed Miss Stanhope to play the piano while the younger people danced. It was, Miss Stanhope decided, a perfect way for Melissa to practice her social skills while having a bit of fun with a small group.

Melissa, who had been dreading seeing John after their awkward conversation in the study, was relieved when he acted as if not one single embarrassing word had been exchanged between them. If anything, he seemed even more good-natured than usual, announcing a dance contest in which people had to dance with an imaginary partner. After the announcement, he winked at her, and Melissa felt unaccountably relieved. Everything was back to normal.

"This seems rather silly," Lady Juliana said, but she

unexpectedly volunteered to go first and seemed to be enjoying herself. Melissa thought that if Lady Juliana would just relax a bit, that sour expression she always seemed to wear would disappear completely. Lady Juliana was a vision wearing a deep golden gown with cream lace trim and beading about the bodice. The underskirt was a rich, deep brown, trimmed with golden lace. Her hair, swept up into an intricate style that Melissa knew she would never have the patience for, gave Juliana an elegance that few women could easily achieve. Melissa, wearing a simple midnight blue gown with few embellishments, felt downright dowdy in comparison. If she'd known there was to be dancing that evening, she would have worn one of her newer gowns.

As Lady Juliana danced, the others laughing at her perfectly executed turns in a complicated country dance, Melissa moved next to John, who watched the display with a small smile. "I do believe I have some competition," she said.

"Lady Juliana is fiercely competitive. You should see her on the archery course. Perhaps Mr. Norris can give you a lesson tomorrow. He's quite good, as well."

"You do not like archery?"

"I do not."

"He may not like it, but he's the only man I know who can outdo Lady Juliana," Charles put in. "But I'd be more than happy to give you what little knowledge I have of the sport, Miss Atwell."

"Thank you, Charles. That sounds delightful." It didn't sound at all delightful, though it should have. She should have been excited about trying something new, but all she could think of was that John had been disingenuous. How could he be an expert at something he disliked? His attempt to push her toward

Charles was obvious and a subtle reminder that she should not have any silly thoughts about one inconsequential kiss. He seemed to be perfectly happy, but John did not look at her. Unexpectedly, she felt her throat ache. When the music stopped, she announced brightly that it was her turn.

"A waltz, if you please, Miss Stanhope."

Charles clapped loudly, urging her on, and Lady Juliana gave her a bland smile before going to stand by John. The two of them began talking quietly together, while looking at her, and Melissa wondered what they were talking about so intently. Her? John let out a laugh, and Lady Juliana smiled prettily. Melissa felt a sharp stab of something she'd never in her life felt before, but that she recognized nonetheless: jealousy.

Once she finished her dance, the others applauded loudly, and John stepped in for a quadrille, having so much fun the others lost themselves in laughter. By the time Avonleigh stepped up, it had turned into a contest of pure silliness. However, *silly* was not a word one would use to describe Avonleigh, and it was that very seriousness that produced such large amounts of levity during his performance of a lively polka. He bowed as if having completed the dance at the Covent Garden Theatre.

"Bravo," John said, clapping loudly. Next to him, Lady Juliana tried, unsuccessfully, to smother a smile as she looked fondly at her older brother. "Well, Miss Stanhope, you are the judge. Who has won the contest?"

"Since Lord Avonleigh was clearly the only one

who gave this contest the solemnity it deserved, I will have to bestow that honor upon him."

Avonleigh almost smiled, and bowed in gratitude. When he rose, he gave John and then Melissa a telling look before announcing, "As winner, I should be granted a prize, should I not?"

John stiffened. "Unfortunately, the only prize is pride of winning," he said.

"I was thinking a kiss," he said, looking at each woman in turn.

"Avon, I hardly think that's proper," Lady Juliana said, two spots of color appearing on her pale cheeks.

Avonleigh gave his sister a lazy smile and completely ignored her words. "I can hardly think that a kiss from my sister, as lovely as she is, could be construed as a prize. And I see that Miss Norris is scowling mightily at me. Given her state of near engagement, that leaves her out." He turned to Melissa. "I suppose a small kiss from Miss Atwell would be more than adequate compensation for my performance."

Melissa gave Miss Stanhope a quick look and was surprised to find that the older woman found Avonleigh more amusing than shocking.

"On the cheek," John growled.

Oh, he was growling, when just that afternoon he'd quite dismissed her concern about kisses. She would show him. She marched up to Avonleigh and aimed her plump, parted lips toward his rather hard and stern ones, but he turned his head just as she was about to meet his mouth, and she ended up kissing his jaw. "A perfect prize," he said softly, his dark eyes pinning her to the spot before shifting past her to look at John.

John turned his head slightly away from the spectacle, so that when Melissa looked up, he appeared bored by the entire show. And then Miss Stanhope, after giving Melissa a cursory frown, began playing a reel, and Charles claimed her for a dance. Avonleigh paired with Laura, and a triumphant Lady Juliana twirled about with John.

Melissa found that after a few measures, her anger with John was quite forgotten, and she gave herself up to the fun of the evening. Her lonely rooms in Bamburgh were very far away at that moment, along with those long hours of staring out the window and wondering what the world held. It was difficult to believe that she was the girl swirling about the floor in the arms of a man she hadn't known just a week earlier. She let out a laugh and caught Miss Stanhope's eyes as the older woman gave her a smile. This was what she'd been missing, the joy of being with other people her age, of feeling beautiful, of being happy.

After dancing, the men begged for a break and headed to John's study for brandy and a cigar, leaving the women sipping sherry and gossiping. Melissa didn't care for the taste of sherry at all, so her sips were quite small, and she didn't know any of the people the other women were talking about, so she remained silent throughout much of the conversation.

Laura turned to her. "We must be boring you with our gossip, since you likely don't know a soul we're talking about. Do we seem dreadfully shallow?"

"Not at all. Simply well informed," Melissa said, and was rather proud when both women laughed. Every day that passed, she felt more confident about her ability to navigate the waters of London society. She was no longer terrified to walk into a room filled with these people, and realized it was only a matter of practice before she became completely at ease.

"I have been wondering," Laura said, "what it was you did all day. There is no society to speak of in Bamburgh, is there?"

"I spent much of my time in our home," Melissa said, feeling only a smidgeon of unease at her prevarication. "I had tutors, of course, and would practice the pianoforte and dancing. I quite enjoy needlepoint, and my father would play chess with me nearly every day. I also read like a fiend. I read every book in our library."

The two women looked at her as if she'd grown another head. "No parties or concerts? Or *shopping*?" Laura asked, aghast.

"Since I had never attended any amusements, I did not miss them," Melissa said. "I think now I would, though. It's quite fun dancing with others about. And simply standing in a small circle with friends is a novelty for me."

"We shall have such fun this season," Laura said, impulsively grabbing Melissa's arm. Melissa didn't flinch or pull away, and she felt as if she'd climbed the highest mountain. Perhaps she could be normal. Perhaps she could get through this season without anyone's suspecting she was different.

"I'm dreading the season," Lady Juliana said, surprising both women.

"Why? You are always so popular, Lady Juliana," Laura said.

"Don't you ever get weary of the constant social whirl? To be honest, I do believe life in Bamburgh would suit me. If someone does offer for me, I shall be perfectly content to live in the country and never go to London again."

"You can't mean that," Laura said.

"I do mean it," she said, and Melissa sensed a deep sadness in her. But any vulnerability she'd shown was quickly masked by a quick lift of her chin and a small, perfect smile. "Perhaps a yearly visit," she said. "No doubt my husband will insist."

"Thomas adores London, thank goodness. He has the most lovely town house, small, but it's quite near Mayfield and very comfortable. I wonder whom you shall marry, Melissa. Oh, I cannot wait until the gentlemen see you. It shall be so entertaining. That is, providing you aren't already spoken for."

It was obvious Laura was hinting about her brother, but Melissa was not in the mood to discuss Charles and his infatuation. This entire business of finding a husband was already so tiresome, and she truly hadn't even started yet. It was the one part of being in society she didn't care for. Oh, she found she adored flirting and dancing, and perhaps even kissing, but the actual thought of spending her life with a stranger wasn't at all appealing. She didn't want to attend balls and be examined by the ton's single men. She didn't want to go on carriage rides with strange men or suffer their attentions. She wished . . .

She wished a foolish wish, one that could never come true. But there it was, this longing for a man, the one man who she could not have, the one who made her blood sing, made her feel things almost frightening. It wasn't an anomaly. It wasn't that John was the first man she'd touched. Was it?

Her experience with members of the opposite sex

was so limited, how could she possibly know what was normal and what was a result of her total isolation? What if the perfect man for her was out there, but she was so fixated on John that she overlooked him?

"Laura," she said, "how did you know Lord Brewster was the one you wanted to marry? There are so many men, how did you pick him?"

Laura's face took on a dreamy look, and Lady Juliana pressed her lips together as if offended by Laura's joy. "I knew the first moment I saw him."

Something that sounded suspiciously like a snort emitted from Lady Juliana. Instead of being insulted, Laura laughed. "It's true. Almost. He asked me to dance, but he was only one of several men at my debut, and I really didn't notice him more than any of the other men with whom I danced. But I overheard him talking with two of his friends, who said I was far too flighty for them to take seriously. And Thomas said, I shall never forget it, 'She has a joy about her, and one cannot help smiling. That is a rare thing.' A rare thing. And that was that."

Melissa furrowed her brow, not thinking much of Laura's story. "You fell in love that quickly?"

"No, not quite. But over the following weeks, I may have positioned myself close by so that he was forced to engage me in conversation, and before we knew it, we were in love," Laura said, hugging herself as Lady Juliana looked at her with a small amount of skepticism.

"Have you kissed?" Melissa asked, and the two women gasped as if she'd asked if they'd made love.

Despite the show of horror at her question, Laura quickly smiled and said, "Yes. Twice."

"And?"

"And what?"

"Was it nice? Did it take you to the stars and make your knees weak?"

Laura gasped again, and Lady Juliana looked shocked. "Has Charles kissed you?" Laura asked, not so much shocked as delighted.

"I'm not talking about myself. I was asking about you," Melissa said, her cheeks flaming. She didn't realize her question was improper. "And no, your brother has not kissed me," she said, her cheeks going even brighter at the lie. Perhaps kissing Charles was not the thing, especially since they'd just met.

"Well?" Lady Juliana asked Laura. "*Did* your knees go weak?" Her eyes glinted with mischief, and Melissa was quickly realizing that Lady Juliana was not at all what she seemed.

"Were they supposed to?" Laura asked, looking from one woman to the other.

"I think it depends upon the kiss," Melissa offered, though she didn't truly believe that. If that were true, the simple quick kiss John had given her should not have affected her in such a profound way. And yet it had.

Miss Stanhope chose that moment to put her needlework down and approach the small group. "Shall I go get the men to resume the dancing?"

All three women turned, each with her color heightened, thanks to all the talk of kissing.

"That sounds lovely," Lady Juliana said sedately, and when Miss Stanhope left, all three dissolved into laughter.

* * *

If John realized one thing that night, it was that he would not be able to make it through a season watching Melissa dance with gentlemen intent on winning her hand. It was torture, a torture he'd never in his life experienced. He was becoming a person he did not recognize and found the effort not to watch her as she smiled up into Avonleigh's stern face an exercise in futility.

She was lovely, even in the drab half-mourning colors she insisted on wearing, and he could not take his eyes from her. He was twenty-nine years old, had attended more balls, more amusements, more concerts with more women than he could count. He had bedded more than a few, been a considerate lover, and said good-bye without one spec of remorse. Or thought. Or longing.

Why, then, could he not get a single kiss out of his mind? Why did the thought that she'd kissed Charles, no matter how briefly, make him want to slam his fist into Charles's mouth? His best friend, no less?

What the hell was wrong with him? He found himself in a state of half arousal most of the time just at the mere thought of her, never mind when she was sitting next to him smelling of spring rain and looking like an angel. He did not recognize himself. He did not get infatuated with women. He did not pine or long or lose sleep over them. Why, then, was this one woman driving him mad? Was it simply because he knew he could never have her? Or was it that she was so damned special, that she touched him in a way no other woman had?

John forced himself to turn to Lady Juliana, who stood by him watching the other two couples dance. His father stood by Miss Stanhope, turning pages, though John suspected the lady did not require his help. John was glad to see his father with them for the evening. He'd joined the men in the library and enjoyed a cigar and a glass of port, and John had thought he would disappear into his study for the evening. Instead, his father surprised him by following them into the drawing room.

The song ended, and Melissa dipped a flirtatious curtsy, and John wondered how she'd learned so quickly the way to attract a man. Even Avonleigh, who had shown little interest in women of late, could not keep his eyes from her. He was far better at masking his interest than Charles, but John could see it clearly. She was lovely and quick-witted and everything a man would want in a wife.

He watched through hooded eyes as she walked over to Miss Stanhope and then replaced the woman at the pianoforte with a delighted laugh. His father looked slightly bewildered, but did as he should and asked Miss Stanhope for a dance. The earl socialized rarely, and when he did it was to further some political cause. Rarely had he seen his father dance for the simple pleasure of holding a woman in his arms. With all the women spoken for, John felt himself drawn to Melissa's side. She was playing a waltz without music in front of her, so he had no excuse for approaching other than a desire to be near her.

She was a confident player, looking up often to watch the others dancing, her eyes delighted by the scene. John swallowed heavily, wondering when he would become immune to her smiles or if he would always be battered by them. Would he ever get used to her being with another man? Would this feeling, this horrible need, ever leave him?

Her hair was piled artlessly upon her head, and the dancing had loosened several curls, which lay softly upon her neck and cheek. Without thinking, he brushed one curl from her face and tucked it behind her ear. And when she looked up and smiled at him, it was all he could do not to bend and press his mouth against hers. Instead, he gave her a tight smile and turned to watch the dancers, irritation growing as Avonleigh raised one eyebrow at him over his sister's head.

When the song was over, the couples turned to Melissa and clapped.

"That was lovely, Melissa," Laura said. "Is there anything you cannot do?"

"I can't ride a horse," she said promptly, with such guilelessness, the others were charmed.

"Oh, my. An Englishwoman who cannot ride a horse. That is something we must remedy immediately," Charles said heartily, and John masked his irritation. Just who was the "we" he was referring to?

"Horses frighten her," John said quietly.

"Oh, but that's simply because she hasn't been near them enough. Did your father not have a stable, then?"

"Yes, but I . . ." Her cheeks flamed, and John understood her mortification that she'd never been in her father's stable. His friends knew she'd been isolated, but they did not know she'd spent nearly her entire life in one set of rooms. They didn't know she'd had to learn to navigate stairs, and even now had difficulty running.

"She was frightened as a girl. Nearly trampled," John said, and Melissa looked first surprised, then grateful.

"Ah," Charles said. "But you must ride."

"Why must I?" Melissa said, laughing. "My legs work perfectly well, and if I have to go a long distance, I daresay a conveyance will do."

"But . . . Of course," Charles said, though he looked rather disconcerted. Charles, who loved his stable of fine horses more than anything in the world, had just realized the object of his affections had a major flaw. Perhaps one he would not be able to overcome. John couldn't have been happier.

"Do you like hounds?" Charles asked as if ticking off items on a list.

"I wouldn't know, as we never had a dog."

"Surely you've been near them," Charles said, looking to John for an explanation. Everyone was looking at Melissa as if she were some strange being. Every well-bred Englishwoman knew how to ride and at least had known one dog in her life. John waited, wondering if he should come to her rescue again or let her rescue herself. This was only a tiny bit of what she would experience during the season.

"I have an adverse reaction to them," she said, and beamed John a smile. "Terrible thing. I get all stuffed up, and my eyes water. And I get itchy. We had a maid who could not eat strawberries, and dogs affect me that way."

"That's horrible," Charles said.

"Yes, quite a tragedy," John said dryly. "I suppose I'll have to put off getting that puppy I wanted. The

Gosslings just had a litter of fine hounds, and I was hoping to bring one home."

"Really?" Melissa asked. She sounded very much like a child who has not eaten an unappetizing dinner, claiming she is full, only to realize her favorite dessert is being served.

"Ah, yes, I'd forgotten about poor old Duncan," Charles said, referring to John's constant companion, who'd recently died.

"Duncan died?" Laura asked mournfully.

"He was sixteen," John said. "He had a good life, and I didn't think I'd want another, but there is something rather empty about a house without a dog. Oh, well. I'll just have to wait until after this season."

"Maybe I will not have the same reaction to all dogs," Melissa said, and John almost laughed. It was quite obvious that Melissa very much wanted a puppy in the house and was regretting her rash explanation. "The dog I reacted to was a hairy beast. And dirty. I don't think a clean little puppy will bother me in the least." She tilted her chin and looked so adorable, John found himself fighting yet another urge to kiss her.

"Still," Avonleigh said, seeing through Melissa as easily as John did. "It isn't worth the risk, my dear. Such reactions can be quite serious. I had a neighbor who nearly died after getting stung by a bee. Quite remarkable, really."

John decided to save her. "I'll tell you what. Why don't we go over to the Gosslings' tomorrow and have a look at the pups? If you feel anything at all, we'll simply leave."

"Oh, wonderful," Melissa said, and John felt his

heart give a sharp tug. She'd never seen a puppy, never mind held a squirming little body in her arms.

"I could use another hound," Charles said, thoughtfully.

John could not immediately think of an excuse for Charles not to go, so it was agreed that he would come.

Melissa stifled a yawn and glanced at the mantel clock, surprised to see it was past midnight. She was unused to staying up so late and was suddenly quite exhausted.

"Shall I escort you to your room, Melissa?" John asked, all politeness.

"I fear I shall fall asleep standing up if you do not," she said. "And I want to be well rested when we look at the puppies tomorrow."

"Perhaps we should all turn in for the evening," Charles said, and the others agreed. Bidding each other a good night, they all headed to their rooms, with John and Melissa trailing. His father had bade Miss Stanhope to remain, and John assumed he was informing the chaperone of Melissa's birth.

Guests turned left, John and Melissa right toward the family wing. He'd been alone with her many times in the past weeks, but was aware in a way he had not been before of their isolation, of the cloak of privacy that surrounded them. When Melissa reached her door, she turned and tilted her head, giving him a smile that seemed almost sad.

"Good night, John."

"Good night, Melissa."

But neither moved. They stood there, looking at one another, until Melissa looked down.

"I am sorry about what I said today in the library.

About that silly kiss. I didn't mean to make you uncomfortable or embarrass you." She looked up at him with a self-deprecating smile. "I'm quite certain any significance I put on it was purely my imagination."

Of their own volition, John's eyes swept down to her delectable mouth, parted just slightly. "Yes."

She nodded, but continued to look troubled. "What if it wasn't?"

John said a silent but fervent prayer, for God to give him strength. The air around them was still, thick, and filled with so much tension, he could feel his body begin to shake. He shoved his hands in his pockets so that he wouldn't reach out and pull her against him, against his raging arousal. "You must stop talking of it, thinking of it. My God, Melissa, it was a simple peck, nothing more. It wasn't even a real kiss, for goodness sakes." He was talking to her, his voice low and urgent, but the message was for himself.

"When other men kiss me, I will feel the same?"

No. "Yes."

She searched his face, almost as if she were searching for the truth. Her breath came out slightly ragged. "John." It sounded like a plea.

He didn't know how it happened, how his hands came out of his pockets, how they ended up behind her neck, how they started to draw her to him. He didn't know how his lips met hers. He only knew that when they did, something in him broke, something that held him in check. That thing, honor or duty, snapped, leaving him exposed and unable to stop himself from deepening the kiss, from pulling her closer, from pressing his arousal against her just for the sheer pleasure of it.

He felt her hands clutching his shoulders, nearly shouted in joy when she let out a low moan and opened her mouth for him. He tasted her, sweet and intoxicating and entirely too addicting. When his tongue met hers, she stiffened slightly, but he could not stop. If the hounds of hell had been ripping him apart, he could not have stopped himself from deepening the kiss, from thrusting his tongue against hers, from moving one hand from her nape to a full breast, from reveling in her gasp of pleasure as her nipple hardened against his palm.

"Yes, John."

Those words, urgent, thick with desire, aroused him to the point that he nearly lost all control. He was a hairbreadth away from opening her door and carrying her to her bed. That close to snapping the very last shreds of decency and honor. With a force of will he didn't know he had—for he'd never had to use it—he drew away, his breath harsh, his eyes glazed with raw desire.

"I see what you mean," he said, finally, after swallowing heavily.

She smiled up at him, her lips swollen and red from his kisses, her cheeks flushed, her eyes, oh, Lord, her beautiful eyes drowsy with need. John folded his hands as if in prayer and pressed his knuckles against his mouth.

He dropped his hands and stepped back, not trusting that he wouldn't draw her into his arms again. "I didn't mean for that to happen. It was highly . . . unexpected. I have no excuse."

Melissa looked slightly bewildered by his words, then she smiled. "It's not just me, then. There is nothing wrong with me."

He let out a humorless laugh. "Hardly."

Her smiled widened, and now it was John's turn to be confused. "Why are you smiling?"

"Because I've just learned I'm perfectly normal. You were affected by the kiss as much as I was. Am I right?"

"I suppose you are."

"Why, that's wonderful."

Why couldn't she ever react the way she was supposed to? Being molested outside her bedroom door by her cousin was not wonderful. It was abhorrent. He must get her to understand that what they'd just done, had anyone witnessed it, would have been tragic for both of them. Perhaps John was not honorable, not anymore, but his father was. The earl upheld his convictions completely, and if he'd witnessed his son making love to his niece, it would have killed him.

"John, are you angry with me?"

He must have looked so, for he was angry with himself. How could he have allowed himself to put Melissa in such a position? He was worse than a cad, for he knew the repercussions of that kiss if it were discovered. His father would never forgive him, and Melissa would be married off to the first person who even hinted at interest.

He lifted a hand to cup her face, but shoved it into his pocket. He didn't trust himself to touch her—and that realization frightened him even more. Even though he knew she was off-limits, he still wanted to have her.

"No, I'm not angry with you, but with myself. I think it is best that we forget about what happened and never discuss it again. There shall be no more kisses between us. No more thoughts of kisses. Do you understand?"

Her expression became slightly mulish. "No."

"We are cousins," he said, exasperated.

"We are not cousins. We share not a single drop of blood."

"We. Are. Cousins."

She grinned. "Kissing cousins?" Something in his face must have finally registered with her, for her smile slowly faded. "I'm sorry. I was only jesting. And I do understand. Truly."

"It is best that we not forget ourselves again, Melissa," he said, sounding very much like a pompous ass. "Good night." He smiled, an attempt to lessen the impact of his cold dismissal.

She turned and went into her room, quietly closing the door behind her, not meeting his gaze. He was glad to see she finally understood how important it was that they not succumb to this ridiculous attraction again. He could no longer put himself in situations where he was alone with her. The strength needed to stay away was simply beyond him. He'd never truly been tested before. But as John walked to his room, he felt a gnawing emptiness grow with each step he took away from her.

Chapter 11

It was almost as if that kiss had never happened, as if she'd dreamt it all. For the next day, when the couples met up to look at the puppies, John was his old self. Jolly. Friendly. And completely at ease.

Melissa, however, felt as if she were teetering on the edge of hysteria. Had it been a dream? Had the delicious sensation of his hand against her breast been her imagination? Every time she looked at John, she saw nothing. No pain, no longing. No interest. He stayed mostly by Lady Juliana's side as they strolled along a country lane toward the Gosslings' house. It was a pleasant walk, taking them through a small woods, the path cushioned by the leaves that had fallen last October. Following yesterday's wet weather, the air was heavy and fecund, and while the sun had yet to break through the clouds, it was quite warm for late March.

They crossed a stone bridge that spanned a sparkling river, and Melissa found herself smiling at the sound of the water tumbling over the rocks. The others didn't seem to notice, but she was enchanted by it and stopped to look over the edge.

"Fine trout in that river," Charles said, peering over the edge as if he might see a trout. "Do you fish?"

"I never have, but it seems as if it would be fun," Melissa said, thinking back on the letter John had written to her all those years ago, those boyish words she'd held so dear.

"Perhaps later today. The fish bite right well after a rain and when it's overcast like this." He called up to John. "Have you been fishing yet this year, John? I thought we could all have a go at it this afternoon."

Lady Juliana smiled. "That sounds wonderful."

"She'll outfish you all," Avonleigh warned.

"That's the point," his sister said pertly.

As they got to the other side of the bridge, Melissa let out a gasp of delight, and John turned sharply to her.

"What a lovely cottage," she said, completely enchanted. "It's like something out of a fairy tale."

John frowned as if annoyed by her enthusiasm. "That's the Gosslings'," he said.

As they approached the cottage, a man stepped out from behind the house and called a greeting. "Here to see the pups, are you, my lord?" he asked.

John introduced the man, known to be one of the top breeders in all of Britain, to his friends. "Miss Atwell may have an adverse reaction to canines, so we'll have to keep an eye on her," he said. "Charles, I'll put you in charge of monitoring Miss Atwell's nose."

"I'm certain I'm not going to," Melissa said, feeling her cheeks redden.

As they approached the garden, the air was filled with the sounds of baying as the dogs, enclosed in a large kennel, greeted them. Mr. Gossling shouted at the dogs, and they immediately became silent.

"Mama's back in here," Gossling said, jerking his head to a small building. He was dressed like a gentleman farmer, and everything but his boots looked expensive and clean. No doubt working with the hounds all day, Mr. Gossling didn't care to ruin his finest boots. As the group entered the building, Melissa hung back, suddenly overcome with anxiety. It was as if an invisible force were keeping her from entering the darkened door. Even as the others calmly walked through, Melissa stood frozen. John, looking back, casually held his hand out to her, and she walked forward as if nothing were wrong. But she grasped his warm hand almost desperately. "The pups, Melissa," he said quietly, as if reminding her that nothing evil lurked in the shadows. She smiled up at him, embarrassed and confused by her sudden anxiety, but stepped through the door.

She could hear Laura oohing over the puppies and Charles chuckling over his sister's enthusiasm. "Aren't they precious?" she said. "Oh, we should come back and get one ourselves," she gushed.

"Perhaps you can return with Brewster and pick out a pup for your wedding present," Charles said, cheerfully needling his sister.

Laura lifted her chin with a bit of defiance. "Perhaps we shall," she said.

Melissa was completely entranced by the squirming little animals who seemed in a frenzy over the people looking down at them.

"The dam is a good mother," Gossling said. "Takes care of the brood well. It's only her second litter. Don't like to overbreed. Not good for the mama." He looked up at John, who studied the puppies with an expert eye.

"That one," John said, pointing to a sturdy, fawn-colored puppy, who, while friendly and curious, was not as frantic as the others, nor as timid as a little one that hung back by its mother.

Gossling immediately began rubbing his beard. "I was considering keeping that one for breeding," he said, and John laughed.

"I'll loan him out to you," John said. "You're not trying to increase your price, are you, Peter?"

Gossling made an effort to appear affronted, then grinned, holding out his hand. While the two negotiated a fair price, Melissa kept her eye on the one John had chosen, trying to determine why that one and not another friendlier puppy. Her heart went out to the shy little one, who looked soulfully up at them from behind its mother.

"I like that one," Melissa said, pointing at the shy pup.

"That's the runt," Gossling said. "Not good for much, typically. You don't want a shy dog, 'cause they won't perform in the field. Most breeders will put 'em down, but I never did have the stomach for it."

"Put it down?"

"Kill it."

Melissa gasped. "But why?"

"Can't breed 'em. Can't hunt 'em."

Melissa was silent for a time, her eyes riveted on the little puppy, who edged forward just a bit, almost as if it were trying to overcome its fear, as if it wanted nothing more than to join its siblings but simply couldn't gather the courage to do so. "But you can love them," she said softly, mostly to the little puppy. She leaned over the rough wooden kennel and held out her gloved hand, and the puppy moved another step toward her.

Melissa ignored another more rambunctious dog that tried to lick her fingers.

As the little puppy approached, she withdrew her hand and peeled off her glove. "There you go," she whispered. "You can do it. I won't hurt you, little one. Courage." After a few more tentative steps, the dog's tail began wagging wildly, and it was licking her fingers. Melissa giggled at the sensation, the pure joy of having a puppy's warm, wet tongue bathe her fingertips. She looked up, her eyes shining, to see John watching her, his eyes warm and smiling. In his arms was his choice, calm and content and looking rather drowsy. A fine puppy, to be sure, but Melissa's eyes went back to the little one.

"How much for the runt?" John asked Gossling, sounding resigned.

Charles was aghast. "It's worthless," he said, and Melissa straightened, her brows furrowed in anger.

"He is not worthless."

"She," Gossling put in. "You can have her, considerin' what yer payin' for the one." He cackled, and John gave him a dark look.

Melissa let out a small squeal, and, unable to contain her joy, gave a hop and clapped her hands before throwing herself into John's arms. He caught her awkwardly but laughed at her excitement.

"You shall have to teach me all about dogs and puppies and how to get them trained. Oh, it shall be so much fun."

"They are a lot of work, you know," he warned, but Melissa could tell it was a halfhearted warning.

"I don't care. I've never had anything of my own before. A living thing to love."

Melissa didn't notice the look that passed over

John's face, as she was far too excited to recognize the mixture of anger and pity—the look he always had when thinking about her isolated childhood.

"I shall name her Darling," she said.

"Darling?" Charles asked, looking at the pup with a bit of skepticism.

"After Grace Darling, the Bamburgh heroine."

"The little girl who saved all those people. You remember her, don't you, Charles?" Laura asked.

"Ah," he said. "Yes."

"A fine name," John said, bending down and scooping the puppy up with one hand before it could skitter away. "Here you go, Darling, this is your new mistress. She doesn't know what she's doing, so you're going to have to teach her." He handed the squirming puppy to Melissa, and she held it up in front of her face, her hands clutching it gently as the puppy's tail wagged wildly.

"She loves me," Melissa said. "Don't you, Darling?" Then she looked up at John, her eyes brimming with tears. "Thank you, John. This is the finest present."

"My father is going to be very displeased," he said. "Not only does he have to marry you off, now he must find someone who will accept an ill-trained, worthless hound."

Melissa gave him a look of mock affront. "Any man would be lucky to get this little beauty." She turned to gaze at Darling. "Wouldn't they?"

John rolled his eyes, and Melissa scowled up at him. "What?"

"If you insist on talking that way to a hound, I'm afraid you're going to drive me to the madhouse long before you find a husband."

"You have to use a stern voice," Charles said. "You have to show her who's in charge."

Melissa hugged the puppy a little closer. "No, she needs a gentle hand."

Charles looked slightly flabbergasted, and glanced at John for support. John, however, simply shrugged as if saying, "It won't be my problem."

Which, of course, was true. Still, that shrug bothered Melissa, making her realize that in a matter of months, she might leave Flintwood House and John and be living with a husband—a husband who might not like an ill-trained dog. Or dogs at all.

"Perhaps it would be best to have a well-trained dog," she said thoughtfully.

"Of course it is," Charles said. "But I still don't know why you wouldn't want one of these other fine specimens." He looked down at the remaining puppies. "That red might end up in my kennel."

"Darling and I understand one another," Melissa said, knowing she sounded foolish. But she was holding a warm little body with impossibly soft fur and couldn't imagine putting her back in place of another. They belonged together.

George Atwell frowned heavily at the invitation before him. It was from the Duke of Waltham, inviting him, John, and Melissa to their famously popular Spring Ball held annually during the first week of the official start of the season. He'd never attended before because he'd never before been invited. The invitation, on thick, expensive vellum, embossed with the ducal seal, held a malevolence that made him physically ill.

He knew. There could be no other explanation as to why, after all this time, Waltham had issued that invitation. Waltham had just been playing with him the day they'd met outside the bookstore. He'd known; otherwise why would he have inquired about her? Of course, George would send his regrets, but why, other than to needle him, had the duke sent the invitation? He surely must know that George would never accept such an invitation.

George closed his eyes, knowing precisely why, even as he wished to deny it. Perhaps someone who had attended the opera had seen Melissa and reported her remarkable appearance to the duke. Just the thought of Waltham's looking at his niece made his skin crawl.

A knock at the door saved him from further torturing himself with thoughts of protecting Melissa from her true father. "Enter."

He stood as Miss Stanhope walked in, her steps efficient and graceful, her face passive. She wore her spinster's uniform of a plain gray dress with black piping. All she needed was a lace cap and the effect would be complete. He couldn't help but recall how pretty she'd looked at the ball when he'd first asked her to chaperone Melissa. Why did she insist on dressing as if she were ancient?

"You wanted to see me?" she asked, her gray eyes direct.

He motioned for her to sit and didn't speak until they were both seated. "A neighbor is coming over this evening for dinner and to play cards. John is usually my partner, but as he is occupied with his friends, I wondered if you might agree to be my partner."

Her mouth twitched as if she might smile. "What game?"

"The Pendergrasts enjoy whist and are quite good at it," he said, subtly asking if Miss Stanhope considered herself a good player. Her smile told all.

"I know how to play," she said.

That smile again. He had to school his features so that she could not see how it affected him. It was rather strange, this physical reaction he had to someone he'd always believed to be a rather plain woman. In fact, he could hardly think of a time in his life when he'd given Miss Stanhope more than a passing thought at all. She had been to many of the same entertainments as he throughout the years, but she'd been no more important than a sturdy chair or well-placed potted plant.

How was it, then, that all she needed to do now was walk in a room and he found himself fighting a rather distracting attraction? Lust of the distracting sort was not something that had had a hold on him since he'd met his wife. It was how he had learned that lust could not be trusted.

"I believe the young people are attending a small concert tonight in the village. The Pendergrasts are expected around seven."

"Of course. That sounds lovely," she said, and rose to leave, her awful gray dress rustling.

"I wonder . . ." He stopped, suddenly uncertain if suggesting a different dress would seem improper. But he truly did not want to be looking at that ugly gray dress all evening.

"Yes?"

"It is not important. Until this evening, then."

She shook her head, as if exasperated. "Please, Lord Braddock, continue with your thought."

"That dress. I wonder if you have another." Yes, he realized instantly he should not have said a word. He could see it in her face, damn it, that he'd insulted her. Her expressive face first showed surprise, then fleeting pain, and finally annoyance.

"My dress."

"It's lovely, but . . . Well, actually, it's not lovely at all, you see. Not that it's important. What you wear is your concern and not mine. It's not as if . . . that is to say you can wear whatever the bloody hell you want." He finished this incredibly ineloquent speech on a note of desperation. When had he become such an idiot?

She tilted her head, and in that moment looked so utterly confused, something tugged uncomfortably in his chest. "I shall wear whatever the bloody hell I want. Thank you," she said with little inflection. And with that, she walked from the room, leaving behind a man who was so thoroughly confused, he let out a groan.

Diane paced her room, anger in every step. Did she have another dress, he'd asked. Honestly. As if that were his concern. She was tempted to wear this dress just from spite, but not being a particularly spiteful person, she stood in front of her wardrobe, her maid, Becky, standing patiently behind her, looking for something *she* liked. She didn't give a care what *he* thought. Perhaps she ought to wear her ugliest dress. She pulled it down, and Becky made a small sound of protest.

"No?"

Becky shook her head. "No."

Diane let out a sigh and took down a deep red velvet dress that she loved but hadn't had the occasion to wear yet. Holding it up in front of her, she gave Becky an inquiring look.

"Oh, yes, my lady."

With her blond hair and gray eyes, the burgundy-colored dress did look rather nice. But she was not wearing it for him. She was wearing it to be presentable in front of company.

"Shall we wear the new comb tonight?" Becky asked. Poor girl, she was quite talented at all sorts of intricate hairstyles, which she rarely was able to show off. Diane would often find her leafing through *Peterson's Magazine*, which showcased the latest fashions.

Diane smiled. Why not look pretty this night? Why not see if she could bring about that stunned look on Lord Braddock's face? It was a heady thought—and a rather foreign one—that she would be able to provoke such an expression from him or any man, for that matter. Not that it meant a thing, of course—she wasn't that much of a ninny—but it would be a novelty to feel desirable. "Yes. The comb. And I'm giving you carte blanche with the style." Becky beamed a smile. "Remember, I'm dining and playing whist, not going to a ball."

Becky nodded her head, still smiling. "You have such lovely hair, my lady. It's a pleasure to work with."

One hour later, at five minutes after the hour, Diane walked down the stairs just in time to greet their guests. Lord Braddock was there already, leading the couple to the drawing room, when he looked up and saw her. And stopped dead. He recovered quickly enough, but Diane's heart sang just a bit as she made her way down the stairs.

Lord Braddock made the introductions, either ignoring or oblivious to the curious looks on Mr. and Mrs. Pendergrast's faces. He did not introduce her as his niece's chaperone, and no doubt the couple wondered at their relationship.

"I am Lord Braddock's niece's chaperone," she said pointedly, extending her hand in greeting. She noted, with a small bit of pleasure, that Braddock frowned at the explanation. Had he wanted the couple to believe they were together? It didn't signify.

The Pendergrasts were a lively couple, charming and vibrant in their midforties. Well traveled, they regaled Braddock and Diane with tales of their latest adventure to Cairo.

"It is the most exotic place I've ever been," Mrs. Pendergrast said with enthusiasm. "You cannot imagine the vastness of the desert, nor the beauty of the Nile. And the pyramids." She sighed. "It was stunning."

"Tell her about the camel, my dear," Mr. Pendergrast said, looking fondly at his wife. They clearly were a pair who enjoyed each other's company and had no qualms about showing it.

"Oh, no, that is your story to tell," the lady said, laughing.

"I was spat upon. By a camel," he said, and his wife clutched his arm and laughed along with him.

It seemed strange to Diane that Lord Braddock would have such lively friends. Stranger still that he would deny that love could exist in marriage when dear friends of his were the finest examples of such a relationship. He seemed to thoroughly enjoy their company, laughing heartily and almost boisterously at their tales.

"I should love to travel," Diane said.

"Then what is stopping you?" Mrs. Pendergrast said.

"Fear," she said with complete honesty. "I cannot imagine making such a trip alone. I know there are brave souls who do it, but I'm afraid I am not one of them."

"Perhaps if you went with a group," Mr. Pendergrast said. "There are quite a few countrymen in Egypt nowadays. I'm certain they would welcome you. We made lasting friendships in the few months we were there. We met Edward Lear there, as a matter of fact."

"The man who writes those nonsense poems?" Diane asked.

"Yes, indeed. Quite a fine artist, too."

"Egypt does sound lovely," Diane said. But she knew she'd never go. "Have you ever been, Lord Braddock?"

"Unfortunately, no."

"But you must. You both must," Mrs. Pendergrast said, and Diane felt her cheeks redden. There was no "both," only her, alone and too frightened to travel.

Lord Braddock darted her a look, perhaps of pity, but Diane looked away before she could decipher it.

"Sir, dinner is served," the butler said, bowing out of the room.

Lord Braddock held his arm out for Diane, and she hesitated only briefly before taking it. "Pretty dress," he said, and he stretched his neck a tad to look to the back of her head. "And hair."

Diane gave him a level look that spoke volumes about how little she cared for his opinion. "Thank you."

He smiled down at her, and Diane's confusion grew, but she gave an inward shrug, deciding to simply enjoy the novelty of walking beside a handsome man who thought she looked pretty.

The two couples shared an intimate dinner, which left Diane more flustered and confused than she'd been in some time. Lord Braddock was acting strangely. Last evening he'd stood by and turned pages for her, then danced a waltz with her, and tonight he was acting as if . . . Her spinster's heart gave a painful twist. Perhaps it was her sad imagination, but it seemed to her that he was looking at her like a man would look at a woman he cared for. Their light banter, his soft laughter, the way he caught her eye—it was all quite disconcerting.

After dinner, the four retired to the library, where a velvet-topped card table had been set up before a warm and cheerful fire. The gaslights were turned up high, and a carafe of wine was set up nearby, four glasses at the ready. And then a thought hit her almost violently: I belong here. It was almost as if someone had punched her stomach, the sickening feeling of hope that churned inside her. One dinner. A few kind words. A bit of flirtation. Really, could she be sillier? She almost laughed aloud at that thought, and instead headed to the sideboard and poured herself a generous glass of wine, hoping the spirits would stop her mad thoughts.

Diane was fiercely competitive, but often rather too aggressive and overconfident when it came to whist. Her partners were forever looking pained whenever she made a bid. But usually she was right about her hand—and lucky when it came to partners. One trick away from disaster and more often than not, her partner would have the one card she was missing.

Lord Braddock dealt the first hand, and Mr. Pendergrast immediately moaned.

"Bad hand?" she asked.

"Pay him no mind," Lord Braddock said. "He groans when he passes and when he bids seven no trump. He thinks it fools me."

Mrs. Pendergrast bid a timid four—much to her husband's chagrin—and Diane bid six and watched delightedly as her partner's eyebrows rose. He gave a small laugh.

"I've never had Miss Stanhope as a partner, but she did assure me she knew what she was doing."

Diane simply smiled, knowing no one would outbid her, and also knowing she had a hand that, with a bit of help from her partner, could easily win. As the four began the hand, it became clear to Diane that the Pendergrasts were formidable opponents, but did not have the cards to stop her run. As the last trick was played, Lord Braddock gave her a wink, and she flushed. She wished, for the first time in her life, that she were more sophisticated and worldly, for a woman in her thirties shouldn't flush like a schoolgirl because a handsome man winks at her.

The longer the couples played, the more wine was consumed, and by the end of the evening, Diane was feeling a bit tipsy. The Pendergrasts, already a lively pair, were downright boisterous after two generous glasses of wine. It was the most fun Diane could remember having in years.

She and Lord Braddock walked the couple to the door, bidding them good night and promising another round of cards in the near future. As they closed the door, Diane caught Lord Braddock's eye and smiled. "That was exceedingly pleasant," she said. "What a wonderful couple." She was rather startled that she was having a bit of difficulty with her enunciation, which, oddly, caused her to giggle. "Oh, my, I do believe I've had too much wine this evening," she said, looking up at the most handsome man she'd ever laid eyes on, who happened to be looking down at her with strange intensity. She might be a tad drunk, but he looked stone sober.

"You had but two glasses," he said.

"Big glasses," Diane responded, holding up her hands to indicate just how big they were.

"You are a bit foxed, aren't you? You're quite an adorable drunk," he said.

She frowned. "No one's ever called me adorable. I am not adorable." She took a deep breath, wishing it would clear her foggy brain.

"You are adorable. And I am very glad you are here." George was slightly taken aback by those words, because he realized with a start that they were true. He liked having her there, a soft woman to listen to him complain, to offer advice. To smile up at him as if he were a desirable man. He could not remember the last time a woman had looked at him and seen him, not his title and not his wealth. She smiled, and yes, she was a bit tipsy. But that only served to soften her a bit, to allow her to let down her guard, to relax that ramrod stiffness she seemed to think was so important.

"When was the last time you were kissed, Miss Stanhope?"

Her cheeks flushed becomingly, but she met his

gaze with her unwavering one. "Quite some time," she said.

"Why?" He was puzzled. She was pretty, intelligent, had a wonderful sense of humor. He couldn't fathom why she had not married long ago. But his question, honestly asked, seemed to make her angry.

"Please do not patronize me, Lord Braddock. I think I should go to bed."

She turned away, but George was having none of it, and he stayed her with a gentle grasp on her upper arm. She gave his hand a quick angry glance, then looked up at him.

"I find you pretty," he said forcefully.

"How lovely." It was not the reaction he had expected. Most women would have smiled up at him. But Diane Stanhope was not most women.

"I find you pretty, and I want to kiss you," he said, sounding rather angry for a man who wanted a woman's kiss.

She turned her head away. "Please do not."

He moved closer to her, and she stiffened, her face still averted. "I want to kiss you," he repeated, this time more softly. "May I?"

"No."

He chuckled softly, and leaned closer, breathing in her softly feminine scent, which did nothing to curb his rather unexpected lust. "Just on the cheek," he said, so low he wasn't certain she even heard him. He pressed his lips against her heated skin, and her eyes drifted closed. He kissed her jaw, then her neck above the collar of her too-chaste dress. He licked her earlobe, and she let out a small sound of pleasure. Her breathing was becoming erratic, and George realized her reaction to his kisses was as much an aphrodisiac as her sweet scent and impossibly soft skin. She turned her head into his kiss, and he pressed his lips against the side of her mouth, just at the corner. If she turned even the slightest bit more, he would be kissing her full on the mouth. He was almost painfully aroused, something that was decidedly shocking, given the fact that he hadn't touched her at all except for his mouth on her skin. It was the breathing, the soft sounds, her scent that made it difficult not to drag her into his arms and kiss her until she melted to the floor.

"Let me . . ."

And she turned, kissing him fully, her arms going around his neck, taking him by surprise. He recovered quickly, slanting his head to gain fuller access, pulling her close, letting her feel his arousal, letting her know he was a man who desired her. She gasped, and he pushed his tongue into her welcoming mouth, groaning in relief and desire. He deepened the kiss and moved his hands to her nicely rounded bottom, pulling her tight against him, so that his cock was pressed against her heated center. God, she was so responsive. He wouldn't have expected that.

"Come to my room," he said against her kiss-swollen lips.

He might have thrown a bucket of icy water on her instead of inviting her to his bed. She pushed away almost violently, her chest heaving, her face a mixture of unspent desire, anger, and mortification. "What are you doing?" she demanded.

He gave her a crooked smile. "I was kissing you."

She gave him a withering look. "No. What do you mean by asking me to your room? Is that what you think of me? That I am a woman of loose morals? Yes,

I had too much to drink tonight, which is evident from my disgraceful behavior. But you, sir, should know better than to accost a woman in your care."

"Accost? I didn't accost you. I kissed you."

She looked flabbergasted. "And then asked me to your bed."

"That is usually what follows such kissing. At least in my experience." That last, perhaps, was a mistake to say.

"As a woman of no experience, I wouldn't know," she said, her voice tightening slightly as if she were trying not to cry.

Now he did feel like a cad. He couldn't remember the last time he'd driven a woman to tears. "I apologize," he said. "I was swept up in the moment. I have no excuse other than that I find you rather difficult to resist."

He'd thought she would smile, but instead she scowled at him. "I have a mirror," she said.

"And what is that supposed to mean?"

"I am not pretty. Nor desirable. I am passable at best. You, on the other hand, are exceedingly handsome, as you no doubt are aware of, and so you think you can seduce the poor, homely old maid. Well, sir, you cannot."

"That is not at all what I was doing."

She raised one eyebrow. "Really? And what, pray tell, were you doing?"

He opened his mouth, then shut it. He *was* trying to seduce her. And she was an old maid. But the way she had said it made him sound like some randy lord taking advantage of the nearest female, and that simply was not the case.

"*Hmph.* No answer." She glared at him rather speculatively.

"Do you think I want to be attracted to my niece's chaperone? Do you think I like being kept awake at night wondering what it would be like to lie with you? I do not. I cannot explain it, but I will tell you one thing, Miss Stanhope," he said, pointing a finger at her. "You are not homely. You are pretty. And when you smile, you are beautiful."

She stood there, staring at him, and slowly her eyes filled with tears, and she shook her head in disgust.

"Diane," he said softly.

She swallowed and looked so torn. "Please don't say another word or I might start believing you."

"Would that be so awful?"

"Yes, sir, it would. Because there is something you may not know about aging spinsters. In here," she said, pressing a fist against her heart, "we are still young. In here, we still dream of a husband and a home and children."

George thought he'd masked his reaction to those words, but either she was quite perceptive or he wasn't as good as he thought at hiding his emotions. She gave him a bitterly triumphant smile.

"No worries, my lord. I have no thoughts of matrimony when it comes to you. Why on earth would any woman willingly marry a man who professes that the emotion of love does not exist?"

"You agreed with me," he said accusingly.

"I lied," she said, nearly shouting, her voice cracking. She took a deep and calming breath. "You needn't worry about me. Let us simply pretend this did not happen. It was wrong of both of us and a grave mistake on my part. But please don't arrange such an evening again. I am not your paramour, and I never will be."

His chest gave a painful squeeze as he realized she was right. No woman had had the capacity to cause him pain in decades. "I am sorry." But he truly didn't know what he was sorry for.

John kept his distance as best he could and watched, his depression growing, as Charles became more possessive of Melissa. It was a subtle thing, really, but whenever the three couples went anywhere or did anything, Charles made certain he was paired up with Melissa. It seemed Charles was constantly touching her. What was worse was that Melissa did not seem to mind. John's fevered mind wondered if they'd kissed again, though he could not think of a time when they could have. It didn't matter how often he told himself she was better off with Charles, for everyone's good. He could not stop his desire, his longing, his near-obsession with her. Fortunately, the houseguests were leaving in two days, which would allow him to depart as well. This constant torture was wearing on him. He wasn't sleeping well, and Avonleigh commented on the dark circles beneath his eyes with a knowing grin.

They had decided the night before when they'd gone into the village to watch a concert that they should go fishing the next day, but it had been raining on and off all morning. John, feeling out of sorts and knowing he was bad company, headed to the library to be alone, only to find the very woman he was avoiding curled up before the fire with a book.

When he saw her there, looking lovely in a white

gown frothed about her, he nearly turned around. "Why aren't you with the others?" he asked, knowing he sounded surly. He didn't care, because frankly, he *was* surly. That's when he noticed Darling curled up beside her, letting out little snores, and he couldn't help but smile.

"She's snoring," Melissa said, looking completely charmed by her little puppy. "And did you know she's already housebroken? Though I daresay she doesn't much care for the rain."

"Most dogs don't. So, she hasn't had any accidents?"

"Just one. But I scooped her up just like you told me, and she peed all the way to the door and finished up outside. She's such a good girl."

He was looking at the dog, resisting the urge to stare at Melissa like some lovesick boy. *Don't look at her. Don't.* But he did, and his heart wrenched in his chest. He didn't know what was happening to him, and he didn't like it. Not at all.

"Charles and the others are leaving in two days," he said, forcing himself to bring up his friend's name. It was quite clear where Charles's thoughts were taking him, and John wouldn't be surprised if the fool proposed before he left. "And I'll be leaving as well. Going to Town. I've had enough of the country."

She looked up at him with those big violet eyes, and damn if she didn't seem to care whether he left today or tomorrow.

"The season starts in just a few weeks. I suppose we'll see each other then," she said, then returned her focus to the book in her hand.

Just at that moment a bright ray of sunshine flashed through a rain-spattered window, like a candle flaring up. "The sun," Melissa said. "It seems ages since we've seen it."

But as soon as those words were out of her mouth, the rain came back in force, pouring down through the sunshine, and Melissa smiled. "Oh, how lovely," she said, watching as the rain, looking very much like falling diamonds, fell from the sky. Then her eyes widened in excitement. "I'm going out in it," she said, carefully getting up so as not to disturb Darling and then rushing over to the French doors that led outdoors. She flung them open and walked outside, immediately turning her head up to the rain, laughing and twirling about as it thoroughly soaked her.

With an indulgent sigh, John strolled to the door to watch her delight in this new experience. When he reached the door, he stopped, mesmerized by the sight before him. She was, quite simply, glorious. She stood, eyes closed, head tilted up to the rain, in the sun-soaked courtyard, wearing a dress plastered against her stunningly beautiful body. Every curve, every swell was clearly defined. His mouth went dry, and his heart nearly stopped. The rain lightened, and she brought her head down, smiling and blinking against the water in her eyes. He stared at her, unable to look away, unable to move. A gentleman would have retreated, would have gone into the house and fetched a coat to cover her. But at the moment, he was a man, hungry for a woman, body tense and aroused.

Her smile slowly faded, and her breathing became heavy, her breasts rising and falling, almost as if she'd been running. He knew raw desire was evident in his face. He knew he should turn and go back into the library. But he stood there, staring at her, feeling more aroused than he ever had in his life. She walked toward him slowly, to where he stood, dry and protected beneath an overhang, her eyes never leaving his, her taut nipples clearly visible beneath her rain-soaked dress. She stopped mere inches from him, and he watched as droplets of water slowly moved down her cheeks, to her chin, and dropped onto her dress.

Without saying a word, he lifted shaking hands and laid them on her breasts, moving his thumbs slowly back and forth across her turgid nipples. She let out a small sound and arched her back instinctively. The cloth was cool beneath his hands. He stood, mesmerized by the sight of his hands on her full breasts. Without thinking—he was far beyond that now—he leaned forward, mouthing one hard nipple and licking it through the wet fabric. She breathed in a sharp gasp, and he felt a hand on the back of his head, pulling him toward her.

John lifted his head and looked at her, seeing only desire. No fear. No disgust. No uncertainty. She moved her head slightly forward and that was all the invitation he needed to kiss her with all the pent-up passion roiling inside him. She let out a cry, opening her mouth, clutching him to her, moving her hips because she already knew it drove him mad. He pressed his arousal against her center, letting out a groan of frustration, for he knew he could not have her, not all of her. He wanted nothing more at that moment than to slip inside her, feel her heat around him, lose himself to the insanity that gripped him unrelentingly.

Her gown was made more pliable by the rain, and he pulled down one side, exposing a breast, then greedily suckled her.

"Oh." That one syllable was filled with wonder and desire and nearly drove John over the edge.

If he was insane, then God help him, he didn't care. He only knew that he had never in his life held a woman like this in his arms and wanted to weep from pure joy. She was so responsive, so innocently provocative, that he had to use all his restraint not to press her hard against the stone of his home. God, she felt so good, moving against him, making small sounds of pleasure.

He needed her to touch him, so he guided her hand to his arousal, letting out a jagged breath when he felt her hand tentatively stroke him. "Yes," he breathed, so taut he thought he just might break. "God, yes."

Melissa felt as if she were drowning in desire. Everywhere he touched her, every sound of pleasure he made, pooled, hot and wet, in her center. She wasn't certain what she wanted; she only knew she wanted something, that touching him, feeling his man-part, hard and so very foreign, was making her giddy with need. His hands touched her on her exposed breast, her buttocks, between her legs. When he touched her there, over her dress, and pressed against her, she felt as if she might faint from pure, raw pleasure. So when she felt his bare hand on her thigh, when he moved his hand up and found the slit of her pantaloons and touched her between her legs, her knees buckled.

"Oh, God," he said as he explored her, moving his hand and touching her in places she hadn't imagined a man would touch. But it felt so good, so right, and so she allowed it, spread her legs so he could gain better access. He slipped one finger inside her, and she let out a sound she'd never heard from her lips. Nothing had prepared her for the feeling of a man, this man, touching her there. He slid his finger in, then out, and she moved her hips in the rhythm he created. She didn't care if that made her wanton, she only knew that it felt good and wondrous, like nothing she'd ever felt before.

And then, it got better. He moved his thumb across the spot that ached the most, releasing such an exquisite sensation, she cried out. He moved his thumb back and forth, and she kept her hand on his man-part as he thrust against her. It was primal, this feeling, natural and wonderful how he matched the rhythm of his finger with his own hips, and Melissa knew she must touch him, not through his trousers, but flesh to flesh. She fumbled with his buttons, and John, realizing what she was doing, made short work of it and his man-part sprang out, hot and hard and velvety to her touch. They didn't speak, and the only sound was their harsh breathing, the rhythmic rustling of their clothing, and the rain falling gently onto the courtyard.

John bent his head and once again suckled her nipples, sending shards of excruciatingly intense pleasure to where his hand moved against her. "Come for me," he said, moving his mouth up to hers, and kissing her deeply, letting out a groan as she squeezed his arousal.

Then, suddenly, the pleasure intensified, and a rush of light and color, explosive in its brilliance, made her body jerk against his hand. It stunned her, for nothing in her life had ever felt quite so good, this pulsing pleasure that flowed from her center, to her toes, to her breasts. She slowly came to her senses, her hand still on his man-part, and she opened her eyes dazedly. John suddenly turned away, pressing himself against the cold stone of the manor house, and let out a deep groan as he clutched himself almost frantically.

In a few moments, his breathing, ragged and heavy, calmed, and he turned his head to look at her, a faint but vaguely apologetic smile on his lips.

"That was wonderful," she said. She should have known he wouldn't agree.

"Oh, God, Melissa, I'm so sorry." He turned his forehead against the stone wall and banged his head lightly, muttering something unintelligible to himself.

"Stop that, you ninny. You'll hurt yourself."

He turned to look at her again, but this time his expression was agonized.

"Don't you dare apologize again. It was wonderful, and you have nothing to be sorry for."

"But I compromised you," he said, apparently stunned that she didn't realize it. "I was supposed to keep such a thing from happening. Oh, God."

The horror of the situation suddenly dawned on her, and she pulled her dress up over her breast as if that would erase what had happened. "Do you mean to say I'm not a virgin anymore?" She knew, from all those lectures from her governess, that maintaining one's virginity was of utmost importance. She didn't truly know what that entailed, but she did know that no man other than her husband was ever—*ever*—allowed to take it. Was that what had just happened?

"Good God," he said, burying his face in his hands.

"John?"

He rearranged his trousers, a faint flush staining his cheeks and making him look almost boyish. "Your virginity is intact," he said. "Just barely."

"Oh. That's good."

He looked at her again, then shook his head. "I

want to kiss you, even now," he said, letting out a bitter laugh. "I want to hold you, lie with you. I want to take your virginity. The thought of another man touching you so drives me mad. I want to drown in you." He swallowed. "But I can't, you see. It's impossible. And even thinking of such things is not only dishonorable to you, but to my father, who trusted me to protect you."

He tucked in his shirt with near-violent gestures.

"Please don't be angry," Melissa said, laying a hand upon his shoulder.

He moved away, out of her reach. "I'm angry with myself."

"I know."

"My father trusted me. I have betrayed him. I have betrayed myself. Don't you understand?"

She didn't understand. Not at all. "But nothing irreparable happened, John."

"Nothing happened?" he said in disbelief. "Nothing *happened*?" He repeated the words and stared at her, shaking his head as if in horror. "I've fallen in . . ." He closed his eyes briefly, and for a terrible moment, Melissa thought he might actually weep. "I've fallen in my own esteem," he said, then let out another sad laugh.

"I wish you would stop," Melissa said, hugging her arms about herself. "I rather liked it, and you're making something wonderful sound sordid. It wasn't sordid."

Suddenly, John slapped his hand hard against the stone wall. "It was. It was wrong. Of both of us, but I'll accept the blame."

Melissa stared at him, hating that he wasn't as pleased as she about what they'd just shared. It hurt.

He looked at her, deadly serious, and tugged at her dress. Then he drew her against him and gave her a quick, hard kiss before pushing her back from him. "That was our last kiss," he said with force. "Do you understand?"

She nodded, her eyes filling with tears.

"Don't cry," he said, softly. "Please don't cry."

"I didn't like that kiss," she said, her voice wavering. "I'd like our last kiss to be nicer." And so she moved to him, laid her hands on his shoulders, and kissed him with everything she felt. Every bit of love, every bit of desire. It was a kiss they would both remember, she vowed. He let out a groan, deepened the kiss, and Melissa felt a small amount of bitter triumph. He might say what they did was wrong, but he wanted to do it again. He wanted to, but she also knew he wouldn't. She pulled away and forced a smile.

"That was a better last kiss," she said, then turned and walked into the library, away from his pain-filled eyes.

Chapter 12

That evening after dinner, the ladies gathered in the Rose Room, a small, feminine drawing room that had seen little use in the past few years. Melissa had discovered the room only two days earlier and had asked that the maids give it a good cleaning so that she might take it over as her very own. It was a lovely room, sun-filled in the daytime, with white-washed walls, deep red cushions on the sofa and chairs, and lighter pink accents. It was an oasis of femininity in this decidedly bachelor house.

Melissa's nerves were rather frayed, and just being in the room was soothing. She was glad the men had gone off to have a game of poker and drink their awful port. If she had to spend one more second in John's presence, she just might scream. He was as solicitous as ever but otherwise completely ignoring her. Anyone seeing him that evening would never have imagined the agonized look on his face after they'd touched.

The women, but for Miss Stanhope, who read by

the fire, sat comfortably, talking about the upcoming season and discussing various people Melissa would likely meet.

"Do you remember when Lady Ashton's daughters both came out the same year?" Laura said, laughing. "That poor father, can you imagine? They are twins. Identical," she said, stopping to explain to Melissa.

"She could hardly have one come out without the other," Lady Juliana pointed out.

"That is true, but I cannot imagine the confusion for all those poor chaps. It was the talk of the ton that year. I remember, even though I was only fourteen at the time. They were beautiful, too, but more than one fellow thought he was falling in love with one when it really was the other that he'd danced with."

"Are they that alike?" Melissa asked, fascinated. She'd never seen a twin before.

"In every way," Lady Juliana said. "They sound alike and dress alike, too. I can't tell them apart. At least I couldn't until they got married."

"Oh, I could," Laura said. "Georgina's hair is parted on the left, and Georgette's is parted in the center. At least I think that's correct. It could be the other way around."

"Georgette and Georgina?"

"Their father's name is George, you see."

Melissa laughed. "And is there a George?"

"Oh, yes, indeed, but . . ." Laura stopped and blushed, shooting a look at Miss Stanhope and Lady Juliana.

Lady Juliana gave Laura a small smile of encouragement, while Melissa looked from one to the other.

"I'm hardly one to repeat gossip," Laura said.

"It's not gossip at this point. It's common knowledge," Lady Juliana said. "And this is something Miss Atwell should know if she is to come out this year."

"Before he died, Sir George was quite ill," Laura explained. "He was bedridden. For years. He fell from his horse shortly after the twins were born and could not walk. Sir George and his wife are both brunettes with brown eyes."

"George junior is *blond*," Lady Juliana stressed.

Melissa knew the two girls were hinting at something, but she still didn't know what.

Laura gave her a look of exasperation. "George junior cannot be Sir George's son."

"Legally, he is Sir George's heir," Lady Juliana pointed out. "So it's really not that much of a scandal, I suppose, even though I did hear rumors that the father was wholly unsuitable. One of their servants, I believe. But it could have been worse for poor George. It's not as if he was born after Sir George died. Then he'd be . . ." Lady Juliana flushed.

"He'd be what?" Melissa asked.

"A bastard," Laura whispered dramatically.

"It could have destroyed the family," Lady Juliana said. "I doubt the twins could have married as well as they did if that were the case."

"I know a girl whose father was a baron, but whose mother was a scullery maid. Do you know how I know her? She works in our kitchen. Papa didn't want to hire her at all, but Mother has a soft heart and Papa relented."

Lady Juliana looked thoughtful. "I suppose it's not the girl's fault her mother was that sort of woman. Though, it's likely she's the same way. The apple doesn't fall far from the tree."

Melissa felt herself growing hot. They could have been talking about her. She was a bastard. She was, and yet she'd never thought of herself as anything other than her father's daughter.

"No one wants tainted blood, you see," Laura explained. "Poor George. His father could be anyone."

"It matters so much?" Melissa asked past a growing tightness in her throat.

"Of course it does," Laura said. "My goodness, you have been sheltered, haven't you? Did no one tell you these things, about fortune hunters and eligible men and such? No one would purposely marry out of their realm and certainly not someone illegitimate. It just isn't done. It only brings heartache. That's why a commoner cannot marry a peer. It upsets the entire order of society. It's why we keep to our own."

Melissa felt her cheeks flush and her stomach give a sickening twist. "What if you were to fall in love with such a person?"

"A bastard? Oh, goodness, no self-respecting person would," Lady Juliana said. "It would never happen. No one would want that sort of blood in their line."

Melissa knew the two girls were not being vicious or cruel, but were simply stating what they believed to be right and true. Unfortunately, every word they uttered only made Melissa cognizant for the first time in her life that she might not be who she'd always thought. She was a bastard, something to be scorned and avoided. She was someone, she realized, who wouldn't even be in this room wearing a fine dress and speaking with these two girls if anyone knew.

"What if someone posed as a peer and you fell in love but found out later that he was . . ."

"Illegitimate?" Laura said, her eyes sparkling with excitement at this apparently lurid conversation.

Melissa swallowed. "Yes. Would you still not love that person?"

"I'd be devastated," Lady Juliana said. "Not only because of who he was, but because he lied." Then she giggled. "But mostly because of what he was. I cannot even imagine such a thing. No bastard would pass him or herself off as legitimate."

Laura nodded. "I think the lie would be the worst. The deception." She looked from one girl to the other. "Have either of you read *Ruth?*"

"No, you didn't—" Lady Juliana gasped. At Melissa's questioning look, she explained. "It's a scandalous book about a girl who has a baby even though she's not married! She gets her comeuppance because she dies in the end, though."

"I thought you didn't read it," Laura said with a laugh.

"Oh, I didn't. But Mary Chalsford has and told me a bit about it," Lady Juliana said. "Did you read it?"

Laura nodded. "I actually thought it was quite horrid what happened to poor Ruth."

"Mary said Ruth got what she deserved."

"I don't think you'd say that if you read the book," Laura said.

With each word the girls uttered, Melissa felt more and more despondent. She was a bastard. Her mother was a promiscuous woman who had lain with the Duke of Waltham knowing he was married. And she was the by-product of that act. If any man knew her background, he would never marry her. He would . . .

A stunned thought came to her, a wave of realization that made her heart contract painfully and the blood

drain from her face. They had lied to her. Her uncle
and John had lied about the reason for her deception.
It was not to save the heart of some duchess, but to
make her marriageable. No one would marry her if
they knew of her birth. No one would want her "tainted"
blood. In a rush of humiliation, she had a vision of
herself, panting and spreading her legs for John,
standing up against that stone wall, her hand on his
man-part, letting him touch her, like some . . . hussy.
She couldn't picture Laura or Lady Juliana acting in
such a wanton way.

They had lied to her, just so they could get her off
their hands, just so they could lie to others if people
noticed the likeness between her and her true father.
She felt sick to her stomach.

"Are you quite all right?" Lady Juliana asked.

"No," Melissa said, shaking her head, feeling hot
tears press against her eyes. "I suddenly feel quite ill.
Perhaps I should retire."

The two women stood, eyes filled with sympathy
and concern—emotions they might not feel if they
knew they were in the presence of a bastard.

"Good night," Melissa said, rising and walking on
shaking legs from the room. Her stomach twisting
from nerves, she went directly to her uncle's library,
where the men were enjoying their cards. She stood
at the open door, feeling as if her world were slowly
falling apart. Would John have dared touch her the
way he had if she had not been a bastard? Was that
the true reason he could not marry her, because of
her birth?

John noticed her at the door first, lifting his head,
his eyes lighting before he lowered his gaze. He
stood, and the other men, seeing her, rose as well.

Melissa looked at her uncle. "May I speak to you and John in private, please?" she asked, hating the quick look of panic that struck John's face. No doubt he feared she would tattle about their encounter. She kept her face passive, wanting him to think that, wanting him to suffer just a little after what they had done. The two younger men excused themselves, Charles leaving only after giving Melissa a searching look. She had no patience for Charles, whom her uncle was duping into believing she was a proper matrimonial candidate. How dare they? How dare they lie not only to her but to Charles, as well? When the other men had gone, Melissa took a step toward her uncle, her throat burning with anger and unshed tears.

"You lied to me," she said, her gaze moving from one to the other.

Her uncle smiled gently. "My dear, what are you talking about?"

"I'm a bastard," she spat. "Shall we go into the other room and make that announcement?"

They looked from one to the other, matching wary expressions on their lying faces. She wished she could slap them both.

"No one would want me because I'm illegitimate. Who my father truly is and the sensibilities of his wife are beside the point."

"Melissa, sit down," her uncle said, taking a step closer to her.

"No, I will not. And I will not be patronized. Tell me that any man would want me as his wife if he knew. Tell me that is not why you lied."

"It is why we lied," John said. "We were only trying to protect you, Melissa. Perhaps we should not have lied, but it was only because we didn't want you to feel the taint of illegitimacy."

Melissa blinked, and two tears fell from her eyes. She dashed them away. "And if a man should come to care for me? If he should ask for my hand in marriage? Do I tell him? Do I keep my secret? Do I lie to the man who has asked me to be his wife?"

Her uncle swore beneath his breath, and John strode over to her, grasping her hand and leading her toward a set of chairs. "Sit down," he said, and exerted a bit of pressure so that she sat.

He pulled another chair over to hers, sitting close. His father did the same. "You haven't been in society, so you do not know the taint of illegitimacy," John said. "It is wrong, I know that. Many people know that. But there are others who zealously defend the treatment of unmarried mothers and their illegitimate offspring. Father and I are working with a group of men to change this, but no one in power wants to listen."

"It is rather futile, my dear," her uncle said, his face lined with worry.

"We thought it best to shield you from that venom."

Melissa looked from one man to the other. She was the same girl she'd always been. Was she supposed to feel ashamed of who she was? People couldn't be that cruel. She couldn't believe it of them, not when her father had loved her so, not when her uncle and John had been so kind. "Would it truly be so bad if people knew?" she asked, her voice small.

"Society has no sympathy toward women who bear children out of wedlock. None," her uncle said. "It is by God's grace alone that your mother was found by my brother. Anyone else would have cast her out, would have let the two of you starve."

"I can't believe that," Melissa said.

John took a deep breath. "Have you ever heard of baby farmers?"

"No, John," her uncle said.

John ignored his father. "Have you?"

Melissa shook her head.

"They are women who prey on those poor souls unfortunate enough to have a child out of wedlock. Our grand society gives such women nothing. Legally, the father has no obligation to aid the woman or the child. More often than not, the women are cast out. They are fired from their positions. They are forced to leave their families. And when they give birth, they are on their own. Such a woman must work to support herself and her child, but no one will hire her. Orphanages will not even take in illegitimate children. These women have no choice but to go to baby farmers."

"John, I don't think Melissa needs to hear all this."

John glared at his father. "She does, Father." He reached out and took one of Melissa's hands. "These women offer to take illegitimate babies for twelve pounds. The mothers believe their babies are being cared for, adopted out, perhaps. But every day, we find babies floating in the Thames. . . ."

"John, for the love of God," her uncle said. "Stop."

"We find them in alleys, wrapped in newspaper, discarded like so much garbage," John said, ignoring his father's plea. "Sometimes the little babes are killed outright. Other times they are slowly starved to death. It is worse for the older children. Many times the mother, desperate to keep her baby, pays these women fifteen shillings a week, thinking her child is safe and one day she will be able to return for it. But they die, almost always. And there is nothing the mother can do."

Tears streamed down Melissa's face. It could have been her, thrown into an alley. Her mother had been desperate, alone, starving.

"How do people let that happen?" she whispered.

John shook his head. "I don't know. Good Christian people turn their heads away, believing such a child is better off dead." Melissa gasped. "Father is working with two doctors to change the laws so that babies are protected. But few people want to listen."

"Why are you telling me this?" Melissa asked, sniffing loudly.

"I wanted you to know why my father and I did what we did. Why your father was so concerned about your well-being. He was afraid for you. My father made a promise to his brother, to protect you at all costs. And that is what we are doing. No one will know of your birth, Melissa. You shall marry a good man, a man who loves you."

Melissa stared at John. "A man whom I must lie to," she said dully.

John squeezed her hand. "Yes."

"And he must never know?" It seemed so wrong. If someone loved her, truly loved her, it shouldn't matter whether her mother was married or not when she was born.

John looked down. "I suppose that is something you must decide for yourself," he said quietly.

"If you married a woman who was illegitimate," she said, "would you want to know?" She stared at him and felt her stomach drop at his expression. "You wouldn't want to know, would you? Because you would think less of her, is that it? Is that how you truly think of me, as simply a bastard to be foisted off on the first unsuspecting man?"

"Melissa, that is enough," her uncle said.

Melissa ignored him. "I'm right, aren't I?" she asked John.

John shook his head, but he could not meet her eyes. "It's an unfair question as I already know who you are and who your father is. But if I'm to be perfectly honest, it is information most men could do without. You would do much better to keep your silence if you wish to marry well. Your birth should not matter, not to a man who loves you. It should not. But it will matter. Life is not fair, Melissa, no matter how we wish that it was."

She gave her head a shaky nod, knowing he was right even as she silently railed against it. She did not know if she could marry someone with this lie in her heart. It shouldn't matter, but Melissa, even with her limited experience of society, knew it would. She didn't know what to do.

"I'm letting Darling out, then going to bed," she said, suddenly so weary she could hardly stand.

"I'll get Sandy and go with you," John said.

"If you wish."

Outside the library, John gave a sharp whistle, and it was only a matter of a few seconds before both puppies come bounding toward them. Darling followed behind, her ears flapping, her tail wagging excitedly, and Melissa smiled and bent down to kiss her pup's head, a difficult task when Darling was bent on licking her mistress's face. She laughed, and John felt his heart tug, glad that all the laughter hadn't been taken from her.

"Come, you two," John said, giving his own dog a hearty pat. They silently walked through the deserted kitchen and out the back door, letting the dogs bound about and do their business.

"Are you all right, then?" John asked, gazing at Melissa as she smiled faintly at the dogs' antics. Her smile disappeared.

"No. I'm not." She crossed her arms, whether from the cold or to shut him out, John wasn't certain. "I had no idea the world was such a cruel and complicated place," she said. "It seems impossible that society would allow innocent babes to die because of their unfortunate birth."

"I couldn't believe it either until I saw it for myself," John said. "If it had been one madwoman, then perhaps. But there are hundreds of baby farmers throughout the kingdom."

"It makes me feel dirty."

John snapped his head around, shocked by her words. "No," he said, horrified that she would think such a thing. "You are the same girl you were. It is society that is foul, not you." He stood before her, his heart breaking at the way she kept her head down. He wanted to rail against a world that could steal her confidence, her joy. "Melissa, look at me."

She lifted her head, and he saw nothing but despair. "Do not let petty people change your opinion of yourself."

"I wish I could go home," she said. "But my home is gone. Sold to someone else. Everything is gone."

He knew she meant more than brick and mortar. All her dreams, all her memories were now tainted.

"You are home," he said, drawing her into his arms, trying to give her comfort and strength. He placed one hand at the back of her head and held her for several long moments, his cheek resting on her smooth, soft, black curls. She let out a sigh, and John pushed back, pressing a kiss upon her forehead.

"I thought we'd have no more kisses."

He smiled down at her, glad she was able to tease him again. "That was the kiss of a first cousin," he said.

"I like the other kind better."

Just like that, desire washed over him, and he took a step back. "I daresay I do, too," he said, his voice uncharacteristically gruff.

"I wish . . ." She stopped, turning her head abruptly away.

"What do you wish for, Melissa?"

She closed her eyes briefly, then gave a small shrug. "Too many things that can never come true," she said softly.

Chapter 13

John spent a sleepless night, worrying about Melissa and wondering if it were true that he'd actually fallen in love with her. His mind was in a bloody war over the matter. He was an intelligent man who knew everything he said and did was a matter of how his brain worked. His heart was no more than an organ that pumped blood. When it stopped, he would die. It was not the place where love was born. But he couldn't help thinking that if love had nothing to do with his heart, why did it hurt so damned much at the thought of Melissa's marrying another?

He sat on the edge of his bed, his hands massaging his temples, as he tried to convince himself that this thing he felt was merely lust. He'd felt lust before, and this was not it. All his adult life, he'd believed that foolish men and women mistook lust for love. He'd seen men and women lose themselves to one another, only to break it off and go on with their lives. Or worse, they married and ended up loathing each other. He'd felt so superior to all those fools who truly thought they'd found love, and rather smug when everything fell apart. If love existed, why were so many people miserable with each other?

Then, the image of the Pickets and their brood of children came to him. That flower Mr. Picket had fetched for his wife, that ridiculous, wilted flower that he'd nearly killed himself to get for Mrs. Picket. Why? Because he lusted for her? Admired her? No. *God, no.* After fifteen years of marriage, a man only did something like that because he loved his wife. *Loved* her.

The way he loved Melissa?

"Bloody hell," he whispered harshly.

Since he'd never been in love, it had been easy to dispute its existence. But now in the throes of what he believed was love, he was rather lost. For the first time in years, he wished he had a mother he could talk to about such things. His mother, dead now for years, would not have been that person. She'd left her husband, abandoned her son, and probably didn't have an ounce of compassion or kindness in her black soul. The few memories he had of his mother were not good ones, but of a woman who was as cold and uncaring as a baby farmer. Had she been born of the lower classes, John had no doubt she would have found the job appealing.

He wished, then, not for his mother, but for another mother. The kind who would lay a gentle hand upon his head, who would smile when he entered a room. Who would pick out the runt of the litter and claim it was the most wonderful pup in the world.

Unable to sleep, John left the manor house as soon as the sky hinted of dawn. He strode to the stables, feeling restless and out of sorts, hoping a good ride would clear his mind and bring him back to sanity. A young stable hand, hair mussed from sleep and rubbing his eyes, came to assist John, but he told the lad to go back to bed. He wanted a distraction, no matter how small, from thinking about Melissa. John had always done some of his best thinking while riding, and he hoped this early morning ride would bring some sense into his addled mind.

It didn't. No matter how fast, no matter how far he rode, he could not get Melissa out of his mind or, yes, out of his heart. His horse, heaving great breaths after an invigorating run, quivered and snorted when he pulled on the reins and stopped the steed. He dismounted, gave the horse a rub on its neck, and stood on a hill overlooking Flintwood House in the distance. It was a fine building, even from so far away, and he felt a swell of pride that it would someday be his. He'd stood at that spot a hundred times, looking down on this land, never imagining himself living there with a family. In his thoughts, it was only him. But now, he could not stop his mind from inserting Melissa into the picture. And their children. He let out a curse, wondering if and when this insanity would end. God help him, he felt like weeping. Over a woman!

"Well," he said to the horse, for it was far, far more difficult to say what he wanted to say to a human. "Looks like there's nothing to do but go to my father." He let out a breath, not wanting to think of his father's reaction when he told him he wanted to marry Melissa. He would try to convince his father it was the best choice, the only choice Melissa had for happiness. He would approach his father and explain his plan as he would a business proposition, with reason and logic, and he would not tell his father that he loved her. His father would dismiss such nonsense out of hand. Yes, people would call his father a hypocrite, and his tenure on the commission reviewing marriages between first cousins would be jeopardized. And his good friend, Mr. Darwin, would likely not be pleased. But, really, what other choice was there?

By the time John returned to the manor, everyone in the house had already been up for several hours and eaten breakfast. The young people, including Miss Stanhope, were out fishing, the butler told him. John grinned. It was the perfect time to seek out his father and tell him of his plan.

He strode into his father's study, pleased when his father smiled at the interruption. He seemed to be in a good mood, which boded well for this conversation.

"I have a solution to our dilemma with Melissa," John said confidently, even as his stomach was a knot of nerves.

"Oh?"

"I can marry her," John said. Instantly, his father frowned, but John forged ahead before he could be interrupted. "Please hear me out, Father, for I've given this matter considerable thought. I do realize that our marriage would jeopardize your work on the commission and could possibly lead to questions about Melissa's birth. But people will have such questions no matter whom she marries. We get on fairly well, and I do believe we could make each other happy. And if I marry her, Melissa will not be forced to lie about who she is and can avoid the humiliation of telling her future husband the truth—and the possible repercussions that could come from such an admission."

His father leaned back with a smile, and for a moment, John thought he'd done it—he'd made his case, and his father would agree. He found that he was painfully hopeful.

"I have never been more proud of you, my boy," his father said, surprising John completely. "But no, I would not ask you to make such a sacrifice."

"It would not be a sacrifice, Father. I do care a great deal for Melissa. And I believe she feels the same," he said, feeling just the tiniest beginnings of panic set in. His father thought he was martyring himself for the cause?

"I'm certain you do. And I care for her, too, but I would never marry her." The earl let out a laugh. "However, such drastic measures are entirely unnecessary, as Charles came to me this very morning and requested Melissa's hand. Of course, I consented."

For one brief moment, John's vision went black, as blood rushed to his head. He quickly recovered, but was left weakened, shaken to his core. "That is . . ." He couldn't bring himself to speak. "What of her birth?" he asked.

His father gave him a curious look. "Are you quite all right, my boy? You have no trepidations about such a match, surely. Charles is your greatest friend. You invited him here yourself for the express purpose of meeting Melissa."

John forced himself to focus on his father, even as his gut churned. "Yes. Of course. But what of Melissa?"

"After long consideration, I thought it prudent to inform Charles of Melissa's birth. No one other than he will be told, of course. He was disappointed, which is understandable given society's prejudices, but he said he loved her and would be able to overlook her birth."

"Overlook it?" John said, feeling a surge of anger.

"Yes, he's rather infatuated with her," George said, chuckling at some remembered comment during their interview. It only served to drive John a bit mad, thinking about Charles and his father discussing Melissa. "And, by the way, Melissa seemed pleased by the arrangement and glad she doesn't have to hold her secret with Charles. Indeed, I could not have asked for a better resolution to the entire problem."

John clutched his chair's arms, trying to process what his father was telling him. Charles would marry Melissa, and she was glad of it. He did not believe it; he could not. He loved her. "Melissa is pleased?" he repeated stupidly.

"Not over the moon, no. But pleased. There won't be a formal announcement in the *Times* until after the season begins. Charles and I agree that Melissa does need a bit more time getting used to social events and interacting with the ton before being deluged with invitations. You know how the women react when someone announces an engagement." He gave a mock shudder. "But, as far as I'm concerned, the matter is settled. I'll have my attorneys draw up a marriage contract immediately. In fact, I'm just now writing to Mr. Henley to start work on it."

"And Melissa is happy with the plans?"

His father shook his head, as if impatient with John's continued questions. "As I said, yes, she is pleased. I think she realizes that her options are quite limited, and the fact that Charles wants to marry her despite her birth is remarkable."

John was taken aback by his father's comment. "Do you think less of Melissa because of her birth, Father?"

"Of course not. But I am a realist. Few members of

the peerage would knowingly marry a bastard, no matter who the father is."

"I am willing," John said, and was horrified to feel his throat aching. He barely recognized the sensation, the raw pain that signified he was near to weeping. *Good God.*

"Yes, and I do appreciate the noble gesture. No need for martyrs though, eh? You've done a marvelous thing for her, John. Marvelous."

John gave his father a nod and stood, feeling as if he'd just been trampled by a speeding carriage. He didn't know how this had happened, how he had allowed himself to fall in love with the one woman who was forbidden to him. She'd told his father she was pleased. *Pleased.*

And he felt as if he were dying.

Melissa's stomach was a bit queasy, and it had nothing to do with the large breakfast she'd had that morning. She and Charles had told no one but Miss Stanhope about their impending engagement, and Melissa felt adrift. She did not know if she was supposed to act happy or grateful. She only knew that had her uncle told her of Charles's request just two days ago, before she understood the full impact of her birth, she never would have agreed to the match. But now she knew no one else would want her.

And yet, Charles did. It should have made her feel wonderful and loved. Instead, for some reason she could not fully explain, she felt even more tainted. He was marrying her in spite of her birth. Although he hadn't said any such thing out loud, she got the distinct feeling Charles felt he was making some sort of grand gesture, that he should be patted on the back and congratulated for still wanting to marry her after hearing the dreadful news.

Perhaps she felt this way because it was all so new, this sense that she ought to somehow be ashamed of who she was. All her life, she had been told she was special; she had felt loved. And now she was supposed to hide who and what she was.

She heard a happy feminine shout, and watched as Lady Juliana's pole bent from the weight of yet another fish. They were all using the same bait—thick, squirmy, pink earthworms—but Lady Juliana was the only one catching anything. Already, she had three fish in her basket, and the men got grumpier and grumpier with every one she caught.

"Oh, a fine trout," she said, expertly taking the flopping fish from the hook. Melissa would never have imagined the proper and unsmiling woman she'd met a week ago was now this grinning hoyden with fish slime on her hand.

The six of them were fishing in a picturesque lake surrounded by weeping willows just starting to sprout their small leaves. Charles hovered by her, teaching her how to bait the hook and toss in the line. Laura sat by Avonleigh, apparently doing so to bother him, and Lady Juliana and Miss Stanhope sat upon a large rock that jutted out into the pond. Only John was missing. It was sunny, finally, and the sun dappled through the trees and onto the grassy bank where they all sat or stood, fishing poles in hand. Laura, incessantly cheerful, regaled the dour Avonleigh with endless happy tales, ignoring his frown and looks of irritation. Melissa enjoyed their banter, his weary sighs as Laura would begin yet another topic he had no interest in. Yet this time, Laura was discussing her wedding, and that topic made Melissa's stomach churn even more.

She wished she felt the joy Laura seemed to feel about her upcoming nuptials. But all Melissa could think was that she was marrying someone she didn't love. She wondered what John would say to her when he learned of the engagement. Would he be relieved? Probably. She knew enough from talking to the other women that men put far less importance on kissing than women did. What she had thought was a magical moment of bliss, John had apologized for. He'd lost his head, but not his heart, obviously. Hadn't even Miss Stanhope dreamed of marriage after allowing a man to kiss her? She, too, had been cast aside.

"Laura, no one wants to know the nonexistent details of your fictitious wedding to a man who hasn't even proposed," Charles said good-naturedly.

Laura wrinkled her nose at her brother, then cast a sidelong glance at Avonleigh. "Am I boring you?" she asked sweetly.

"Yes." Avonleigh was not a man to jest, and so Laura pretended to sulk even though Melissa suspected she'd known all along Avonleigh had absolutely no interest in discussing her wedding plans.

"Perhaps we should discuss *your* wedding, then, my lord," Laura said. "Do you want a large one or a small one?"

"I don't want one at all," Avonleigh replied dryly. "What of you, Charles? Are you still racing to the altar?"

Melissa stiffened, for Avonleigh wasn't looking at Charles with his hooded gaze, he was looking at her.

She always had the feeling the marquess knew far more than he let on.

"I'm certain I'll get there before you," Charles said with a laugh, then looked at Melissa warmly. She wished that look caused a thrill in her heart instead of a sickening lurch in her stomach.

Charles stood, waving at John, who approached the group, a ready smile on his face. No doubt his father had already told him the good news of her pending engagement.

"Any luck?" he asked. They all grumbled, except for Lady Juliana, who held up her basket half full of fish.

Melissa stared at him, willing him to look at her. Did he know of the engagement? He must. Then, he met her gaze and looked quickly at Charles, before offering her one of his easy grins. He knew. And he was happy, obviously. A burden relieved. A problem solved. Perhaps, even, a temptation removed. Melissa wished she could leave this happy scene, go to her room, and cry for a day. Life had been so much simpler when she'd lived in Bamburgh with her father. Each day had been very much like the one before it, with no surprises, no heartache, no arguments. She'd been content, unaware an entire world existed that she didn't know and could never understand. Now she understood far too much. She understood what it felt like to love someone who did not love you back. She knew shame and the uncomfortable feeling of deception. Her uncle had told her no one but Charles could know of her birth. That meant living a lie for the rest of her life.

"Hey, ho!" Charles shouted, his pole bending nicely, indicating a big fish.

"Set the hook properly," Lady Juliana said, clearly teasing him.

"It's set, all right," Charles said, and in a matter of minutes a large fish was flopping about helplessly on the grass. "That's a big bastard," he said, full of excitement. Then he looked at Melissa and his cheeks flushed. "Oh, sorry," he mumbled, to her horror.

"Such language," John said, lightly. "And in front of the ladies."

"Yes. I did apologize," Charles said.

"So you did," John said blandly.

Melissa felt a rush of humiliation and terrible awareness that for the rest of her life, each time someone used that word, Charles would give her a searching look, a mumbled apology. "What kind of fish is that?" she asked, grateful her voice did not betray the pain in her throat. It was an odd-looking creature with a large, flat head and some sort of tentacles sprouting from near its ugly mouth.

"It's a catfish," John said. "See the whiskers?"

"Fine eating, too," Charles said, holding up the fish and showing it to Melissa, who wrinkled her nose and backed up a step. Charles laughed. "There's nothing to be afraid of, Melissa. Haven't you ever seen a fish before?"

"Of course I have. On my dinner plate."

"This is her first time fishing, Charles, you know that," John said.

"Oh. I'd forgotten," he said, sounding almost sullen, and Melissa gave him a questioning look. Charles had been a wonderful companion these past days and had never even hinted a criticism. "Come here, then, and take a look, Melissa. It won't bite."

It looked awful to Melissa, like some sort of abomination of nature with its whiskers and flat head, its mouth opening and closing as it gasped for air.

"She's a beauty."

"It's a girl?" Melissa asked dubiously, silently thinking it silly to call that ugly fish "a beauty."

John laughed. "Hard to say. But it is a fine fish and delicious. That one's big enough to almost feed all of us. Would you like to touch it?"

Melissa looked at John with horror. "Goodness, no!"

"Come on," he said, holding out his hand.

Melissa pressed her lips together, and did as he asked, allowing him to bring her hand to the fish's slimy surface. She wrinkled her nose, but giggled. "See?" he said, looking at Charles, who held the fish out to her. "You just have to be patient."

Melissa's eyes were on the fish, so she missed the look that passed between Charles and John.

"It feels just as slimy as it looks," Melissa said, laughing up at Charles. She called over to Lady Juliana. "I don't know how you can take one of those things off the hook. It's dreadful."

Lady Juliana was putting on a worm at that moment and bent to rinse her hands in the lake's clear water. "Practice," she said briskly.

Melissa didn't think she'd want to practice such a thing, but she was willing to try to forge her way in this new life. Charles seemed to enjoy so many things that were foreign to her and was genuinely shocked when she didn't know the simplest things they all took for granted. The only skills she had were used in the confines of a home. But those skills didn't seem to mean much at the moment.

"Fishing is boring anyway," Laura said, glumly looking at her slack line. "I don't know how many times I've been, and I hardly catch a thing."

"You've been fishing four times," Charles said.

"Because it's so boring," Laura countered, making Melissa smile.

Lady Juliana let out another shout. Honestly, that woman must be doing something none of the others were. "It's not boring for Lady Juliana," Melissa pointed out.

Laura moved her pole, and it bent, producing a gleeful shout from the previously bored woman. "Oh, I've got one. I've got one." She pulled, jerking the pole, and pulled some more.

"I think you've got a root, not a fish," Charles said, laughing, and going over to his sister to help. "Honestly, Laura."

Laura stuck her tongue out at her brother, and he simply laughed, taking the pole from his sister's hands and maneuvering farther down the bank in hopes of dislodging the hook.

"Having fun?" John asked, coming up to stand close to Melissa.

"Oh, yes."

"Liar."

Melissa gave him a searching look and saw nothing but good humor. No suffering. No longing. And certainly no love. She looked back at the lake, feeling ridiculous. "You've heard," she said softly.

"Yes." He was silent for a long moment. "You are pleased?"

"Oh, yes, very," Melissa said brightly, looking out on the lake with new intensity. If she looked at John, she knew she would cry. It took a few moments before she could bring herself to glance at him and flash him a smile that she prayed was believable. How mortifying if he somehow suspected she was madly in love with him and that the thought of marrying Charles was breaking her heart.

"Good, good. It's what my father and I hoped for."

Those words were like small knives plunging into her heart. Suddenly, she was angry with him, raging in fact. How could he stand there so blandly when just yesterday he'd been touching her, kissing her, moaning into her mouth as if he'd die. How *could* he?

"I think I fell in love with him the moment I saw him," she said, lifting her chin. "And I'm so glad you showed me, um, things, so that I could be more prepared on our wedding night. I'm ever so grateful." Her throat aching, she hauled in her line and walked with determination over to Charles, noticing Avonleigh staring at her. She stared right back and gave him a brilliant smile.

John swore to himself as she walked—or rather stalked—off, using all his willpower to look as if nothing of import had passed between them. She was angry, no doubt wondering how a man could ravish her one day and be happy about her engagement to another man the next. Well, she was going to have to keep wondering. She was Charles's now. She'd agreed to the marriage; his father was having the contract drawn up; the announcement would appear in the *Times* within a matter of weeks.

The ache in his heart, this wrenching pain that

stunned him as much as hurt him, would go away. No doubt one or two weeks in London carousing with his chums and he'd be good as new. It had been unnatural to think he wouldn't be attracted to such a beautiful woman. He'd never spent so much time with a woman alone, never mind one so desirable. What had his father been thinking, that John was made from stone? Of course he was attracted to her. Of course he'd developed certain feelings. He was a man, and this was lust. It had to be.

Because if this aching, dying feeling was love, then he was doomed to live the rest of his life missing her, seeing her with his best friend, knowing Charles was having what he never would. Knowing Charles was making love to her, touching her, smiling at her in the morning and holding her at night. God, how could he bear it? How? Charles had better be good to her; he'd better never make her feel anything but cherished and loved, or there'd be hell to pay.

This would pass. Dear God, it had to pass.

John hadn't realized he was glaring at Melissa and Charles until Avonleigh purposely put himself in his sights. He wrenched his eyes away and stared out at the lake, tensing when his friend sidled up to him. "Get a grip, man," Avonleigh said, his voice tight and low. "Every lustful thought is as plain as if you were holding a sign."

John nodded, swallowing heavily. "They're to be married," he said, his throat raw. To his dismay, tears burned in his eyes. Avonleigh, looking decidedly horrified, took his arm and said loudly, "Sure, let's try fishing down here."

They moved down the lake perhaps fifty yards before Avon stopped and stared at him, his dark eyes intense and kind. "Why are you allowing it?"

John clenched his jaw, refusing to give in to the misery that was tearing at his heart. "Because it is what she wants. What my father wants. What Charles wants. Everyone is *bloody* thrilled." They were far from the others, and John glared at the happy group, whose cheerful shouts he could still hear.

"Do you think Charles has an inkling about who her father truly is?"

"Yes. My father told him. He's still willing to marry her." A rush of despair hit him as he recalled going to his father and telling him that he would marry her. John wondered if he'd told his father the truth—that he loved her and had compromised her—whether things would have turned out differently. Probably not. In fact, it would have been far worse. He would have been left with a father who felt betrayed and sickened by his son's actions—and Melissa would still be marrying Charles.

"Perhaps it's best, then."

John looked at his friend, not understanding.

"Love is fleeting. You know that. You *believe* that."

"I did."

Avon shook his head. "John, you're my friend and the only man who, I thought, truly believed what I do—that love is a phantom, something that weak men invented to explain temporary insanity."

John let out a laugh. "You're probably right. I do feel a bit mad right now."

"It will pass. It *always* does."

John looked up the lake, to where Melissa stood next to Charles, hating this feeling of complete helplessness. "What if it doesn't?"

"Hell isn't such a bad place to live, my friend. I do it every day."

Chapter 14

Melissa looked at her reflection as a seamstress made small corrections to her ball gown, the one she would wear to her debut in two weeks. It was royal blue held aloft with a cage crinoline covered by two petticoats that peeked beneath the cream lace scalloped about the bottom. The bodice was rounded and modest, showing only the barest hint of the swell of her breasts, and the waist seemed impossibly small, thanks to the rather brutal corset she wore.

"The color is perfect," Miss Stanhope said. "Your eyes are absolutely beautiful."

Melissa looked at her reflection and smiled. Although her father had hired a woman to come to their home each year to present her with the latest fashions, she'd never owned a ball gown; she'd never had reason to have one. She'd been back in London a week now, and the season's first ball was in one week's time. She'd thought two weeks was plenty of time to get ready, but realized now they should have ordered her wardrobe weeks ago. Many of the dresses she needed would not be ready for another two weeks or more. It was only the generosity of her uncle—and his willingness to pay top dollar to get her needed gowns done quickly—that allowed her to have enough clothes to wear during her first week in Town. She was a bit overwhelmed by the amount of clothing a woman needed to wear when in the city. There were day dresses and walking dresses. Dresses one wore to ride in a carriage around Hyde Park, and dresses to wear to the opera. There were ball gowns, and riding outfits (she would have one, even though it was completely unnecessary), and dresses she would wear to dinners. And, of course, every gown required the proper hat and gloves and parasol and fans. Silk stockings, yards of expensive lace, overcoats, and shawls. It was a veritable mountain of clothing. And it all had to be new because everything she had was either black or outdated.

Most disconcerting were the nighttime things she was supposed to wear once she was married. She couldn't imagine being so very naked in front of Charles, wearing items that were so flimsy and see-through. She was building, Miss Stanhope said sternly, a fine trousseau.

Miss Stanhope had a list, and she would check off each item as soon as it was purchased. It all seemed so excessive, but Miss Stanhope insisted every item was absolutely necessary.

"Not the riding habit," Melissa had said stubbornly.

"My dear, your future husband is one of the foremost experts in horseflesh and one of the finest riders in the kingdom. You will learn to ride."

That pronouncement only depressed Melissa, for it reminded her of that day in the stable, when John had been so patient with her, letting the horse gently take bits of carrot from her palm. She wanted John to teach her to ride. She wanted . . . well, she wanted John. She knew she was being unfair to Charles, but she couldn't help what was in her heart. It seemed like forever since she'd seen John, though he was often in her thoughts.

When the small group had left Flintwood House, she'd been both relieved and terribly lonely. She missed John, missed the way he made her feel clever and beautiful. She missed their talks, the lessons he'd given her on simple things like how to skip a stone on a pond or train her puppy to stay. Or how to kiss. Everything seemed to remind her of John, even her puppy. Darling was such a good dog, and she loved her mightily, but every time she saw her, she longed for John. Tonight, for the first time in weeks, she would see him, for he was having dinner at home. It was foolish and futile to wish things were different. She knew she should be happy and grateful Charles wanted to marry her, that he loved her.

But she couldn't help wondering *why* he loved her. They hadn't spent all that much time together. How was it possible for him to love her when all they'd shared was a few walks and four dances? Even their single kiss had been unremarkable. There'd been none of the breath-stealing, heart-stopping, body-throbbing passion she'd felt with John. Nothing but mild pleasantness.

Standing in her ball gown gazing at her reflection, Melissa was happy with what she saw, but she didn't wonder what Charles would think of her. She only wondered about John.

She'd not seen him since they'd all left Flintwood, even though she'd been in London eight days in his father's town house. John, she was told, had rented his own place for the season. Still, she would see him. In fact, he was to escort her to the ball, where they would all meet up with Charles and his family. Melissa was a bit nervous about meeting Charles's family, even though she adored Laura. She couldn't help wondering what Charles had told his parents about her and whether they knew about her birth.

Charles had visited twice since her arrival, awkward meetings that left Melissa feeling discontented. While they had all had jolly fun in the country, seeing Charles without the others had seemed strange. They'd had little to talk about, and conversation had been strained.

Today, she would be riding out with him in Hyde Park and wearing a new carriage dress—another item she hadn't needed in Bamburgh, since she'd never had cause to ride in a carriage.

"All done, miss," the seamstress said, stepping back to look at her handiwork. "It is lovely on you."

"Yes, it is," Miss Stanhope said. "Please deliver the dress by Thursday, along with any other items that are completed." The woman immediately began undoing the tiny seed buttons that ran down the back of the gown. Once her corset was loosened, Melissa gasped for breath. She'd never in her life been so constrained.

"We'd best hurry. Mr. Norris will be at the house in one hour, and I daresay we hardly have time to get home and get you ready."

"I'm famished," Melissa said, fearing she wouldn't have time to eat before her ride with Charles. It was nearly teatime, and they planned to leave for Hyde Park at five.

"I'll have the kitchen send something up while you dress. Thank goodness, your carriage dress was prepared in time."

In a flurry of activity, the two women rushed from the dressmaker's, climbed aboard their coach, then waited in thick traffic as the vehicle edged its way toward Piccadilly.

"It would have been much faster to walk," Melissa grumbled.

As soon as they reached the town house, they disembarked and stepped briskly inside, Miss Stanhope hurrying to the kitchens, and Melissa going up the stairs to change yet again. She didn't know why she couldn't wear the dress she had been wearing; she had been in a carriage, after all. But no, she had to wear the dress specifically designated as the "carriage dress," along with her pretty green velvet hat with the jaunty black plume, and matching parasol and gloves.

Her maid made quick work of getting her out of her day dress and into her carriage dress while Melissa drank a cup of tea and ate a sugared scone Miss Stanhope had sent up. Her dress on, her hair fixed so that it complemented her new hat, her maid pronounced her ready just as a footman knocked on the door and announced that Mr. Charles Norris was waiting in the Blue Parlor.

"Goodness gracious," Melissa said, giving her reflection a quick look. "That was fantastic, Clara." The scone had done little to fill her, and her stomach grumbled in quite an unladylike fashion. She giggled and looked at her maid. "Did you hear that?"

"The thunder, miss?" Clara smiled, and Melissa laughed aloud.

When Melissa stepped into the Blue Parlor, Miss Stanhope was already there, talking politely to Charles.

"Good afternoon, Mr. Norris," Melissa said, dipping a small curtsy. Charles stood immediately, his gaze warm and inviting. He was a handsome man, and today he looked rather dashing in his fawn-colored pants and dark brown coat.

"If I might be so bold, you look lovely, Miss Atwell," Charles said, his cheeks going ruddy.

"Thank you. Shall we go? This is my first carriage ride in Hyde Park, so you will have to tell me all about it. Miss Stanhope tells me it is all the thing, especially once the season begins."

"That is true. It gets quite crowded in May and most especially in June," Charles said, donning a top hat and picking up a silver-headed walking stick. "Hopefully that will not be the case today."

Visiting Hyde Park was another strange ritual that Melissa did not understand. Apparently, men and women rode in their best carriages or on their finest horses, wearing their best clothes, and nodded to passersby. The park attracted society's elite, and it was not unheard of to see a member of the royal family. Miss Stanhope told her she should maintain a pleasant look, be certain to ask who people were, and be extra careful never to ignore someone of higher rank. She would help Melissa understand whom and whom not to acknowledge as they went about the circuit. It sounded rather tedious to Melissa, who wouldn't know a soul but for the passengers in her own carriage.

They entered the park from Kensington Road, turning onto a wide dirt path that was crowded with carriages and smartly dressed riders.

"This is Rotten Row," Charles said.

"Is it?" Melissa asked.

"Is it what?"

"Rotten."

Charles did not find her amusing, though Miss Stanhope let out a chuckle. "I really don't know where it got that name, but no, it's definitely not."

Melissa grinned at Charles, who was positioned across from them, his back to the liveried driver sitting like a statue on his elevated seat. She thought he would smile back at her, but instead he looked slightly annoyed. She wondered where the besotted man had gone, the one who had hung on her every word and found everything that came out of her mouth utterly charming.

"This is a lovely carriage," Melissa said, not knowing if it was or not, as it was the first of its kind she'd been in. The black-lacquered vehicle trimmed in gold certainly seemed luxurious enough. Thus far, she'd ridden in a train and covered coach, but never in an open carriage. "And the horses seem fine, too."

"They are the best-matched team in London," Charles said proudly. "It's all in the breeding, you know. A superior line absolutely must be maintained for the proper result. Our stables . . ." He stopped abruptly and looked sharply away. "I do apologize."

It took Melissa a few moments to understand what he was apologizing for, and when she did realize, her face flamed. Next to her, Miss Stanhope cleared her throat.

"It certainly is a lovely day for a ride in the park," Miss Stanhope said with forced cheer. Obviously she, too, realized that Charles was apologizing for mentioning superior breeding when Melissa was a human mutt.

"You cannot continue to apologize every time you say something that I may or may not interpret as some sort of criticism or slight regarding my parentage," Melissa said, her voice tight.

"Miss Atwell, this is not the place for a public disagreement," Miss Stanhope said sternly, but in a whisper only she could hear.

Melissa snapped her mouth shut, clutching her parasol fiercely in her hand as she looked stonily at the passersby.

"I do apologize," Charles said fervently. "Please forgive me."

Melissa relaxed, now feeling quite horrible for losing her temper. "There is no need, Charles. Truly. If we are to be married, it should be something we make light of, not agonize over. Until very recently, my father's identity was completely irrelevant. Each time you apologize, I feel dreadful."

"I'm sorry." And then, realizing he'd apologized again, he let out a sigh and mumbled, "sorry" again.

Miss Stanhope touched her sleeve. "That's Lord Chantilly. He and his wife are hosting the first ball of the season," she said, nodding toward a luxurious carriage across the way. "He is one of your uncle's staunchest allies in the House."

And so it went, for nearly two hours. Two excruciatingly long hours. Melissa, who had been schooled in the art of sitting still and quiet, had never sat quite so still and quiet for so long. Her arm hurt from holding her parasol perfectly still; her hands sweated inside her green velvet gloves; her back and neck ached. She noticed many women riding on horses wearing smart riding outfits and dashing little hats, and for the first time thought how wonderful it would be to be riding a horse, rather than sitting in a carriage.

"I should like to learn to ride, I think," Melissa said, looking enviously at one young woman who was trotting by at that moment. She didn't have to carry a parasol.

"That would be marvelous," Charles said, full of enthusiasm. "We'll have you up on a horse in no time. Laura's smashing good and could give you some pointers. I'm afraid I don't know much about riding sidesaddle."

"I am quite fearful," she said, already reconsidering. She didn't want to ride a horse, but rather she wanted the freedom riding a horse allowed.

"Once you're up, it'll be like second nature. You'll see."

Melissa looked at a passing horse dubiously, her doubt growing. Horses were huge. And the riders so high. How did one steer such a large animal? "Perhaps someday."

"You must learn," Charles said. "Every woman in England knows how to ride."

Melissa laughed. "Surely not every woman."

"Women of quality, I should say."

Melissa gave him a sharp look, wondering if he'd meant what he'd said, or if she was simply being overly sensitive. He did not apologize, and this time she wished he would. But perhaps he had not intended to insult her. Or perhaps he had, and that was why he did not apologize.

"Melissa," Miss Stanhope said quietly, but with an urgency that was startling. "Please look over to the right. And do not look back until I tell you to."

Melissa did as she asked immediately. "What is it?"

"The Duke of Waltham is passing on our left," she said conversationally in a low voice. "Perhaps you could move your parasol slightly? There, that should do it."

Melissa felt her entire body flush and stiffen as she lowered the parasol to hide her face. Her father. Her real father was passing them by, right at this moment. He might be looking at them, at the girl holding the parasol in front of her face, wondering who it was. She felt her skin prickle, almost as if she could somehow feel his gaze upon her. Next to her, Miss Stanhope chatted with Charles as if nothing were wrong. Or at least they were trying. Their conversation was stilted at best, and Melissa could sense their discomfort. It seemed like forever, as if the crowded Row would never allow them to slip past the duke's carriage unnoticed.

And then, "He's passed."

Hot tears pressed against Melissa's eyes as she realized she would be forced to behave in such a manner her entire life. Her father, just a few feet away, and she couldn't even look at him. Suddenly, the true nature of her birth struck her in a way it hadn't before.

"My dear, all is well," Miss Stanhope said soothingly.

"I don't know what he looks like," she said in a small voice. "What if I should encounter him when I am alone? What should I do?"

Charles pressed a handkerchief into her hand. "Be discreet," he urged, indicating the cloth, and she looked at him in dismay. "People talk."

"He is right, my dear," Miss Stanhope said, calmly. "You must never cry in public."

Melissa stared at the handkerchief in her hands and tried very hard not to allow any more tears to fall.

"I've just told a joke, Melissa," Charles said. "Laugh."

She did, laughing delightedly, then pressing the handkerchief against her cheeks as if so overcome with mirth she was crying. Strangely, the pretend laughter turned into real laughter, for Melissa had never in her life been in such a bizarre situation.

"That's enough," Charles said, rather harshly. "You're making a scene." He looked about nervously.

Melissa was not making a scene. In fact, no one looked their way with anything other than mild curiosity.

"No need to worry, Mr. Norris," Miss Stanhope said.

He nodded, but appeared to be upset. Again, that sullen look she hadn't seen until quite recently showed itself, and her uneasiness grew. Charles had told her father that her birth didn't matter, but it was becoming clear to Melissa that it did. It was small things, the slips, the veiled criticism, the worry that she wasn't acting entirely correctly. Just the other day he'd looked at her perfectly respectable gown, one that Miss Stanhope herself had picked out and deemed modest, and suggested mildly that it wasn't appropriate for a walk along Mayfair. She'd looked down uncertainly, seeing nothing untoward, but felt self-conscious for the remainder of the day. He wasn't being intentionally cruel, she knew that, and perhaps she was simply overly sensitive to every look and comment that could be construed as criticism.

Finally, the carriage turned onto Kensington, and the group made its way back to her uncle's town house on Piccadilly. Charles leaped from the carriage and assisted first Miss Stanhope and then herself down—not an easy feat with their voluminous skirts. He walked the women to the door, gave a bow, and bid them good-bye, seemingly in a hurry to leave.

Once the door was closed, Melissa leaned up against it and closed her eyes. "That was perfectly dreadful," she said, pulling off her gloves and sighing with relief.

Miss Stanhope agreed. "It certainly was not the most pleasant drive, was it?" she asked, in that brisk way of hers.

"This is far more difficult than I thought it would be." She heard the frantic clicking of Darling's nails on the floor and bent to greet her puppy. "Did you miss me, Darling? I missed you. Next time, I'll bring you. What do you say to that?" Darling wiggled her little body so much she nearly fell over.

The thought of another carriage ride sent dread into Melissa's heart. She'd stupidly thought seeing her true father would be a wonderful thing, but that was before she'd learned it was very likely he wouldn't acknowledge her. London was not such a big place, and for the rest of her life she would be fearful of running into him, or into his daughter who apparently looked so much like her. Her lovely room in Bamburgh called out to her, those safe walls that kept all ugliness and sadness away.

"Ah, there you are. How was your ride?"

Just like that, John was there by her side, acting as if all was well, as if they hadn't been separated for nearly three weeks. He bent over to give Darling a good scrub, then straightened.

"Awful," Melissa said feelingly.

"Waltham was in the park," Miss Stanhope said, pulling off her hat and setting it on a nearby table.

"Did he see you?"

"No. I hid behind my parasol." Melissa picked up the green parasol with black lace and snapped it open to demonstrate.

"That must have looked rather suspicious," John said, laughing.

Melissa closed the parasol and smiled a genuine smile for the first time all day. "Perhaps I should start wearing a mask. I would become very mysterious, and the ton would go mad with curiosity. 'I wonder if she's afflicted,' 'I wonder if she's too beautiful to behold?' And I'll wear a different wig to each event so no one will be certain if I'm one woman or several."

"An ideal plan," John said, smiling down at her. But even though he smiled, and let her make light of it, she saw real concern in his eyes, and loved him all the more for it. It was so *good* to see him.

"I'm very glad you are here, Lord Willington. You are the only one who can make Melissa laugh," Miss Stanhope said warmly. "Now, my dear, we must change for dinner. No doubt we're both full of dust."

John stood at the base of the curving staircase and watched the two women ascend, Darling awkwardly following behind them. His smile slowly faded once they were out of sight. He knew the instant he heard her voice that he should not have agreed to dine with his father that evening. He'd truly thought being away from Melissa for three weeks, going to his clubs with his chums, and generally doing anything he thought would get his mind clear of her, would work. It had not. He had been miserable, had had trouble sleeping, and had not been able to bring himself to have sex with a rather lovely barmaid who offered herself up to him in the most blatant manner possible.

He'd come to the conclusion that it was not lust driving him, but love. He loved Melissa enough to let her be happy. That was what he told himself—that Charles would make her happy, would protect her, would love her.

John knew she and Charles had been spending time together because his friend had regaled him with droll stories about their various adventures. Everything seemed to be going along just swimmingly, and John would have forced himself to be happy for his friend if it weren't for the odd things Charles would say now and again.

He'd mentioned, for example, Melissa's clothing. Charles had asked, with complete sincerity, if Melissa dressed in a fashion that was a bit "fast." That was his word. Fast. It was ridiculous. From John's point of view, her gowns were rather too modest—but perhaps that was because he so enjoyed looking at whatever flesh he could. It could also be that John had seen quite a bit of Melissa that day in the rain, and even that had not been enough.

And then Charles had casually asked what John knew of her mother. In honesty, John knew next to nothing but that she'd come from an impoverished family of high birth and had been forced to work as a governess. She'd had the misfortune of being hired by Waltham, who, if rumors were correct, made a habit of forcing himself on his female servants. The younger, the better.

"Are you having second thoughts about Melissa?" John had asked carefully.

Charles had seemed genuinely surprised by that

question. "Good God, no. It's just that I want to know more about her. We are to be married, after all."

John had ignored the rather sharp stab of disappointment he felt. Charles clearly was still in love with Melissa, and John felt slightly ashamed for thinking his friend would abandon her.

John went to his father's study, grateful it was empty, and flung himself onto a settee. She'd looked damned beautiful today. Her cheeks had been flushed, her eyes sparkling, even though she'd had an awful time on her carriage ride through Hyde Park. The thought of her sitting there, hiding behind her parasol as her father drove by, made his stomach clench. Poor Mel. He wished he'd been there to hold her hand, to give her courage. She should never have to hide from anyone, and the thought of her cowering from Waltham made his blood run hot.

Yet, she seemed happy. Wasn't that what he wanted, for Melissa to be happy? What kind of a cad would endanger her position in society simply because he wanted her so badly it was a physical ache? And what of his father? Should he ruin his father's reputation, simply because of his own selfish needs?

Yes, he should, he screamed silently.

But he wouldn't.

"Ah, there you are, my boy." Speak of the devil, John thought.

"Father." His father gave him a hearty embrace as he always did when they hadn't seen each other for a few weeks. They had an easy relationship, one his friends envied, actually. Perhaps it was because it had been just the two of them for so long, living in a bachelor house, relishing all their manly pursuits without worrying about the female gender. Having so many females about lately was disrupting their calm life in ways neither could have imagined.

"Waltham passed by Norris's carriage today in the park," John said. "He didn't see Melissa, but it was a close call. She actually hid behind her parasol."

"What the devil was Waltham doing in Hyde Park, for goodness sake?" his father asked rhetorically. "Let's go into the study, shall we? I've got a nice cognac I want you to try. It came highly recommended."

The two men didn't speak until two snifters of the fine cognac were poured. "It's Courvoisier," George said, lifting his glass. "To Melissa's happy marriage."

John was in the process of lifting the glass to his lips, but upon his father's toast he stayed his hand. "Of course," he said, taking a large swallow.

His father looked at him curiously. "You don't seem very enthusiastic about the marriage, even though you acted as the matchmaker."

John shrugged and stared into his glass, letting the warmth of the cognac hit his stomach before he said another word. "I worry about Waltham, and about whether Charles will be able to deal with him should the duke meet Melissa. Then again, I don't know if I could deal with Waltham. I've heard he's rather volatile."

"He's evil," George said. "I don't know if we'll be able to avoid Waltham, since he's in Town and likely to be attending the same entertainments as we. I'm not certain it was a good idea to let Melissa have her season, after all."

"She'll have to face him at some point," John pointed out. "She could be a countess someday, and it is very likely they will meet. Perhaps it would be good to simply get it over with. This waiting for the ax to fall is not good for Melissa. She shouldn't have to hide her face. It makes her feel . . . tainted somehow."

George took another appreciative sip. "Fine, very fine," he said, indicating the cognac. "But as far as Melissa goes, I pray all goes well. That girl tugs at one's heart."

John smiled thoughtfully into his glass. "That she does."

"Say, I was wondering if you would like to join Miss Stanhope and me later on for some whist. Melissa does play, rather badly, but it will give her a distraction after what happened today. Miss Stanhope is a fierce player."

"Oh?"

"We're undefeated."

John raised his brows. "I hadn't realized you and Miss Stanhope had been partnered," he said, surprised his father had spent so much time with the woman.

"I wouldn't call us *partnered*," his father said, and John was rather shocked to see his father's cheeks grow pink. He could not recall ever seeing his father blush in all their time together. Lord George Braddock did not blush—ever. "But I do admire her bloodthirsty tactics when it comes to whist. Quite amazing, really."

"I don't know if Melissa even knows the rules. Not very sporting of you, Father," John said, but he knew he wouldn't pass up the chance to spend time with Melissa. He was quite masochistic when it came to her, it would seem. "Just how many matches have you two had?"

His father smiled. "Let's see now. At least twenty."

"Twenty?" John said, flabbergasted.

"Perhaps more."

"You've spent nearly every night since I left Flint-wood House playing whist with Miss Stanhope? Father, I think something more is going on here." John was joking, but realized he'd caught on to something when his father blushed—again. "There is something going on, isn't there?"

"I do enjoy her company," his father said evasively, and John noted his father was looking at his cognac and not at him. "She's the only woman I've met in twenty years who didn't bore me, or worse, annoy me," he said gruffly.

"You have surprised me, Father," John said.

"It's cards, John, nothing more."

"I never suggested otherwise, Father," John said, giving his father a knowing smile.

"Get that smirk off your face."

John grinned, then downed the rest of his drink. "I haven't the vaguest idea what you could be talking about, Father." He walked to the door. "By the way, I notice you appear quite clean shaven this evening. Hmmm."

He walked through the door with the sound of his father chuckling behind him. Imagine, his father shaving for a woman. In all his life, even when his father attended obligatory balls, he'd never taken the time to shave twice in one day. It was more than interesting.

Chapter 15

Diane wasn't stupid. Naïve, perhaps at times. Stupid, no. It was almost as if a veil had been held up in front of her for weeks, but had finally been lifted. It had begun when she and Melissa had come home from their ride. She noticed, but didn't give it a thought, how happy Melissa was to see John. How he'd looked down at her with real concern—concern Charles hadn't shown. No, Charles had been more fearful of what people would think of Melissa's shedding a tear or two. John, she knew instinctively, would have done anything to comfort her. And then, it was the way Melissa had laughed, the way her eyes shone when she looked at him. It was the look a woman gives to a man she loves.

It was a rather startling observation, but Diane, being suspicious of love in general, took it upon herself to watch the subtleties of their interactions. And she found it wasn't what was said or even the looks that passed between them. No, it was rather the way they looked at one another when they thought themselves unobserved. If she was not mistaken, it appeared as if Melissa and John were in love and trying not to show it to anyone—particularly to one another.

Diane was not stupid, and so she realized she might be seeing love where it didn't exist because she was so very much in love with Lord Braddock and trying just as desperately not to let him know. The kiss they'd shared had been a mistake of monumental proportions—not simply because it was inappropriate, but because now Diane could not get that kiss out of her head. It was disconcerting that all he'd had to do was give her that crooked grin of his and she'd agreed to continue being his partner in whist. Worse, in all the evenings the two of them had shared since, Lord Braddock had never looked at her with anything but fondness. Clearly, he enjoyed her company. But he enjoyed the vicar's company, too.

Because it was an intimate dinner, they all sat close together at one end of the dining room table. Lord Braddock had abandoned the head of the table to dine across from her and next to his son. Melissa and John sat across from one another, each taking turns devouring the other with their eyes when they thought no one was looking. They couldn't have been more obvious had they announced to her and Lord Braddock that they were in love. She hoped that was as far as it had gone.

How very tragic, she thought. She understood, then, why Melissa always seemed so very sad, even when she was facing the prospect of marrying a very fine gentleman. It reminded her of her own niece, who had been secretly in love with one man while engaged to marry another. Diane had been taken completely by surprise by her niece. But, as the saying went, fool me twice, shame on me. And Diane wasn't about to be fooled twice.

She could almost feel their love, like an intangible thread that connected them to one another. This could not end well, not for either of them.

Still, she could be wrong. It could be her overactive imagination, which would be understandable given the hell her poor niece had gone through. And the hell she herself was going through, to be honest. Imagine, falling in love with a man who claimed the emotion did not exist. It was almost amusing.

"Melissa," she said brightly, forcing herself to stop thinking such depressing thoughts. "While we were out this afternoon, the modiste sent over another gown. It is lovely. We're going to have to start thinking about your wedding dress, you know." She watched John from the corner of her eye, and it was as if he'd received a small blow before he instantly recovered with a smile.

"Have you set a date?" he asked. To someone who wasn't already suspicious, that would have seemed like an innocuous question. But Diane saw the tension in his face, the way his knuckles shone white as he held his fork and calmly took a small bite of roast pork.

And Melissa, the dear girl, pasted on a very similar smile. "No, we haven't. I haven't even met his parents yet."

"That will be amended tomorrow," George said, then turned to John. "We're having a small dinner party. Lord and Lady Hartley just arrived in Town yesterday. Unfortunately, the older boy is too ill to travel to London. I do expect you to be there, John."

John looked as if he might argue, but nodded. "Of course. Are you nervous, Melissa?"

Melissa shook her head, even as she said, laughing, "Terrified."

"No need," George said heartily. "They are a fine family. Lord Hartley is quite down to earth and very easy to get along with. No airs. I tell you, it will be rather pleasant to have them part of our little family. It's been just the two of us for long enough, eh, John?"

John gave his father a level look, one Diane couldn't begin to interpret. "Yes," he said softly. "That is true."

"And I can come visit any time," Melissa said, looking from one man to the other for confirmation.

"I'm certain you'll be quite busy setting up house and having babies and being a good wife," John said with impatience.

"Of course she will," George said, appearing slightly confused by John's tone.

"You're the only family I have," Melissa said, looking uncertainly from her uncle to John. "It would be dreadful not to see you."

"Perhaps," John said, his jaw clenching. "Charles will be your family, dear cousin. And, of course, Laura." He threw down his napkin and stood. "If you will excuse me."

"You will always be part of this family," George said to Melissa, then gave his son a chastising look. "Really, John."

"I'm not very good company tonight," John said tightly. "I do apologize."

"Will we not play cards, then?" Melissa asked, and John drew in a breath, then smiled, his expression softening considerably.

"Of course. Say in an hour? I need a breath of fresh air, that is all." He gave a small bow and left the dining room, leaving those still at the table looking at one another in confusion.

"Well," George said. "I don't know what that was all about. Very unlike John to act so disagreeably."

"Perhaps he is simply tired," Melissa said, turning toward the door where John had disappeared.

Diane made a decision, one she prayed she would not regret. She had seen firsthand how devastating it could be to keep a man and woman apart who were deeply in love. She would not be party to such heartbreak again.

John sat sullenly at the card table, gazing at a terrible hand, and wishing he were in his own town house. In bed. With a buxom, willing woman. He was not a sullen man. He was not a man who brooded. But this night, he could not bring himself to pretend he was happy that the woman he loved was marrying someone else. That she wanted to "visit" them after she was married, perhaps with her husband in tow, perhaps with her belly swelling with Charles's child, perhaps happy and glowing and driving a jagged piece of metal into his heart each time they looked at each other.

"John, it's your trick," his father said, giving him a searching look. He didn't care. He didn't care if his father stared at him all night. His father was the reason, after all, that John couldn't claim Melissa as his own. It was his father's damned sense of honor, his vital work on that damned commission, his damned friendship with Charles Damned Darwin that was causing all this heartache.

"So it is," he said, throwing in a random card.

"John," Melissa said, miffed.

Apparently he'd thrown in the wrong card. "What was trump again?"

"Clubs," Melissa said, looking pointedly at the two of clubs he'd led with.

He could feel them all looking at him. He knew they were wondering what was wrong, and he didn't care. His father had forced him to attend this dinner and forced this ridiculous card game on him. Just as he was forcing him to attend dinner the next evening so he could watch Melissa be introduced to her future in-laws. Just ducky all around.

They finished playing the hand and once again his father and Miss Stanhope won, much to his father's glee. Across from him Melissa gave him a look of exasperation, and he had to smile. She was so adorably angry at him for losing yet another hand.

"I thought you were a good player," Melissa said.

"He is," George said. "When his mind is on the game and not elsewhere. Just where is your mind tonight, son?"

John's eyes flickered to Melissa, before he gave a small shrug. "I'll try to do better."

It wasn't easy, for he was trying very hard not to look at Melissa, knowing that how he felt was likely written plainly on his face. But they were sitting across from one another, and they were partners, so it was fairly difficult to avoid looking at her altogether. Everything about her delighted him. From the way she studied her cards so carefully, wrinkling her nose when she didn't like what she saw, to the way she meticulously organized her cards, to her very poor bids.

"It's best not to use up all your trump," Miss Stanhope said during one hand.

"I've got plenty more," she said, so innocently John laughed.

"You shouldn't let a player like Miss Stanhope know what you're holding, silly goose," he said, and Melissa laughed.

"It truly doesn't matter," she said, impishly laying down yet another trump card.

"Oh, my, I believe the girl is holding a rather excellent hand," his father said.

"Why didn't you bid more?" John asked. "Miss Stanhope would have bid seven on such a hand."

"I'll get it whether I bid it or not," Melissa said pertly, and John was certain that made complete sense to her.

"But I could have outbid you," Miss Stanhope pointed out.

"But you didn't."

"But she could have."

Melissa shrugged, for she truly didn't care one way or another. She was having fun, and that was all she cared about, clearly. With a handful of trump, Melissa won the hand, giving a triumphant "hoorah" at the end of play.

"I think we should quit while we're ahead," Miss Stanhope said. "Why don't you escort your cousin to her room. Tomorrow is a big day, with her future in-laws coming, and Melissa needs her rest."

John frowned at Miss Stanhope, both at her mention of Charles's parents, as well as at her forcing him to be alone with Melissa. It was the last thing he wanted—and the thing he wanted most.

Melissa, oblivious to his anguish, readily agreed, her cheerful attitude beginning to grate. Couldn't she feel even a tiny bit miserable? Was this love so unrequited then? John had never felt so foolish in his entire life.

He bowed before her, and she took his arm with a smile, bidding his uncle and Miss Stanhope a good night.

"You are a terrible card player," he said, smiling down at her. She let out a gasp of outrage.

"I won that last hand, if you recall," she said. "And all I need is a bit of practice. That was the first time I've played pairs, you know. I think I did rather splendidly."

Her hand on his arm, warm and small, was a subtle torture. She had a habit, he noticed, of squeezing his arm when she spoke, an unconscious thing that was like a caress in his fevered mind. He found himself walking unaccountably slowly, simply to prolong the trip.

When they reached her room, she dropped her hand and lifted her face up to him, her brows furrowed. "What is wrong, John? You were not yourself tonight. Have I done something to make you angry with me?"

"I'm perfectly well, and of course I'm not angry with you."

"Oh." It was almost as if she were disappointed.

"What on earth would I have to be angry about?" he demanded, sounding rather angry even to his own ears.

"See? You are angry. Is it about Charles?"

He could feel his cheeks redden, but he forged on with his lie. "Of course not. Charles is my best friend."

"And you are happy we're to marry?"

"Ecstatic."

She nodded, and to his love-addled mind, she

seemed relieved. Relieved that he was giving her his blessing. *Bloody, bloody hell.*

He gave her a curt bow and knew he should say his good nights before he lost the ability to keep his hands by his sides. She couldn't have looked lovelier at that moment if she'd tried, gazing up at him with those eyes that drove him mad with want. Almost against his free will, his eyes drifted down, past her pretty nose, to her full lips, slightly parted as if ready for a kiss. He felt himself sway toward her before staying himself and taking another step back.

"I shouldn't walk you to your door," he muttered.

"No." A whisper, breathy and soft.

"Because it's too much of a temptation."

She said nothing, but grew impossibly still, her eyes never leaving his.

"Because I want to kiss you." Oh, God, what was he saying?

"I know."

"I want to do more than kiss you. I want to make love to you." He clenched his fists by his sides, and he nearly groaned when she took a step back.

"Stop it," she said, angry suddenly. "You've made your decision."

"What decision?" he asked, feeling his own anger surge.

"Never mind," she said, turning toward her door. He reached out without thinking and grabbed her arm.

"What decision?" he repeated, this time more gently.

"It doesn't matter. I'm marrying Charles and glad of it."

"If you are glad, then I am glad," he said, shocked

that he didn't choke on those words. "I only want you to be happy."

She swallowed, and looked down at her arm, where his hand still lay like a manacle holding her in place. "Then let me go," she said, bringing her clear gaze up to his. There was a wealth of meaning in those words, and John felt his heart beating leadenly in his chest as he dropped his hand. He could have held on. He could have kissed her. He could have told her he loved her and would do anything for them to be together. Instead, he stepped back and walked away without uttering another word.

Melissa, nervous beyond words, stood by her uncle and greeted Charles and his parents, Lord and Lady Hartley. Their greeting was warm and welcoming, and Melissa knew instantly Charles had said nothing about her birth. She wasn't certain whether she was grateful or bothered that he'd kept it from them. It was probably best, she thought. Though Charles had insisted they wouldn't mind about her birth, Melissa knew they would have. And in the end, so had Charles, apparently.

Lord Hartley looked like an older version of Charles. He was still a handsome man, younger than Melissa had imagined, and just beginning to grow thicker about his waist. Melissa could tell that his hair, now shot with gray, had once been the same hue as Charles's. His mother was petite, with lively brown eyes and an enormous amount of dark brown hair piled artlessly atop her head. Melissa liked her instantly. Even though Laura took after her father more, Melissa felt the same warmth from the mother as she had from Laura. Her uncle had been right—they put on no airs at all, but she couldn't help wondering whether their attitudes would change if they knew the truth. It was such a terrible thought to have, but it somehow entered her mind as she smiled back at her future in-laws. She told herself it would be nice to be part of this family, to have a sister and a husband and people she could come to love as a mother and father.

But then John walked into the large foyer dressed immaculately in a black coat, forest green vest, and dark gray trousers, and her heart felt as if it stopped. He gave her a grim smile, before smiling in earnest while greeting Lord and Lady Hartley. Clearly, they were all good friends. How nice that she would be able to visit with John and her uncle, that everything would be so amiable, that she would be able to break her heart over and over again.

Melissa smiled and forced herself to stop her torturous thoughts. Why couldn't she be happy that a good man with a warm and welcoming family had asked her to marry him? She wished she could simply turn off her feelings for John, that the three weeks they'd been apart had proven to her that what she had felt had been nothing more than her first infatuation with a man who'd paid attention to her. She knew it was possible that the entire newness of feeling desire, of being desired, was enough to make her believe she was in love. After all, she had so little experience with such feelings.

Her uncle led the small group to the parlor, and Melissa listened as they chatted about a new grain mill being built on Braddock's property in Flintwood.

"Charles tells us you spent your childhood in Bamburgh," Lady Hartley said. "How exciting London must seem to you."

"Oh, yes," Melissa said. "It's a bit overwhelming at times, but I am getting used to the noise and crowds. Your son has been an excellent guide."

"I must say, this is all very exciting for us all. I truly despaired of seeing Charles marry," Lady Hartley said with a fond look at her son. "I can hardly wait to tell my friends, though I do understand the need for postponing the announcement. I'm afraid the news will cause quite a flurry of activity surrounding you, and Charles tells me you are not quite ready for all the hubbub."

"I don't know if I shall ever be ready," Melissa said, smiling down at the older woman.

"None of us ever is, my dear," Lady Hartley said kindly.

The two families were comfortably ensconced in the home's most formal parlor, Charles sitting next to her on a settee, the two elder men standing by the fire, with Miss Stanhope and Lady Hartley sitting across from the young couple in a pair of matching wingback chairs. John stood slightly apart by a tall window, staring out at the traffic as it rolled down Piccadilly.

"So, John," Lord Hartley called out jovially, craning his neck to look back at John. "With Charles biting the bullet of matrimony, you're next, eh?"

"I do believe I will forgo the institution if at all possible," John said, still looking idly out the window.

"But you must marry," Charles said. "My children will need cousins to play with."

A muscle twitched in John's jaw before he turned and gave Charles an easy grin. "I'm certain Laura will provide plenty of playmates for your children. I do believe she's already named all four of them."

Charles laughed, and Lady Hartley frowned mightily. "I do wish Laura would stop telling everyone she meets that she is nearly engaged. What if it doesn't happen? The poor girl will be humiliated."

"I don't believe she's even given that possibility a passing thought," Charles said. "Where is the girl, anyway?"

Lady Hartley looked a bit uneasy at the question. "She was supposed to have attended a play with Brewster, but he cried off at the last minute, claiming he had to remain home to help his ill mother."

The men in the room gave one another a knowing look that Melissa didn't understand. "Mama's boy," Charles said.

"Charles, really. There is nothing wrong with a young man's attending his mother. If I became ill, I would think it quite nice of you to stay home with me."

"Really, Mother?" Charles asked, raising one brow, and Melissa smiled. Charles, she realized, was much more amusing to be with when they were in a crowd. He was witty and intelligent, and these attributes showed even more when with others. It was only when they were alone that Melissa found him less than desirable. Perhaps, she thought with sudden insight, he was nervous when it was just the two of them. Why anyone would be nervous around her, she didn't know, but perhaps that explained why he was so charming in a crowd.

Lady Hartley gave in with a laugh. "I suppose most men would not stay home with their mothers."

"Especially when he could be out with someone as lovely as Laura. I think I should call him out for changing their plans so abruptly."

"Yes, a duel for a broken appointment," John said as if mulling the possibility. "Pistols at dawn or swords, do you think?"

"Fisticuffs," Lord Hartley said, joining in the banter.

Melissa hid a smile and looked over at John, and was startled to see he was staring at her. He averted his eyes, but not before she saw the heat of his gaze. She flushed, a rather shocking rush of desire sweeping quickly through her, and she moved uncomfortably in her seat. She reminded herself forcefully that lust was not love. She knew John desired her, but he did not love her, and *he* had not asked her to marry him. Certainly, she should not be having carnal thoughts about John when she was sitting next to her intended.

"Surely a broken appointment doesn't call for a duel," Melissa said.

"Of course not. They are simply being foolish men," Lady Hartley said.

The conversation turned to the coming season, with speculation about whether Laura would truly be engaged by the end of it. Melissa had thought, given Laura's complete confidence in the matter, that her marriage to Lord Brewster was a foregone conclusion. But she realized Lady Hartley was not as convinced about either a forthcoming engagement or whether Brewster would be a good match for her daughter. Melissa found this fascinating, the interaction of the group, the dynamics between Charles and his parents.

She felt quite like she was a scientist observing animals in their natural habitat, rather than a participant. Her own family life had been so very strange compared to anything that occurred outside her sheltered life in Bamburgh. For all her life, she'd thought it completely normal to have a father visit her once or twice a week. While she had adored her father, theirs had been a formal relationship compared to the warmth she detected between John and his father and Charles and his parents. As they talked about various topics, the conversation was often interrupted by hearty laughter and amusing side stories, and Melissa was delighted by it all.

It made the prospect of marrying Charles far more attractive. She would be part of his family. She would be their daughter; she would have a sister to gossip with, a mother to shop with. Even if she never came to love Charles, she at least could be content to be part of such a family.

Her gaze went to John, standing so still and stiff by the window. He was probably bored by this ritual, forced to attend this dinner when he likely had other, far more interesting amusements awaiting him in Town. She wished, briefly and fiercely, that he was the one sitting next to her.

Because no matter how hard she tried, she could not picture herself married to Charles, breakfasting with him each morning. Making love. She could not picture their children, those little golden-haired babies with brown eyes and broad smiles. Perhaps it was because she'd had so little contact with children. Or perhaps she simply did not want to picture children who looked like Charles when what she truly wanted was a little boy with chocolate-colored hair and bright gray eyes.

The group was enjoying a witty tale delivered by Charles, when Darling came loping in. She'd grown from a roly-poly puppy to an awkward, gangling girl, her tongue hanging out the side of her mouth as if smiling and happy to see her mistress.

"Oh, my," Lady Hartley said when Darling put her front paws on Melissa's knees.

Melissa, oblivious to Charles's disapproving look, bent over and let Darling slather her cheek with devoted kisses as she laughed.

Charles snapped his fingers and gestured to the dog, and a footman hurried over to take Darling.

"Oh, she can stay. She adores people," Melissa said. "Don't you, Darling?" She scrubbed the dog's ears, and Darling closed her eyes in doggy bliss.

"Don't tell me you allow this animal in the house," Charles said, his comment directed to John.

"I can't tear them apart," John said, smiling warmly at Melissa.

"Animals belong outdoors," Charles said, his tone level and assured. It was as if he were talking about trees or chipmunks, as if there could be no argument.

"Not Darling," Melissa said, a bit of coolness entering her tone. "She'd be so lonely. Wouldn't you?"

"I think you should get used to the idea that she cannot be in the house, Melissa."

Melissa turned to Charles and smiled brightly. "And you should get used to the idea that Darling belongs with me. I don't plan to sleep in the barn or the kennel."

John let out a laugh, and Charles glared at him.

"I wonder who will win this little argument," Lady Hartley said, half amused by their tiff.

"We'll discuss this later, shall we?" Charles asked stiffly, and Melissa felt an unaccountable surge of anger.

"As there is nothing to discuss, I don't see the point," she said sweetly. Darling, who'd been leaning against Melissa's knees, no doubt getting dog fur all over her gown, looked back at her with complete devotion.

"John, talk some sense into your cousin," Charles said, sounding slightly flabbergasted.

John grinned. "As you can clearly see, I've already lost this argument."

"That's because you are not firm enough," Charles muttered, but Melissa heard him clearly.

John heard him, too, but he chose to ignore his friend. He didn't know whether he was bothered because he felt Charles was wrong or because Charles believed he could enforce his rigid rules on Melissa. Or was it that he was sitting too close to the woman John loved? He hoped Melissa could hold her own against Charles. His friend was a stubborn man who felt his opinion was not, in fact, simply an opinion. John and he often had heated arguments about one matter or another, with Charles rarely being swayed from his original stance.

John only knew that if Charles upset Melissa one more time, if he caused that little crease to form in her forehead, if he tried to exert his power over her, John just might make a fool of himself by losing his own temper.

As the new family group chatted and got to know one another, John watched Melissa. He stood behind the others, so no one but Charles could see his perusal, and he was careful to look away when Charles looked up at him. He didn't know why he was here, didn't know why he was torturing himself. Perhaps it was to reassure himself Melissa would be welcomed. He liked the Norrises quite a lot. Growing up, he'd spent numerous hours at their estate and had learned a great deal from Lord Hartley about horses and good breeding practices. His own father was very much a city man, whose interests were almost entirely in legislative and political matters. John had political interests, but he found he was just as happy in the country dealing with estate matters as he was in London.

Yes, Melissa would be with a good family. But that thought gave him no comfort, when all he truly wanted was for her to be with him.

John had lost track of the conversation, but his heart contracted painfully when Melissa laughed at some quip by Lady Hartley. He knew she had very few memories of her own mother, and Lady Hartley would be a warm and welcoming mother-in-law. Still, he could not help wondering what would happen to that warmth if the Hartleys knew she was a bastard. He'd seen the kindest people he knew turn cruel when confronted with those they considered to be below their social status. It wasn't a matter of whether they discovered the truth, but when.

John swore silently. He could see no good end to this. Charles was playing a dangerous game if he thought his parents would not discover her parentage before he and Melissa walked down the aisle. John only hoped he would be able to comfort her when things went wrong, which they assuredly would.

Chapter 16

Lady and Lord Chantilly owned one of the most impressive mansions in St. James Place, set across from Spencer House, home to the Earl of Spencer. While their home was not quite as grand as Spencer House, on this night it was lit up for the ball, its white marble façade brilliant against the dark sky. Melissa felt only a small amount of trepidation as the carriage they were in finally settled in front of the mansion.

She wore her new ball gown, one Miss Stanhope said was beautiful, but she had some small doubts as she looked down at the mountains of material flowing around her. Her uncle sat across from them, looking uncomfortable, as if he couldn't wait to get out of the confines of the carriage and breathe some fresh air. John was meeting them at the ball, and Melissa couldn't help feeling a stab of disappointment that he wasn't with them to bolster her courage. She hardly needed it, but it would have been nice.

"You'll be fine," Miss Stanhope said, patting her knees, and Melissa gave her an uncertain smile.

"I do hope Laura and Lady Juliana are attending. I won't know a soul otherwise."

"I'm certain they are," her chaperone said. "It's one of the best-attended balls of the season, my dear."

That news only worried her more, for what if her true father was amongst the guests? Her uncle had assured her the duke rarely attended such events, especially since he had no eligible daughters to marry off. It would be at least another year before her look-alike half sister attended such functions.

"But what if he is there?" she'd asked worriedly.

"Then we shall leave immediately," he'd said. "But please don't worry yourself, my girl."

The carriage stopped, and Melissa felt a small dip as a footman hopped from the conveyance, and soon after heard the noise of the steps being dropped, seconds before the door was swung open. The first thing Melissa saw was John, looking pensive and utterly handsome in his top hat and tails. His eyes pinned her momentarily, and then he grinned and any fears that plagued her were instantly dispersed. "John's here," she said.

"So he is. Ladies, if you will?" her uncle said, indicating the door.

Miss Stanhope stepped out first. She was lovely this evening, her blond hair piled atop her head. She wore a dark, plum-colored gown that did wonderful things to her pale complexion. Melissa stepped down next, smiling at John, who held out a pristine, white-gloved hand. She grasped it, loving the strength she felt, the added confidence it gave her. He squeezed her hand and leaned toward her ear, and for one wonderful moment Melissa thought he was about to kiss her. Instead, he whispered, "You are stunningly beautiful this evening, cousin."

Melissa gave him an impish smile at the word "cousin." "You are rather dashing yourself, Lord Willington."

"Such formality. No need to worry, my darling cousin, word is a certain duke was invited and is not expected to attend."

"Thank goodness," she said feelingly.

John offered his arm, and she readily took it, feeling joy bubbling inside her. She was attending her first London ball, surrounded by society's elite, on the arm of the man she loved. For that moment, she could almost believe nothing bad could ever happen, that all her fears and worries were groundless. Walking up the shallow marble stairs, she was simply one of dozens of young, unmarried women, all hopeful the night would end well, that they would be asked to dance every dance.

They entered a grand hall, and Miss Stanhope led her to a table where they collected their dance cards, gilded little booklets with a golden tassel attached.

"Yours will be filled in no time, my dear," Miss Stanhope said. "I would reserve at least two dances for Mr. Norris and one for both your cousin and uncle, of course."

"A waltz, if you please, Melissa," John said from behind her. The words were low and meant for her ears only and caused a telling bit of color in her cheeks. Why did her entire body react in such an embarrassing manner each time he said something to her?

"The fourth dance, then," she said, taking the small pencil and putting his initials down. She turned to find he was standing only inches from her, so close she could see small specks of gold in his gray eyes.

"And eighth. Two waltzes, if you please," he said, grinning at her like a naughty boy.

"But that would mean I'd only have one waltz with Charles. Miss Stanhope, wouldn't that cause gossip?"

"Not at all," she said briskly, but turned her head when John raised a questioning brow.

"I thought you were a stickler, Miss Stanhope," he said thoughtfully. "I see I was mistaken."

Twin spots of red showed on the older woman's cheeks, but Melissa couldn't begin to know why they'd appeared.

Melissa was jostled a bit, but felt none of the panic that had bloomed when she was at the opera. "It's a bit of a crush, is it not?" she asked, feeling rather sophisticated.

"Lady and Lord Chantilly always invite far more people than can squeeze into their home, large as it is," Miss Stanhope said. "Goodness, it's warm." She opened the fan that hung from her wrist and moved it rapidly in front of her face.

Melissa, who still wasn't used to wearing such a tight corset, heartily agreed. She could hardly hear the orchestra above the general rumbling of the crowd.

"How are you faring, Mel?" John asked softly.

She smiled slightly, liking that he called her Mel. It seemed such an intimate name, one that only he would use. "Quite well," she said. "But don't leave me, if you please, because it just might be your presence holding my panic at bay."

"If you insist," he said, pretending to be put out, even as he stepped closer to her. He laid a hand on the small of her back, moving his thumb back and forth in such an intimate gesture, Melissa shivered, closing her eyes briefly.

"Ah, there you are, Miss Atwell," Charles said, coming up to them. John dropped his hand and stepped slightly away. "I'm here to claim my dances," he said loudly, then leaned in and added softly, "and my beloved's attention."

Melissa forced a smile, feeling horrible that she couldn't be happier to see Charles, that she was achingly aware of the empty place where John's hand had been.

"You look quite pretty," said Charles, giving her an admiring look. "Like a princess."

Despite herself, Melissa blushed and warmed beneath such praise, even as another stab of guilt assailed her. Charles was a nice fellow and deserved to have a woman who loved him. Perhaps once they were married and away from John, she could fall in love with him. Charles was in his formal wear, a red satin vest beneath his black tails, and looked quite dashing. He was a handsome man—except for that nose, of course.

He looked around the crowded room. "It appears you are causing quite a stir, standing here talking to two of the most eligible bachelors in London," he said, laughing. Indeed, both women and men were looking at Melissa curiously. London society was a close-knit bunch, so the appearance of a newcomer would be cause for keen interest.

"If only Lord Avonleigh were here, tongues would be wagging in a frenzy," she said.

"Melissa! My God, must you always be so beautiful?" Laura gushed, leaning in for a quick kiss.

"I do so try to be plain, but Miss Stanhope insists on dressing me like this," she said, looking down at her gown as if it were the most wretched thing.

"She could wear a potato sack and still look lovely," Charles said. Next to her John let out a strangled cough.

"You don't think so, John?" Laura asked, mimicking his oft-raised brow. His eyes sparkled with amusement at the gesture, and he gave her a small bow.

"I daresay Melissa would look lovely in nothing at all," he said, and smiled when there was a collective gasp.

"Hey, I say, John. That was rather improper," Charles said. His tone was light, but Melissa could tell he was angry.

John looked devilishly shocked. "I certainly meant no insult," he said. "I meant only that she needs no adornment."

Charles gave his friend a hard look before turning to Melissa. "I would like to request the honor of the first dance," he said formally.

"Of course, sir," Melissa said, giving him a small curtsy. "If you will excuse us. Lord Willington. Miss Stanhope."

Diane watched the couple move off, indecision tugging at her. "That remark was improper," she said in her best chaperone voice.

"I'm aware of that."

Her eyes were still on the couple. "And I'm aware that when a young man is in love, he's likely to say foolishly improper things." She slowly turned her head to look at John. He met her gaze levelly, then shook his head slightly. "You deny it?" she asked kindly.

"I do not."

The happiness that had been in his eyes slowly leeched away as the orchestra began to play the Grand Promenade. Following this formal dance, the ball would begin in earnest, and Charles would stake his claim by dancing with Melissa for all to see.

"I don't think she loves him," Diane said conversationally. "I do believe she's in love with someone else entirely."

John grew impossibly still. "How could you know such a thing?" he asked tensely.

"Because I know how a woman acts when she's desperately in love with a man and is trying her best to hide that fact—especially from him." Her eyes were on the dancers, who were going through the formal steps of the promenade, but she felt John's steady gaze on her.

She heard him let out a breath. "It doesn't matter," he said. "We're first cousins."

Diane pressed her lips together, anger surging through her at this farce. She would bet her best figurines that by the season's end not a person in the ton would believe John and Melissa were first cousins. Too many people knew Waltham, and too many people had seen his daughter. Word would spread, as would speculation.

The two of them stood together as the first set began, and Diane noted John was not watching Melissa dance with Mr. Norris, but rather looking at the floor, his face set. The ballroom was filled with beautiful young women, many of whom cast John longing looks. Three dances were done, and still he stood, staring blindly ahead, his misery almost palpable.

"The fourth dance, my lord," Diane said softly.

"Miss Stanhope," came a deep voice behind her.

She turned and smiled up at Lord Braddock. "I hate to interrupt your discussion, John, but I must borrow Miss Stanhope for a few minutes."

"Of course." John disappeared into the crowd, and Diane's heart broke a bit for him. He was so clearly miserable, and his father was so clearly oblivious to his son's pain.

"Your son seems a bit out of sorts," she said.

"Really? I hadn't noticed anything. Look, he's gone to claim his dance with Melissa. And I am here to claim my dance with you."

"You must have a favor to ask of me," she said pleasantly.

"The favor is that you spend some time with me. Every widow has been batting her eyes at me since we walked in the door."

Despite herself, Diane laughed. "You are such a romantic man. There I was giving you the perfect opening so that you could claim your undying love, and you admit you are simply using me to avoid matrimony-minded widows."

He grinned, and in doing so, looked ten years younger. Diane wished he wasn't such a handsome man. She wished she could forget that kiss, that drunken kiss that he so obviously regretted. In the weeks that had followed it, he'd given no indication that he desired her, that he intended to kiss her again. That she was anything more than a female chum to spend time with. For all she knew, he simply liked winning at whist.

"They are a determined lot. It's one reason I have shied away from such events for so many years."

They moved around the dance floor easily, as if they'd been dancing together for years. He was a fine dancer, and his hand, large and warm on her back, was a delicious torment. She hadn't felt such an attraction in ages, and it was getting more and more difficult to school her features each time he walked into a room, or smiled at her, or asked her to dance. The pair passed by Melissa and John, who at that moment were both laughing delightedly at something. They looked so completely happy, Diane felt her heart tug again.

"They certainly do enjoy one another's company," Diane said cautiously.

"John gets along with everyone. It's his gift."

Diane nearly rolled her eyes at how obtuse one man could possibly be. If he couldn't clearly see the love in their eyes, he would never recognize it in her own.

The waltz ended, and Lord Braddock gave her a bow. "Would you care to join me in the garden, Miss Stanhope?" he asked.

Diane narrowed her eyes. "Are you attempting to lead me astray?" she asked, half joking.

"Of course."

"Then of course I'll join you," she said, her blood singing when he let out another hearty laugh. Diane had never in her life been very quick with a quip or engaged in sophisticated repartee. But tonight she felt empowered and just a bit wicked. She would go out to the garden with Lord Braddock, and if he wanted to kiss her, she would allow it.

With her gloved hand on his strong arm, she went with him through the large French doors and to the terrace and garden beyond. The garden was lit with paper lanterns, flickering brightly in the gentle breeze. "Why, it's lovely," she said.

"At the risk of sounding like a bounder, Miss Stanhope, I would like to say that the candles dim when compared to your own loveliness."

Diane frowned, which only made Lord Braddock smile. "You do hate compliments, don't you?"

"I do not trust them," she said honestly.

They were walking down a dimly lit path, with no others within sight. "I find you quite lovely," he said, stopping and looking down at her, his expression suddenly fierce. She couldn't help it; she smiled.

"Yes, Diane," he said, "please smile. It makes you rather difficult to resist."

She had her lips pressed together, fighting that smile he was working so hard to see. But at this last, she let it fully bloom. He took a sharp breath.

"My God, Diane," he said, right before pulling her against him and pressing his mouth urgently against hers.

She went willingly, letting out a small moan of need, as his hands pulled her close, as his tongue entered her mouth in such a blatantly carnal action, her knees nearly buckled. He dragged his mouth from hers, nudging her head back so he could kiss her jaw, her neck, as he pulled her bottom and settled her hard against his arousal.

"I cannot stop thinking of you, Diane. I feel as if I've gone a bit mad," he said hoarsely against her throat. "Why? Why do you do this to me?"

It seemed a rhetorical question, so Diane remained silent, reveling in his words, his touch. He stopped suddenly and placed a hand on either side of her head, peering down at her with such blatant lust, Diane wondered why she hadn't been set afire by it. What he said next, though, jarred her from her lust-filled reverie.

"Are you a virgin?" he asked, urgent and low.

"Yes." Her voice, even to her own ears, sounded shaky. He pressed his forehead against hers and uttered a mild curse.

"You are sure?" he asked, laughing a bit.

"Quite."

"I don't suppose you'd be up for a romp, then?" His eyes were sparkling with good humor, as if this were a conversation he had every day with women.

"A romp?" She knew what he meant. Sex without consequence. Sex without commitment. Sex just for the pure enjoyment of it. Her body was tingling with desire; she ached for his touch; she was on the verge of taking his hand and placing it on her breast just for the relief it would give her. She was on the verge, she realized with humiliation, of proclaiming her love. And he wanted a romp.

"No. I suppose not," he said, reading her expression accurately.

"It's not as if you're asking me to partner you in whist, you know," she said a bit crossly.

"We do suit."

That hurt. Yes, they suited. Quite well, as a matter of fact. But, obviously, they suited just enough for a game of whist or a tumble. Not for anything more permanent. What sort of woman did he think she was? She was thirty-two years old, a spinster and a virgin, and he wanted a romp. A *romp*?

She was outraged and angry and far, far more tempted than she should be. But, no. She would not, even as her aching body urged her to reconsider.

"Thank you for your kind invitation, Lord Braddock, but I do believe I will decline." With that, her knees still a bit wobbly, she walked away from him. He let her go perhaps twenty feet before following her, and by the time they reached the terrace, he was silently offering his arm.

"I haven't . . . I don't . . ." He let out a sigh. "I'm a cad," he said, finally. "I don't know what's come over me. I've never acted in such an ungentlemanly way in my life. If you want to slap me, you may."

Oh, drat. He was making her love him even more. "Perhaps another time," she said calmly. "I'm certain you'll do something in the future to warrant it."

He threw back his head and laughed, and she swore when he looked down at her, she saw something in his eyes that looked very much like love.

"Walk with me in the garden," Charles said after fetching Melissa a cup of watery punch.

"I have to find Miss Stanhope," she said. "Do you know where she is?"

"We're practically engaged, Melissa. Surely you don't need to have your chaperone trailing your every movement."

She smiled. "Surely I do, sir. Miss Stanhope—and John—gave me very explicit instructions on what is expected of me during a ball."

He let out a sigh. "All right then. Go and find Miss Stanhope. I'll be over by the doors."

Melissa took a thorough look around the ballroom, and quickly determined her chaperone was not among those dancing, nor those sitting along the sidelines. She walked around a bit on the ground floor, finally seeing Laura and relaxing at the sight of a familiar face.

"Have you seen Miss Stanhope?" she asked.

"Sorry. You could try the Pink Parlor. I saw quite a few ladies in there as I was passing. It's right down this hall."

Melissa thanked her and turned down the long hall, peeking into each room to determine if it was the Pink Parlor; she imagined the color would give it away. A man was coming in the opposite direction, and she felt the frisson of familiar tension that came upon her whenever she encountered a stranger. She never knew where to look, or whether to greet the person. As she was passing, she looked up to see a middle-aged man, tall and striking, with ruthless good looks and jet-black hair.

"Caroline, what the devil are you . . ." His harsh voice trailed off, startling Melissa, for he was clearly addressing her. The man stopped suddenly, blocking her way. The only way 'round him would have been to squeeze by rudely.

"I beg pardon, my lord?" Melissa said, trying to quell the frantic beating of her heart. She had no reason to fear this man, but for some reason she had the urge to flee his penetrating gaze.

"What is your name, child?" he asked, still staring intently at her.

"Melissa Atwell."

"Atwell." His eyes sharpened, and it was at that moment Melissa noted their color—a beautiful and quite unusual lavender. They were precisely the same color as her own eyes.

"*Atwell*. My God," he said, stumbling back, taking in her features with an intensity that was frightening. "It's impossible. But your face. You're my . . . My God."

Realization of who the man was struck Melissa at

the same moment that he was apparently making the connection, and she mirrored his movements, stepping back, eyes intent, mouth open in pure shock. Her father—her real father—was standing in front of her. She stood there dumbly, staring, not knowing what to do or say but feeling a terrible sense of the inevitable. This was her father, this tall, imposing man with the cruel mouth and beautiful eyes.

"Christina's daughter," he said raggedly. "I am correct, am I not?"

Melissa could only nod, even though she knew she should deny a connection.

"She never told me. I never knew," he said, his voice filled with confusion and anger, as if her mother had somehow betrayed him. "Christina's daughter. All that time, I never knew you were mine. How could it be that I never knew?"

Melissa swallowed and looked behind her. People were milling about, passing by the hall, but they took no notice of the two of them standing there.

His eyes swept her form, and Melissa took another tentative step back. He was not looking at her as a father should look at a daughter, even one he'd apparently not known about.

"Oh, but you need not fear me. I am . . ." It seemed he couldn't bring himself to say it, so Melissa did.

"You are my father."

The duke held out his hand, and Melissa stared at it, holding her hands tightly together, a familiar panic hitting her at the thought of touching another person, even with her gloved hands. He smiled reassuringly, then took her arm, leading her into a small study. Melissa didn't resist—he was a duke and her father, after all. But her instinct told her she should have resisted. She had a sudden urge to break away from him and run, even as her mind told her she was being foolish. "A hallway is no place for this meeting," he said as he quietly closed the door. The room was lit only by a single wall sconce, creating eerie shadows about the duke's face. "It's quite remarkable," he said, studying her again. "It is your eyes, of course, that mark you as mine. Did you know you look very much like my own daughter?"

She nodded, finding his words—*my own daughter*—strange. She was his daughter, too.

"I wonder why no one has noted it?" he said, studying her face. "Why did I not know? Why didn't she tell me? I would have made accommodations. I would have welcomed you."

Melissa shook her head, for she had no answers to his questions. "I only recently learned you are my father. My mother never mentioned you, and I lived in Bamburgh until my father's death just last year."

"Father," he spat, and Melissa's eyes grew hard.

"He was the only father I knew," she said, lifting her chin.

He forced a smile, one she suspected was calculated to appease her. "Of course," he said. "It is only a shock to me to find that the one woman I have ever loved bore me a child and then chose to hide the truth from me. Surely you can see that I would find this upsetting."

Melissa focused on his phrase, "hide the truth." Yes, her mother and father had gone to great lengths to hide the truth from her and the rest of the world. Why?

"I cannot get over your resemblance to Caroline. In fact when I first saw you, I thought you were she.

Quite remarkable," he said, studying her face as a man might a fine work of art. "I wonder why no one has mentioned to me that my daughter has a twin."

"This is my first ball. I've been living in Bamburgh quite isolated until this year."

He smiled, but that smile did not reassure her. Instead, it made her even more wary. But that made no sense. It was just that he was looking at her so strangely, as if he were looking at a juicy bit of prime rib instead of his bastard daughter. She suppressed a shudder. "I should be getting back. My fiancé is waiting for me."

"Fiancé?"

"Charles Norris. Perhaps you know him? His father is Lord Hartley."

He shook his head, never taking his eyes from her. "You sound like her, like your mother," he said softly, taking a step closer. She backed up until she was pressed against the door, her hands behind her clutching the latch. She didn't know why she was so frightened, for he was calm, his voice soothing. But something in the way he looked at her, spoke to her, was making her flesh crawl.

He put his hands on her shoulders, effectively trapping her, and he closed his eyes. "Say something," he said. When she remained silent, he squeezed her shoulders painfully. "*Say* something."

"You're hurting me," she whispered.

"Yes, you sound like her," he said, his voice strained. He leaned forward so that his mouth was nearly against her ear, his eyes still closed, and she turned her face away. "My God, you smell like her. Christina." She squeezed her eyes shut and began shaking as he nuzzled his head against her hair, breathing in and out harshly, his hands gripping her shoulders with brutal strength. It was almost as if he were trying to inhale her, and the thought sickened her.

"You're just like her. Like Christina," he said softly.

"She hated you," Melissa said, instinctively knowing this was true. Her mother had feared this man, had feared discovery.

He chuckled softly, and for some reason that frightened her even more. "That's not true. We were in love. I know it," he said, taking another deep breath.

Melissa stood, stiff and shaking, her hands clutching the latch. But it did no good, for the door opened inward, and he had her pressed against the door. Then she felt him, his stiff *thing*, against her thigh. And then, thank God, she heard voices just outside the door.

"Release me," she said loudly. And he did, looking dazed, as if he'd forgotten whom he'd been assaulting. Melissa didn't hesitate; she spun around clutching the latch. He grabbed her wrist, squeezing her painfully, but she wrenched it away and ran out the door. Once in the hall, she knew she was safe, for there were people there—a girl and her mother making a quick repair to a bow. Walking toward them, she tried to calm herself as she made her way to the ballroom. She had but one thought: find John.

John stood and watched the dancers until he was certain Melissa was not among them. He spied Charles, looking impatient and miffed, by the doors leading to the terrace, but Melissa was not by him. John had begun skirting around the edge of the crowded room when he saw her and knew immediately something was horribly wrong. Her face was tense, her eyes darting about the room, and he saw her visibly relax when she saw him. It took him only a few moments to reach her, but it seemed as if everyone he passed was trying purposely to thwart his progress. Finally he was at her side.

"What has happened?"

"The duke is here," she said, her voice quavering.

John looked about the room and saw his father entering the ballroom from the terrace. He motioned to him, and in a matter of moments, his father and Miss Stanhope were there beside him. Charles, seeing them together, started making his way toward them, but John ignored him and led Melissa away from the crowd and to the relative privacy of Lord Chantilly's library.

"Waltham is here," John said when the four of them were in the library. "He saw you?"

Melissa could only manage to nod as she nearly collapsed onto a settee. John sat next to her and grasped her hand. Something more than a simple meeting had taken place, he was certain of it.

"What happened, Mel? What did he say to you?"

She swallowed, her eyes filling with tears as she shook her head. "He is dreadful. The most dreadful man."

John looked up at his father, feeling helpless to ease her pain.

"He . . . he . . . touched me," she whispered, and John's heart stilled as a slow-burning rage grew.

She shook her head again, over and over, and tears streamed down her face as she looked beseechingly at him, as if he could somehow take away whatever had happened. "It was nothing. Nothing. But . . ."

"What did he do, Melissa? Be calm and tell us." His father's voice, strong and firm, did calm her, and John felt her trembling subside.

"I was looking for Miss Stanhope. Charles wanted a walk in the garden, and I thought I might find you in the Pink Parlor. That's when I saw him. He knew almost immediately who I was, and he led me to a small study. He told me I sounded like Christina, my mother. He wouldn't let me leave and he . . ." She stopped and looked as if she might vomit, staring unfocused at the carpet. "He kept smelling me, saying I smelled like her, like my mother." She looked up at them, each in turn. "I think he's mad."

John drew her into his arms and held her, not caring that what was in his heart would be clearly visible to anyone watching. "It's all right, Mel. You're safe now." She clung to him, burying her head against his shoulder. John looked up to his father, his gut burning with the need to do violence. "I want him to pay," he ground out.

His father's face was a mask of well-contained fury. He gave John a hard nod, and John had no doubt his father would somehow make the duke pay for what he'd done.

All four were startled when the library door opened, revealing Charles. He looked from John, still holding Melissa in his arms, to John's father. "What has happened?" he demanded.

"Waltham is here, and Melissa had a disagreeable encounter with him," John said, not wanting to reveal any details of what had transpired.

"Waltham is here? Did anyone else see you? It would be a disaster if my parents learned of this before we are wed."

"Charles," John bit out. "He assaulted her."

Charles looked stunned. "What?"

"I'm fine," Melissa said, pulling away from John, who reluctantly let her go. "He frightened me, that is all."

"He touched you," John said, nearly losing his tight grip on his temper.

"Touched? What do you mean? You cannot mean that he . . ."

John's expression was stony, and he silently willed Charles to shut his mouth.

Charles's expression grew taut. "He's a monster," he said. "I'll kill him."

"You'll do nothing of the sort," John's father said harshly. "The possibility of scandal is contained at the moment, and Melissa is rattled, but fine. He will pay, let me assure you, Mr. Norris, but please let me handle this in my own way. Waltham is a powerful man and ruthless beyond anything a gentleman can imagine. I do not want Melissa harmed."

"Of course," Charles said. He walked over to Melissa and took up her hand. "I am sorry this has happened, Melissa."

She gave him a shaky smile. "It frightened me more than anything. I am perfectly fine." John stared at their clasped hands, fighting the terrible urge to rip them apart. He had no right to, though. None. Charles would be her husband, and he had every right to offer her comfort.

"I'm going to call for the carriage," John's father said. "You should all stay here, and if anyone should come by, simply tell them you are feeling unwell."

"Sir," Charles said.

George turned toward Charles, lifting his head in inquiry.

"What if Waltham should tell people about this encounter? What if he claims her as his daughter?"

George's look was nearly incredulous. "Even Waltham would not be that foolish."

"But what if he does?" Charles persisted. "Everyone will know and . . ." His voice trailed off, because John could see there was murder in his father's eyes.

"We shall deal with such a happenstance should it occur," his father said finally and with such coldness that Charles blushed.

"I will not hold you to any promises made," Melissa said, her voice strong, her eyes steady.

Charles looked truly regretful he'd even hinted at such a thing. "There will be no need. No need," he said. "My devotion will remain constant no matter what happens."

For the first time, John wished Charles were not such a good man, for many men would have walked away from Melissa under these circumstances. And he wanted nothing more than for Charles to walk away.

The drive home from the ball was markedly different from the trip there. For one, John sat next to his father, his eyes never straying from Melissa, as he tried to gauge how she was faring. He could not let her out of his sight, and this feeling that he had failed to protect her made him nearly ill. Though he trusted his father to do something to Waltham, John feared he would not be satisfied with whatever course his father took.

"I think, perhaps, I should forgo any more public

events," Melissa said on a sigh. "Each time I appear in society, something terrible happens."

"That is only because you keep wandering off and putting yourself in danger," John said.

Melissa shot him a dark look. "The opera was my fault. But this was not. You all told me my father wouldn't be there, and how was I to know he would accost me?"

"Why did Charles allow you to wander about by yourself? And where the hell were you, Miss Stanhope, when all this was happening?" John demanded, his anger and frustration making him surly.

"John, that is markedly unfair of you," his father said.

"Is it? We all failed Melissa, me most of all. I was keeping my distance so that she could be with Charles, but I should have known he wouldn't be able to protect her."

"No one is to blame but Waltham," George said.

John beat a fist upon his knee, wishing he didn't feel so utterly helpless. The thought of Melissa's being at the mercy of such a man was like acid burning in his gut. What sort of man would accost his own daughter? It was beyond depraved. If John had been with Melissa, if he had been the one asking her for a walk in the garden, he would never have let her go off on her own. He stared at Melissa, at her profile as she looked out the carriage window. As they passed the gaslights, her face was illuminated by the soft light, and she looked so ethereally lovely his heart was wrenched. To think that madman had touched her, had made her cry. How could he let her marry Charles? How could he live each day of his life without her?

The answer was simple. So simple, a surge of pure joy filled him. He *couldn't* live without her. He couldn't let it happen. He could not and would not allow Charles to marry the one woman on earth that he would ever love. What kind of fool was he to almost let her slip away from him? He was no fool, and he was done making decisions to please others. He loved Melissa, and he was quite certain she loved him. What the *hell* had he been *thinking*?

She turned to him then, just as he was coming to this conclusion, and he knew that what he was thinking was written clearly on his face. She stared at him curiously, her expression slowly softening until he saw what he was feeling reflected clearly in her eyes. And then she smiled, as if silently saying, "It's about time, you great buffoon."

He let out a laugh, and she joined him.

"Something is amusing now?" his father asked testily.

"No, Father, not amusing," he said, his eyes never leaving hers. "Something rather better than that."

Chapter 17

It was all John could do to sit there and not drag her into his arms. He would ask for his father's blessing, but if he didn't get it, he would take her to Gretna Green or Canada or America. He felt as if a dark, murky cloud that had been surrounding his soul for weeks had dissipated. He loved Melissa. *Loved* her. And he'd be damned if anything or anyone kept him from her.

As they entered the house, his father and Miss Stanhope headed directly to his father's study.

"Father, Melissa looks impossibly weary and I am as well. I'll bid you good night and walk Melissa to her room," he said, keeping his voice as level as possible, considering he was walking on clouds.

"Oh, yes. Good night then," his father said distractedly.

Miss Stanhope gave John a searching look before turning and following his father down the hall that led to the study. When John and Melissa reached the top of the first landing, he stayed her with a gentle hand on her arm.

"I need to tell you something," he said, looking down at her, completely and utterly in love with her, and praying she felt the same. He couldn't be mistaken, could he? He took a deep breath, letting it out in a shaky release of pent-up tension. "I love you," he blurted. "And it will be a cold day in Hades before I let Charles marry you. That is, of course, if you love me. Otherwise, you may marry Charles, for I only want you to be happy. Though of course I wish you wouldn't." He closed his eyes briefly as he realized what a muck of it he was making.

Melissa stood very still, looking up at him with those solemn, beautiful eyes, and she gave him the smallest of smiles. "What of your father?"

"I don't care. I can make him understand. Or perhaps not. Likely not. But I cannot live without you by my side. I cannot allow you to marry another, not when the very thought makes me die inside."

She looked down at her hands. "You don't believe in love, John. How can you be certain this is not some misguided bit of chivalry because of what happened this evening?"

"Misguided . . ." he said, stunned. "If you believe that . . ."

"I don't, but you've spent a great deal of time and effort trying to get me to understand your feelings about love and marriage." Melissa looked up at him, searching his countenance for the truth.

"I have been fighting this . . . this . . . *thing* I feel for you for weeks," he said roughly. "I didn't believe in love, Melissa, because I'd never felt it before. I've never felt anything like this madness that tells me I would do anything to make you happy. Anything. Even allow you to marry Charles if you love him, even though I swear my heart will be torn from my breast if you do."

"That's rather gruesome," she said, smiling up at him. Why wasn't she relieving his torment? Did she not love him? Was she trying to figure out a way to spare his feelings? Shouldn't she be throwing herself into his arms and declaring her undying love? By God, if she didn't love him, she ought to tell him now before he shattered. He was starting to breathe a bit harshly, and his hands were clenched by his sides to stop himself from dragging her into his arms and kissing her until she relented.

She stepped closer to him, and he stiffened, even as she kissed his cheek; he was bracing for the blow that would break his heart. "I do love you, John," she said softly. He took her shoulders gently and pulled her away so that he could look at her face. "I've loved you since the day your horse took that carrot from my palm. I just didn't trust my feelings because you were the first young man I'd ever known."

A broad smile slowly formed on his face, and he finally allowed himself to pull her against him and kiss her silly. It was a rather unsatisfying kiss because they were both smiling like fools. They ended up laughing together, there on that landing for anyone to see should they happen by. But at that moment, neither cared.

"A very happy ending to a very terrible day," Melissa said, burrowing her head into the crook of his neck. And he thought he could stand there forever like that, with her warm body pressed against his, with her head resting on his shoulder in complete trust. He put his hand up to stroke her hair as he had wanted to do so many times.

"Tomorrow you will break it off with Charles, and I will tell my father that we are to be married."

"Can't we simply hie off to Gretna Green?" she asked hopefully.

"No," he said grimly. "We are going to hurt two people who trusted us. I am going to lose my best friend and my father's esteem, but I don't care."

"I do know that Charles will be angry, but your father, surely he will understand."

John smiled down at her, but that smile was for her sake only. He knew what was coming. He knew Charles would likely hate him for the rest of their lives. And he knew his father, a man he had never wanted to hurt, would feel betrayed. John wasn't certain he could make him understand, but he knew he had to try. "I'm certain I can turn him around. And if not, we'll be taking that carriage ride to Gretna."

He took her hand and led her to her door. "I want more than anything to go into your room with you—you do know that?" He burned for her in a way he'd never burned for another, but he would not cuckold his best friend. Tomorrow night, however, after Charles had been informed that the engagement was off, well now, that was a different story entirely.

George Atwell, Earl of Braddock, did not like it when things went awry, and things had definitely gone awry. His brother's request had seemed so simple when he'd written that letter pleading with his older brother to help his only daughter find a good marriage. It had been so easy to write back and tell Rupert that, of course, he would do what he could to ensure Rupert's daughter was happily and safely married and that no one would hear a whisper of her illegitimate birth. Very few members of the ton even remembered George had a brother, so the idea of presenting his niece to society, of seeing her safely married, seemed such a simple one. He never could have anticipated that his niece was the Duke of Waltham's daughter, that she would resemble his legitimate daughter so strikingly, or that the damned duke would discover her practically on the eve of her wedding to a fine young man who truly seemed to love her. It was messy and unpredictable, and he hated messy and unpredictable things. It was one reason he'd so diligently avoided marriage all these years. That thought, unaccountably, bothered him even more and gave him an unwanted reminder of last evening with Miss Stanhope.

It was only after their kiss in the garden, after his ridiculous burst of elation, that he'd begun feeling the noose get a bit too tight. So last night before they retired for the evening, he'd thought it would be a good idea to put things right between them. To be clear about where he stood. And so he'd told her as she sat stiff-backed in his study and he'd stared into the fire. Yes, he'd been a tad abrupt with Miss Stanhope. *Diane.* No doubt he wouldn't be seeing her smile up at him so guilelessly again. He refused to feel bad. He refused to remember how she'd looked at him when he'd told her flat out that, while he was attracted to her physically and would enjoy making love to her, he had no plans of making their relationship permanent. She'd nodded in that no-nonsense way of hers and bid him good night. He'd thought, at first, that she'd taken his announcement rather well, until he saw her eyes change just as she turned away. She'd been stricken, perhaps even on the verge of tears, and that had bothered him. It had bothered him far more than he would like to admit, if he were honest. He'd been tempted, God help him, to call her back, to tell her he'd broken things off with his mistress weeks ago. In fact, the day after their first kiss. And that made the noose pull even more tightly.

Frankly, the woman made him nervous. She made him yearn for things he thought were long forced out of his hardened heart—things like quiet walks and making love and waking up next to the same smiling face day after day. She would be a lovely old lady, one of those women who aged well, who retained an elegance and grace so many others didn't. And she wasn't so old that she couldn't bear him a child or two. Perhaps a girl with blond hair and blue eyes. He shook his head firmly, pushing away such thoughts. He could do without all that nonsense, thank you very much.

And so, when John knocked on his study door at half past eleven in the morning, he was grateful for the distraction. He enjoyed his son's company, for John was one of the few truly intelligent, logical men he knew who shared his core beliefs. John was his rock.

"Good morning," he called out, pulling out a blueprint for the grain mill he was building in September. "Take a look at this." He pushed the drawings toward his son, who gave them a cursory look.

"A fine mill," he said. "Father, I have something I need to talk to you about."

"You haven't been out carousing lately, have you?" George asked good-naturedly.

"It's about Melissa."

George's heart sank. He truly didn't want to talk about Melissa or the problems that now plagued him regarding his niece. He fully planned to write to Charles that day and move the wedding date up. He'd received the marriage contract from his solicitor just that morning, and given the events of the previous evening, he felt the matter of their wedding was becoming rather urgent.

"Really, John, everything's been settled." He'd thought that would put an end to the conversation.

"No, Father, it hasn't. You see . . ."

George looked curiously at his son. He actually looked quite ill, and George wondered if John had stayed up late and imbibed too much port. John nervously wetted his lips, then looked him straight in the eye. "I'm in love with Melissa and want to marry her."

George shot him a half smile. "We've discussed this, John. There's no need . . ."

"You're not listening, Father. I love her. I've loved her for a long time. Quite desperately. I want your blessing. We both do."

George looked at his son as if someone else had somehow gotten into John's skin. The noises coming from his mouth sounded like John, but the words made absolutely no sense. "That's impossible. You know that."

"No. It's not. I cannot allow her to marry Charles, not loving her the way I do. I cannot live anything resembling a normal life without her."

George barked out a laugh. "My God, John, do you hear yourself? You're lusting after a girl—quite inappropriately, by the way—and now you have convinced yourself you love her. You and I both know love is a fleeting, worthless emotion that doesn't exist beyond the first time you bed a woman."

"No, Father, you are wrong. I have lusted after many women, but I've only loved one. I only agreed with you all these years because I had never been in love."

George threw up his hands. "Oh, for God's sake, John." He stared at him in disbelief. He didn't mean to be cruel, but really. "If it were any other girl, I'd say bed her and be done with it. But I'm afraid that's impossible."

"I have compromised her."

His son's face was like stone, and George knew he was not lying. A building anger burned in his stomach. His son, whom he trusted with his very life, had done the one thing George could not have imagined. "Are you telling me you took your cousin's virginity?"

"She is not my cousin," John said forcefully, and tearing his gaze from George's expression of disbelief, he added more softly, "She is yet a maid."

"Thank God for that." George felt nearly limp with relief. This was not irrevocable.

"Father, you do not understand. I want your blessing, but I do not require it."

George's entire body stiffened, and he looked at his son as if he'd never seen him before. Who was this ardent young man proclaiming his undying love? What sort of insanity had overtaken him? This fervent, ridiculously naïve man in front of him was not his son. "You cannot mean that," he said softly.

"I do." And this time, John looked directly into his eyes. "I do understand the consequences of such a marriage. I know that either Melissa will be considered a bastard or you will lose your standing in your commission. I do not come to this decision lightly, Father.

But I have no choice. I cannot allow the woman I love, the woman who loves me, to marry another simply because you or society tells me I should."

"I don't know who you are," George said, stunned beyond bearing that his son could betray him in this manner. "You promised to *protect* her. I *trusted* you."

John looked truly pained by his words. "I know. And I have betrayed that trust. Every time I looked at her, every time I touched her, thought of her, I betrayed that trust. It is killing me, Father, but I cannot choose you over her, and I pray you do not ask that of me."

George stared blindly at his desk. "Leave me now."

"Father, please, your esteem means much to me."

"I said leave!"

John did not start at the shout, but nodded calmly and turned away from him, pausing at the door just before he left the study. "I would never willingly do anything to hurt you, Father," John said, his voice low and filled with raw emotion. "I love you, and this has been one of the most difficult decisions of my life. Please, Father. Please forgive me and give us your blessing."

He left, shutting the door quietly behind him, leaving George to stare in hopeless disbelief at the spot where his son had stood.

Chapter 18

The flowers arrived just before noon. Baskets filled with a bright yellow flower, already beginning to wilt. The butler looked at them in dismay, but directed several footmen to bring them into the main parlor where Melissa sat restlessly and worked her needlepoint. Miss Stanhope, in an unusually quiet mood, read a book.

When the first footman entered, Melissa smiled at the bright flowers that filled the pretty white basket. Miss Stanhope had told her to expect such offerings from the gentlemen she'd <u>danced</u> with the night before. But five more baskets followed, all with the same flower—celandine.

"Who on earth would send a girl baskets filled with weeds?" Miss Stanhope said, staring at the profusion of flowers that most British gardeners pulled up and discarded.

"Joys to come," Melissa said softly. She wouldn't have thought John would have made such a gesture, but the meaning of these flowers was clear. She'd spent long, wonderful hours with *Le Langage des*

Fleurs, poring over the drawings of flowers, fascinated by the idea that even something as simple as grass could have a meaning.

"The card, Miss Atwell," the butler said, handing her a card.

Melissa smiled, her heart skipping happily. But her smile faded and her heart dropped when she read the name written in bold, eloquent script. *Your devoted servant, Waltham.*

"No," Miss Stanhope breathed, getting up and looking over Melissa's shoulder at the card. Melissa put it down on the chair's arm as if it had caught fire. If their meeting had been a pleasant one, the flowers—and their meaning—would have warmed Melissa's heart. But the flowers' meaning had a rather ominous taint given the man's despicable behavior.

"What a horrid man," Miss Stanhope said, marching over to the door. "Please remove these weeds immediately and put them with the garbage."

In less than one minute, the flowers were gone, but Melissa could not get the image—and the sordid message—from her mind.

"Where is John?" she asked.

Miss Stanhope shook her head. "I would expect he has gone home," she said.

"Oh." How could he have left without saying good-bye, without letting her know how his discussion with his father had gone?

Melissa was staring morosely at her needlepoint when the butler reentered the room. "Mr. Charles Norris is here, Miss Stanhope. Are you in?"

Dread filled her, but she nodded. "Could you please have Mr. Norris wait in the Blue Parlor? Thank you."

"You look rather ill, Miss Atwell. Are you quite well? Did those onerous flowers upset you? Perhaps it would be best to put off your drive with Mr. Norris," Miss Stanhope said.

"It's not the flowers, though I did find them upsetting," Melissa said, letting out a rather miserable little laugh. "I'm breaking it off with Charles."

Miss Stanhope, surprisingly, did not seem stunned. In fact, Melissa realized, she appeared almost pleased. "I see," was all the older woman said.

"I don't believe we would suit, and with all that's happened, it's not fair of me to ask him to keep his word on a proposal that hasn't even officially been given." Melissa waited for Miss Stanhope to argue with her, but the usually opinionated woman simply nodded in agreement. "Shouldn't you be urging me to change my mind?"

"Why would I urge you to marry a man you do not love?" she asked sensibly.

"I don't understand," Melissa said, feeling as if her entire world had gone a bit topsy-turvy.

Miss Stanhope gave her the gentlest of smiles. "You're in love with someone else, aren't you, my dear?"

Melissa nodded slowly. "But how did you . . ."

"One would have to be blind or an old, stubborn fool not to have seen it," she said, sounding oddly bitter. "I've suspected for quite some time that John was in love with you. I only recently realized that you return his affections."

Melissa smiled hopefully at the older woman. "And you approve?"

"Wholeheartedly. However, my blessing is quite irrelevant, is it not? I do believe Lord Braddock, stubborn man that he is, will not be as forgiving of this change in plans. But if the two of you are truly in love, you can weather this. It will not be easy," she warned. "You not only have to deal with Lord Braddock, but also with a society that can be unforgiving of scandal. I have no doubt that your father's identity will be common knowledge quite soon. You should both be prepared for some negative social consequences. Then again, with Lord Braddock's public support— and mine—no doubt any censor that does occur will pass. You will also have the support of my niece, the Duchess of Kingston, and her husband."

Melissa went over to Miss Stanhope and gave her an awkward embrace, a gesture that seemed to pleasantly stun her chaperone. "Thank you, Diane," she said. "You have been a true friend."

Charles was sitting patiently in the Blue Parlor when she entered, quietly closing the door behind her. This alone caused his eyebrows to rise, no doubt because propriety dictated that she should have kept the door open. He stood, smiling uncertainly, and Melissa's heart did a little tug. She liked Charles, and she did not want to hurt or humiliate him as surely her rejection would do.

She stood at the door, hands behind her back, and gave him a small smile. "I cannot marry you, Charles," she said simply.

His expression changed subtly, as if he thought he hadn't heard her correctly, or as if he couldn't believe the words that had just sprung from her lips. "Beg pardon?"

"I cannot marry you." She prayed he would not ask why, that he would accept her word and go on his merry way and find another to marry. He shook his head, as if the words still did not make sense.

"If this is because of what happened last night, I would like to assure you . . ."

"It's not," she broke in. "Not entirely, anyway. I could tell you that I won't marry you because it is not fair to you to make you marry a girl whose birth isn't acceptable." He started to protest, but Melissa held up her hand to stop him. "It isn't fair, but that is not my reason. I do not love you, Charles."

His face grew tight, and he looked completely taken aback. "While that is unfortunate, it does not make a difference to me. I love you, Melissa, and I know in time you will come to love me."

"Please, Charles, this is so difficult." She wrung her hands in front of her, wishing she did not have to explain.

"I don't understand. You are a . . . ," he stopped abruptly, his face turning slightly red. "You are illegitimate. You cannot expect to marry well—if at all. And yet you refuse my hand simply because you do not love me? I can give you my name and perhaps even a title one day. You will be my wife, live in a fine home."

"It has nothing to do with you," she said.

"Then tell me what it does have to do with. You are refusing me, so pray tell me how this decision of yours has nothing to do with me."

"I love someone else," she blurted.

That news stunned him to silence, and he visibly stiffened.

"We did not think it was possible for us to be together," she said miserably. "But we cannot deny what we feel."

He let out an audible breath. "John."

Melissa nodded as her eyes filled with tears. She did not want to hurt Charles, but could see no other way. "He feels terrible about this, about hurting you. I beg you to forgive him if not me. I fell in love with him before I met you. I did try not to."

"How you must have suffered, being forced to attend to me," Charles said bitterly.

"Not at all. I like you; I enjoy your company. And for a while I truly believed I could be happy with you. But that was before . . ."

"Before what?"

"Before I realized John felt the same way as I."

He shook his head and stared at the floor. "This was not well done of you," he said, sounding horribly close to tears, though she saw no evidence of such in his eyes. "Of either of you."

"We do feel dreadful."

"You've made a fool of me," he said, finally showing anger.

"Very few people know of our engagement, and those who do will no doubt be understanding." She was desperate to assuage his hurt. "I'm so sorry, Charles. You cannot know how much."

He stared at her, hurt and anger in his brown eyes. "I'll see myself out, shall I?" he said with fierce dignity.

Melissa moved away from the door, wishing she could say something that would make this better all around. He stopped at the door, his hand on the knob. "I could have made you happy, Melissa."

"I know," she said softly. He walked from the room, shutting the door quietly behind him, still acting the gentleman. When he'd gone, Melissa went slowly to the nearest chair and collapsed into it with a sigh. Moments later, Miss Stanhope looked in on her.

"I saw him leave. He didn't seem overly distraught."

"No. He took it rather well," Melissa said, still

feeling unaccountably sad. Never in her life had she hurt another person so, and she found it was not a good feeling at all.

Diane gave Melissa a searching look, for it did appear she was rather more upset about the breakup than Mr. Norris. Diane had a feeling the gentleman, as much as he'd insisted upon his devotion, was likely a bit relieved at this moment. He was a good man, but he had found it difficult to accept the fact that his intended was born on the wrong side of the blanket.

A polite knock and the butler's entrance again interrupted their conversation. "Miss Stanhope. Lord Braddock is requesting your presence in his study," he said.

Diane gave an inward sigh. In all her life she'd never experienced such drama. She wished she'd never accepted Lord Braddock's proposal that she chaperone his niece. Had she known accepting such a request would bring such heartache and headaches, she would have politely declined, then walked briskly in the opposite direction. He requested an audience, did he? She was quite, quite certain that it wasn't to apologize for his boorish behavior of the previous evening. No doubt he wanted to discuss his son and his ward's future.

She ought to let him figure it all out for himself. After all, hadn't she warned him about leaving the two of them together? Hadn't she done her best to prevent what he would certainly see as a debacle? At least until it was too late and their hearts had already been fully engaged. If she'd been allowed to do her job, they never would have had the opportunity to fall in love. As it was, the two of them had spent long hours together—two beautiful, young, intelligent people ripe for the picking. Honestly, how could Lord Braddock act upset or shocked? He, himself, had nearly succumbed to her own charms, such as they were.

No, she reminded herself. He had not succumbed to anything but lust for a woman in close proximity. She was sure he would have responded the same way to any moderately attractive woman. Diane, whose heart was so fully engaged it constantly ached, knew well that she had not captured Lord Braddock's heart. And if she hadn't known, his little speech the evening before certainly had given her a large dose of reality.

"While I find your presence diverting and would be more than happy to share a few hours in pursuit of physical pleasures, Miss Stanhope, I do hope you realize that I have no interest in anything permanent. Or even long-term." Worst of all, perhaps, was that it hadn't been said in a haughty tone, but rather a kind one. And that could mean only one thing—that he greatly suspected she was in love with him and that he could in no way return those feelings. But a good romp? Then, of course, he would be at her service.

He couldn't have been clearer. And yet . . . he seemed to like her quite a lot. He seemed to seek out her company. And sometimes he would look at her the way a man looks at a woman he loves.

"Balderdash," she muttered, chastising herself, just before she entered his study following an efficient knock on his door. She did not wait for him to invite her inside, but pushed through, her face set in her sternest old-spinster lines. Then she looked at him, at his anguished expression, and her heart was immediately engaged once again.

"What has happened?" she said, going to where he stood staring at the cold, empty fireplace.

"My son fancies himself in love," he said with such derision, any warm feeling that had snuck into her heart was chased away.

"I believe he *is* in love, my lord. And I also believe I expressed some concern about allowing the two of them to be together. Alone."

He quickly took out his watch and snapped it open with a practiced motion. "Ah. Ten seconds before you gave me your 'I told you so's.'"

She raised one eyebrow. "If that is all," she said, turning to leave.

"That is not all," he shouted, and she turned slowly back toward him, raising one elegant brow. "What am I to do? He's threatened to marry her one way or the other."

"Then give him your blessing," Diane said calmly.

"My blessing! Good God, woman. My *blessing*? Not only has John betrayed me, I have betrayed my brother. John is so concerned about being in love," he said mockingly, "that he's lost sight of everything he believed in."

Diane stared daggers at this man she loved, wondering if she could choke some sense into him. "I'm sorry, my lord, but I simply do not understand why falling in love with a beautiful girl is such a tragedy."

"Because now everyone will know she is a bastard, for they damn well know I would never sanction such a thing otherwise. And until his madness took over, John believed as much as I do that love does not live past the first fuck."

Diane flinched, for she was unused to hearing such language and certainly not from a peer.

Lord Braddock swore again, this time beneath his breath. "I apologize," he said curtly.

Diane let out a weary sigh. "Regardless of your invalid beliefs, you cannot be as obtuse as you are acting. After last night's ball, there is no one in London who isn't talking about your niece and speculating on her parentage."

"I haven't heard a thing," he said, outraged that she would suggest such a thing.

"No, you would not have. But I did. I do have some friends who are unaware I am Miss Atwell's chaperone, and I heard from two that the Duke of Waltham's by-blow was attempting to pass herself off as your niece."

He turned startlingly white. "Why did you not tell me last night?"

Diane let out a weary sigh. "Hadn't we all been through enough?" she asked, feeling unaccountably on the verge of weeping. "Waltham also sent her several baskets of flowers this morning, which I promptly had thrown in the garbage. You could never have known Melissa would look so much like her half sister. Unfortunately, enough people have met Lady Caroline that their likeness cannot be easily overlooked. Especially with Waltham's sending her flowers the day after her first ball. He signed his name."

George walked behind his desk and sat down heavily, resting his head against his palms in a gesture so defeated, Diane couldn't help feeling badly for him.

"How has it come to this?" he asked, looking up at her. "I was only trying to honor my brother's last wish. How did it all get away from me?" He gave her a searching look. "Nothing about these past few months has gone as planned." His eyes flickered lightly over her face. "Nothing."

"Lord Braddock. George. May I be frank with you?"

He gave her a small smile. "When have you been anything but?"

"No matter what you believe or don't believe about love, I'm telling you right now that John and Melissa love one another. Their love may not last; you are right about that. We've both seen too many unhappy people to believe it always does. But I have seen love," she said, thinking of her own parents.

"He wanted my blessing. I couldn't give it."

"You can, my lord," she said briskly. "And you must."

"It is unfathomable to me, how he could be so swayed by a pretty face."

Diane fought another surge of anger. "Do you really have so little faith in your son that you think he would believe himself in love with Melissa simply because she is lovely? My God, you must have loved your wife to distraction to have become so utterly jaded."

He lifted his head sharply, his eyes filled with undeniable anger. "You are wrong," he said succinctly.

"Am I?"

"Don't you see that proves my point? I was young and foolish, not much younger than John, and I allowed myself to believe in such fairy tales. I was a fool. I am not bitter; I am a realist, so please do not look at me with pity." He slammed a fist atop his desk. "*Goddamn* you." He'd quite lost his temper, but Diane was having none of it.

"Are you finished?"

He took a few bracing breaths before nodding.

"I was not looking at you with pity, you great fool of

a man. I was looking at you with love. So if anyone is
to be pitied, sir, I would say it is me."

"You can't," he said roughly. "You don't."

"Of course, you are right, Lord Braddock. You are
always right about all things."

"I have never made such claims." He looked downright aghast.

"It is just that you are so opinionated. And if
anyone dares to offer an opposing opinion, you are
ready with a long list of reasons why they are wrong."
Diane felt weary of a sudden. "I did not wish to turn
this conversation toward myself. I am here to discuss
Melissa and John and to urge you, for once in your
life, not to act like an ass."

With that, her back straight, her eyes dry, she
walked from the room.

George sat for a long moment staring at the closed
door as if paralyzed. "Foolish woman," he mumbled
after a time, then stared blindly at the paperwork on
his desk, He felt a rather foreign ache in his chest,
and thought, for a moment, that he was ill. And then,
with a small, disgusted sound, he realized that the
ache in his breast just might be his heart, completely
thawed and able to feel pain for the first time in
nearly thirty years. He let out a strangled sound.

She couldn't love him. He refused to believe it. *Refused*. He was too old for such nonsense. How dare she
say such a thing to him when she knew full well he had
absolutely no interest in reciprocating those feelings.

"Love," he said, making the word sound like a
curse. "Poppycock."

And then he let out a small chuckle. What gall

Diane had, telling him such a thing without even the smallest bit of warmth in her voice, as if she'd been rather appalled herself. He had to admire her courage, standing before him and arguing and then admitting to him that she . . .

"Loves me," he said softly. The ache that had dwelt in his heart for so long eased just a bit. "Bloody hell."

Chapter 19

John supposed he deserved it, but damn, Charles could hit hard. He gazed in his mirror, his valet behind him looking concerned and just a bit angry (it was difficult to shave a man when he sported a large bruise on his jaw). "Not broken," he said, waggling his jaw a bit. Though it hurt like hell, he wasn't angry with Charles, and he certainly hadn't reciprocated.

He'd been surprised when he'd returned to his town house to learn that Charles was waiting for him in his study. He'd gotten out: "Charles, my God, I'm so sorr—" before his friend's fist hit his jaw with such force, he slammed against the wall. He was momentarily stunned as Charles shook out his hand, looking quite pleased with himself.

"S'pose I deserved that," John had said, gingerly touching his jaw.

"I suppose you did."

"I want you to know I went to my father before I knew of your engagement with the intention of offering for her. That's when my father told me of your plans. I love her."

"And you don't think I do?"

John had stepped away from the wall and walked to a side table where he poured two generous portions of brandy. "I know you do. She's a difficult girl not to love." He had offered Charles the snifter and been relieved when his friend took the drink.

"Hell, John," was all Charles had said before tossing it back. Somehow that summed up how both felt about the situation. By the time Charles had left, they had come to an unspoken agreement to remain friends.

"As much as I hate to admit it, I think she'll be happier with you," Charles had said.

"I do hope so." John had offered his hand, and Charles had taken it without hesitating.

It couldn't have ended better, John thought, even though his jaw ached. Now he could marry Melissa with a freer conscience.

He stepped from the mirror with a sheepish grin on his face when he caught sight of his valet's frown. "It couldn't be helped, Walter. Do you think it'll be gone by week's end?"

Walter tilted his head and studied the bruise. "Hardly, sir."

"Hmm. That's too bad. I'm getting married in five days, and I wanted to look my best."

Melissa had not seen John all day and was going mad with worry. It seemed so very long ago that she'd sat with Miss Stanhope in the parlor; it was as if she were in some awful state of limbo. It was nine o'clock at night, and no one had disturbed her since she'd removed herself to her rooms several hours ago pleading a headache. The house seemed unusually quiet, the only sounds the distant striking of a grandfather clock that chimed lightly on the quarter hour.

Having spent nearly her entire life confined to a set of rooms, Melissa found it difficult to keep herself cloistered now. She still wore the same dress she'd donned that morning, a mint-green creation that was far more cheerful than she was feeling at the moment. She remained dressed only because she was trying to garner the courage to speak to her uncle herself. If he wouldn't listen to his son, perhaps he would listen to her.

What if her uncle had convinced John not to marry her? What if he simply could not endure hurting his father? She paced back and forth, chewing on her thumbnail, and stopped suddenly at her door. Staying in her room was solving nothing. She must know what had transpired between her uncle and John. Pulling open her door, she let out a small scream to see a tall man standing outside it.

"Oh, goodness, Uncle, you frightened me near to death," Melissa said, gasping.

"I could say the same for you," he said on a laugh. "I was just about to knock when you yanked the door open. I need to speak to you. If you wouldn't mind coming with me to the library."

He allowed her to precede him down the hall and stairway, and she used every bit of discipline she had not to ply him with a dozen questions. It was his stern countenance more than anything, however, that kept her silent. He did not seem to be in a jovial mood, and she feared she was about to learn there would be no marriage to John.

When they reached the library, he indicated a

chair for her to take. To her surprise, John sat in a matching chair, looking as pensive as she felt. The expression on his face, a mixture of despair and dread, did nothing to make her feel better about this interview. She gave him a tentative smile, which he returned in a rather miserable way, as her uncle sat across from them.

Her uncle looked from one to the other, his eyes steady, his hands folded in front of him, resting lightly on his lap.

"You have my blessing."

The two remained frozen for a moment, as if not quite believing the words that had just come from the older man's mouth. Then John leaped up, an expression of complete joy on his face. "Father, do you mean it?"

"No," her uncle growled. "I don't. However, it has come to my attention that I may be mistaken. Or at least that I should allow you to find out for yourselves what I found out years ago. So while I am not pleased with this outcome, I give you leave to marry and make yourselves miserable in five years' time. Or sooner."

John walked over to his father, and Lord Braddock stood as the two men gave each other a hearty embrace. John grabbed his father's head roughly and said in a jagged voice, "Thank you, Father."

Then John turned to Melissa, a broad smile on his handsome face, and she flew into his arms with a squeal of pure joy. She kissed his cheek soundly, then pushed back, feeling happier than she could ever remember. Turning to her uncle, she smiled up at him, knowing he was struggling mightily not to smile. "Thank you, Uncle. I shall make it my life's work to prove you wrong about love."

"Hmph."

"Oh, come now, Father. You cannot remain so cynical when proof of the existence of love is standing in front of you."

"I simply see two fools," he said with a grumpiness that seemed rather forced.

John reached into his coat pocket and withdrew a ring, showing it first to his father. "If I may, Father," he said. George looked at the ring with a wistful smile.

"Of course," he said gruffly.

And then John got down on bended knee, making Melissa laugh in delight. "Would you do me the great honor of becoming my wife?"

"I would," she said with a firm nod.

"Father, turn away. I'm going to give my fiancée a rather improper kiss."

"Why don't I simply leave the room? For no more than five minutes," he ended with a warning note.

Once his father had left, John pulled Melissa into his arms and gave her a deep kiss that made her legs go weak. "It was my grandmother's ring," he said. "And by all accounts, she loved my grandfather until the day she died."

Melissa gazed down at the beautiful ring, a large oval emerald surrounded by diamonds. "I could tell it held great meaning for your father. Thank you." She brought her head up for another kiss. "I want to make love with you," she whispered against his lips, teasing him into another smile.

"As do I. Which is why I spent today obtaining a special license. Will five days be enough time to prepare?"

"Miss Stanhope will kill me," she said, but she was grinning. She simply couldn't stop it. "And if she doesn't kill me then the modiste will. I don't know if it's possible to have a gown readied in time."

"It will be ready," he said firmly, pulling her to him for another staggering kiss. "I'm afraid if I have to wait any longer to have you, I will perish."

Melissa let out a laugh. "You will not *die*, John."

"I will. I can wait five days to have you, but no more."

The door opened without warning, and George glared at the happy couple, who reluctantly stepped back from their embrace. "We're to be wed in five days, Father."

"Impossible," Lord Braddock said.

"I've already obtained a special license," John said, waving the document triumphantly. "Which, by the way, was no easy task."

"Don't you realize how much scandal is already attached to the two of you? I think it rather imprudent to marry so quickly. Perhaps in September when . . ."

"Let them marry when they choose. There will be no less scandal in September." All three turned to see Miss Stanhope standing at the door.

Lord Braddock glared angrily at the interruption. "This is none of your concern," he said, and Melissa was taken aback by the anger in his tone. Diane turned pale but for two spots of pink on her cheeks.

"You are, of course, correct. However, given the volatility of Melissa's true father, I would suggest a quick and quiet wedding. We do not know how the duke will react if the banns are posted ahead of time. If she were my daughter, I would want her safely married and under John's protection as soon as possible."

"She is not your daughter and, again, this is not your concern."

"Father," John said, looking at his father with disbelief. "Miss Stanhope makes a valid point. One that I'm certain was made with the best of intentions."

Lord Braddock's expression was stony. "It is only that this is a family matter, and Miss Stanhope is not part of this family."

Melissa thought she heard a sharp intake of breath from Diane, but when she looked at her, Diane appeared calm. Almost too calm, given the fact that her uncle was being unaccountably rude to her. "Uncle," she said softly. "Miss Stanhope has become a dear friend, and I value her opinion."

"Only because it corresponds to your own opinion," he grumbled.

"Lord Braddock is correct. I am not part of this family, nor will I ever be," Diane said, her words frosty. "However, I've never been one to remain quiet when I believe my input will benefit the outcome of an event." She softened as she looked at Melissa. "And I thank you for those kind words, Melissa."

"If you are finished submitting your unsolicited opinions, I would bid you good evening," Lord Braddock said, his tone just as frosty. John and Melissa looked at each other, clearly wondering why the older couple was sparring.

"I have not finished," Diane said.

"Then would you do so? Please."

"Father. Diane. Would you two stop bickering so that we may come to a decision about our wedding?"

"Five days is fine," George shouted, making everyone else in the room jump slightly.

Melissa knew better than to express any kind of happiness over that pronouncement, but she squeezed John's hand to let him know how pleased she was. She didn't know what was going on between her uncle and Miss Stanhope, but she was thrilled Diane had managed to persuade him.

"Well, if you don't mind, I'll be heading home now," John said. "Wouldn't do to stay here when we're engaged."

"I'll walk you to the door," Melissa said, suddenly fiercely wanting to remove herself from her uncle's and Diane's presence. They were casting a pall on what was a glorious ending to a trying day.

She didn't notice John's jaw until they were standing beneath a gas sconce by the door, and she let out a small sound of dismay. "However did you do that?" she asked.

"Not to worry, love." He looked terribly guilty about something.

"It was Charles, wasn't it?"

"It was," he said, holding up his hand to stop her from expressing her dismay. "But we're still friends. I figured I deserved something like this," he said, touching his jaw. "And it could have been worse. He could have blackened my eye, and just how would that have looked on our wedding day?"

At the mention of the wedding, Melissa smiled. "Our wedding."

"Our wedding," he said, kissing her on the nose. He drew her into his arms, letting out a low sound that did all sorts of wonderful things to her insides. Then she felt him stiffen, and she drew back.

"What's wrong?" He was staring at a thick envelope with a fancy seal upon it sitting on the silver platter that normally held the home's correspondence.

"It's likely nothing," he said, and walked over to retrieve the envelope. Melissa wasn't overly concerned until she heard him curse.

"Waltham," he said, snapping the ducal seal. "It's addressed to you, but I hope you don't mind."

Melissa didn't mind at all, for just touching something her father had touched would certainly make her skin crawl. "What is it?"

"An invitation. One I believe you will not accept. I hope you don't mind if I go in your stead," he said with deadly calm. He tucked the envelope into his jacket.

"Just throw it in the fire, John. Let's pretend we didn't see it." She'd never seen John look so coldly determined, and she feared he would do something rash.

"This ends now."

"Please, John. Whatever you're thinking of doing, don't. He cannot hurt me once we are married."

John laughed. "I'm not going to kill him, if that's what you're thinking. Though I wish I was the sort of man who could. No. Don't worry," he said, his eyes warm. He pulled her into his arms and kissed the top of her head, but his body was rigid.

Melissa let him go without another word, but she *was* worried. It was almost as if that invitation was an evil presence that should be destroyed, not held onto. When John held it, she saw a man she did not recognize—a man who could kill for something he loved.

"If my presence here so offends you, I will leave tonight," Diane said, anger coursing through her. She often felt angry, but she rarely showed it. She was showing it now.

"I will not stop you. It's obvious to me that your

ability to properly chaperone a young girl is suspect at best."

Diane knew that if thoughts could make a man burst into flame, Lord Braddock would explode in a dazzling inferno. "How dare you criticize me when it was I who warned you about your son. You have the audacity to blame me when it was you, and only you," she pointed out with triumph, "who fostered this state of affairs. Which, by the way, I believe to be a wonderful conclusion to an otherwise difficult situation."

"You would," he said with disgust.

"What is your meaning?"

"My meaning is that I asked you to chaperone Melissa only because I believed you to be a practical woman who would not succumb to the romance of this catastrophe and would realize this is perhaps the worst possible outcome. I asked you and only you because you appeared to be a woman who no longer believed in fairy tales and had her mind settled on the sensible, not the sensational."

If Diane had been a different woman, she would have burst into tears then and there. "Just because a woman is not married does not mean her heart has turned to stone. How dare you assume such a thing about me? If I acted seriously, if I rarely smiled, it was only because my heart has been broken so many times. . . ." She stopped abruptly and turned away, using all her strength not to cry. He did not deserve the tears she longed to shed. He was a mean, despicable cad, and she didn't know how she'd allowed herself to feel even affection for the man, never mind being stupid enough to fall in love with him. Good God, how could she have been so foolish?

All was silent behind her. No doubt he was looking

at her with pity. Or disgust. Either was untenable. Without looking back at him, she began walking steadily toward the door, telling herself she would never walk back in. She was done. Well and forever done with allowing herself to love any man who didn't love her in return. She would pack this very night and stay at a hotel. She would leave London tomorrow and return to her gentle and quiet home in Flintwood. She would . . .

"I'm sorry."

He sounded wretched, but Diane didn't care. Didn't. Care. She had nearly reached the door when she felt his hand on her arm.

"You cannot leave," he said, his mouth so near her ear she could feel his warm breath.

"I can and I will," Diane said, suddenly not meaning a syllable. If he were to turn her around, if he were to kiss her, she would melt into his arms and give him that romp he so wanted. She would, and then she'd spend the rest of her life trying not to regret it.

"What if . . ." His arms came around her, a warm band of steel holding her stiff body in place. "What if you stayed?"

She shook her head, staring at the door, hating the fact her vision had blurred with unshed tears. *Damn him.*

He turned her slowly in his arms, and she did not resist, even though she stiffened even more. "Why are you crying?" He sounded unabashedly terrified by those tears. She couldn't speak, so she simply stared at his shirt, wishing he would let her go and wishing he would draw her more tightly into his arms.

"Do you realize how difficult this is for me?" he said, sounding almost angry.

She looked up at him then, with a glare that would have made another man flinch.

"Do you realize how absolutely terrifying it is for a man such as me to come to the ridiculous conclusion that he's in love? Do you? And you were going to walk out that door and leave me without allowing me to tell you. Are you trying to drive me mad?"

Diane allowed herself a sharp intake of breath. "Beg pardon?"

"I asked if you were trying to drive me mad," he repeated gently, with the smallest of smiles tugging at his lips.

Diane closed her eyes briefly. "Yes," she said. "I am. How am I doing?"

With a groan, he pulled her close and kissed her, his strong hands pressing her against him, nearly knocking the breath from her. "I'm very angry with you, you know," he said, dragging his mouth to her neck.

"I know."

"I suppose you won't settle for a romp."

"No. I don't suppose I will."

He stepped back and looked at her, agony warring with pure happiness. "I do love you."

"I thought you might." She was trying not to lose control, but it was so very difficult in the face of his love. She wanted to throw herself into his arms, to laugh and dance around the room, arms outstretched, until she collapsed in a puddle of pure joy. Instead, she kissed his cheek and said, "I love you, too."

"And you'll marry me?"

She gave him a level look, then smiled. "I will."

And so, when Melissa, curious about why it was so quiet in the library, chanced to peek through the door to make certain all was well, she found herself rather surprised to see two people, who'd just been fighting, kissing each other rather enthusiastically.

Chapter 20

Melissa lay in her bed and turned her head to look at the empty space beside her, glowing softly in the light of her bedside lamp. She'd been reading, and now the book lay by her side forgotten, for she'd been unable to keep her thoughts from John. How strange, wonderfully strange, it would be to turn and see John there, sleeping beside her. She wondered what he looked like when he was asleep. Did he snore? Her father had, great rumbling sounds that traveled even to her rooms down the hall from his.

Five days. In five days she would become Viscountess Willington, and eventually a countess. But for now she suspected her chaperone would make a very fine countess indeed. At least she hoped they would marry. She prayed her uncle would finally realize what a wonderful woman Diane was. As a woman madly in love, Melissa wanted the world to be madly in love and could not imagine two people kissing with such abandon if their hearts weren't completely engaged.

She hugged herself, remembering that day in the

rain, the way John had made her feel, that wondrous flood of ecstasy that had left her feeling so pleased and John so horrified. She giggled, stopping abruptly at a sound at her door, a light tapping. Cocking her head, she listened intently until she heard it again. Swinging her legs over the side of her bed, she padded over to her door, grabbing her wrap on the way. As she tied the silk belt, she whispered, "Who is there?"

"John."

That single word made her heart pick up a beat, and she immediately opened the door. His expression was grave, his hair damp as if he'd been outside walking in the fine mist that fell. Without a word, she stepped back, allowing him to enter.

"I thought you'd gone home."

"No. I went to see Waltham. He's dead."

Shock nearly made her knees buckle. She took a step back, as if she could run from those horrid words. "Oh, no, John, what happened? What did you do?"

Incongruously, he smiled and stifled a laugh, which only confused Melissa more. "Good God, Melissa, *I* didn't kill him." He hesitated. "It was his heart. But he's dead, and I wanted you to know."

Melissa laid a hand on her heart, which still beat crazily in her chest. "You frightened me half to death, John Atwell." She searched his eyes to be certain he told the truth. Something was there, a flicker of something hidden. "When did he die?" she asked, trying to keep any suspicion from her voice.

"Shortly *before* I arrived," he said, seeing the doubt in her troubled gaze. He looked at her with affectionate exasperation. "Did you truly think I could have killed the man?"

"Actually, yes. You had a murderous glint in your eyes."

John grimaced. "Truth be told, I don't know what I planned. I suppose I did feel a bit murderous." He rubbed a hand across his forehead. "I would kill for you, if need be, to protect you. I would die for you."

Melissa's eyes flooded with tears. "Don't say such things, John."

He pulled her into his arms and kissed her. It was a gentle kiss, as if he were asking for understanding and forgiveness. It felt so good to be in his arms, to feel his strength, to breathe in the scent of him. When he deepened the kiss, she instinctively followed suit, opening her mouth and welcoming his tongue with hers. His hands cupped her buttocks and drew her closer, close enough that his rigid arousal pressed against her center, causing a shard of pleasure so intense she cried out.

He lifted his head and gazed down at her. "I want to make love to you."

"Yes."

He gave her a quick, pleased smile, then slowly drew her wrap down, skimming his hands down her arms, watching his progress with drugging intensity. The wrap fell soundlessly to the floor.

"I want to see all of you."

Melissa pressed her lips together, suddenly shy. Her lamp cast them in a golden glow, and she could see that his eyes swept her form hungrily.

"Please."

"Since you are being so polite," she said, trying to sound light, but feeling terribly nervous. She lifted the gown over her head and stood naked before him. She needn't have worried about any embarrassment, for the look in his eyes, the need, the love, kept her from feeling any emotion except desire.

"My God, Melissa. You are impossibly perfect." His breathing was ragged, and his hand shook slightly when he reached up and touched one breast, his thumb moving tantalizingly slowly over one turgid nipple. She let out a small sound and closed her eyes, overwhelmed by the pleasure of that one touch.

"I like the sounds you make," he said, before he kissed that same nipple, drawing it into his mouth and sending another wave of desire through her. She stood there bathed in lamplight, naked, while he was fully dressed. For some reason, the contrast was intoxicating.

His hand slowly moved to her thigh, the outside where her hips gently curved, and then inside, to between her legs, to where every bit of pleasure seemed to pool. He let out a sound of satisfaction, for Melissa knew she was slick and that meant she was deeply aroused. She knew this now, this wicked bit of information, and it gave her the courage to take her hand and press it against his erection. He let out a growl, and she chuckled, loving that she could evoke such a response.

With one quick movement, John lifted Melissa up into his arms and gently laid her on her bed. He gave the lamp a speculative look, then looked down at her and was lost. The light would stay on, and it would take the Devil or God Himself to make him douse it. She was beyond anything he could have imagined. Her skin was smooth and flawless, her breasts rounded and lovely. The curls between her legs a shade darker than the hair on her head.

"I cannot believe you're mine," he said at last,

emotion making his words ragged. He didn't care. He didn't care if he started weeping. He would never forget this moment, this pure feeling of joy, looking down at Melissa as she looked up at him with such love and desire. "Don't you dare move." He waved a warning finger at her and smiled. Within a minute, he had discarded all his clothing and stood beside the bed, his arousal straining in front of him. Her eyes swept down his form, skittering a bit nervously over his cock, and she swallowed.

"Don't worry, love," he said, lowering himself down onto the bed. He kissed her, a long, thoroughly intoxicating kiss, while his hands moved between her legs, touching her sensitive nub lightly. Her eyes were closed, her face intent, her hips moving just slightly. He bent and took a nipple into his mouth, laving it with his tongue, loving the way she gasped, the way her hips began moving more frantically. When he abandoned her nipple, and withdrew his hand, she let out a small sound and opened her eyes.

"John?"

He kissed her belly. "Yes, love?"

"Why did you stop?"

"I haven't." He moved down her torso, kissing her smooth, flat belly, wondering if she would stop what he longed to do more than anything. Instinct drove him, this need to taste her, to draw her into his body, to feel her throb against his mouth. He'd never been tempted to do this to a woman, never wanted to, really. But it seemed he couldn't stop himself. She was driving him mad with her sounds and her moving hips and her scent. He took a taste, she gasped, and he let out a groan. With his mouth on her, his finger inside her, he pleasured her. He'd never wanted to please a woman as much as this one. Never wanted to lose himself so much. But this was Melissa. His Melissa. And so he kissed her and licked her and lost himself as she let out gasps of raw pleasure, as she clutched his head and brought him closer, as she jerked her hips and pulsed violently around his finger.

When the trembling subsided, she let out a long breath, as if she'd forgotten to breathe entirely. "That was wondrous," she said, her eyes still closed, her legs still wantonly spread for him. Never had he been so close to coming with so little physical stimulation. He moved up between her legs, his erection pressing against her wet heat.

"This may hurt you, love," he said, and he pushed inside her, cringing when she stiffened and let out a small sound. "I hurt you."

"No," she said. "Well, a bit. But not now. It's . . ." She shook her head as if searching for the correct word. "Right. It's right." She smiled up at him, and he moved back, watching her reaction intently. He did not want to hurt her again. She didn't cringe, just stared at him with a light look of wonder on her lovely face. He was shaking from the need to move quickly, but he used all his strength to go slowly, to think of anything but how hot and wet and tight she was around him.

"Oh, God, I can't," he said, then began moving frantically, the need to find completion overcoming anything else. When she wrapped her legs around him, he was undone. His release came, filling him with such intense pleasure, he buried his head in the pillow beside hers and cried out.

The large grandfather clock in the hallway chimed twelve times, and John slowly withdrew, kissing

Melissa to distract her just in case he'd hurt her. "Four days," he murmured against her mouth. "God, I love you."

Melissa's eyes filled with tears. "I'll never get tired of hearing you say that. Never."

Later that day, John had just arrived home from his tailor when he was informed by his butler that his father had requested he meet with him. He had a moment's trepidation that his father had somehow found out about his night with Melissa, then shrugged it off. His father, while a moral man, was not overly religious, and he could not imagine his father calling him to task for making love to Melissa. They were to be married in four days, after all.

But when he walked into his father's study, he grew faintly alarmed. His father seemed irate. "Sit down," he said, and John immediately sat. It was that sort of tone.

"Waltham is dead, and I want to know what you had to do with it."

John sighed. What was it about the people he loved that made them think he was capable of murder?

"I didn't kill Waltham." And then he recounted what had happened the night previous.

The Duke of Waltham's town house was only a short ride away from John's rented town house in Mayfair, so John had left his mount in his own mews and had walked to the duke's mansion. It had been too late to abruptly show up at Waltham's door, but John wanted this mad obsession to end. He'd decided he would not see that look of fear in Melissa's eyes again, not while he still had a breath in him.

For a man to desire his own daughter was so far beyond anything of John's experience, it was difficult to comprehend. He knew only that the mere thought of the duke's looking upon Melissa was enough for bile to form in his throat.

The last thing he'd expected when he'd turned the corner to pass in front of the massive home was to see it lit up as if for a party. John had known, though, that something was wrong, for there were no people milling about, no fine carriages, no footmen awaiting orders. It was eerily quiet but for the snort of a horse attached to a plain black surrey. With a small amount of trepidation, John mounted the stairs, listening intently for the sound of a party, but there was nothing. He pulled on the knocker, a gargoyle head so gruesome he wondered at the purpose of it. The knocker hung between fanged teeth and came down upon a lolling tongue. Grimacing, he waited for the door to open. He was about to knock again when the door opened, revealing a solemn-faced butler.

"I have an invitation from His Grace," John said, pulling out the envelope and showing the butler the seal. The man didn't bother glancing at it.

"His Grace is indisposed," he said blandly.

"Who is it, Peters?" From behind him, a woman dressed for the evening appeared, and the servant backed away with a bow.

John felt himself flush. The last thing he'd wanted was to have to speak to the duke's wife. Good God, what a horrible idea this had turned out to be.

"Sir?" she'd asked politely.

She was a lovely older woman, with silver hair and brown eyes. Her dark brows gave her an almost exotic look, and she raised one brow elegantly in inquiry.

"Lord Willington, at your service, Your Grace," John said with a bow.

"Lord Braddock's son?" she asked, and it seemed to John that she was almost trying not to laugh, though he couldn't have said why.

"Yes, ma'am. I was unaware you were acquainted."

"We are not. To what do we owe this visit?"

"We received an invitation from His Grace," John said, feeling ridiculous standing there at the door. He tried not to shuffle like a schoolboy being questioned by the schoolmistress.

"We?" That brow arched up again.

John cleared his throat. "It is for Miss Atwell."

The duchess gave him a steady look, then backed away, indicating that he should enter the foyer.

"Perhaps this isn't a good time. I came to see His Grace, and if he's not available I could make an appointment with his secretary perhaps."

"His Grace is dead," she'd said with as much inflection as if she were commenting on the weather.

"My God. That is horrible."

"Hardly," came her mild reply. "If you would join me in my parlor, Lord Willington."

John could hardly refuse, so he'd found himself following the duchess, his mind rapidly going over the events unfolding. They were silent until the duchess took a seat and nodded for him to join her. "My condolences," John said.

"Thank you." She gave him an assessing look. "Now, then. Why are you really here?"

"As I said, I came here to speak to His Grace."

"May I inquire about what?"

"About a private matter," John said, for he'd still been unwilling to explain to the duke's wife that

Waltham had held an unnatural attraction to his daughter.

"But His Grace is dead. Any private matter with him is now within my purview. Perhaps I can help you."

She almost seemed to be enjoying his discomfort. And when she let out a musical laugh, he knew he was correct. "I'm sorry, Lord Willington. I shall stop teasing you. You came here to tell my husband to leave your cousin alone. Or rather, for the duke to leave his daughter alone. Is that it?"

John was startled that she was aware of the situation, but he'd nodded gravely. "Yes, ma'am."

"My husband was quite ill. That's what his doctor called it, an illness. I'd say he was simply a mad deviant. He enjoyed certain activities that I found despicable. Indeed, most of humanity would. I tried my best to protect the females in this household. The young ones in particular." She gave an elegant shrug. "But I had limited success." She seemed completely at ease, but when she pushed an errant strand of hair from her eyes, John noted that she trembled.

"He is . . . was . . . a powerful man, my lady. Please do not fault yourself for his failings."

She gave him a calm smile, even as her eyes filled with tears. "I protected my daughters. I protected my Caroline."

John swallowed, feeling sick inside. What sort of evil man had his children living in fear of being accosted? "He can no longer do anyone harm, ma'am."

Suddenly, a keening sound, distinctly girlish, reached them, and the duchess raised her head. "A difficult evening for her," she'd said softly. "She blames herself."

"I don't understand. How did His Grace die?"

She'd given him the most serene smile. "I killed him, of course."

"You . . ."

"I was protecting my daughter. I tell you this in the strictest confidence and will deny this conversation ever took place should you repeat one syllable of it." She'd smiled again, but this time her eyes were hard. She was silent for a long moment. "His physician will testify that he hit his head following a heart attack. He's an old friend of mine. It's good to have friends, Lord Willington." She let out a sigh and stood. "You may tell Miss Atwell she is safe. Good evening, sir." She'd walked from the room, head held regally, clutching her skirt with fisted hands.

"That's the truth?" his father asked.

"Yes, sir. She told me in confidence."

His father gave him a nod. "All right then. I've something else I'd like to discuss. Something that affects you."

"Oh?"

Suddenly, his father couldn't meet his eyes. He cleared his throat and moved his hands restlessly over his desk. "Miss Stanhope and I plan to marry," he said grimly.

John raised his brows in complete surprise. "You. And Miss Stanhope? Whatever for?" He was truly and completely baffled.

"It has occurred to me that I . . ." and he mumbled something beneath his breath that John couldn't quite make out but that sounded insanely like "love her."

"Pardon?"

"I said I love her," he said angrily.

John felt his mouth drop open and then a smile grew on his face. "You love her."

His father lifted his chin. "Indeed."

"Love. *Love.*"

George snapped his mouth into a firm line. "As I said."

John stood and pointed an accusing finger at his father. "After giving me such grief about Melissa. After belittling me for my feelings. You are in love?" he asked with incredulous glee.

His father shook his head and closed his eyes, then threw up his hands in disgust. "I don't know how the hell it happened, so don't ask. As for my treatment of you, I apologize," he ground out. "I was wrong."

John crossed his arms and gave his father a full smile. "You devil," he said, chuckling.

"Yes, well. I'm telling you so that you are aware that if we have a son and something happens to you, your own children may have quite a wait for the title."

"Children?"

"She's still young enough," George said, looking decidedly uncomfortable. "And I'm still young enough."

"If you say so," John said with skepticism he didn't feel. He was happy for his father. Tickled, really. "Congratulations, Father." He gave his father another disbelieving look. "However did she do it?"

His father gave him a sharp look. "I realized that my life seemed rather dull and endless without her about."

"That would never do."

"It would seem so. What a couple of fools we are, eh, son?"

John smiled. "Fools in love, Father. Fools in love."

Did you miss Jane's first book in the series?
Go back and read *When a Duke Says I Do*!

Miss Elsie Stanhope resided in Nottinghamshire, an area so rich in titled gentlemen, so felicitous for marriage-minded mamas, it was called "the Dukeries." Indeed, Elsie had been betrothed since childhood to the heir of a dukedom. She had no expectation it would be a love match. Still less that she would enter into a shockingly scandalous affair with an altogether different sort of lover. And the very last thing she imagined was that the mysteries of his birth would be unraveled with as many unforeseen twists and turns as the deepest secrets of her heart . . .

Books by Bestselling Author
Fern Michaels

__**The Jury**	0-8217-7878-1	$6.99US/$9.99CAN
__**Sweet Revenge**	0-8217-7879-X	$6.99US/$9.99CAN
__**Lethal Justice**	0-8217-7880-3	$6.99US/$9.99CAN
__**Free Fall**	0-8217-7881-1	$6.99US/$9.99CAN
__**Fool Me Once**	0-8217-8071-9	$7.99US/$10.99CAN
__**Vegas Rich**	0-8217-8112-X	$7.99US/$10.99CAN
__**Hide and Seek**	1-4201-0184-6	$6.99US/$9.99CAN
__**Hokus Pokus**	1-4201-0185-4	$6.99US/$9.99CAN
__**Fast Track**	1-4201-0186-2	$6.99US/$9.99CAN
__**Collateral Damage**	1-4201-0187-0	$6.99US/$9.99CAN
__**Final Justice**	1-4201-0188-9	$6.99US/$9.99CAN
__**Up Close and Personal**	0-8217-7956-7	$7.99US/$9.99CAN
__**Under the Radar**	1-4201-0683-X	$6.99US/$9.99CAN
__**Razor Sharp**	1-4201-0684-8	$7.99US/$10.99CAN
__**Yesterday**	1-4201-1494-8	$5.99US/$6.99CAN
__**Vanishing Act**	1-4201-0685-6	$7.99US/$10.99CAN
__**Sara's Song**	1-4201-1493-X	$5.99US/$6.99CAN
__**Deadly Deals**	1-4201-0686-4	$7.99US/$10.99CAN
__**Game Over**	1-4201-0687-2	$7.99US/$10.99CAN
__**Sins of Omission**	1-4201-1153-1	$7.99US/$10.99CAN
__**Sins of the Flesh**	1-4201-1154-X	$7.99US/$10.99CAN
__**Cross Roads**	1-4201-1192-2	$7.99US/$10.99CAN

Available Wherever Books Are Sold!
Check out our website at **www.kensingtonbooks.com**